PRAISE FOR
AND THEN
CAME PEACE

"'When peace comes to Jerusalem it will come to the whole world' is an old saying. This exciting and well-researched novel by Greg Masse makes clear just how difficult this is in the face of terrorism and repression, but it also offers a message of hope. If only we could draw upon the spiritual resources that the great religions share, then peace is possible. My prayer is that this work of fiction is a prophetic vision of future reality."

—Reverend Dr. Marcus Braybrooke
President of the World Congress of Faiths

"And Then Came Peace by Greg Masse is the gripping story of a man caught up in seemingly irresolvable violence and conflict, who discovers in a series of strange encounters both his own peace and a message of peace for the world."

—Dr. Robert Hunt
Director of Global Theological Education
Southern Methodist University

AND THEN CAME PEACE

A NOVEL BY
GREG MASSE

Enlightened
PUBLISHING GROUP

Published by Enlightened Publishing Group
St. Petersburg, Florida
www.enlightenedpublishinggroup.com

Distributed by Greenleaf Book Group LLC

For ordering information or special discounts for bulk purchases, please contact Greenleaf Book Group LLC at PO Box 91869, Austin, TX 78709, 512.891.6100.

Cover design by Greenleaf Book Group LLC
Cover images © iStockphoto.com/zepperwing (Jerusalem) and Ig0rZh (background)

Publisher's Cataloging-In-Publication Data
(Prepared by The Donohue Group, Inc.)
Masse, Greg.
    And then came peace : a novel / by Greg Masse.—2nd ed.
    p. : map ; cm.
    1st ed. published by: Enlightened Publishing Group, c2012. This is the 1st ed. published by Greenleaf; ed. statement transcribed from book.
    ISBN 978-0-9894513-0-7
    1. Assassins—Jerusalem—Fiction. 2. Terrorism—Jerusalem—Fiction. 3. Religious awakening—Jerusalem—Fiction. 4. Religious tolerance—Fiction. 5. International relations—Fiction. I. Title.

PS3613.A774 A54 2013
813/.6   2013940224

Part of the Tree Neutral® program, which offsets the number of trees consumed in the production and printing of this book by taking proactive steps, such as planting trees in direct proportion to the number of trees used: www.treeneutral.com

TreeNeutral®

Printed in the United States of America on acid-free paper

15 16 17 18 19 20 10 9 8 7 6 5 4 3 2

Second edition.

For my grandfathers

FACTS:

What follows is accurately sourced from the Torah, Talmud, Bible, Qur'an, Hindu Vedas, Buddhist Sutras and Confucian Analects.

In recent years, Israel has freed over a thousand Palestinian prisoners in exchange for a few captured Israeli soldiers.
Those released include terrorist leaders and organizers of suicide bombings, and today, some continue to plague our world with terror.

This story is not intended to offend but, rather, to enlighten and bring humanity closer.
Knowledge feeds freedom and starves tyranny.

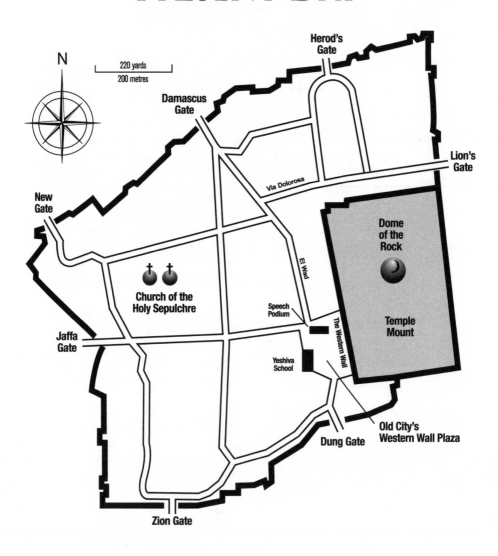

THE OLD CITY IN JERUSALEM PRESENT DAY

N

220 yards
200 metres

Herod's Gate

Damascus Gate

Lion's Gate

New Gate

Via Dolorosa

Dome of the Rock

El Wad

Church of the Holy Sepulchre

Speech Podium

Temple Mount

Jaffa Gate

The Western Wall

Yeshiva School

Old City's Western Wall Plaza

Dung Gate

Zion Gate

I

THE OLD CITY

To everything, there is a season,
And a time to every purpose under the heaven:
A time to be born and a time to die . . .
A time to kill and a time to heal;
A time to break down and a time to build up . . .
A time to cast away stones and a time to gather stones together;
A time to embrace and a time to refrain from embracing . . .
A time to love and a time to hate;
A time of war and a time of peace.

King Solomon
The Bible
Ecclesiastes 3:1–8
Jerusalem, 940 BC

ONE

THREE DAYS PAST EASTER SUNDAY, Mikha'il bin al-Rashid peered through the scope at the flags of Israel, the United States and Palestine, roughly a hundred yards away. Behind a podium sat a row of a dozen chairs. He positioned the crosshairs at the empty space just above the podium and adjusted the settings until the microphones surrounding it were in focus.

"Perfect shot," he whispered to himself on the isolated balcony, four floors up in the Yeshiva School, where, before the building had been closed for renovations, Jewish youth had studied the Torah and laws of their forefathers. With the sun behind him, the small balcony was in shadow, well hidden from the sight of security. He had an ideal, unobstructed shot to the main plaza below, to the gathering center of Jerusalem's Old City.

The Old City was less than half a square mile and, surrounded as it was by towering walls of stone, accessible only through one of seven ancient gates. Scores of workers and security officials were busy preparing for the dignitaries who'd be arriving the following afternoon. While the workers set up chairs, barriers and sound systems, the officers gazed in every direction and spoke into miniature microphones clipped to the cuffs of their sleeves, their focus in stark contrast to that of the people praying among them.

Across the bustling court, those facing the revered stone wall paid no heed to the activity behind them. Silently, they stood before the remains of their ancient temple, carrying on with the ritual of prayer, as generations had before them.

As Mikha'il scanned the scene from the famed Western Wall to the open square of the Old City, he thought about the bitter strife among Jews, Christians and Muslims. All believed this land to be the holiest of sites. In the decades since the declaration of a Jewish state in 1948, the pain and destruction had been unceasing, death and despair spreading as Israelis and Palestinians refused to give up what was, to each, their rightful homeland. No family was left untouched; the scars of suffering were everywhere.

But tomorrow, the latest attempt at peace talks was being announced. The Israeli prime minister, the appointed leader of the Palestinian Authority and the American secretary of state would address a hopeful, yet skeptical, audience.

Mikha'il turned his attention back to the stage. Again he looked through the scope, but this time, he softly depressed his forefinger, taking first one shot, and then another, before pulling his head back to look at the two images in the display box of his Nikon D3-Pro camera. He decided he couldn't ask for better results and wondered if the same would be said of coming events.

He stretched his neck to one side, working out a kink, when something odd caught his attention. He brought the camera back to his eye and saw he was not mistaken. Perched on the roof of the building behind the stage was a large golden eagle.

"What are you doing here, my friend?" Mikha'il murmured.

He pressed the shutter button, and the Nikon snapped ten images. He caught the majestic bird opening its wings and gracefully rising into the air above.

Mikha'il thought it odd that this bird would ever approach a city the size of Jerusalem. It should be flying above the sprawling vistas and endless terrain outside the city's domain, where it would reign supreme over all below.

While the eagle glided out of sight, Mikha'il packed his bag with cameras, lenses and a folding tripod. They were the instruments of his trade, and he considered himself fortunate that his hobby was his profession and with it, he made a good living. At least he thought so, even if others did not.

He started to hurry. He didn't want to keep Jasmine waiting at the airport, and he still had to set everything up in the hotel room.

Stepping over scattered bricks and steel rebar, Mikha'il walked the few short steps to the waiting elevator, the only access to the tiny balcony. The balance of the floor was blocked off by two heavy fire doors, both locked and chained. Mikha'il assumed this was a security measure in preparation for the next day. It was strange that access to the small balcony remained open, but someone's oversight was his gain.

Mikha'il took the elevator down the four floors and made his way through the vacant lobby. Exiting the empty building—the workers had been excused for three days—Mikha'il bent under the yellow chain holding the Access Restricted sign.

"You there!" called a tall, burly man dressed in the standard black suit, shirt and tie of an upper-level security officer. He strode toward Mikha'il with a coffee cup in his right hand. "Show me your credentials."

"Of course, no problem." Experience had taught Mikha'il to cooperate with security personnel. He rummaged through his equipment bag. "I have them right here."

"You really should be wearing them." The agent set his cup on the ground.

"Yes, I know. I will next time," Mikha'il said, pulling the documents from his bag and handing them over.

"And your name, in full?"

"Mikha'il Patrick bin al-Rashid."

The man reviewed the papers. "You're a photographer? You make a living selling your photos?"

"Yes, that's right."

"You make a good living at it?"

"I get by," Mikha'il replied, thinking to himself, *Not him too,* but realizing the intimidating agent was just sizing him up.

"Where did the Patrick come from? Odd combination, isn't it?"

"I guess. It was the name of my grandmother's brother."

5

The officer looked at him, expecting more of an explanation.

"It's a long story." Mikha'il raised his shoulders once in a shrug, hoping that would suffice.

The agent nodded, paused for any forthcoming details and then returned his eyes to the documents.

Mikha'il controlled his impatience. He was thinking of Jasmine waiting for him, but he knew it was best to remain calm and keep a smile on his face. Passing the seconds leisurely glancing around, he noticed a young boy off to his left, staring up at him.

Only fifteen feet from Mikha'il and the security officer, the boy, no older than seven, stood apart from those praying at the wall. He was a Hasidic Jew, from the fundamentalist sect that considered itself the purest of the pure. They maintained that God's presence was universal and that every act and word should serve God. The child's long locks of brown hair flowed from under a wide, black hat, and his soft eyes fixed on Mikha'il.

Mikha'il looked at the faces of those nearby to try to determine who the boy was with, but he seemed to be alone. Mikha'il gave a friendly nod, but the boy offered no returning sign.

"Citizenship?" the security officer asked, breaking the spell cast by the boy.

"Ah, American."

"Birthplace?"

"Vietnam."

"Birth date?"

"July 2, 1970," answered Mikha'il, remaining confident yet calm.

"Okay, the announcements are tomorrow. How come you're here today?" He held Mikha'il's gaze, likely to gauge his response.

"Always best to be prepared."

"And why were you in that building?"

"Just checking the place out."

Mikha'il knew his odd background—an American Muslim, born in Vietnam and named after an Irish Catholic relative—would have raised a red flag, but not enough to make him appear a true threat.

As he predicted, the officer pointed at the Yeshiva School and shook his head. "Can't you read the sign? That building is off limits. I could have you arrested for that."

"I'm sorry. I meant no harm. Just trying to find an angle for a good shot tomorrow," Mikha'il said, lifting his bag.

The agent tilted his head and pressed into his right ear. Then he raised his left wrist to his mouth. "Roger that, Control. My ETA at Lion's Gate is five minutes."

Mikha'il knew the Old City of Jerusalem well. The Lion's Gate was at least a five-minute walk from where they stood, so the questioning was obviously coming to a close.

"You're free to go." The officer handed him back the documents. "Just stay out of that building."

As he turned to leave, Mikha'il saw that the young Hasidic boy, still staring at him, had moved even closer. Somehow, the boy's presence was more unnerving than the agent's questioning.

Within a minute, Mikha'il had reached the main entrance to the plaza. Approaching the security checkpoint, he realized what was odd about the small boy. He bore an uncanny resemblance to himself as a child. Mikha'il stopped, turned and scanned the plaza, but didn't see him.

The buzz of his phone intruded. It was a text from Jasmine.
Sorry. Had 2 work this am. Now in @ 9. xo.

Though relieved she wasn't early so he didn't have to rush to the airport, he felt a pang of disappointment that, once again, he was second place.

TWO

AFTER LEAVING THE PHOTOGRAPHER and knowing that the Temple Mount, with its two grand mosques, was sacred to Muslims—and off limits to Jewish people—Major Rubenstein went around it. Along the northern perimeter, he walked the Via Dolorosa, the narrow cobblestoned street over which Jesus had carried the cross on the way to his crucifixion.

At the end of the modest lane, Rubenstein passed under the Lion's Gate arch, his thoughts absorbed with a personal sense of duty, the preparations for the day ahead and the sacrifice to come. He ignored the dozen young soldiers gathered around the entrance.

At the age of eighteen, men and women are called to mandatory service in Israel's military—a necessity to protect their vulnerable nation. With the approach of the major, this cluster of young soldiers, M-16s strung over their shoulders, ceased their conversations, backed off and made a wide path for him. They all knew of Major Jacob Rubenstein.

To them, he was not just any security officer. Rubenstein was considered the ultimate Israeli soldier. Achieving top-of-the-class marks during his early training at sniper and explosives school, he went on to excel in counterintelligence and to be recruited by the army's elite Special Forces unit, the Sayeret Matkal. His family was legendary, and he had become not only highly decorated and well respected but a prominent-ranking officer in the Shin Bet, Israel's internal security service, whose motto was *the defender that shall not be seen.*

As he entered the Central Command trailer, Jacob felt the soldiers' eyes still on him. He wondered to himself, *If I'm exposed tomorrow, what will they think of me then?*

Inside the confined space, Commander David Caplan was studying the map of the Old City on the large, wall-mounted video screen. He turned to greet the major. "Hey, Ruby!"

"Commander." Rubenstein rubbed his forehead with his right hand.

"Commander?" Recognizing that his protégé seemed distracted, Caplan asked, "What's with you? You okay?"

"Sorry, David. I'm just thinking about all of the plans for tomorrow."

"It's not like you to second-guess yourself. You sure you're all right?"

"I'm fine. Just a head cold I'm shaking, that's all."

Dismissing his concern, Caplan moved on. "The roads surrounding the Old City are packed. It seems there are more protesters than we expected."

"Yes. I've seen them. My early planning reports had anticipated this."

"It's not just the Palestinians protesting. There are several from our side, too. Israeli extremists and those from the settlements."

Rubenstein huffed. "True, but our release of so many prisoners has strengthened the Palestinians' hand." He shook his head. "Letting go thousands of Pali militants in exchange for a handful of our captured soldiers . . . It makes no sense. They've killed so many of our people. No peace will be good enough for them. They only want to annihilate us—they're just waiting for the perfect time to strike."

Caplan contemplated an appropriate response. In recent weeks, he'd noticed a change in Jacob, a growing skepticism in those leading the peace process. Still, Jacob had always been professional, never allowing anything to interfere with his duty. With so much required the next day, Caplan decided it wasn't the right time to risk provoking his security leader. *Perhaps after tomorrow*, he thought. *Jacob's due for some time off anyway.*

"Intel shows no real threat," Caplan replied evenly. "It seems the Palestinians are only waiting to hear terms for peace talks. Just like us."

"Well, if there is peace, how will it last?"

"One can only pray, Jacob. One can only pray."

Turning to the video screen, Rubenstein said lightly, "If peace does last, you'll be out of a job."

"You, too." Caplan laughed, relieved to see him back. "I've been told you have everything in order here."

"Yes, sir." Rubenstein pointed to the map. "You'll be sitting here, behind the prime minister. Alpha Perimeter is the protective shield of our agents surrounding the stage."

Caplan nodded.

"Those agents are also responsible for the arrival route through the Dung Gate and onto the stage. Bravo Perimeter is the entire plaza. It'll be patrolled by uniformed police and our undercover agents. Most protesters will be outside the plaza, here and here," Jacob said, pointing. "They won't get through security screens with their signs and banners."

"And where will military support be?"

"Close," Rubenstein responded with confidence. "Two Sayeret Special Forces teams ready to deploy—one at the Lion's Gate and the other at the Dung. We'll have another eight assault vehicles within one mile of the outer perimeter."

"And Air Defense?"

"Attack choppers, Black Hawks and F-16s on standby."

"I see. Well, I have a new directive," said Caplan firmly. "We have to move all military personnel out farther and keep Air Defense completely out of Jerusalem air space."

"What? Even with more protesters expected?"

Caplan turned to his friend. "I don't like it any more than you do, Ruby, but I'm getting flak from the prime minister. He doesn't want any military presence visible because, and I quote, 'We're about to announce peace talks.' Apparently, it's not enough that we've moved our command trailer here."

Rubenstein's face tightened. He didn't say anything.

"Is something wrong?" Caplan asked.

"No, I suppose not. You're the boss."

"Good. Now what are the deployment tactics for a security breach?"

"First breach—Alpha Perimeter goes into lockdown, and the dignitaries are evacuated up the El Wad and out the Lion's Gate. With a second breach, the two Sayeret Special Forces units are released into the thick of it. If there's a third breach, all eight of the STAV assault vehicles will be deployed and Air Defense scrambled. But only if required, sir."

"We won't let it get to a third breach," Caplan replied assuredly. "And if by chance it goes to a second breach, I want it contained without the Sayeret teams. We have enough police and Shin Bet agents throughout both areas. The prime minister has been very specific. He doesn't want our military making matters worse."

"Still, is it wise to move them so far out? They'll be at least three if not four minutes away, depending on the crowds."

"With no sign of terrorist activity, I can't see a situation where we'll require them. The only breach should come from protesters, which we can handle on our own."

"And if we can't?" Rubenstein could barely contain his frustration.

"Deploy the Sayeret teams, but only if you can't contain a second breach." Caplan looked his protégé in the eye. "However, you will not let any situation get out of Shin Bet control, and you will not require the deployment of military forces. Are we understood?"

He hesitated lightly. "Completely."

"Good. Radio transmission and Lead?"

"I'll personally have the Lead. I'll direct Radio Control and call for any deployment necessary."

"You'll lead Control from the ground then?"

"Yes, where I always am—dead center of it all."

"And the security cameras?"

"I've covered each camera position myself. Before I go home tonight and first thing in the morning, I'll double-check every camera feed and clear the Sayeret vehicles and STAV troop carriers."

"Very good. I wouldn't have expected anything less."

"Thanks, David. Just doing my job."

"Well, make sure you look after that cold and get some sleep tonight. We're going to need you at your best tomorrow."

THREE

"PLEASE, GENTLEMEN, PLEASE. Just take a minute to relax." Virginia Adams tried to control her frustration. "You're only making matters worse."

The meeting had been going on for just under an hour in a secure room of the Knesset, Israel's legislative building. The Israeli prime minister, Aaron Kessel, sat on the sofa beside her while Umar Abu-Hakim, the recognized head of the Palestinian people, sat alone across from them. What had started with friendly dialogue and a review of the sequence of events for the next day's activity had turned bitter as the sun set handsomely outside the large window behind them.

"What do you expect, Madam Secretary?" barked the Palestinian leader. "Their Ministry of Justice has been editing my speech. They won't let me say what needs to be said and instead are writing in words that aren't mine. How just is that?"

Turning to Kessel, ten years her junior, Adams asked politely, "Are these changes that necessary? It is, after all, his speech, and he's not reviewing yours."

Abu-Hakim bowed his head and smiled at her, showing respect and gratitude for her support.

Peace in the Middle East was Virginia Adams's personal goal and political mandate. She was determined to revive the stagnant talks. It meant she had to understand both men and stay impartial while being empathetic to the objectives of each.

Although easily excited, Abu-Hakim was a tough negotiator and, at seventy-two, well aware of the history and repression of his people. A strong advocate for nonviolence as the answer to claiming an independent Palestine, Abu-Hakim had long struggled as a minority voice among his people. After more than thirty years in politics, he knew how to get what he wanted.

The Israeli prime minister only hardened his stance. "The changes are absolutely necessary. Any reference to final borders, the return of refugees and the future of both Jerusalem and its Old City will only cause instability. These points cannot be in his speech—or we'll simply not allow him to speak."

Virginia was grateful Abu-Hakim remained silent. Maybe she could still work this out. "Mr. Prime Minister, not granting him the opportunity to speak will have far worse consequences. Fifty thousand are expected tomorrow, not to mention the international media."

The Palestinian leader coolly added, "We've been discussing this for years. These issues are not unfamiliar to your government."

Aaron Kessel nodded. "Yes, and we've made great progress, which is why we're announcing a path to peace tomorrow."

"My people are expecting more," continued Abu-Hakim, agitation clearly apparent.

"They will get more . . . in time."

"You've been saying that for over forty years," answered the Palestinian.

Virginia observed both men, waiting to see what would happen next. She had tried to alleviate the evening's pressing tension. It was now up to them. If they were to erupt in heated debate, she would have to douse the flames at the appropriate time.

Abu-Hakim started. "For fifty years, the United Nations has called for your withdrawal from the lands you took in the Six-Day War. You can keep your beloved state of Israel. Just give us back our land in the West Bank and Gaza—and with it, our freedom. But you won't, will you? You talk of peace, but continue to build Israeli settlements on our lands. You put up walls, restricting us from traveling on our own roads. All around the world, they call out that this is wrong and insist that you stop, but they only watch while you continue."

Although exasperated by the rhetoric, Virginia stayed quiet, hopeful that Kessel would parch the Palestinian leader to a point where she could intervene.

At Ben Gurion Airport—named after Israel's first prime minister—a similar display was occurring, though on a very different scale.

Mikha'il watched as two boys played tag through the maze of benches and pillars in the international arrival lounge. The sandy-haired boy, dressed in black trousers and a white shirt—an Israeli Jew, Mikha'il assumed by his appearance—darted with arms outstretched, in an endless figure-eight around two pillars. The other boy, slightly larger and with a dark cowlick, leaped out from behind the closest bench, and the two collapsed in a laughing heap. They wrestled for a moment and then resumed their game of chase, making airplane noises as one neared the other, giggling and calling out—one in Hebrew, the other in Arabic.

Mikha'il was writing his grandfather in New York City while waiting for Jasmine's plane to arrive. His grandfather found email a nuisance and appreciated hearing from him the traditional way— by hand, on writing paper, folded neatly in an envelope, personally addressed, stamped and mailed.

I must have been about their age when I met my grandparents, Mikha'il thought, remembering that long-ago meeting at the airport in Vietnam.

Mikha'il's father, an American medic on a Huey helicopter, had been killed while trying to rescue four downed airmen behind enemy lines. His father's death had come before Mikha'il was born, and although his father had proposed, he hadn't yet married Mikha'il's mother, a young Vietnamese woman he'd met the year before. Loving her fiancé as she did, Mikha'il's mother had given their child the name his father had chosen.

Mikha'il's earliest memory was the sweet smell of burning spice from the incense sticks his grandmother and mother sold to those going to the Buddhist Temple in the Saigon slum they called home. Mikha'il was different from both the Vietnamese children in his neighborhood and the half-Yank children born to Vietnamese mothers. He was marked by his Muslim name and was often the victim of beatings administered by local bullies.

In his early teens, well after leaving Vietnam, Mikha'il discovered that his mother had refused to accept offers of financial aid from his father's parents. But, looking back, Mikha'il realized it had made no difference to him. In their one-room, sheet-metal home, love and comfort abounded. His mother and grandmother adored him, and they often cuddled together under one blanket, telling him stories well into the night.

Survival had been difficult in the disease-infested slum. One morning, his grandmother did not wake with the rising sun. Sometime later, his mother became very ill. She sat him down and explained that she couldn't look after him any longer. He would have to leave her, before she left him.

The last time Mikha'il saw his mother was in an airport waiting room, smaller and dingier than the one he sat in now. She had handed him over to an unfamiliar, older couple. They were his grandparents, and they had come to take him to the great United States.

Abu-Hakim's fury continued. He waved his hands excitedly and sharpened his tone in a frustrated outburst. "Israelis cry for their dead when five times more Palestinians have been killed. Millions of our people have fled as refugees. And you refuse to let them return. Four million more live in the lands Israel occupies, but they lack the rights your citizens have."

His voice grew louder. "We can't vote, can't own property without fear of confiscation . . . We can be held in your prisons without trial. More than half of our people live below the poverty line, and still your people are allocated five times more water than ours. Our unemployment rate is over forty percent, and our youth can't afford an education. Instead, our children are killing and being killed." Abu-Hakim finally paused to regain his composure and concluded, "While you thrive, we suffer. All of this is in the name of your cause: protecting the state of Israel, supposedly promised to you by God."

The Israeli Prime Minister sat back on the sofa, bringing his hands together and resting them at his chin. After a seemingly eternal delay, he lowered them and chose his words carefully. "In the absence of peace, humanity is destroyed and people suffer. God knows how our people have suffered in the past decades and centuries. Protecting our state has been our survival. Israel is but a sliver of a country with only eight million people surrounded by a dozen Islamic states with a hundred times that. Some of these—who have shown their distaste for our existence—are, once again, growing unstable. We need to respect the liberties of all peoples, and we will. But these issues require much more review, a firm direction agreed upon by both of our delegations, and then must be passed as law."

"It disgusts me—politics getting in the way of what is right," Abu-Hakim rebuked. "Well, it won't last. Change has come to our neighboring countries. My Muslim brothers won't stand for this much longer."

Shifting to the edge of the sofa, Aaron Kessel leaned forward and looked Abu-Hakim straight in the eye. "I'm sorry, my friend, but you and I are allies here. My coalition government is supporting your cause but only by a narrow margin. Other political parties are deeply rooted in protecting the state of Israel and constantly point out that attacks of terror remain a huge threat. They argued vehemently against our release of prisoners, and they would like nothing more than my removal.

"Umar, we are doing our very best against great odds. It is difficult to keep this ship steady and all on board. Please, I beg of you, don't be the one to rock the boat now when so many others are trying to sink it. Have patience."

Umar Abu-Hakim sighed. "What's left, then, to announce tomorrow?"

This time, Virginia didn't wait to let Kessel respond. "What's left is the solidarity in your mutual declaration of a developing peace for your people, for our humanity and for the hope of a new tomorrow."

Abu-Hakim sat quietly, and the prime minister moved back into the sofa.

"Let's finalize both our speeches together," Kessel added in compromise. "We still have a few hours. What do you say?"

"I guess that'd be fine," Abu-Hakim grunted in acceptance of the evening's truce.

Prime Minister Kessel clapped his hands once and stood up. Extending his right hand to the P.A. leader seated across from him, he said, "Shalom."

Abu-Hakim stood and took Kessel's hand. "Salaam."

Virginia had always found it odd that these two warring peoples, with such different languages, shared the same root word for greeting—and for *peace*. Relieved that the confrontation had eased, she stood as well. Looking at her watch, she said, "Seeing as it's already 8:30, I'll leave you two gentlemen to your work. Call me when you finish, and I'll inform the president of your progress."

"I like that one." A child's voice interrupted Mikha'il's thoughts.

Mikha'il turned toward the voice behind him and recognized, with a start, the serene face of the Hasidic boy he'd seen earlier. But before his mind could properly register the unlikely coincidence, the boy's face transformed into that of the Palestinian boy who'd been playing tag. Following the child's pointing finger, Mikha'il looked at the screensaver photo change on his computer.

"You do?" The screen changed again, and Mikha'il clicked the setting for his screen and pressed the Back key a couple of times.

"There, that one," he said in broken English. "What kind of bird is it?"

"It's a golden eagle."

"I wish I could fly like that." The boy opened his arms and spun around.

"Have you ever been in a plane?"

"Nope, but my mom's on one now," he answered, flying off, his arms still extended.

Mikha'il chuckled and then ripped a page from his notepad and made several intricate folds. When finished, he held a well-engineered paper airplane. He launched it, and the plane soared brilliantly, landing smoothly at the Palestinian boy's feet.

The boy looked at it and then at Mikha'il. Smiling, Mikha'il nodded, and the boy bent to claim his gift.

"Thanks for that," said the man sitting to Mikha'il's right and observing over the top of a folded newspaper. "My son loves anything to do with airplanes."

"It's nothing. I used to make them when I was a child."

"Where you from?"

Mikha'il never really knew how to answer the question. "Uh, New York City. You?"

"East Jerusalem. Who are you waiting for?"

"My girlfriend's flying in from London."

"My wife the same. You got kids?"

"No," Mikha'il said, hiding a wince with a friendly smile.

"Good thing. I'm sure it would be terrifying having kids in the States."

Mikha'il looked at him, curious. "Why do you say that?"

"With all the shootings there, you'd be afraid just to send them to school. Terrible thing," the father said, pointing to a story in the newspaper about the most recent U.S. school shooting, this time in a Charlotte, North Carolina, suburb.

"Yes, sure," Mikha'il replied, not really wanting to comment. He observed the Jewish boy hiding behind a pillar, watching with envy his playmate throwing and retrieving his new prized possession.

Mikha'il ripped off another page and, again, began to fold.

The father went back to his newspaper.

When Mikha'il finished, he threw the plane toward the Jewish boy, who promptly picked it up and launched it toward his Palestinian playmate.

After watching for a moment or two, Mikha'il returned to his letter, the father's remark on his mind. The young Jewish and Palestinian boys engaged in an aerial dogfight of folded paper, laughing together in their innocence. No thought of bombings and missile attacks in their homes and schools, while the father of one apparently thought them safer here than in the United States.

Mikha'il knew the threat in the U.S. was very real to the man beside him—such was the power of the media in forming people's perceptions.

He ended his letter, folded it into an envelope and made his way to the arrival gate.

Standing in front of the frosted sliding doors, Mikha'il's smile broadened as he watched Jasmine walk among the arriving passengers, towing her luggage behind her. He recognized the signs of fatigue around her eyes and in her stride, but she still stood so far out from the rest. She always looked so classy and beautiful to him—her slender frame, olive skin and big brown eyes, her head confidently up and dark hair flowing down her back.

Approaching Mikha'il in her navy business suit and high heels, she was close to his height. She let go of her luggage and threw her arms around his shoulders. Their lips touched for the first time in two weeks.

"Hey, butterfly," Mikha'il whispered in her ear. "You okay?"

"I'm beat. I've been working my butt off and almost missed the plane. Add to that endless lines with security and customs . . ." She pulled Mikha'il closer and looked into his eyes. "But I'm all right now."

FOUR

"EXCUSE ME, MA'AM," announced Virginia Adams's aide as he entered the royal suite of the King David Hotel. "Prime Minister Kessel is calling for you."

"Good." She reached for the phone. "Hello, Mr. Prime Minister. How did things end after I left?"

"We just finished ten minutes ago, and all went well."

"Great news. I'll call the president."

"Goodnight, Madam Secretary. We'll see you in the morning. And, hey, Virginia, thanks for your help."

"Tonight, it was you two who made this work."

She looked at the clock beside her bed: *11:35 p.m., 4:35 p.m. D.C. time.* The president would be in the Oval Office before leaving for a long weekend at Camp David. She summoned her aide to request the secure satellite phone.

Three floors below, Mikha'il opened the door to their room and ushered Jasmine inside. A bouquet of her favorite—white roses—was arranged beside two candles on the table, and their favorite music played on his iPod.

"It's beautiful! You're so thoughtful."

"Well, it *is* our four-year anniversary, and we did meet here." Mikha'il lit the candles.

For the second time that night, she threw her arms around him.

Mikha'il slid off her jacket, gently unbuttoned her white blouse and tenderly kissed the skin above her lace bra. "Let's get you out of these clothes and into a hot bath."

"What good things did I do to deserve you?" She raised his head and pulled him closer.

The couple had first met at the King David Hotel four years before. Less than half a mile west of the Old City, the hotel was a landmark of Israel.

From its earliest days in 1931, it had hosted royalty and the political might of the world. The British governing body of the Palestine territory moved its administrative offices in, and in 1946, terrorists fighting for the establishment of a free Jewish homeland bombed the hotel, killing over ninety people.

After the attack, the hotel remained of strategic importance. When the British flag was lowered in May 1948 and an independent Israeli state declared, war broke out with the resisting Arabs, and the building was transformed into a Jewish military stronghold.

Following the armistice, Jerusalem was divided in half, with the coveted Old City on the West Bank side of the line and completely in Muslim control. The King David Hotel found itself on the edge of no-man's land for nearly twenty years until, with the 1967 Israeli victory in the Six-Day War, Jerusalem was reunited, the Old City reclaimed and the hotel's glory renewed.

Some forty-five years later, Aaron Kessel and his newly formed government had held a media reception in the hotel's garden. The event took place in the middle of a sweltering day, unusual for mid-April, and Mikha'il, contracted by an American newsmagazine to cover the turbulent election, attended.

He'd first noticed Jasmine standing at the patio bar, waiting for a drink. Moving near her, Mikha'il said nothing but casually glanced at her name badge—*Jasmine Desai, Assistant Producer, BBC World News, London.* Keeping an unassuming distance, he watched her mingle with politicians and media acquaintances around the pool.

In the sunshine, her beauty overwhelmed him. She was an enchanting presence, wearing a soft chiffon dress that clung to her slim figure and a white, wide-brimmed hat that framed her perfect face. Mikha'il found himself aiming his camera her way and taking shots every chance he could. Once, he zoomed in and saw her staring back at him, her eyebrows rising in either disdain or curiosity.

She excused herself from the group she was in and approached him. "Hey. You've been taking pictures of me for almost half an hour. What gives?"

"Uh, in the sun, the contrast of your hat to your hair is stunning. It makes for good . . . composition," he blurted out awkwardly. Her confidence caught Mikha'il off guard, and feeling embarrassed, he lapsed into silence.

"I see." Jasmine nodded, a sudden warm smile making her eyes sparkle. She held the top of her hat and glanced to the sky. "This sun is quite hot, though. Maybe if I sat under that big tree over there, I could take my hat off and enjoy my lemonade."

Jasmine brushed past Mikha'il and looked back over her shoulder as she headed toward a single bench shaded by the bowing canopy of a large tree. "Would you like to join me?"

"I guess so" was all he managed to say.

She'd had no more use for her hat that day. They'd talked for hours, trading stories of their lives. Mikha'il told of growing up in Vietnam and New York City and of becoming a photographer, first with the Associated Press and then as an independent. Jasmine recalled her life in India, recounting her family's history and how she'd come to chase her dream with the BBC. Until the sun eased behind the hotel, they sat together on the bench, only to rekindle their conversation and laughter three hours later, over dinner.

By the time they walked back to the hotel, it was after midnight. Mikha'il reached for Jasmine's hand, and for the first time, they touched. A light drizzle filled the warmth of the quiet night, and a haze gave the streetlights a transcendent glow. The sprinkle turned to gentle rain, and Mikha'il stopped Jasmine to softly wipe her face.

He lightly kissed her lips and raised his jacket over their heads. They'd been a couple ever since.

Jasmine, relaxed but still exhausted, walked from the bathroom wrapped in a plush white robe. Seeing Mikha'il stretched out on the bed with his eyes closed, she whispered, "You asleep, babe?"

"No, just thinking."

Jasmine walked over to the bed and sat on the edge. She lowered her bathrobe to her waist. "Can you put on my moisturizer for me?"

As Mikha'il smoothed the lotion onto her back, he told her of the two boys at the airport and what the one boy's father had said. "It's so wrong that the media influences people that way. I can't stand how they focus on the bad in the world."

"That's what sells. It may not be ideal, but it's how the news system works," she murmured, enjoying the sensation of Mikha'il's hands warming her softened skin.

"It didn't used to be like that. News was a public service until cable news turned it into entertainment."

Here we go again, Jasmine thought. "It's what the people want, babe," she said with a sigh.

"Don't you see?" asked Mikha'il. "It's all about selling advertising. But by sensationalizing everything, they're influencing our perception of reality. By continually showing us so much bad in the world, the media are making that the only truth, and people can't help but react to it."

Feeling the discussion intensifying, she pulled up the robe and turned to face him. "And to protest, now you only take photos of what you see as good."

"What's wrong with that?"

"For starters, the people we work for aren't interested in that." Jasmine's tone sharpened. "What's going on is mostly bad. That's what they want. And that's what the public wants."

"Well, I don't like it!"

"Look, like it or not, it's how we get paid," Jasmine snapped. "And I'm tired of working my butt off for a promotion so we can buy a flat and finally make a home together, while you play to your own ideals and refuse every opportunity to make real money."

"Hey, I work, too."

"No, you don't. You keep taking pictures you can hardly sell, because you say no one else will do it. You're traveling more and making less. You used to be one of the top international news photographers. Your photographs were everywhere. They weren't just the news. You were recording history."

Mikha'il thought of his days in Bosnia, his work in capturing the devastating images of violence in Somalia and Rwanda, in Afghanistan, Iraq and here, his prize-winning photos of the aftermath of so many suicide bombings. He had seen and recorded so much destruction and suffering—all of it permanently etched into his subconscious.

"You were highly paid. You could make ten times as much as you do now. But, no. Instead, it's all me. And you find the nerve to criticize what I do, when I'm trying so hard to make a life for us. We don't need to be rich. I'd just like a normal life with you. That's all. But you make me feel like I'm awful for trying to succeed." Jasmine paused. "You know I love you. You're selfless, kind and caring. You constantly put others before yourself, but sometimes you're . . ."

"I'm what?" he asked quietly.

"Well, sometimes you're too good for your own well-being."

Mikha'il did not argue. Instead, his thoughts turned inward. He remembered stealing money from his mother so he could pay the bullies to stop beating him. How she had caught him, only to hug him tightly and tell him how much she loved him, that he was special, that he should have pity on the bullies and not accept their words nor weep after their childish attacks. Instead, he should respect his true self—it didn't matter that he was different.

That talk with his mother had deeply affected him, and since that day, he'd always avoided confrontation. True to form, Mikha'il withdrew from the conversation and sat sadly, silently, barely hearing Jasmine speak.

"Why can't you ever do anything bad? Why do you always have to be so good?" She reached out and gave his shoulder a little shake. "Can't you say something, instead of just sitting there?"

Mikha'il could only shrug, his lone offer of retreat and apology.

"Damn you!" Jasmine swiped angrily at the tears on her face and rushed to the bathroom, slamming the door behind her.

She sat on the edge of the tub, hunched over, her elbows on her knees, her palms pressed against closed eyes. Her thoughts were torn—a heart begging yes, a mind reasoning no. She loved Mikha'il and all that was good in him, but, now in her mid-thirties, a fulfilling life with him seemed less and less likely. He never allowed discussion to segue into talks of marriage and family. Perhaps because of his awkward upbringing, she made excuses for him. But his perspective on career and life—so inconsistent with hers—could not be ignored.

Colleagues had begun to suggest Jasmine move on—that Mikha'il was not right for her. Whenever she spoke of it with him, Mikha'il replied, "It shouldn't matter what others think." But it did.

Now here, at the King David, she'd hoped he might propose. Then others would see he truly loved her. Any question of how she might have replied didn't matter now.

When Jasmine came out of the bathroom twenty minutes later, Mikha'il was on the far side of the bed, facing the other way, with the covers up to his cheek.

She turned off the music, blew out the candles and slipped between the sheets. In a gesture of reconciliation, she cuddled up to the warmth of his back. Thoughts of life without Mikha'il continued to plague her. She tried to silence them, snuggling up behind him, hoping he would turn, knowing he would not.

———

In a small, one-bedroom condominium, Jacob Rubenstein remained awake late into the night. Staring at the ceiling fan, he lay on his bed, thinking of his family.

His grandfather had fought in the war for Israel's independence and had been killed liberating the Old City from the Palestinians. But it was Jacob's father who'd entrenched the Rubenstein family into Israeli military legend when the tank battalion he commanded broke through the Egyptian lines and into the Suez during the Yom Kippur War, sparking the subsequent Israeli victory. Killed during the assault, Jacob's father had been hailed a hero. To honor both men, Jacob had pursued a military career.

As his trance grew more hypnotic with the spinning fan, he reminisced about love and the loss of it. The one time he'd shared his life, she, too, was taken. It had been many years ago, but he still missed Rachel so very much.

During the eighteen months they'd been together, his life had had meaning, and he'd looked forward to his tomorrows—right up to the moment she and eight of the children she taught were killed by a suicide bomber who'd stopped his van next to their bus at a downtown traffic light.

On so many lonely nights, Jacob had visualized the face of his lovely Rachel looking out the window as the bomber pressed a button to detonate the explosives behind him. In his mind's eye, Jacob watched Rachel screaming for his help while shards of metal ripped through her face, her body parts torn asunder among the dismembered limbs of the young children. Just as he could not have prevented the horror, he could not erase the vision or stop it replaying in his mind.

They had all sacrificed so much.

Their God had witnessed them give up their lives to serve his cause and to protect their beliefs, people and land. To carry on in the purpose of God and to honor the principles of those who'd died, more needed to be sacrificed.

This prime minister had betrayed his people. He who would repudiate their God by giving away the land promised to them would undo all of the sacrifices made by those to protect it. Kessel and his compromise of peace had to be stopped. Tomorrow, he *would* be stopped.

Praying to his God, Jacob repeated a mantra over in his mind. *We are your chosen people, and this is the land you promised to us. With your help, I will be strong and persevere to defend it for my people.*

FIVE

MIKHA'IL AND JASMINE WALKED through through the crowd of protesters at the Dung Gate and approached the security barrier. After her purse and his equipment bag were x-rayed, they entered the plaza of the Old City. She reached for his hand.

He took it in his and squeezed.

Searching for words to break his silence, Mikha'il looked up to the brilliant blue sky. "It's a beautiful day for this, isn't it?"

"Yes, it is." Looking at him, Jasmine smiled. She was clearly happy to hear him speak.

Mikha'il had been quiet since their quarrel the night before. He disliked arguing with Jasmine, not wanting to hurt her. Whenever a discussion grew tense, he drifted away—unable to express himself, his sadness or shame—only to return with the regularity of an ocean's tide. He didn't want to lose her. Jasmine was all that he hoped for, but, inside, something was preventing him from committing the way she wanted him to. Something he did not understand.

Hand in hand, they made their way through the crowded plaza to the Yeshiva School. Mikha'il pointed up. "There's the balcony I want to shoot from. We can wait here until about thirty minutes before the speeches begin. Then I'll head up."

"Sure, whatever you want."

Mikha'il once again fell silent. As he looked to his right, toward the Western Wall, the memory of the young Hasidic boy flashed in his mind, and he half expected to see him there. He shook his head at his fancy and focused on the scene before him. Although

29

the speeches would not begin for at least an hour, thousands had already arrived. The prevailing hum was one of excited anticipation; despite the protests outside the wall, these people had come to wait in peace.

Jacob Rubenstein wove his way through the mass of people. He raised his hand and spoke into the microphone clipped to his cuff. "Lead to Control."

"Control here. Go ahead, Lead," the radio transmitter squawked in his ear.

"Perimeter and station check?"

"All stations have been checked—ready and clear."

"Speech launch mark?" Jacob asked and looked at his watch: *2:25.*

"On cue at fifteen hundred hours, T plus thirty-five."

"Order check?"

"Unchanged. Daffodil on lead, Professor on two, and Fisherman on closing."

"Roger that. I'm holding stationary on the west side of the plaza. Report threat activity only until final check at T minus five minutes." Jacob was pleased that all had gone according to plan. There had been discussion that Prime Minister Kessel, code name Fisherman, would speak first. Jacob preferred that the prime minister not get the chance to reach the podium.

As he continued to weave his way through the throng, he reassured himself that he was taking the righteous path. The assassinations of the U.S. secretary of state and the Palestinian leader were necessary sacrifices. With the death of their beloved Virginia Adams, the American people would demand aggressive retribution, and a Palestinian quest for peace would die with the killing of Abu-Hakim. The additional slaughter in the Old City would scar both sides, ending any desire for peace.

The prime minister would be left without support. If he were killed, he would become another martyr, and like others' before, his agenda encouraged. Kessel had to be left alive, to fall on his own.

With his demise, the yearning to give away the lands that so many had sacrificed to defend would be thwarted. All the Promised Land would remain with the people of Israel.

The best part of the plan, Jacob thought, was that the Palestinians would be blamed. The night before, he had planted explosives and detonation devices commonly used by them in the two Sayeret vehicles and the eight STAV armored troop transporters. He'd checked them earlier that morning. This is what he had been trained for—there was none better positioned than he.

This was his destiny.

And God was on his side.

Jasmine felt Mikha'il's hand move from hers.

He checked his watch. "It's 2:30. I should be going to get set up. Hopefully they'll start on time."

"Okay, I'll wait for you here. Good luck." She looked into his face.

Mikha'il glanced back at her, kissed her forehead and walked toward the Yeshiva School.

"Hey, you," Jasmine yelled as she watched him leave.

"Yeah?" Mikha'il replied, turning.

She mouthed across the crowd, "I love you."

Mikha'il read the words on her lips, smiled and nodded back.

As she watched him walk away, Jasmine felt a surge of emotion. She wanted him back in her arms as soon as possible. He ducked under the security chain and disappeared into the building.

Jacob also made his way toward the Yeshiva School, but instead of using the main doorway, he approached a concealed entrance in the south corner. He removed a pair of thin, black nylon gloves from his pocket, drew them snug onto his hands and entered the building through the opening used by construction workers. Once inside, he climbed a workman's ladder, unscrewed a ventilation cover and removed it. Reaching into the duct, Jacob pulled out the duffel bag he'd placed there the previous day. He had scheduled a check of security cameras throughout the area, which had allowed him a window to casually carry the black bag through the plaza. If any agent or officer had noticed him, they'd have assumed he was delivering the bag to a security location and would think nothing of it.

Now he made his way to the elevator. As he rode up, he pulled a key from his pocket; when the elevator stopped on the fourth floor, he inserted the key into the control panel, turning it to lock mode.

Jacob knew how these elevators worked. Once locked, the elevator would not allow access from the lobby, but to enable evacuation, access down would still be available.

Squatting behind the balcony wall, Mikha'il was pulling a camera lens from his equipment bag when he heard the elevator doors open.

"Hey, you there!"

Mikha'il turned but, startled, was lost for words.

"What the hell are you doing here? I told you yesterday this building was off limits."

"I . . . I'm sorry," said Mikha'il, recognizing the security officer. Mikha'il held his arms out. "I'm not a security risk. You can check. I'm clean." Holding up his camera, he asked respectfully, "Can I stay? This is a perfect location to get a couple of good shots. I won't be long."

"No way. Not here," Jacob answered sternly. "You media people think you get access anywhere you damn well please. Now get out of here before you find yourself forgotten about in a Shin Bet jail cell."

Mikha'il found Jasmine waiting where he'd left her.

"How come you're back so soon?"

"Busted by Security."

"That's too bad. Is there anywhere else you can get a good shot?"

"I don't think so." Glancing around the busy square, Mikha'il frowned. "I cased the plaza out yesterday, and that was the best spot. Besides, it's too late to find something else now. The speeches will start in ten minutes. With some luck, I might get a few shots through the crowd."

"Good! You can watch with me," Jasmine said, happiness in her voice.

Waiting for the proceedings to begin, they quietly stood, no different from the thousands of others who'd gathered around them.

Alone on the fourth floor, Jacob opened the duffel bag. He removed his jacket and pulled on a tight-fitting black sweater. Reaching into the bag again, he took out two weapons, an AK-47 automatic assault rifle—the Palestinians' affordable weapon of choice—and a Russian-made Dragunov sniper rifle. Placing the assembled weapons over one shoulder and an ammo belt over the other, he moved with practiced precision. Sliding on his stomach, he inched his way to the balcony.

Jacob looked over the crowd. He was pleased with the balcony's orientation. Due to its obscure angles, with the sun at his back and wearing all-black operative gear, he was virtually invisible.

The whole of the plaza, the building and entrance were covered by security cameras, but he'd ensured the tiny balcony and temporary workmen's entrance were just missed. As a senior officer, he knew that satellite recon would not pick up full detail of the balcony. At best, it might show an unidentifiable human form in black.

The shots would echo through the plaza, making their origin impossible to pinpoint. Jacob would remain unseen and unheard. His position had been slightly compromised, but the photographer shouldn't suspect anything. Regardless, Jacob had come too far to stop now.

He looked at his watch—*2:55*—and raised his cuff. "Lead to Control, cue minus five minutes. Ready all perimeter checks."

"Roger that, Lead."

For the next three minutes, the radio operators checked with all perimeter locations and assigned agents, and Jacob sat with his back to the wall. He instinctively held the Glock in his side holster, ready for any offensive attack against him.

Only he knew what was to come. Taking out the two dignitaries would spark Breach One and perimeter lockdown. He would then spray bullets from the AK-47 into the crowd three times, creating Breach Two. His plan had had to be modified because of Caplan's changes. He would be on the balcony longer than he'd hoped, but there was no other way. Only after the continued gunfire would the breach be deemed uncontained, giving him reason to call for the two Sayeret units.

After they passed the gates, the GPS detonators he'd planted the night before would go off and the vehicles would explode. Breach Three would be automatic and the full military response launched. The STAV combat vehicles would rush toward the panicking crowd. Unknown to those troops, they would be delivering more bombs that would go off when the vehicles reached their marks. Even if the plan was thwarted before all the bombs were detonated, there would be enough blasts to cause scores of casualties in the crowds rushing out of the Old City.

The disastrous scene could not be averted.

"Control to Lead." The voice in Jacob's ear interrupted his thoughts.

"Go, Control."

"All stations ready to go."

"Keep frequency clear, emerg and action only. I'll call the ball," Jacob ordered.

He could feel the pounding in his heart. *I am not afraid. This is my destiny.* He breathed deep and slow, praying for strength.

"Beruchim habayim beshalom, chaverim. As salaam alaykum ya sadiqaee," Jacob heard over the loud speakers, as Virginia Adams spoke her welcome in both Hebrew and Arabic and then in English. "Welcome in peace, friends."

Jacob lifted his rifle.

"We are all gathered together today . . ."

He peered through the high-powered scope. The crosshairs targeted her heart. He took a breath and held it as he had been well trained to do. With his right forefinger, he gently squeezed the trigger. Before the first clap of the sniper rifle reached the crowd, Jacob found his second mark and squeezed again.

As the two shots echoed, the U.S. secretary of state and the Palestinian leader were thrown backward. The bullets blasted through their bodies and sprayed flesh, bone and blood out their backs.

The words were screeched into Jacob's ear. "Daffodil and Professor down. Repeat, Daffodil and Professor down."

Sitting safely out of sight with the sniper rifle resting on his lap, Jacob confidently gave orders. "Breach One, Breach One. Lock down Alpha Perimeter, emerg evac through Lion's Gate."

"Roger that, roger that," Control replied and began transmitting orders.

The crowd was oddly hushed, too shocked to realize what they had just witnessed.

Jacob moved the sniper rifle to one side and reached for the AK. He stood, aimed and opened fire into the thousands of innocents below. He counted to himself as he fired. *One, two, down.*

Repeated training had taught Jacob to expose himself for only a two-count to avoid being seen. In those two seconds, he unloaded most of the thirty rounds from the clip and returned behind the balcony wall.

"Automatic shots fired in Perimeter B, central plaza," came Control's voice.

"Go, Breach Two, but do not deploy the Sayeret teams. All eyes alert for unfriendly fire." Jacob clipped the next magazine into his weapon, counted another twenty seconds and rose to unload it.

At the first sound of automatic gunfire, Mikha'il had pushed Jasmine to the ground.

When the clamor of the second rapid-fire came, he held her down, covering her body with his. *Thank God I'm with her.* He shot a quick glance up to where he would have been. To his shock, he caught a glimpse of someone in black, pointing a weapon and then dropping behind the balcony wall. *The security officer. His large bag . . .*

"Jasmine, stay here! Don't move!"

He jumped up, looking for the nearest security agent or police officer. In the panicked frenzy all around him, Mikha'il saw none. All the while, his mind whirled. If the attack was from the Shin Bet itself, he couldn't trust Security anyway.

With determined desperation, Mikha'il forced his way through the mayhem, dropping his camera bag at the entrance of the Yeshiva School.

"Continued automatic gunfire in Bravo Perimeter. Request orders!"

Jacob had to wait as police and his agents tried frantically to source the unfriendly fire. Ninety more seconds would do it and then the last attack and an unavoidable military response. "Locate unfriendly fire and contain," he insisted to Control.

"Repeat, Lead. Repeat!" Control excitedly requested confirmation of his order, expecting instead an order for the deployment of the Sayeret teams.

"I repeat. Locate and contain unfriendly fire!"

"Roger that."

"Are you checking video? Do you have anything yet?"

"Negative."

"That gunfire is coming from someplace. Find it fast and report!" Jacob ordered briskly. "We don't want to deploy the military."

"Yes, sir."

"And keep my channel open! I want to hear all activity."

Jacob waited, secure knowing that he would be warned of any approach to his position. He had originally planned to be gone by now, returning to the plaza after calling for the deployment of the two Special Forces units after the second breach, but with the last-minute changes, he now had to wait before ordering them in.

He jammed the last magazine into the AK and waited as the long seconds ticked by. On ninety, he rose to position. This third and final time, he took an extra second to empty the full round, shooting hot lead into the frantic crowd below.

He ducked behind the balcony wall, breathing steadily and easily, immune to the screams of terror and pain rising from the plaza.

Control excitedly confirmed the gunfire. "Attacks again in Bravo Perimeter uncontained. Repeat, uncontained—many civilian casualties."

This was the point Jacob had been waiting for. He raised his wrist to call in the Sayerets. The next stages of his plan were unstoppable.

Just as he was about to give the order, the elevator doors opened behind him. *But the elevator was locked.* He swiveled in disbelief and, for a split second, froze at the sight of a wild figure hurtling toward him. In that instant, Jacob pulled the Glock from his holster. He fired three times in quick succession at the rapidly approaching figure, but it kept coming.

For the first time, Jacob's cool was shaken. *It's that damn photographer. I just shot him three times—he should be down.* Why isn't he falling? He fired three more times and hit the intruder with only the final shot, red spraying from the head of the now leaping man.

Jacob readied for the blow.

Mikha'il met his target with such force that both men flew over the balcony wall and hurled toward the concrete of the Old City plaza square below.

SIX

THE BRILLIANT SUNSHINE was just a blur in his blood-filled eyes. He clenched the ground with both hands and spit out a mouthful of blood that coagulated immediately in the sand by his face. Mikha'il felt no pain, but his body was slow to react.

He rolled onto his back, bewildered as the realization set in that there was no sound in the still air, no panicked voices, no one rushing to his aid. He raised his hands and wiped his forehead, drenched with blood. Sand mixed with the fleshy matter above his left eye. He could feel the coarseness of the grains abrading the open wound, but still he felt no pain.

He closed his eyes to the intense sunlight in the clear sky above him, trying to comprehend what had happened. The last thing he remembered was falling, falling toward the concrete plaza with the shooter beneath him.

Am I dreaming? He attempted a deep breath but heard soft bubbles escaping through his open chest wounds. This didn't feel like a dream.

The red of the sun behind his eyelids softened.

Mikha'il opened his eyes and looked up. A large bird hovered over him. A scavenging vulture was his first thought, but no. It was a golden eagle, the majestic bird he'd seen the day before. He watched as the bird circled and then vanished into the sun's center.

Mikha'il felt pressure as something pushed against his open wounds. Then he heard words.

"Are you him?"

Silhouetted by the sun was an old Bedouin woman, who poked him with a stick.

"What?" Mikha'il forced the word through his lips.

"I said, 'Are you him?' " the old woman repeated, still prodding Mikha'il's oozing chest.

"Look . . ." He could barely breathe. "I need . . . help. Please."

"I believe you to be him."

"Who?"

"But perhaps not. We shall see." The Bedouin pushed her stick into the sand.

"I don't know . . . what you're . . . talking about," Mikha'il said, coughing and spitting out more blood. "You've got . . . the wrong person."

"Maybe so, but this is not for you to decide."

"I need help. Please."

"You will be taught and judged. Still, you will have to choose."

"Choose?" Anger mixed with fear. *What is this woman saying?*

"Then I will know. Then we will all know."

Mikha'il's eyes closed, wanting the surreal scene to disappear. When he opened them, the woman was gone. Other than her stick, discarded in the sand, all that remained was an empty desert and a lone bird in flight.

SEVEN

ALMOST TWO MINUTES had passed since Virginia Adams and Umar Abu-Hakim had been hit. Above the chaos of the screaming crowd, apparent order had settled on the stage. While Prime Minister Kessel was evacuated, Shin Bet and U.S. Secret Service agents formed a protective ring around the two downed peacemakers as medics desperately attempted to stabilize the two bloodied bodies for evacuation.

David Caplan was organizing the arrival of two stretchers when his earpiece radio sounded.

"Caplan here."

"Commander, Lead is not responding. Request orders."

Caplan was both surprised and concerned but wanted to avoid deployment of the Sayeret teams and a full military response. "Locate and contain unfriendly fire. Hold off added deployment until my order. I'll take Lead until the major returns. Where was his last known location?"

"West side of the plaza, near the Yeshiva School."

Caplan looked to the mayhem in the plaza. "I'm on my way there. Ensure evac route is secure. Fisherman's going through now. Daffodil and Professor are on their way. Make sure trauma teams are ready at the Hadassah."

"Roger that."

David leaped off the stage and into the plaza.

He slipped through the hysterical masses, barking orders to galvanize police into maintaining order. Other officers and agents scoured the plaza with their weapons drawn, searching for the source of the attacks.

There was carnage everywhere, the wounded helplessly screaming and bloodied. Many lay motionless in the plaza. Some were being dragged to safety by family members; others staggered on their own. One thing was apparent: the bullets had shown no prejudice as they struck down the young and old, Jew and Muslim alike.

He'd almost made it to the buildings along the west side of the plaza when the receiver in his ear came alive. "Control to Lead."

"Go, Control."

"Major Rubenstein's down, sir."

"Location?"

"Base of the school."

"His condition?"

"Unsure, sir."

"I'm almost there." His pace quickened as he passed a shrieking woman covered in blood rocking a small body in her arms. Shaking his head in despair, he asked Control, "Any containment?"

"We remain uncontained, sir."

He could no longer delay the deployment of the two Sayeret reinforcements.

Jacob could not move. His chest and vital organs had been crushed by the combined impact of the photographer and the cement floor of the plaza. Throbbing pain beat through his body, but what sickened him was a sense of defeat. The Sayeret and military deployment had been avoided, and the bombs not launched. Praying his actions may have been enough, he heard the screams of the people blend with the transmissions on the radio receiver in his ear.

"Deploy the Sayeret teams," came David's order. "I repeat. Deploy the Sayerets."

Flooded with the relief of triumph, Jacob whispered to himself, "Well done, my friend. Thank you."

He thought of the sacrifices of those he loved, the heroics of his grandfather, his father and all who had given so much for their cause. He had now joined them. A sense of peace descended upon him as images of Rachel, his only love, passed through his dying mind, the shards flying away from her face and restoring her perfect smile. He hoped that he would be with them all soon.

Mikha'il's twisted body lay beside that of the gunman. Yet somehow, Mikha'il could see himself lying there. The desert was gone; the eagle was gone. It seemed to him that he was gazing down, as if from high above, at the chaos of the crowd surrounding his own stilled form. The gaping wound in his forehead and his clothes were saturated in blood, but the pain he felt did not come from his broken body. All he could feel was a pulsation emanating from those around him. He sensed their presence and their individual battles for life, while his own existence felt spectral. *Is this death?*

He searched for Jasmine, but through the pandemonium of the scattering crowd, he couldn't find her. She'd likely been pushed toward the south gate by the crush of people trying to get away. Mikha'il felt the man beside him greeting the death that awaited him, and to him, Mikha'il sent his thoughts. *Hold on, friend. Find the strength.*

As he focused on the dying man, the thoughts and emotions he felt from those around him eased, edged out by the single force of the one suffering beside him. Mikha'il was flooded with an awareness of the man's pain: the deaths of all whom he'd loved, the tragedy of war, his anger and lack of forgiveness, mixing with retribution and the completion of his mission.

The shooter! Mikha'il stopped himself from recoiling and continued to will a message of strength into the man's mind. *Hold on, friend. Don't let death take you. Don't surrender to it.*

Jacob Rubenstein felt the strange presence inside him. Bewildered, he attempted to ignore the insistent message, but it only intensified. Jacob's glory in fulfilling his destiny and any tranquility he felt in the acceptance of his own death were eroding, being replaced instead with intrusive thoughts. He could feel them radiating from the inert body beside him.

Remembering the strength of the photographer on the balcony, Jacob painstakingly focused his eyes on the motionless clump next to him. The words and their source filled his soul. He felt prickles of panic rushing through him and, in a blaze of revelation, understood the magnitude of the acts he'd just unleashed, acts that he'd believed to be in the service of his God.

Grasping the horror of his actions, Jacob pleaded to the spirit beside him for salvation. His words were faint. "Forgive me. Oh, please forgive me. I'm so sorry, I am so very sorry for what I've done."

Two agents tended to Jacob while others surrounded the scene. Panting from his run across the plaza, David asked, "Situation?"

"Looks like the major brought him down, sir."

David gestured toward Jacob. "How is he?"

"He's pretty bad. I don't think he's going to make it."

David grimaced. He looked toward Mikha'il. "And him?"

"Don't know, Commander. Medics are on the way."

"Is he alone?"

"I think so. No signs of any other suspect. We're locking down the building now."

David knelt by his friend. "Hey, Ruby, buddy."

"I'm so sorry," Jacob whispered.

"Help is on the way. You got him. You did great." David tried to reassure his dying friend.

"Please forgive me."

"Just hold on. Fight."

David's words intermingled with those Jacob was hearing through Mikha'il's presence. This was his chance for salvation. He had to stop the detonation of explosives.

His plea was garbled. "The Sayerets, the STAVs. Stop them, David. Please stop them."

David strained to hear his dying friend. Even with his last breaths, Jacob was trying to manage the operation.

"Don't worry, Jacob. We've already deployed the Sayeret teams for support . . ."

"No."

". . . but we won't need full military launch. We're locking down the school now. You got him. You contained the breach."

Jacob's next words were drowned out by the frantic cries of a woman who forced her way through the agents and dropped to her knees at the suspect's side.

"Oh no, God. Please no. I'm here, Mikha'il."

Feeling her beside him, Mikha'il tried his best to ease her fear. *Don't worry. I'm okay . . . I love you.*

But before his thoughts could reach her, Jasmine was pulled back and forced to the ground. The skin of her right cheek tore as her face skidded along the concrete.

Mikha'il's focus immediately shifted from the shooter to the threat to Jasmine.

"Cuff her," David ordered and, standing over Jasmine, demanded, "Who is he? Are you alone?"

"What? It wasn't him. He's innocent!" She shouted in disbelief as one of the agents held her down, his knee jammed into the back of her neck.

"Get her out of here," David snarled.

The agent dragged Jasmine away as two news crews arrived and began recording.

Standing below the balcony, a senior agent was on the radio with his team above. He reported the information to David. "Sir, we have complete containment. They found the sniper rifle and an AK-47 on the fourth-floor balcony above us. The major must have taken him over in the struggle to stop him."

"Good work, Captain. Get the media back and set up a perimeter."

David breathed a sigh of relief. He could halt the Sayeret deployment and avoid any military advance. Just before giving the order to cancel the approaching teams, he looked toward Jacob and the men tending him.

Shaking his head, a medic glanced up. "I'm sorry, sir. He's gone."

David gave a slow nod of acceptance. He pushed his grief deep inside and raised his cuff. "Lead to Control."

"Go ahead, sir."

Watching as Jacob's body was covered with a dark blanket, David gave the order. "We have containment. Halt the Sayeret teams."

"Roger that, Commander."

Control had just got the words out when the ground shook with a thunderous explosion. David could only watch as flames and smoke shot into the sky behind the Temple Mount.

EIGHT

"WHAT THE HELL WAS THAT?" David yelled into his sleeve.

"Sir, the first Sayeret team has been hit! They're all down!"

"Where are the dignitaries?"

"Fisherman is out. Daffodil and Professor still approaching Lion's Gate."

"Get the other Sayeret team in as fast as you can. Hold on Breach Two but do not deploy military."

"Roger that."

David surveyed the mayhem in the plaza. Sirens wailed in the background while cameras began feeding live footage to their country's news networks, the journalists struggling to maintain their calm despite the horror of violent disruption on a day set aside for peace. As they tried to make sense of the senseless, the Old City plaza was rocked by a second explosion, this time, from the south.

David tried to block out the screams of the crowd. He held his hand over his ear so he could hear Control's report. "Commander, the second Sayeret team has been attacked."

"Condition?" He yelled above the noise.

Control paused. "It's bad, sir. They're all down."

This was it. He had no choice. "Go Breach Three. Full military scramble. Deploy the STAVs and Air Defense."

"Roger that," responded Control and transmitted the order through all frequencies. "Breach Three. Scramble, scramble, full deployment!"

———————

The agents surrounding the scene at the base of the Yeshiva School linked arms and stepped forward in an attempt to push the cameramen back. Two more medics had arrived and were treating Mikha'il. Watching them, David checked his watch: *3:07*.

In just six minutes the world had been turned upside down. He regretted altering Jacob's orders the day before. *Perhaps he'd still be alive. He would've ordered deployment earlier, and the military would've been here by now.* David waited in defeat for their needed support, every second of delay agonizing while he considered the possibility of more attacks.

A screeching roar filled the sky as two F-16s flew low and banked for a second approach, the menacing sound adding to the terror below. They were so close to the ground, the panicking crowd could see the pilots look down from the safety of their cockpits.

Over the noise of the planes, David heard the beating of the helicopters coming from the west. Regathering his composure, he barked orders to Control. "Locate attack source! Report unfriendlies on sight."

"All eyes alert, Commander, but nothing yet."

"Damn it, where are they?" he shouted in frustration.

"Right here, sir," a soft voice answered, but not from his earpiece.

Looking down, David saw a lone Hasidic boy standing at his side. Somehow, he had slipped beyond the gathered agents. Completely without fear, and in absolute contrast to those around him, he stood, gazing into David's taut face.

"What? Where did this kid come from?" David looked around to the agents, but no reply came.

"I saw what happened," the small boy went on.

David squatted beside him.

The boy did not blink. His eyes were large and honest. Under his wide-brimmed black hat and flowing curls, his face revealed nothing of fear or any other emotion. David felt an immediate shock of recognition. He knew this boy. *Impossible!* He shook the thought from his head.

"You did? What did you see?" Maintaining gentle eye contact, David carefully questioned the boy.

"I saw everything," he said softly and then turned to Mikha'il's motionless body. "It wasn't him."

"Who then?" asked David, focused solely on the child.

"It was that man." He pointed a tiny finger at the blanket-covered mound. "He shot the lady speaking and the man sitting beside her. Then he shot the people."

"You mean the man under the blanket shot the people? Are you sure?"

"Yes, sir, from up there." His arm and finger rose toward the balcony.

"And what about him?" David gestured toward Mikha'il.

"He saved us."

David stared at the boy, his mind racing for explanations to refute the words. The radio squawked into his ear.

"Commander, Daffodil and Professor trapped in evac. Too much damage near Lion's Gate from the Sayeret explosion."

"Other exits?"

"Not good, sir. Crowds are spilling everywhere, and Dung Gate is blocked by the second explosion."

Three Apache attack helicopters flew in from the west, thundering low over the roof of the Yeshiva School just as a Black Hawk arrived from the north.

Forgetting the boy, David looked up at the Black Hawk hovering over him. He ordered to Control, "Evac them to the Temple Mount. Land the Hawk there and get them out!"

"On the Temple Mount. Are you sure, sir?"

"Yes, I'll take full responsibility. Have the Apache gunships provide cover."

"Roger that."

Commanding the helicopter group and piloting the Black Hawk, the captain was confused by the order he'd just received. He turned to his copilot for guidance.

The copilot only shrugged.

"Repeat order," requested the captain.

"Hawk One, land on Temple Mount and hold for Daffodil and Professor evac. Apache One, Two and Three, in for cover. Confirm!"

But the captain would not confirm the order. The Temple Mount was the holiest of sites to his people and had been sacred for three thousand years. Landing a helicopter on it would desecrate the hallowed place and violate many Jewish laws. He stalled, pondering his next move, protecting the sanctity of the Temple's location and disputing any authority that tried to usurp God's.

The small child looked up at the Black Hawk. Still betraying no emotion, his eyes remained open wide. He held his hat and tilted his head back farther.

David's gaze followed the child's. He raised his hand to shade his eyes and squinted against the sun. Expecting to see the choppers moving toward the Temple Mount, he was surprised to find they weren't. But more surprising was what engaged the interest of the boy.

Above the helicopters, an eagle soared, peacefully circling the bedlam below. As David watched the boy, the full impact of the young child's words sank in.

He recalled Jacob's dying plea. *The Sayerets, the STAVs. Stop them.* David looked toward the body of his fallen friend and saw what he hadn't noticed before: a black operative glove. Jacob's covered right hand peeked out from under the blanket.

David stared at the gloved hand. He yelled into his mic, "Lead to Control, stop the STAVs! Repeat. Stop the STAVs and report."

"Yes, sir. Aborting STAV advance."

David waited for Control's report and the advancement of the helicopter formation to the Temple Mount.

Within a few seconds, Control came back. "All STAVs stopped. Request action."

"They may be wired with explosives. Have them return to initial locations. Do not deploy personnel until cleared. Is that understood?"

"Understood, sir."

"Good. Now why the hell aren't those choppers advancing to the Mount?"

"Their captain is stalling. He doesn't want to land there."

"Damn! Put me through directly to him."

"Go ahead," Control responded, connecting him with the Black Hawk.

"This is Commander Caplan, director of the Shin Bet. Can you land that thing? We have digs condition critical for evac."

"Not on the Temple Mount. Approach too dangerous."

"Look, I have full authority here. Now land it!"

"Sir, request alternative landing instructions."

"The U.S. secretary of state is one of the casualties. We have no other approach, and we still don't have containment. So land it on the Mount, or I'll have a Shin Bet sniper take you out, and your copilot can land it."

There was a pause before the captain's response. "Landing on the Mount."

The Black Hawk turned toward the Temple Mount. The Apache attack choppers followed closely behind.

David looked around for the young child, but he was gone. "Find that kid for questioning!" he ordered.

"Which kid?" the senior officer next to him responded.

"The young Hasidic I was just talking with. And find his family, too!"

The medics were having difficulty stabilizing Mikha'il.

He was aware of their presence but paid no attention. With Jasmine's departure and the death of Jacob, his attention was focused on the scores of wounded. He felt their pain as if it were his own.

Although astounded by his own transformation, Mikha'il recognized that he had to act quickly and seek understanding later. His concern was with those near death—the secretary of state, the Palestinian leader, thirteen bystanders dying from gunshot wounds and the burned Sayeret teams.

Mikha'il felt each individual's desperate struggle to cling to life. On behalf of each, he fought against the grip of death. He didn't know how he was accomplishing this, but he was determined that no more would die there.

"So, who is he?" David asked the agent standing guard over Mikha'il.

"Don't know, sir, but looks like he was passing himself off as media."

One of the medics turned. "Well, whoever he is, he isn't going to make it unless we get him out of here, and fast."

David was frozen with indecision. If the boy was correct, his suspect may have been a savior, not a terrorist.

"Get him to the Mount. The Hawk is landing there for evac. And hurry. Because they won't wait for him."

Agents carried Mikha'il on a stretcher through the crowd, medics running along each side, adjusting the equipment and ventilating the air bag, while officers guarded the front and rear.

Maintaining his hold on the lives fading around him, Mikha'il became aware of a new force, strange and unrecognizable. A large mass was moving through the mayhem, a tremendous snorting and growling emanating from it. Defiantly, the creature weaved its way through the crowd toward the stretcher. Broad horns, tipped with razor-sharp points, rose from the huge head of the bull-like beast. Its sweating body was all muscle, and its piercing, bloodshot eyes were fixed on Mikha'il. He was puzzled at the lack of reaction from the crowd and then realized that nobody else could see it. He was filled with the same sensation as earlier, when he had the vision of the woman in the desert.

He watched in fascination as a second form appeared on the back of the bull—a manlike shape. Like the bull, the man was large and muscle-bound. Wrapped in lion and tiger skins, he carried a spear in his right hand. A hissing cobra, flicking its tongue past its fangs, looped around his neck. On his chest, beneath the slithering snake, lay a necklace made of wood, and woven into the left side of his long dark hair was a golden half-moon.

As the escort team rushed Mikha'il to the helicopter on the Mount, the apparition paced behind—never taking their eyes off him.

"We're losing him," yelled the medic pumping Mikha'il's air bag. The team halted and another medic injected Mikha'il's upper arm with more Adrenalin.

"Leave him or get him in now!" someone shouted from the helicopter. "Our orders are to evac after the other two are in and secure."

Mikha'il still sensed the rider and bull, the bull clawing at the ground, blocking access to the helicopter's opening. The rider raised the spear and pointed its tip directly at Mikha'il's face.

Seemingly oblivious to the vision, the helicopter crew reached for the stretcher as the medics scrambled up beside it. The creature shifted sideways, and the security officers rammed his stretcher into the open doorway.

"All clear!"

Before the stretcher was strapped in or the door closed, the Black Hawk ascended rapidly, leaving the square of the Temple Mount behind.

Through the open door, a disoriented Mikha'il fixed his gaze on the rider, still pointing his spear at him. The unknown hunter's twisting hair and animal skins blew in the dust from the rising helicopter.

———

"He is Shiva the Destroyer, Lord of Death. He has come for you. He is headstrong and will not give up easily." The gentle voice came from Mikha'il's right side. "Like you, saving so many here from his grip, I defend you," continued the voice. "I am Vishnu the Protector, the Lord of Preservation."

Mikha'il felt his right hand seized in a powerful grip.

Vishnu did not let go until the medic's words came.

"We got him back!"

NINE

THE BLACK HAWK WAS MET by trauma teams on the roof. OR teams, already fully briefed on the condition of Virginia Adams and Umar Abu-Hakim, waited below. Mikha'il was taken last and hurried to the ER.

"Gunshot wounds. Two in the chest, no exits. Another through the right shoulder, and one to the left forehead, no exit. Compound fractures to both tibias and left collarbone, heavy internal abdominal bleeding," the medic who'd accompanied Mikha'il in the helicopter briskly reported and then scurried off once the team moved into action.

Inside the ER trauma room, an intern jabbed an IV into Mikha'il's jugular, providing his craving body with red blood cells and platelets while a nurse hooked up an ECG and another attached Mikha'il's breathing tube to the ventilator.

Behind the team, and flanked by two armed Shin Bet agents, a doctor pushed aside the curtain.

"This one's critical," the attending intern promptly reported.

"No. This one's a terrorist. He's the last priority. We need you out there. Casualties from the plaza are coming in." She looked down. "You've done all you can here, anyway."

Less than thirty minutes after the interruption of his morning run, President Daniel Robinson stood in front of a large television, his ears alert for either the sound of Marine One landing or his aide bringing him the phone with the Israeli prime minister on the other end. Dressed in a modest business suit and tie and ready for the West Wing, the president waited impatiently, angry at himself for having been at Camp David while events unfolded in Jerusalem. A break was quite irregular for him, and he regretted letting the secretary of state talk him into it. But she'd been so insistent that she could control the proceedings.

Now, his inner cabinet was meeting in the Situation Room, reviewing the collapse of her dream, and he was watching coverage on CNN.

"This day of peace has turned dreadfully wrong. The carnage is everywhere. We have unconfirmed reports that Israeli forces brought down a single terrorist minutes after the shooting started. Identified as Mikha'il bin al-Rashid, he is a forty-two-year-old American Muslim—"

"Sir, Prime Minister Kessel is on the line."

"Thank you." The president reached for the phone. "Hello, Aaron, are you all right?"

"As far as one can be under the circumstances."

"Right." The president quickly moved on. "Madam Secretary—how is she doing?"

"She's in surgery. I've been told the bullet grazed her heart. I am sorry to say that her condition is critical, but she couldn't be in better hands."

"I appreciate that. Please make sure that I am personally informed at the first sign of any change in her condition. And the other casualties?"

"Many wounded, some critical, but only one death so far. A Shin Bet officer."

"And Abu-Hakim?"

"Also critical and in surgery."

"Good God, Aaron, how did this happen?"

"All of our investigation teams are on it. I am waiting for further information from them."

"I'm told you got the terrorist."

"We have a suspect under guard at the hospital. They don't think he'll make it."

"Was he acting alone?"

"We don't know yet. Right now, we have his girlfriend in custody and are questioning her."

The aide entered the room and whispered, "Mr. President, Marine One is here."

"Okay, Aaron. Let's talk again when you have more information. In the meantime, stay strong. I'll say a prayer."

TEN

"YOU! I HAVE COME FOR YOU!" Shiva shouted fiercely, astride his raging bull, as they burst through the curtain.

The intrusion startled Mikha'il, but before he could react, a figure with luminous blue skin materialized protectively in front of his bed. The apparition grabbed the horns of the bull and thrust it toward the doorway.

The bull clawed and struggled for traction as the blue figure forced it backward until the bull crashed against the opposite wall in the hallway. Shiva sneered and growled, angered by his defeat, and then vanished into nothingness.

Vishnu pushed through the curtain and returned to the trauma room, passing two guards on the way.

The soldiers saw none of the violent battle, only the slight billowing of the curtain. Curious, one raised it and looked in. Nothing had changed since the trauma team had left; the terrorist lay still on his deathbed.

But towering over Mikha'il's prone body, Vishnu stood tall and lean. A shining crown sat on twisting curls of light brown hair, and bands of gold covered his bare chest and arms. His majestic form was reinforced by the jade-colored robes draping his shoulders and body. Most striking about him was his skin. It was the color of the deepest sky, except for a fiery dot of red in the center of his forehead.

"You have done well, my friend, but the medicine men have left you to die. Knowing that, Shiva will continue in his quest to steal your breath and transform your spirit."

Mikha'il grimaced in confusion. "Transform my spirit. What are you talking about?"

"He is death, coming to take you," Vishnu answered bluntly, staring down at the blood-soaked, bandaged body that was, and was not, Mikha'il.

Taped over his mouth, a thin plastic pipe systematically pumped air into his lungs while wires and tubes flowed to and from his unconscious body. Mikha'il remained sternly defiant. "Let the rider come. I'm not afraid."

"I know you aren't. Your stubbornness may prove your strength or perhaps your weakness. We shall see."

"And who are you? How can I be awake and unconscious at the same time? What's happening to me?"

"The rider of the bull and I are of the Hindu Gods. The one who loves you most prays to us for your survival."

Mikha'il drew a deep breath, trying to reassure himself. How the whole impossible sequence of events that brought him here could have occurred was beyond him—the vision in the desert, the uncanny sense of oneness with those suffering in the plaza, the stalking bull and its malevolent rider. And now, this strange blue form calling himself a god.

None of this is true, he thought, *none of it. This is an elaborate unholy nightmare, and I will wake up at any moment in bed beside Jasmine.*

"This is what it is," the blue god's voice resonated in his mind. A soft but powerful surge of compassion and strength washed through Mikha'il. Soon, a realization, an acceptance he'd been resisting, occurred. This was not for him to question. It was for him to experience, to absorb.

But there were things he needed to know. "Jasmine, where is she? Is she all right?"

"She will be fine."

"You'll make sure of that?" Mikha'il questioned forcefully.

"Yes, of course."

"And the victims, how are they?" Mikha'il was aware once more of those from the Old City who were near him in the hospital. "I feel so much pain. And before, many dying."

"You protected them from the rider's grasp."

"You're saying I saved them?"

"The wise man of Muhammad will survive, but the woman of Christ's gospels remains in a struggle for life. Twenty-four soldiers of Moses were burned. Their lungs will be restored, but severe scars will remain. Forty innocent spectators were hit with bullets. Twelve were mortally wounded, and death should have taken them. But you prevented that."

"Twelve mortally wounded, and I prevented their deaths?" Mikha'il paused, remembering all that he had sensed just a short time before. "But . . . I felt thirteen."

"You felt the other one?" Vishnu asked inquisitively.

"Yes. What happened to him?"

"He was taken beyond your reach."

"He's dead then?"

"No, just moved."

"That's right—an older man, a Muslim," recalled Mikha'il. "He was shot in the stomach and his companions carried him away . . . to some small room, but that's all I remember."

"You see well." Vishnu nodded approvingly.

"And what of the agent from the balcony? Did I save him, too?"

"No. You could not, for he did not want to be saved. Only those with a will to live could you protect and save. And, even then, only when destined to do so."

"What do you mean? How can I do this?" Curiosity and incomprehension combined as Mikha'il impatiently probed further at what, until now, had seemed only illusions.

"Chosen by destiny, and on this day you chose to accept destiny." Vishnu's tone was gentle and yet strong. "Through you, a presence surges in the will of the mortally wounded, halting the penetration of death. But if their will falters, you can be of no help to them. The dying agent had lost his will before he sensed your spirit, but with its emergence, he truly realized what he had done."

"You speak of destiny, as if I were meant to do this. If this is true, why me?"

"There are those who are watched through time. Most are not called, for either they are not needed, or they do not choose well. But you have always chosen well, as you did in this holy place and on this day of need."

With lingering disbelief, Mikha'il considered what he'd heard. He could not reject it, for it clearly was his reality. "You say that I've fulfilled my destiny by saving these people. Then I am ready for death. I can feel my injuries, and I know how life will be if I survive. It's not how I want to live. You promised me you'd take care of Jasmine, so just let me die in peace. Let Shiva, this rider, and his bull approach."

"You may die in peace, but not on this day," Vishnu replied, shaking his head. "As it was your duty to save the lives of those today, it is mine to save yours. Worry not, my peaceful warrior. We need to preserve your strength. So now rest."

"Rest! How can I rest with all that you have told me?"

Vishnu did not answer. Instead, the blue prince simply vanished, as if never there.

Jasmine sat alone. With no windows, the interrogation room was dark except for the light from a single bulb above the table. Her passport, purse and phone had been taken. She had told the agents who initially questioned her what had happened, but they had said nothing.

Worrying about Mikha'il, she had spent the past three hours pacing around the room, pounding at the steel door and wall mirror or sitting, frustrated by her helplessness. Periodically, a flood of tears escaped, and she winced in pain from the large abrasion along her right cheek. She prayed to the Hindu Gods not to take Mikha'il from her.

Finally, the door opened, and a large man in a dark suit sat down across from her.

"What am I doing here? What's happened to my boyfriend? How is he?" Tears again flowed as her fears overtook her.

"I'll ask the questions here."

"Do you know who I am? I'm an associate producer with the BBC."

"That doesn't matter here. What does matter is what you are. What you and your boyfriend were doing in the Old City."

Jasmine explained once more the events that led up to Mikha'il running from her side.

When she finished, the agent spoke with no consideration of her story. "You are a Hindu, born in India?"

"Yes, that's right."

"Tell me, why does a Hindu from Delhi have a Muslim boyfriend?"

"Why? Is that a crime in this country?"

"Your real name is Sudha, correct?"

"Yes, Sudha Desai."

"Sudha is a nice Hindu name," sitting back in his chair, the gruff Shin Bet interrogator mused. "So why does a Hindu woman take a Muslim name? Jasmine is a Muslim name, yes?"

"What? You think we're Muslim terrorists?" Jasmine snapped. "We're innocent. My boyfriend was there to get some photos, and I was just with him. That's all. That's it. No more."

"When did you take the name?"

"In my teens, but I'm sure you already knew that."

"As a sixteen-year-old, why would you change your name?" demanded the agent, relentless in his questioning.

In August 1947, when Jasmine's mother was a child, British control over the province of the Raj officially ended, and the nations India and Pakistan were born. But in that moment of liberty, the lands became a killing field, when ten million Hindus and Muslims, who for centuries had lived, worked and socialized together, gave up their homes and migrated across the new border. Law and order collapsed. Riots, massacre and slaughter erupted. Friend became foe, and neighbor, enemy. Within one month, two million people lay dead on the fields of their homeland.

The family of Jasmine's mother was friendly with a neighboring Muslim family. Both had daughters, born only seven days apart in the sweltering heat of two August nights, nine years before the partition from British rule.

From birth, the girls were inseparable. The villagers laughed and referred to them as the twin stars fallen from the pure night sky. They were the sparkle of youth.

One morning, in the days between their ninth birthdays, as the two chased each other through fields of sunflowers, their daily play was interrupted. The Muslim child was hastily lifted up by her father and carried away. Not a word was spoken, not even a goodbye. In their innocence, the two girls' eyes remained locked on one another until the tall flowers closed the space between them. Within a few hours, Jasmine's mother and her family left their home, never to return.

For thirty years, Jasmine's mother searched for her friend, writing letters unanswered, poring over newspapers and tracking down other former neighbors. Then one hot summer day while she was pregnant with Jasmine, a letter arrived at their Delhi home.

From her long-lost friend's older brother, it told of how he alone had survived the migration. Bitterness toward Hindus remained as he described the horror that he was forced to watch. His sister was brutally raped and killed just days after the family's departure, while her parents were held down in clear sight and then slaughtered afterward.

Seven days after receiving the letter, Jasmine's mother gave birth.

ELEVEN

PRESIDENT ROBINSON SAT at the head of the long mahogany table, one level below the executive offices of the West Wing. His chief of staff, Matt Whelan, sat to his right and the vice-president to his left, while other key members of his team occupied the remaining seats. Although they, and others, had come and gone over the past three hours, the president had not left his chair since first arriving at 9:25 that morning.

An impressive array of flat-screen monitors lined the walls and showed encrypted uplinks of GPS video mappings and satellite reconnaissance. The men discussed the events before them, their mood somber as they awaited further reports on the condition of Virginia Adams.

CIA director Tony Vasquez entered the room and before sitting down, he began to speak. "We're getting interesting intel. Seems the Israelis aren't sure what happened. Our embassy team is getting conflicting stories from their Mossad sources. We didn't know what to make of it until we got a download from one of our recon satellites. My techies have been working on it for an hour."

The president watched as the video started. From above, the crowds and stage in the plaza came into view. The screen zoomed in on a shadowed figure on a tiny balcony. The cloudy recording went to half speed.

The indistinct form raised a long rifle, and two thin streaks of light burst from its tip. He changed weapons. The video was sped up, and he fired three more times into the crowd. It slowed again when a figure in lighter clothes rushed the shooter, who fired back with a revolver, and the two went over the balcony.

"That doesn't show anything we don't already know," the vice-president commented.

"Yes, but watch this," said Vasquez. "It's media footage from a crew early on the scene."

This video was focused and clear. Although badly bloodied, the "suspect" being guarded wore faded blue jeans and a safari-type shirt. Next to him lay the body of the Shin Bet officer, dressed in operative gear. "Look how they're dressed. That's the photographer in beige. The Shin Bet officer is in black."

"Come on, I'm waiting. Why did you change your name?"

Jasmine sighed. *Is this a story I can tell an Israeli interrogator?* "It was my nickname," she answered somberly. "Hindus couldn't use Muslim names when I was born." She hesitated, choosing her wording carefully. "The name is in honor of my mother's childhood friend. She died when she was nine. I took her name when I finally could."

"The girl, she was a Muslim?"

"Yes."

"You're a Muslim sympathizer then . . ."

"Yes, I can sympathize with the Palestinians." Jasmine stiffened in the chair. "And I abhor the oppression of any community of human beings by those like you. But that doesn't make me a terrorist, you, you fool!"

The agent smiled, pleased he was making headway in loosening the self-restraint of his obstinate suspect. Calmly, he said, "Ms. Desai—or may I call you Jasmine?—being in the media, you certainly must be aware of rumored interrogation tactics used in the questioning of terrorist suspects, particularly pretty ones like you."

"You wouldn't dare." Jasmine sneered, attempting bravado despite a sudden increase in heart rate.

The agent continued through his tobacco-stained teeth. "Yes. You see, well, they really aren't rumors. We don't even have to tell anyone we have you. Now, I want the facts and I want them immediately. Or we will resort to different tactics."

The door opened and a second man entered. He nodded to the interrogating agent. "That's enough. You can leave us."

"So, who are you? The good cop?" Jasmine clenched her teeth but could not stop the quiver in her chin.

"I'm in charge here. I had your boyfriend evacuated out on a helicopter with the U.S. secretary of state and Palestinian leader."

"How is he? Is he okay?" she begged.

"He's alive and has been taken to the Hadassah Hospital."

"Oh, thank God." Jasmine's voice cracked, and tears welled in her eyes.

"You'll have to forgive the behavior of my agent. As I'm sure you can appreciate, we are somewhat anxious around here. But my job is to find the truth about what happened today."

"I want to see him!"

The door opened again, and a woman stood in the entrance. "Sir, Major Milner is waiting for you in the screening room. He says it's quite urgent."

"Good. Thank you, Deborah." David turned to Jasmine. "You're going to have to stay here until I have more information." He passed the female agent holding the door open. "Make sure she's comfortable. Have her escorted to the ladies' room, clean up her wound and get her something to eat."

There was a quick murmur around the Situation Room as the significance sank in. "A rogue agent?" asked the vice-president. "Looks like the Israelis may have a mess on their hands."

"Yes, it does," confirmed Vasquez. "We believe him to be Major Jacob Rubenstein of the Shin Bet. He was the top man on the ground, responsible for overseeing security of the entire event, ideally placed to pull this off."

Rubenstein's photograph, personnel files and military record appeared on the screen while Vasquez reviewed his background and career history.

The president remained silent. In instances such as this, other than asking a question for clarification, he preferred to listen, reviewing all of the pertinent information before he commented.

"Any connection to the suspect?" asked the vice-president.

"None that we know of. Looks like the photographer was there doing his job and, witnessing the attack, did all he could to stop it," replied the CIA director.

"Tony, are you saying an unarmed photographer, with no military training, attacked a decorated commando officer armed to the teeth and threw him over a balcony, just like that?" asked the vice-president, skepticism clear in his voice.

"Looks like it. And apparently the man was unstoppable. Watch the satellite feed again. I'm going to run it frame by frame. It's remarkable."

The monitor, now in super-slow-motion, showed the photographer advance and three shots come from the shooter. They saw the white figure jerk backward as bullets hit his body, but he scarcely slowed. They watched in fascination as Rubenstein fired three more times. The photographer jolted again, and a small spray of red could be seen, but he still advanced, barreling into Rubenstein and forcing him over the balcony.

TWELVE

"HOW DOES IT LOOK, MORT?" asked David Caplan.

The pudgy director of the Shin Bet Investigation Unit had never made a good field agent, but David knew when it came to analyzing evidence, none was better.

"The girl's story holds true. The elevator video was turned off, but the trip memory card indicates one rider up at 1430, and plaza cameras show her boyfriend entering the building seconds before." Milner pointed to one monitor and then another. "At 1443, we have Major Rubenstein heading toward the Yeshiva School, roughly ten seconds away. Then we lose him.

"Two minutes later, the elevator memory shows another entry. The fourth-floor button is again pressed and the rider carried up. But this time the elevator is put on lock mode. While in that mode, the elevator remains on the floor and won't allow access from the lobby. However, for safety purposes, it'll still allow for exit in the event of an emergency. The rest of the building was in lockdown— hallways, fire doors, stairwells, all chained and bolted. After locking the elevator, anyone going up would be completely secure.

"But the elevator button was pushed fifty seconds later, taking one rider to the ground floor. When the doors opened, the lock was automatically turned off. Construction workers had set the bypass so it would unlock when they came down after-hours, in case they needed to go back up. They're not supposed to do this, but apparently, it does happen from time to time when buildings are being renovated. Clearly, whoever locked it didn't know that the lock was bypassed."

"So, who came down, turning off the lock?"

"It was bin al-Rashid. His girlfriend said he'd planned to get photos of the speeches from the balcony, but he was caught by Security."

Milner again directed David's eyes to the monitors. "On video, we see him leaving and rejoining his girlfriend at 1449. There's no more elevator activity until just after the attacks started. At that time, bin al-Rashid runs from his girlfriend, here, and then runs back, here.

"The elevator goes up to the fourth floor. Once it opened, bin al-Rashid would have startled the shooter, who believed himself secure. The elevator wasn't used again until we contained the site."

"Have you found the elevator key?"

"Yes—in Major Rubenstein's pocket."

"Why don't you have video of Jacob entering the building?"

"There was an entrance in the south used by construction workers. It was to be blocked off. He likely entered there."

"Then why aren't you showing me video of that or of the balcony?"

"We don't have any."

"How can you not have any? Every inch of that plaza was under video surveillance."

"Commander, that's just it. The major approved the camera locations. That entrance and the balcony were missed."

"Damn." David shook his head as the evidence against his friend mounted. "What do you have from ballistics?"

"It's also incriminating. Testing of the weapons indicates they were used in the attacks, but there are no prints. Major Rubenstein was wearing gloves and an operative sweater. His suit jacket was found on the balcony with a duffel bag. Residue from both the rifles and his sidearm was found on the major's gloves and sweater. Also, he was the last to inspect the STAV transporters and Sayeret vehicles. He had the opportunity to place explosives inside and—"

David interrupted, "There are radio transmissions from Jacob calling orders. You're saying he made them while firing?"

"There are no sounds of gunfire during any of them. He's heard asking if the source of the attacks had been reported. He would've known right away if his position was compromised, giving him time to react. Also, having the Lead, he controlled the deployment of the Sayeret teams."

"But he didn't give that order. I did."

"He would have, had bin al-Rashid not stopped him. And you changed the order." Milner paused briefly. "Why did you think to change it?"

"Something that Hasidic boy said. Has anyone found him yet?"

"No, but we have him on video talking with you. He must have disappeared into the crowd."

"Any other witnesses?"

"No, not yet."

"Any evidence that Jacob and bin al-Rashid may have been accomplices?"

"On the contrary. We have them on cam yesterday afternoon. Major Rubenstein is checking his credentials, which in itself is strange—not his responsibility and out of character."

The two men turned again to the monitor.

"You see—he's checking his credentials. He didn't know him. Also, Major Rubenstein failed to follow protocol. He didn't record the check. Here, he's shaking his head and pointing in the direction of the school. A minute before, the elevator's memory card shows someone coming down from the fourth floor, and we have bin al-Rashid on video leaving the building. It was just past 1500 hours, the same time the speeches started. He was probably checking settings for today."

"Consistent with the photographs time-stamped in his camera."

"Which we thought implicated him."

"Has the photographer survived?" asked President Robinson, finally speaking.

"He was still alive at last report," answered Vasquez. "His injuries haven't been a priority. We're only just putting this together. However, we did think it odd that he was evacced on the Black Hawk with Virginia and Abu-Hakim."

"Perhaps somebody suspected something at the scene," suggested the vice-president.

"Regardless," Vasquez continued, "this will prove disastrous for the peace advancement. Protests will intensify when the Palestinians learn the attacks were from within the very agency responsible for preventing them. It's going to look like a cover-up—especially with the blame pinned on a Muslim. The longer the truth is withheld, the worse it will be. Who knows how people in nearby Arab countries will respond. It may be too late already."

There were a few moments of silence as the men considered the options.

President Robinson signaled to the duty officer. "Get the Israeli prime minister on the phone."

A few minutes later, Robinson was greeting Kessel and asking for an update. "How is the madam secretary? Any word yet?" Everyone in the room listened to the conversation from a speaker at the center of the table.

"She'll be out of surgery soon. All has gone better than hoped. We remain optimistic."

"Good. I knew we could count on your people for their prompt and professional response."

"Thank you, Mr. President."

"Aaron, the CIA has just analyzed satellite feed from today's events."

"Yes, Mr. President."

"It indicates a Shin Bet officer may be the assailant and your civilian suspect the one responsible for stopping him. Do you have any insight into this?"

Kessel paused before responding. "No. I have yet to receive full reports. Can you have the feed sent to my office as soon as possible?"

"We're doing that now." The president waved to Vasquez. "And Aaron," he added squarely. "This photographer . . . I remind you, he is an American citizen."

Milner turned the monitors off. "Commander, the evidence is conclusive. Major Rubenstein was the lone attacker. We would never have known had bin al-Rashid not stopped him. Without containment, the major would have ordered in the Sayeret teams. After the first explosions, the eight STAV vehicles would have been deployed to further disaster.

"Once we identified the detonators used, we would have blamed the Palestinians. We probably wouldn't have cared so much about the missing surveillance video. There would have been no proof of the major's involvement. Even if he had been suspected, at worst, with such a clean record, he would have only been forced to an early retirement. That was his only risk."

David remained professional, hiding his regret. "Thanks, Mort. Your people have done good work here."

"I'm sorry. I know you and Jacob were close," said Milner quietly. He waited only a moment and then carefully gathered his evidence and left.

David sat alone, trying to wrap his mind around Jacob's betrayal. All the years of closeness, the affection he'd believed existed between them—all of that now cast into doubt.

His phone buzzed. Shaking off his personal sorrow, he answered.

"Commander, the prime minister wants to talk with you."

Once connected, David told Kessel of the evidence just detailed to him, and the prime minister shared his news of the American satellite feed.

The prime minister was direct. "It's essential that we be seen as preemptive and not reactionary. Arrange a press conference for first thing in the morning—and by that, I mean before nine. Keep a lid on it until then. This announcement has to come from us."

"Shall we include the satellite recon?"

"If it's not too explicit. I'll have it sent to you. Where is the photographer now?"

"Under guard at the Hadassah."

"Make sure he's getting the best treatment possible. It'll be a disaster if he dies."

THIRTEEN

THE MEDICAL TEAM WAS SURPRISED that Mikha'il's condition had not worsened. In the five hours since his arrival, the only attention he'd received had been from a nurse who'd changed his bandages and checked his vital signs. While arriving casualties were given priority, Mikha'il stayed at the bottom of the list.

Now, however, the full team worked to stabilize his body and prepare him for surgery.

The guards watched the frenzied pace as another nurse dashed in. "Doctor, you wanted me?"

"Find Dr. Levine," said the head of the ER. "Tell him we just got directive from the Shin Bet exec that this guy is our highest priority. Have him ready his best surgical team. X-rays are on the way up. We lose this guy, heads will roll. Now go!"

The motorcade pulled up to the hospital's emergency entrance and came to an abrupt stop. The agents marched Jasmine inside. They were met by more agents, and the entourage proceeded to a waiting room on the surgical floor. Two agents remained in the hall while the female agent ushered Jasmine inside.

"How's Mikha'il?" she continued to ask her. "Do you know what's wrong with him?"

"Be patient, Ms. Desai. A doctor will be in soon."

But soon did not come for several long hours.

Seated across from the agent, Jasmine was in turmoil. One minute she felt hopeful. *He will be fine. He's so strong, so healthy. This can't be the way we end.* But the next, dread threatened to overwhelm her. *It's been way too long. I treated him so badly last night. He's gone. I know he is.*

Finally, a break in the agony came as a doctor entered the room. "Ms. Desai?"

"Yes?" She leaped to her feet.

"I'm Dr. Levine, chief of surgery and intensive care. I supervised Mikha'il's surgery."

"How is he? Is he all right?" she asked, feeling the pounding of her heart throughout her entire body.

"He's just been taken to recovery." Dr. Levine turned to the agent. "Miss, can you give us some privacy?"

"Certainly." The woman left the room.

"Please tell me he's okay!" Jasmine implored of the doctor.

"Remarkably, he's alive. Your boyfriend has a strong will. His injuries were extensive, including broken bones from the fall, all of which will mend. We were able to remove the bullets from his body, but—"

"Bullets? And a fall? What happened to him?"

"You don't know?" he asked, surprised.

"No, they've kept me locked up. No one has said anything!"

"Mikha'il was shot four times, once in the shoulder, twice in the chest and once more in the forehead. He then fell from a fourth-storey balcony."

"Oh my God." Jasmine raised her trembling hands to her face. "How did this happen?"

Dr. Levine ignored the question. "His condition remains critical. Although we removed the bullets from his body, a few microscopic fragments and bone splinters remain in his head. They're in areas too dangerous to access. We might try again when the swelling subsides."

"When will that be?" Jasmine asked, trying desperately to retain focus, not knowing what questions she should even ask.

"I'm not sure. He's too weak to undergo further surgery. Both lungs collapsed, and he didn't breathe for some time."

"What does this mean? How are his chances?"

"You should be prepared for the worst." The doctor's voice was soft but direct. "If he does recover, there is a strong possibility of brain damage."

"How bad?" She clenched her jaw and swallowed tightly, attempting to fight back her tears.

"It's hard to say. The brain is a complex thing. Even if he does well over the next few days, we won't know for a month or so."

"Can I see him?"

"Yes, but only for a minute or two."

Although weakened from the surgery, Mikha'il remained aware of Vishnu's presence. He sensed the strong hand of the godly prince in his.

"There is another to take your hand for a moment, my new friend. But I will stay near." Mikha'il felt the solid grip of his protector's large hand release his, but it was replaced by another, much smaller one.

Jasmine held the hand of her beloved. She leaned over his motionless body, touched her lips to his right ear and whispered, "Mikha'il, it's me. I'm here." All she could see of him was his ear and his right eye, blackened over a swollen cheekbone. White bandages wrapped his head and covered the left side of his face. His dry lips and nose were covered with tape to hold in place the tubes that were his lifeline. Green surgical drapery tented his body, and wires and tubes ran to machines and hanging bags. The only sounds in the room were the rhythmic bursts of air pumping through the breathing apparatus and the monotonous beeping of other life-sustaining equipment.

A single teardrop rose from the corner of his right eye and trickled down the side of his face. Jasmine bent over him and kissed it away.

Thinking of how strong he'd seemed only hours before, she was unnerved by the sight of his helplessness. Stunned, she stood over him, deep in anguish and lost for what to say.

Dr. Levine gently touched her arm. "Come, dear. You can get a few hours of sleep. The sun will be up soon."

She did not look up, nor did she move. She only stood still at Mikha'il's side, staring down at him, not wanting to leave.

Dr. Levine coaxed further. "We have a guest suite prepared for you, here in the hospital. Come, Ms. Desai. You can return in the morning. We need to have someone look at that cheek of yours, too."

She finally turned. "Thank you, Doctor."

He took her elbow in his palm. "The officers will show you the way. We have done all we can for now."

FOURTEEN

THE BEAUTIFUL SOUND OF CHANTED PRAYERS from more than two hundred mosques enveloped the city in song as the sun rose over East Jerusalem. One early ray broke through a tear in the curtain of an apartment window and touched the face of a sleeping man. Blood had soaked through the white cotton sheets over his stomach. In a chair at his side slept a second man, his arms folded and head slouched.

In the bed, the wounded man awoke. He turned his head painfully toward his companion. "Tariq, what has happened?"

The man in the chair opened his eyes with a start and quickly got to his feet. "You're awake?"

"Yes, with morning prayer. Where am I? What's happened?"

"You were shot yesterday at the ceremony in the Old City."

"By who?" asked Yazid Abdul-Qadir, his voice raspy and slow.

"An American photographer, although they say he's a Muslim."

"A Muslim shot me? Why?"

Tariq Nur al-Din, Abdul-Qadir's second-in-command, explained, "You weren't specifically targeted. He first shot the American secretary of state and Abu-Hakim. He then sprayed gunfire into the crowd, and you were hit. Explosions followed. Many have been hurt. It was a well-planned attack."

"All by one man? Why didn't I know about this?" Abdul-Qadir coughed.

"Nobody knows anything about him, and no group has claimed responsibility. He apparently acted alone."

The renowned jihadi leader fell silent and then tried to lift his head to see out the window. "Where are we?"

"A safe house in the east of the city. You refused to be taken to a hospital. You put up a good fight, so we brought the doctor here." Nur al-Din helped the weakened man sit up in the narrow bed. He set an extra pillow behind his head and poured a glass of water.

"Yes, I remember now." Abdul-Qadir winced with his movement.

Nur al-Din raised the glass to the cracked lips of his injured leader. After drinking, Abdul-Qadir took two heavy breaths and pointed at the bloody sheet. "And how am I?"

"The bullet lodged between your kidney and spleen. Although the doctor was able to remove it, the surgery was difficult. You need to rest."

"I feel nothing. The bullet was small." Abdul-Qadir fidgeted and stubbornly pushed his elbows into the lumpy mattress to raise himself.

"You shouldn't rise. You've lost much blood." Nur al-Din reached to assist the middle-aged man, worn well beyond his years.

"I'm fine!" Abdul-Qadir snapped. "I will not rest." Struggling to lift himself, the notoriously headstrong Palestinian got out of bed.

Jasmine awoke from her restless sleep. She lay on her back atop the comforter, exactly where she'd landed earlier. Still dressed in her clothes from the day before, she turned to the clock on the bedside table: *9:26*. She jerked upright—it was much later than she'd thought.

She jumped from the bed, peered through the bedroom door into a modestly decorated sitting room and, finding it empty, approached the front door. Reaching for the handle, she expected to discover it locked. To her surprise, it turned.

Standing outside were two agents she hadn't seen the day before. But seated across from them was the female agent who'd escorted her here. "Good morning, Ms. Desai. Did you get some sleep?"

"A little," Jasmine replied, her voice slow, trying to sense any ill will behind the courtesy.

"Good, I'm glad. Can we talk when you feel up to it?" the agent asked politely.

"Sure. How about we talk right now," Jasmine said, gesturing to the open door while noticing the woman hadn't changed clothing either.

The two entered the suite, and Jasmine lowered herself onto one of the matching gray sofas, as the agent sat on the other. A brass table with a glass top separated them. A simple gas fireplace was unlit beside them and impressionist prints inside thin chrome frames hung on the walls.

"I am Special Agent Deborah Barak," the woman began. "Before anything else, I want to tell you that I'm very sorry for the way you were treated. I apologize on behalf of our country."

"I don't even know why I was detained in the first place. I know nothing of what's been going on—how Mikha'il could be hurt so badly."

Agent Barak nodded. "Of course. In view of Mikha'il's involvement in the events at the plaza, we had to detain you, taking every precaution. We now have conclusive evidence that he had nothing to do with the attack. In fact, our investigation has revealed that Mikha'il singlehandedly stopped the shooter. Our commander, who you briefly met yesterday, held a press conference thirty minutes ago. It'll be all over the news by now."

Jasmine pressed her fingertips to her temples, trying to take in what she was hearing. "But how did Mikha'il get shot? I don't understand how he could have found the terrorist before your people did."

"Pure luck, we suppose. He must have seen the assailant shooting from the balcony of the Yeshiva School."

"The shots came from that balcony? Yes, that makes sense," Jasmine said, almost to herself. "He was up there yesterday, planning to take photos of the announcements."

"It was an incredibly brave thing that he did. Your boyfriend took several bullets before managing to reach the sniper. In the struggle, they both went over the balcony."

Jasmine nodded in understanding and felt tears once again drop to her cheeks.

The agent paused, as Jasmine tried to digest the significance of what Mikha'il had accomplished. A surge of pride welled within her, but it was immediately displaced by worry. "I want to see him."

Jasmine brushed her palms along his warm arms, avoiding the many catheters, wires and other tubes. She listened to the machines breathing for him and watched his chest rise and fall, thankful for the evidence of life in him.

A nurse brought her a phone, and she called her parents and Mikha'il's grandfather. She detailed the events and her concern over Mikha'il's condition, and, grateful to finally hear her voice, they told her of how the world was reacting. Commenting on the barrage of reporters in front of their homes, they spoke of the endless news reports and their horror at the vilification of Mikha'il until the subsequent change of opinion after the satellite video had been broadcast. "The world is calling it a miracle," said her mother in Delhi, "that no one except the Israeli traitor was killed."

The call to her BBC colleagues fell short of expectation. Any concern for her or Mikha'il quickly waned, replaced with pestering for an exclusive scoop. Jasmine found an excuse to get off the phone as fast as she could.

Time, if it mattered at all, seemed to stall as she spent the day watching him, uncertain of what to do or expect next. Before she left, she touched her lips to his ear and whispered, "I love you. Stay strong, sweetheart."

Two tears rolled down his cheek.

———

In the hallway, the female agent jumped to attention.

"You're still here?" Jasmine asked.

"Yes, ma'am."

The spry agent showed no signs of fatigue. Her short, dark hair framed a round face set with brown eyes. A black business suit, with fitted jacket, matching pants and white blouse, showed off her tall, boyish figure. "I have your identification, personal items and phone for you."

"Thank you. I forgot about them."

"The agents will escort you back to your suite. I can have your things picked up at the King David and brought here, or if you prefer, you're free to go back to the hotel. But I suggest you let our agents accompany you. This has become a big story, and the press are gathering in great numbers. They won't respect your privacy."

"I'd rather stay here, close to Mikha'il," Jasmine said, wearied.

"All right. I'll be back this evening. Our prime minister would like to talk with you then, if you don't mind."

The prime minister. Jasmine was taken aback once more at her involvement in such an important event. "That will be fine, Agent . . . I'm sorry, I forgot your name."

"Deborah," she replied with a kind smile.

In her suite, Jasmine walked to the window, pushed back the drapes and glanced toward the entrance of the hospital complex. Behind guarded barriers, reporters stood in front of a multitude of cameras and trucks carrying giant satellite dishes. Just a short time ago, she'd belonged to that group.

She was glad not to be among them. Jasmine felt betrayed by those she worked with and was troubled that her loved ones were being harassed—and that there was nothing she could do to help. For the first time, she shared Mikha'il's disgust at their employers.

Refusing to get sucked into the endless news coverage, Jasmine didn't turn on the television. Instead, she curled up on the sofa and closed her eyes tight.

Soon, she found herself wandering endless canyons where Mikha'il's cries echoed off sheer cliffs. From jagged crevices, a faint ringing came. The sound grew louder as the images faded.

Suddenly alert, she grabbed at the telephone. "Hello."

"Hello, Jasmine. It's Deborah . . . uh, Special Agent Barak. Sorry to disturb you. Do you need anything . . . Can I get you something to eat?"

Jasmine hesitated, finally accepting that she was hungry. "Soup and some toast perhaps? And a hot tea would be wonderful."

"I'll have them brought up. I'm right outside if you need me for anything at all."

"Thanks, I'll be fine."

"Jasmine, the prime minister would like to speak with you. Is now a good time?"

Jasmine answered after a short pause. "Okay." She sat up and waited for the connection, watching the glow of the flames trapped in the gas fireplace.

"Hello, Ms. Desai. This is Prime Minister Kessel."

"Hello, Mr. Prime Minister."

"I wanted to call to tell you how deeply sorry I am for your sacrifice. Our people are indebted to you and your boyfriend. We want to help in any way we can."

"Thank you, sir." She thought of how terribly she'd been treated earlier and could find nothing more to say.

"He'll get the best care possible. You are welcome to stay with us as long as you like. If there is anything you need, we are here for you."

"Thank you again. I'm just so tired right now." She wanted only to get off the phone.

"Of course. Please know that our prayers are with you and Mikha'il."

After finishing half of her light meal, Jasmine sat in the emptiness. Tears once again threatened as they had so often since her argument with Mikha'il just two nights before.

She wished she could go back to that moment. Instead, in the quiet suite of the Hadassah, with Mikha'il's presence so close yet so distant, she played his favorite music, dimmed the lights and drew herself a bath.

FIFTEEN

THROUGHOUT THE FOLLOWING WEEK, the media aired stories of Mikha'il's selfless act and his unusual background. The diverse cultures and faiths of his past all laid claim to the emergent hero: the Vietnamese and Buddhists, because he was born and raised among them; the Americans based on his citizenship; the Muslim community, for his stated faith; the Vatican due to his grandmother's religion and his middle name; and the press itself, thanks to his award-winning career.

While hundreds held vigil in prayer, placing flowers, cards and candles at the Hadassah entrance and below the balcony at the Yeshiva School, the media preferred to report on the great numbers of Muslim protesters gathered along the Old City walls, the Knesset and the prime minister's residence. Angered by the false accusations against a fellow Muslim, they shouted conspiracy theories and tyrannical oppression, masquerading behind the illusion of peace.

Mikha'il drifted in a strange state of awareness. He had no concept of time passing, except the few moments when Jasmine whispered in his ear. He'd tried to reach her through his thoughts, but he felt she wasn't able to sense his reassuring words.

At all other times, Vishnu was his companion, and, stepping out of time and space, he followed the Hindu god into the halls of the hospital. All the while, Shiva and his bull lurked in the shadows.

"You two are part of the Hindu Trinity?" Mikha'il asked.

"Yes. You are familiar with the Hindu religion and Trimurti, the great Hindu Trinity—the cosmic forces of creation, maintenance and destruction?"

"Only a little. Jasmine's a Hindu."

Mikha'il sensed the two of them sauntering through the halls, passing unperceived among the patients, doctors and nurses.

"It dates to before 3000 BC, well before the mighty Greek and Roman gods. While these pagan gods fractured into myth with the advance of Christianity, Hinduism survived."

Mikha'il was aware of the bustle around him but ignored it as he listened to Vishnu's teachings.

"It was Brahma, the supreme one, who made the universe. He created Atman, the first man, whose soul was re-created to fill all man. Brahma, the Creator, is the third of our trinity. Shiva and I are second only to him. I am the maintainer of life and Shiva the re-creator of it. Hindus believe in the immortality of the universe and the eternal soul, so life does not die. It is merely re-created or transformed."

"Reincarnation then, a new life after death?" asked Mikha'il.

"Yes. Atman is the human soul, one's true self beyond the reality of worldly existence. It is the conscience—the superego, as later science describes it. It explains your presence here with me now, for it is the essence of your soul that walks these halls by my side. In man, that essence follows a perpetual sequence of rebirth from one form into another. In these rooms, we see death, but not infinite death. Rather, the soul is transformed into rebirth. And in this place, we also witness that birth. As people die, people are born."

"So the same souls that die here are reborn here?"

"Not necessarily. The Atman is not linear but rather abstract in time and space. So perhaps another day, another year, another place."

"How is it decided, this rebirth?"

"The goodwill of mankind is critical to Hindus," answered Vishnu with the pride and practical understanding of a seasoned professor. "If one demonstrates a life of well-being, or good karma, then one will be rewarded with a better existence in re-creation. However, the opposite holds as true. If one does ill toward his fellow man, one will be punished with rebirth as a lower life form. A thief may come back as a small animal. The ethical duty and morality of man is recognized—good, the victor over evil.

"To release the soul upon death, bodies are cremated, mated in creation. The ashes are thrown into a body of water—a river, a sea, an ocean—where destiny and karma determine rebirth."

Vishnu stopped. The two stood by a room guarded by four officers, who continued their quiet conversation, oblivious to the existence of the peculiar tutor and his student. But behind the door, the woman opened her eyes.

"Do you feel the woman in this room, the one called Virginia?" asked Vishnu.

"Yes. All week I've felt her pain and tried to strengthen her will."

"You have chosen well to save her. She is full of positive karma and delivers goodwill to her fellow man. She is now out of danger and will again serve as an agent of peace."

"There are no deaths from the attacks then?"

"They have all been saved," confirmed Vishnu confidently.

"What about the other, the thirteenth one? The Muslim man shot in the stomach. You said he was out of our reach. Has he too been saved?"

"For now, but not by us."

"He'll die then?" Mikha'il asked.

"Not on this day, for your paths may cross again."

"Cross again?"

"Yes, just as with good and evil, life and death intertwine in a never-ending duel for supremacy."

"When?"

"You get ahead of yourself," Vishnu said. He hesitated briefly and then resumed. "As I, too, get ahead of myself. For you, my peaceful warrior, you have done well here. The lady no longer needs the presence of your will. Just as she and the others no longer need you, you no longer need me. My time with you is at its end."

"Why? Where are you going? What's going to happen?" Mikha'il asked. "And what about them?" He looked around, searching for the dark pair that had been stalking him all these days.

"The bull and rider have left your shadow."

Mikha'il looked once more. "They're gone!" He turned back to Vishnu, but the blue Lord had vanished, leaving no trace.

Jasmine watched the stillness of Mikha'il's features. After a week of not being shaved, his beard had turned from stubble to soft hair. She'd never seen him unshaven for that long and didn't like it. To her, it seemed an added barrier between the two. "How long will you keep him unshaven?"

Standing on the opposite side of the bed, Dr. Levine looked from Mikha'il's face to Jasmine's. "Until we change the bandages next."

"Can I do it?" she asked. "Can I shave him?"

"Let's let the nurses do it, at least until the stitches are out. Perhaps you can then."

"I'd like that."

Dr. Levine walked around the end of the bed. "We have the results from the preliminary testing. Would you like to discuss them now, or would another time be better for you?"

With a sudden thud in her stomach, she met the doctor's eyes. "No, now," she said quietly.

"Mikha'il is healing as well as can be expected. His broken bones and gunshot wounds are mending. But he's still on the respirator. We don't want to attempt more invasive surgery to remove the fragments from his head."

"What about after the swelling of the brain comes down? You said you'd try then."

Dr. Levine hesitated. "I know I did . . . but with the complication from the trauma of the gunshot to his head, we simply shouldn't risk it—especially since the EEG, CAT scans and MRI continue to show only minimal brain activity—"

Jasmine paled. "You're saying he's brain dead?"

"I wouldn't go so far as to say that. We can do more tests over the next couple of weeks to determine the severity of damage."

Dr. Levine saw the last of her optimism flee. "I hope at some point you can find comfort in his goodness and the fact that he saved so many. The secretary of state is out of danger now. She is conscious and would like to meet you."

"I'm thankful she's better, but not now."

"I understand. I'll pass along your good wishes. You know the prime minister's office has given instructions for you to be allowed to stay here as long as you want. Let us know if there's anything we can do for you."

"Thank you, Dr. Levine," Jasmine said, the one thing she wanted, unobtainable—Mikha'il well and whole by her side.

"Please, it's Dr. Ben. Come with me, and I'll get you some cream so that scab on your cheek won't leave a scar."

"No thanks," she said abruptly.

Yazid Abdul-Qadir coughed into the white handkerchief, adding more blood to the already crimson-stained cloth.

Nur al-Din passed him a glass of water and two pills. "You strain yourself too much. The doctor has said that although he's removed the bullet, he's worried about infection."

"My health is of no concern now." Trying to ignore the throbbing in his abdomen, Abdul-Qadir waved his hand, refusing any medication. "What *is* our concern is the future of Palestine! Israel's quest for peace is a charade. They release us from prison, only to set us up, to make us the villain in the eyes of the world. It is the will of Allah, foiling their plot. These Jews are devious, and the West shares their wickedness. Allah has shown us the way. All over the world, our people awaken."

Nur al-Din nodded slowly. "The time is right, Yazid, for new leadership."

"The attack in the Old City is our blessing. And with it, we shall strike. We'll lure the West into a conflict they don't have the stomach to win. We will stretch their aid to Israel until it snaps and end their evil grasp over all of Islam for good. Israel will be left to fall on its own. The plans we talked about in prison, how fast can they be put in place?"

"Just waiting for your word."

"Let the infidel fall. We'll drop them from the skies and watch them squirm."

II

AN EYE FOR
AN EYE

You are to take life for life,
Eye for eye, tooth for tooth, hand for hand.

Moses
The Bible
Exodus 21:23–24
Sinai Peninsula, Egypt, 1440 BC

An eye for an eye makes the whole world blind.

Mahatma Gandhi
Political and spiritual leader, father of modern India
Delhi, India, AD 1927

SIXTEEN

SWEEPING HIS HAND ALONG THE COOL ROCK, Mikha'il felt his way through the rugged corridor forged before the existence of man. The passage meandered but remained narrow, no more than eight feet wide. The hanging cones of limestone brushed the top of Mikha'il's head as he ducked to pass them. Wearing pajama bottoms and a faded gray New York Giants T-shirt, he cautiously advanced. His shuffling feet kicked the odd stone, skipping it ahead, echoing into the emptiness. The dust he raised filled the air, and the dampness made breathing difficult. Forcing as much oxygen into his lungs as possible, he inhaled with deep breaths, and then coughed as his body filtered the stale air.

He was moving through the gloom toward a slight glow when he heard a baby's cry.

Mikha'il still wasn't accustomed to the strange state he'd found himself in. He was, however, aware of his physical condition in the hospital room and the hopeless results from the prodding he received there. He knew with each test, Jasmine became more worried and more deeply depressed.

But, here, alone in this other existence for the first time since Vishnu had left him, Mikha'il walked further into the cave. The crying grew louder and the glow brighter. He followed a bend in the passage, and, in front of the light, he saw the source of the cries.

Thrashing and kicking, a baby lay naked on the cold cave floor. Mikha'il's pace quickened. From the opposite end of the cavern, the light advanced at the same accelerated rate. As he neared the child, Mikha'il saw that the white light emanated from a tall figure.

They reached the baby at the same time. Mikha'il instinctively bent to lift the child, but the bright figure raised a hand and pushed Mikha'il back.

"Who are you?" Mikha'il demanded. "Why has this child been left alone here?"

The figure stood silently, staring down at Mikha'il. It was draped in pure white. Although there was no breeze, the luminescent robes billowed back and forth as if carried by a soft wind. The figure itself was also white, except for the tender blue of its eyes and pink hue of its full lips. Smooth skin and high cheekbones were framed by shoulder-length, white flowing hair. The face was flawless, strong, chiseled and confident. Male, Mikha'il decided when the figure spoke.

"I am not here to harm the child but, rather, to provide him with nourishment," the figure said in a deep, rich voice, stretching his arm toward the infant and touching the forefinger of the baby's right hand.

Mikha'il watched as a milky white liquid erupted from the baby's finger and squirted over the cave floor. Ceasing its cries, the baby placed his finger in his mouth and began sucking.

The glowing figure straightened and looked into Mikha'il's face. They stood two feet apart. For some seconds, neither moved, until the illuminated figure nodded, smiled and dimmed its transcending light. Without it, the cave went black.

"Hello, folks. This is Captain Simon Burke. We're thirteen hundred miles from New York City and will be landing at JFK in two hours and fifteen minutes, at 10:05 p.m., local time. We've taken advantage of an unexpected tail wind and have made up thirty minutes of our delay. I thank you for your patience and hope you enjoy the remainder of the flight."

El Al Flight 011 had been scheduled to land at 8:40 p.m., but had been delayed in Israel because of thunderstorms over Ben Gurion Airport, an unusual occurrence.

For the second time, Naomi Kaufman took the plastic baby bottle from the woman traveling alone with her two-month-old son. "He's been pretty good for his first flight," she said.

"Yes. Not a peep." The young mother looked up to the flight attendant and then down at her new son, resting his head on her shoulder. "I hope he stays that way for his grandmother. She wanted to come to Jerusalem but couldn't make the long flight."

"He's a little angel. I'm sure she'll love him to bits," Naomi said, smiling at the picture of loving mother and baby. "I'll be back in a couple of minutes with his formula."

After heating the formula, Naomi headed back down the aisle. Before reaching the waiting mother, she felt a heavy rumble underneath her. The floor buckled and a tremendous blast blew her off her feet. Screams filled the cabin. Losing her hold on the bottle, Naomi threw her arms up to protect her face from the loose objects battering her; then she felt herself being sucked through the fuselage. She grasped at seats and legs rushing by. A passenger grabbed her.

Gripping his calf, she met his terrified eyes for a quick second until she turned and looked through the fuselage. The front half of the plane was gone, and anything not bolted down—including bodies—was being pulled through the gaping hole. Try as he might, the passenger was unable to fight the force of the vacuum. He let go.

Naomi flew out of the opening, into the vast sky of pink and orange. In the sudden silence, she held consciousness for a few seconds until the combination of the minus-fifty-degree temperature and empty air pressure shocked her bodily functions.

Through a dusk-lit sky, at one hundred and ninety miles per hour, Naomi's lifeless body tumbled down into the heavy waves of the Atlantic.

From the blackness of the cave, Mikha'il was transported to open ground. He stood on an arid hillside. The sky was bright and cloudless, and from behind him, a warm breeze blew through the scattered trees. There was no sign of the cave from which he had come. Before him was the broad curve of a rocky peak with what appeared to be a wooden table of simple design on top.

He heard footsteps and turned. Two men almost knocked him over. They passed within inches, oblivious to his presence. As they continued up the slope, Mikha'il followed close behind.

One was a teen; the other, in his later years. His once-broad body now slouched, and his white beard grew halfway down his chest. He leaned on a staff and rested his other arm across the shoulders of his younger companion. They walked in silence until they arrived at the wooden table. There, they embraced for a long moment.

The bearded man nodded at the youth. The younger man pulled his robe down below his chest, and allowed the other to bind him and lay him on his back atop the table. Staring into the eyes of the teen, the older man paused, motionless. From his belt, he pulled out a knife and placed the blade at the neck of his victim, who willingly, patiently, awaited death.

"No!" Mikha'il shouted, darting toward them, but before he could attain full stride, he stopped.

The shining figure from the cave had materialized, hovering over the table. The older man raised his face and, bathed in the pure light, stood transfixed, listening to the figure speak.

Mikha'il could hear no words.

The old man, tears of joy and gratitude on his face, turned and lifted the teen, cut the twine and held him tightly. Above them, the angelic figure slowly vanished, leaving the two men clutching each other.

Malcolm Polson studied the data on his laptop and keyed a few more numbers into his spreadsheet. He'd been working every hour he could over the past two days. Since he wouldn't be arriving in Jordan until late the next afternoon, Malcolm hoped to work quietly at his seat through the early hours of morning and then catch a few hours of sleep before finishing his analysis. Luckily, he'd managed to secure an aisle seat, despite his last-minute flight change.

Seated across the aisle and one row ahead of him, a Middle Eastern businessman pulled a briefcase from the overhead storage. As he did, his backside jostled Malcolm's computer, but the man did not apologize. Malcolm glared at him as he shuffled toward the bathroom, briefcase in hand.

When the businessman returned, Malcolm leaned away so his laptop wouldn't get knocked again, but the man did not return the briefcase to the bin. Instead, he passed it to a second man and sat down.

The two men bent over the briefcase and began working at something inside. Malcolm noticed two other men, sitting beside them, doing the same thing in a second briefcase. None of the men spoke. All were conservatively dressed, in their mid-twenties with short dark hair and clean-shaven faces.

Malcolm leaned forward. "Hey, is everything all right? Did one of you lose something?"

The man who'd knocked Malcolm's laptop looked up briefly but didn't answer and calmly returned to the briefcase.

His concern accelerating to alarm, Malcolm unbuckled his seat belt and stood to get a better view.

With the unwelcome intrusion, one whispered, "Now!"

The sudden blast brought instant death to the four businessmen, Malcolm and several nearby passengers. The explosion that followed, though, was a hundred times greater. The Airbus buckled, and the fuel reservoir between the wings exploded, severing the plane in two. The pieces fell through the freezing night air, trails of blazing wreckage and burning fuel swirling behind.

Mikha'il walked from the rocky crest.

Suddenly, he felt the terrain change and looked at his bare feet. The ground was transforming, becoming darker and more rugged. What few trees had been present had disappeared, and although he still stood on a hilltop, not any more or less high than the one he had just been on, everything around him had changed. The dry air was hot, and the sun beat down on him. Already, he could feel the sweat escaping his body. Disoriented, he struggled to the peak to view his surroundings.

Rounding the top, he looked down the other side.

Not far away, in the center of a clearing, the same old man he'd seen before raised a knife to the neck of another man. Lying on sticks and dried palms, this young man was at least ten years older than the previous would-be victim. He was more muscular and wore a trimmed beard. His full hair was not a light brown but a heavy, dark black. He, too, did not resist his fate.

Above their heads, the midday sun grew brighter. Both the old man and his soon-to-be human offering shielded their eyes. From the sun's rays, the radiant figure of light descended and grasped the old man's hand.

Once more, the duo embraced joyously.

The glimmering figure drew back into the sky, but before disappearing, it came close to Mikha'il. Just as in the cave, it nodded and then, gently smiling, merged into the middle of the sun.

SEVENTEEN

"HEY, WHAT'S THAT AT TEN O'CLOCK?" Ensign Tommy Esparza pointed past the captain, seated at his side in the low-flying U.S. Coast Guard search and rescue plane.

Captain Roland Caruso lowered his night-vision goggles and squinted slightly to his left. "Too bright for a star, and it's moving fast."

"Well, whatever it is, it just disappeared."

Sitting behind the two men, the navigator declared, "I have a radar signal lost at three-zero miles and minus six-two degrees."

"You don't think it can be another one?" asked Esparza.

"Radio it in," the captain ordered grimly.

"E-City Station, this is Rescue Owl Four. We just caught sight of a bright flash going out in the sky at two-niner-eight degrees from our position, and our radar indicates a lost signal from five-zero miles out."

"Roger that. Hold, Owl Four."

Captain Caruso maintained the easterly course of the white and red Coast Guard plane. Searchlights from a large commercial fishing ship illuminated a watery grave of drifting bodies among twisted wreckage and floating luggage.

"E-City Station, this is Rescue Owl Three. We confirm the same at minus seven-zero degrees and five-three miles to the point," chimed in the copilot of another Hercules.

Four HC-130 search and rescue planes had been scrambled six hours earlier from the Coast Guard station in North Carolina. For almost two hours they'd been flying in a grid above the debris site of the crashed El Al flight, searching the dark and cold waters.

"E-City to Owls Three and Four. Air Traffic Control just reported the signal loss of a second commercial airliner. New coordinates on your grid. Owls One and Two, hold course. Air Force F-15s have been scrambled from Langley Base and will support all. Arrival, plus four-zero minutes."

Esparza lowered his mouthpiece. "A second plane down. This is crazy! Think there's something out there?"

"Don't know, but they're sending in the cavalry to watch our butt." Captain Caruso banked the quad-turboprop, and the mammoth Coast Guard plane headed for the new mark.

Dr. Ben Levine clicked the penlight on and off, aiming into the dilated pupils of Mikha'il's eyes.

Mikha'il had been moved to a larger private room. The ventilator tube, once running down his throat and taped in place around his lips, was now attached to a plastic fitting in the center of his throat. He lay motionless, his head resting on two pillows and his torso on a slight incline from the rise of the bed. Both arms rested neatly alongside his body and outside the unruffled sheets.

Dr. Levine returned the penlight to his pocket. "I'm sorry, Jasmine. He remains completely unresponsive."

For two weeks after the attack, Jasmine rarely left Mikha'il and gave no interviews. Earlier in the third week, the Israeli government had provided her with a private jet to return to London and gather some clothes and personal belongings. While there, she checked into her office at the BBC and provided an on-air statement, thanking all for their prayers of hope. She'd visited her parents in New Delhi afterward but had stayed only a couple of days, anxious to return to Mikha'il.

She'd returned to her hospital suite late the night before but got up early to see him. Her spirits were high with the obvious improvement in his appearance.

Dr. Ben could see the optimism in her face and chose his words carefully. "I realize he looks better now that the bandages aren't as bulky. The swelling and bruising have come down nicely, and his stitches have been removed. But we've finished all the tests. His CAT scans, MRI, apnea and sensitivity tests are all conclusive. I know it's difficult to accept, but he hasn't improved."

"How can that be? Whenever I whisper to him, he cries."

"I'm sorry. Every test we've done indicates that his conscious brain has ceased functioning. Tearing is an involuntary response— when his eyes are dry, they tear." Dr. Ben hesitated. "At least that's the scientific answer. If it's important for you, spiritually, you can believe what's best."

"So there's hope?"

Dr. Ben bit his lip, regretting that he'd crossed the line between science and faith. He should have known better. "Professionally, I'm afraid not. I'm a trained physician and have to rely on science, not faith."

"I see," Jasmine said curtly. "Well, I am not ready to give up. He looks so alive to me, like he's just sleeping."

"He does, doesn't he?" agreed Dr. Ben, smiling empathetically.

She straightened the already straight sheets. "Thanks for putting his clothes on him. He loves his Giants. Do you think I can shave him today?"

"Sure, I'll ask a nurse to show you how."

The phone on President Robinson's bedside table rang. After another day of tense meetings and phone calls about recent events, he'd retreated to the upper residence of the White House. Reaching for the receiver, he noticed the time: *2:27*. He'd scarcely had an hour of sleep when the ringing woke him. "Hello."

"Mr. President, you asked me to wake you if we had any developments on the Israeli plane."

"Yes, Matt."

"Tony's also on the line with us," Whelan added.

Vasquez said flatly, "Sir, a second plane has gone down."

The president squeezed his eyelids in weariness. "Is it Israeli?"

"No, sir. One of ours, a US Airways Airbus. It left New York three hours ago en route to Jordan. The Coast Guard is reporting debris floating fifty-five miles northeast of the El Al site."

Not wanting to disturb his wife, the president rose from the bed and walked to the parlor. "They're that close?"

"Yes, that close, and in the north Atlantic deep water ditch, where depths can reach four miles. Recovery and investigation will be difficult."

"Any signs of survivors?"

"No, sir. Both planes would have been at least thirty-five thousand feet up when they blew. I'm afraid there won't be."

"Any more ships at the crash site yet?"

"Two freighters, one Italian and the other French, have joined some Canadian fishing ships. Our rescue ships will be there by this time tomorrow."

"There won't be much left by then." President Robinson paced back and forth. "Was the US Airways plane full, too?"

"Yes, sir. Two hundred and ninety passengers and twelve crew," answered Whelan.

"Damn, Matt, with the Israeli plane, that's over seven hundred lost souls. Still no one claiming responsibility?"

"No, sir," Vasquez replied.

"Could they have been shot down?"

"Unlikely. We have no indication of unfriendly aircraft, ship or submarine threats in the area."

"So, bombs on board?"

"We believe so, sir."

"How the hell could anything like that get past security, considering all the measures we've put in place?" A moment of silence followed the president's unanswerable question. "Tony, I have a couple more questions for you, but, Matt, can you get the joint chief on the line."

While Whelan made the call, the president continued. "You think this has to do with Jerusalem, don't you, Tony?"

"Yes, sir. With the targets being an Israeli plane and a Jordan-bound U.S. plane, Islamic militants with Palestinian ties are likely responsible."

"Anything on them?"

"We've gotten a lot of chatter with the Old City attack but nothing concrete."

"I have the general on the line," announced Whelan.

"Hello, Mr. President. Matt just brought me up to speed."

"Okay, Stan, where's our closest carrier group?"

"Carrier Group Ten would be the closest. That's the *Harry Truman* and Escort Squadron Twenty-Six. She's just been refitted and they're on their way to relieve the Bush Group in the Mediterranean."

It was unprecedented that a U.S. naval carrier group joined the recovery mission of a commercial airliner crash, but, with the second downed plane so close, Whelan had anticipated the request. "With fourteen ships, the Truman is just on this side of the Azores and only nine hundred miles from the crash sites."

"Thanks, Matt. Stan, how long for them to turn around and reach the sites?"

"Twenty-seven hours."

"All right, have them diverted to aid in recovery and investigation. Their air wing can add reinforced security and recon."

"Yes, Mr. President. On it now."

"Mr. President, we have FAA holding on the other line," Whelan went on. "They want to ground everything."

"Disruption is exactly what these terrorists want." President Robinson contemplated his next decision. "Ground only Middle East–bound flights, and have each thoroughly checked."

"Yes, sir."

EIGHTEEN

YAZID ABDUL-QADIR removed his reading glasses and sat up on the small bed. He closed the Qur'an, the religious text of Islam and, to Muslims, the verbatim word of God.

For twenty-five years, he'd carried this Qur'an with him. It had been given to him by a freedom fighter minutes before he'd exploded the C-4, stuffed with hundreds of tiny nails, strapped to his chest. Along with the jihadist, three Israeli soldiers and two bystanders were blown to pieces at a checkpoint outside Ramallah. It was the first of many suicide bombings Abdul-Qadir would order.

He could no longer remember the look of the young man awaiting his reward in paradise, but Abdul-Qadir kept the Qur'an near him as a reminder of the commitment and sacrifice required to fulfill their beliefs in the causes of Palestine and Allah.

Out the dirt-stained window, he watched children play in the slum streets so similar to where he'd been born. His father had operated a modest trading business in the West Bank. After his father's death during the Six-Day War, Yazid's mother had taken her young family to Saudi Arabia. In Riyadh, they'd found safe haven in the care of a close colleague of Yazid's father, who soon after, in accordance with Muslim tradition, married his friend's widow.

With the Saudi oil boom, the business of Yazid's stepfather flourished, and he traded with the Americans expanding their military bases to protect the vital resource. The new family moved to a posh neighborhood, and Yazid attended the best schools. While he was at university in France during the mid-seventies, the Americans asked his stepfather to aid their efforts to strengthen the Shah of Iran's government, and Yazid's stepfather moved the family to Tehran.

The Shah's regime fell to the Ayatollah Khomeini and his devout Shia followers. The Shah fled the country, leaving his supporters to face the barbarism of the Shia mob. In the mayhem, Yazid's sisters were raped and, along with their mother, brutally murdered, while his stepfather was executed by hanging.

For this, Yazid Abdul-Qadir would never forgive the Shia and vowed vengeance against Western influence in the Middle East, blaming the West for putting his family in harm's way.

With an inheritance from his stepfather, he had returned to his birthplace and focused attention on the Jewish occupation of Palestine. During the First Intifada, the rebellion against Israel in the eighties, he'd quickly risen in status—his wealth financing operations and his brutish tactics leading to many successful bombings. By the Second Intifada, erupting in 2000, he had grown in reputation, fanatic in his cause and merciless in his terror until, near the end of the five-year uprising, he'd been captured in a Shin Bet raid.

Although connected to the deaths of scores of Israeli citizens, in dozens of attacks, he'd been acquitted on most due to a lack of corroborating evidence and missing witnesses. He was, however, convicted on six counts of murder and sentenced to life in prison.

After serving eight years in a tiny cell, where disdain for his Jewish captors only festered, he'd been freed with over a thousand Palestinian prisoners in a swap inspired by the hope of new peace talks. Despite the number let go, it was his release that sparked controversy and long debate.

Now, Abdul-Qadir sat alone in the small bedroom where he'd lain for the past three weeks. He grimaced in pain as he stood to dress. Death had been close numerous times, and he had fragmented recollections of frantic voices around him, mixing with strange dreams of something, or someone's presence, that had kept him alive while he was rushed out of the Old City.

A doctor had come to remove the bullet lodged so close to his spleen, but without the sterility of a hospital operating room, infection had set in. It hadn't been the bullet that nearly took his life but the poison that flowed through his veins.

But now was the time to end his recovery. The attacks on the two airliners had been successful, and he could not wait to depart the confining walls with their peeling paint. Soon, he would release the video he'd made the day before while standing in front of the only piece hanging on those walls—a photograph of the Kaaba, the holiest place to Islam, taken during the Hajj pilgrimage, when Muslims retrace the footsteps Muhammad took upon his triumphant return to Mecca.

In the glass of the photograph, Yazid could see a reflection of the slum outside. He could just make out the rows of crumbling buildings where decaying balconies were tied together with lines of laundry and drying bed linen.

Abdul-Qadir finished dressing and waited for Nur al-Din's arrival. He cringed at the laughter he heard through the paper-thin walls.

Hasan, the smaller of the five-year-old twins, wiped the jam from his arm. "Hey, that's not funny."

"Yes, it is." Hussein giggled and smeared more on his brother's face. "You look so silly, Hasan."

"Don't play with your food!" Across the table, a man in his late teens slammed his hand on the table.

"I'm sorry, Uncle," they replied in unison. Hussein's broad grin turned downward, and Hasan started to tear.

The boys sat side by side on milk crates at an old table. Hasan scrunched his now-solemn face, twisted his shoulders and turned away as his mother pushed a rag across his cheek, cleaning his face while rocking her infant daughter. "Oh, Ramzi, leave them alone. They're just children."

"I tell you, Fatima. You aren't strict enough with them." Ramzi was quick to criticize his sister-in-law.

Waving the rag full of holes, she looked her husband's younger brother in the eye. His face, with only the soft fuzz of a beard on adolescent cheeks, reminded her of the man who'd captured her heart years before.

She spoke quietly so their guest could not hear. "It is difficult enough with their father taken away because of his association with *them*," she hissed, gesturing toward the other room. "Now you bring him here—he who has caused so much shame to Islam. We struggle to live in this one room while you have this excuse for a man taking up the other. So, no! Don't be yelling at my boys and then explaining to me how to be a good mother!"

Ramzi pushed his chair back and huffed. Before he could respond, the door of the dingy room opened and his attention shifted away from starting another vicious argument with the Shia wife of his brother. "Tariq, it is done!" Ramzi stood and opened his arms. "We did it. Praise be to Allah."

"Yes, my friend, success." Standing at six-foot five-inches, Nur al-Din dwarfed Ramzi. He seemed to fill the small room as he approached the table, removed the full duffel bag slung over his shoulder and placed it at Fatima's feet. He took two chocolate bars from his pocket and gave them to the twins, smiling at their mother. "I have brought some food for you and your family. Allah thanks you for your sacrifice."

"And I thank you for the food, but that is all." Standing firm in front of him with her head held high, Fatima was resolute. She did not return Nur al-Din's smile, although, with his well-groomed beard and his confident eyes, his charm was hard to resist. She detested armed resistance but appreciated the generosity Nur al-Din showed where others did not. Her children did have to eat.

With little care for her response, Nur al-Din turned to Ramzi. "How's your guest? I heard his recovery has been difficult."

"He's still weak but insists he's fine. He's waiting for you."

For twenty years, Tariq Nur al-Din had been loyal to Abdul-Qadir. Although with others, Nur al-Din never discussed his past, he had shared his family history with his mentor, fifteen years his senior. As they compared tragic lives, the similarity of their losses had only tightened their bond.

Nur al-Din's father had eked out a living as a tanner in Ramallah until the poisonous fumes of the dye claimed his life, and his young family was forced into poverty. Tariq's mother followed to an early grave, and, sent to different orphanages, Tariq was forever separated from his siblings.

At twelve, Nur al-Din ran away, surviving in the streets any way he could. By nineteen, he'd turned his surrogate family of petty street criminals into an underground cell of freedom fighters, attacking Israeli soldiers every chance they could.

Soon, Abdul-Qadir, recognizing both the intellectual prowess and physical stature of the rough Palestinian, included him in his inner circle. In the years following the Second Intifada, Nur al-Din was rounded up and sent to prison before being released with Abdul-Qadir.

In the small room, Nur al-Din scrutinized Abdul-Qadir carefully. The man's narrow shoulders were hunched and his color sallow. Darkness surrounded sunken eyes, and much more gray had spread through his beard and hair. In three weeks, the leader of Islamic jihad in Palestine had aged ten years.

But his will had not left him. Abdul-Qadir raised his head and laughed in excitement. "Ah, Tariq, we have done it."

"Yes, we have." Nur al-Din approached the bed. "And you look well, Yazid."

"Never mind your foolish compliments," said Abdul-Qadir as he glanced over to the chair by the bedside table. "Come, sit, and tell me of our success."

"On both planes, four of our men each had two condoms containing a high grade of concentrated nitroglycerin stuffed in their rectal cavity. Even the most advanced security scanners would not detect the abnormalities."

"This is brilliant," interrupted Abdul-Qadir, grinning and wide-eyed.

"With batteries from a portable DVD player, they detonated the nitro using passenger headphone wire. They were seated over the wing, to ensure the explosions would ignite the fuel reservoir below. Other than the nitro, all traces of which will be lost, only materials regularly found on planes were used."

Abdul-Qadir stood, clapping his hands in delight, but, wincing, sat back down again, trying to hide the pain that wrenched his body. His breath ragged, he congratulated the younger man. "A good start, Tariq, a good start."

"Start?"

"We must bring the West to their knees, not in prayer, but in pain. We'll continue to strike terror into their people. Their support of Israel will dwindle and their influence in our region will collapse." Abdul-Qadir straightened, more slowly this time. "Yes, Tariq. This is just the start, and it is time we warned them of what is to come."

"Shall we prepare a video?"

"I already have. Ramzi filmed me here yesterday. He'll leave soon to deliver it to the IBA."

"The local television network? Are you sure you want him to deliver it there?"

"Yes," Abdul-Qadir said firmly.

"But it's too dangerous. Exposing him like that, he'll be forever marked. His brother won't be released from prison for some time. Ramzi is needed to provide for his family. Why not send the video through our usual contacts? The Israelis may not even air it, or at least not in its entirety."

"I've sent a copy to Al Jazeera. It'll be delivered there soon after Ramzi makes his delivery, and a letter addressed to the Israeli network will make them aware of the copy going to Arab media. I'm sure the IBA will be quick to air it." Abdul-Qadir was methodical in addressing Nur al-Din's concerns. "I have confidence in Ramzi.

I've spent much time with him these past weeks. After he makes the delivery, he'll join us in Syria and then on to Iraq."

"Syria? Iraq? You're not ready to travel. The doctor's informed me that there's an abscess next to your spleen. The infection almost killed you. You have been safe here. Why leave now, before you're—"

Abdul-Qadir raised his hand. "Stop. Do not oppose me. Ramzi will deliver the tape in two hours. After that, we won't be safe here. We'll join the insurgents in Iraq. They'll protect us. Prepare the guards. We leave immediately."

"What about his brother's family?"

"We have no need for women and children. Especially Shia ones. They stay," barked Abdul-Qadir, his temper shortening.

"Shia or not, she's still Muslim. We should at least leave some guards to help them escape if needed."

"No. All the guards come with us."

"She will be arrested." Nur al-Din remembered being left with no parents at too young an age. "Her children will be left with no one to care for them."

"So be it. Now hurry yourself. We leave at once."

"Why so quick?"

"Shin Bet will be onto us soon after the tape is released."

"You seem certain."

"I *am* certain."

NINETEEN

BITING HIS THUMBNAIL, David Caplan watched the television on the credenza in his office. The executive news producer at the IBA had called him just after the network received the Abdul-Qadir tape. Upon hearing a copy was being immediately delivered to Al Jazeera, David reviewed an encrypted digital copy and approved its airing to preempt the Arab news channel.

Within fifteen minutes after its delivery, world news networks were broadcasting Abdul-Qadir's rant.

David's eyes did not leave the screen. He watched the face of a reemerging foe and listened to the translation.

"With the unprovoked attacks in our beloved Old City of Jerusalem three weeks ago by Israel's security force, it is now obvious that Israel does not want peace with Palestine. Instead, they continue to tyrannize our people and occupy our lands. Any talks for peace are purely a distraction from their real cause, the utter destruction of our Islamic state.

"Meanwhile, America and its allies continue to support Israel in its cause. This wicked wind grows around us, attempting to smother our nation in a storm of dust. In the name of Allah and for the sake of his messenger, Muhammad, may peace be upon him, we cannot, and will not, allow this threat against our people. The time has come for us to fight against its evil grip. In defense, we wage war against the state of Israel and its infidel allies from the West.

"We will defeat our enemy over the water, between our shores. The skies will collapse around them, and the ocean will swallow their souls. Let them forever burn in their hell as they cry out to an unreachable heaven.

"To my brothers and sisters of Islam, join us. Let us unite under our Muslim cause. Take up arms against our enemy wherever and whenever you can. Allah is with you. Praise in the name of Allah, most gracious, ever merciful, and praise to his messenger, Muhammad."

Within seconds, Caplan's phone began ringing. He glanced at the call display and answered, "Hey, Mort. You watching?"

"We never should have let them out. At least not him, and now they're blaming us for Rubenstein's attack in the Old City."

"We've been seeing that response everywhere. All of the protests—it's as we feared. Jacob was Shin Bet, so it's our fault."

"How convenient for them," Milner added. "But I think I saw something. Go back to the beginning."

David rewound and pressed Play. "Got it. What's up?"

"Check out the picture on the wall behind him."

"Looks like the Kaaba?" David asked.

"It is. Now look at the reflection in the glass. I think it's East Jerusalem."

David saw the vague reflection of a cityscape. "Damn him to hell. Last we heard he was training Islamic insurgents in Syria. Now he's back?"

"Can't say for sure. We're reviewing it now. Should be able to pinpoint exactly where it was taped. Can you get the original for us?"

"Already on it."

A nurse pushed an elegant woman in a wheelchair down the quiet hospital corridor. Dressed in a navy skirt and blazer with a bright yellow blouse, the woman was impeccably made up.

The nurse knocked softly on the open door of the room they'd come to.

Seeing Jasmine curled up under a blanket, sleeping in the chair beside Mikha'il, the woman whispered to the nurse, "Not now. I don't want to wake her."

Jasmine opened her eyes. "That's okay," she said. "I was just getting some rest."

"I'm sorry, Ms. Desai. I can come back later."

Recognizing her visitor, Jasmine stood up. "It's all right, Madam Secretary. Come in."

The nurse left the room and closed the door.

"Please, please, sit down, Jasmine, and you must call me Virginia."

"I am glad you're all right . . . Virginia. You look well."

"Tough old ladies like me take a little longer to recover, but you still can't knock us down. Dr. Levine tells me it's you who's been the pillar of strength."

"I don't know about that. I still don't sleep so well, and I seem to cry a lot."

"I'm so sorry for you. It must be terribly difficult for you to see Mikha'il like this. I'm sure you realize what a special person he is and the sacrifice he's made. You should be so proud of him. He truly is a hero."

"I don't really care about that right now," Jasmine said. "I just miss him."

"I'm sure you do," Virginia said, as the young woman's eyes strayed to the still body of the man she loved. Virginia could understand—she, too, had known loss. Almost to herself, she repeated quietly, "I'm sure you do."

Some note in her voice must have resonated with Jasmine because she turned to look at Virginia with a curious expression.

Although Virginia hadn't discussed it in some time, she suspected it might help Jasmine to tell of her own past. It had been so long ago, but still Virginia's voice cracked when she started. "When I was twenty-one, I lost my husband." She straightened in the wheelchair, attempting to catch her emotion. "We hadn't been married two years when his helicopter was shot down in Vietnam. I thought my life had ended. All seemed hopeless.

"It was so difficult at first, but I eventually found new purpose . . ." Virginia explained how her husband's sacrifice in a tragic war became her inspiration. Staying close to his family, she never remarried, and his father, a distinguished politician himself, convinced her to run for Congress. She'd lost the first time but celebrated victory the next. She'd gone on to win her father-in-law's Senate seat when he'd retired, and her appointment to Secretary of State resulted from a faithful pursuit of peaceful solutions to any conflict. The memory of her husband's death was never far from her mind.

The two women grieved in their shared losses, each comforting the other. After more than an hour together, Virginia realized she had been there longer than she'd intended and, reluctantly, readied herself to leave. "I do hope we can meet again, Jasmine, and, somehow, in happier circumstances. I'll be leaving soon for Washington, but I want you to call my office if there's anything I can do for you. They'll always know how to reach me."

"Thank you for that. I will and, well, you've surprised me. I thought you'd be here, just doing your duty, but it really felt good talking with you. These weeks have been so hard, and it's nice to be able to open up with someone."

"You're welcome, dear." Virginia paused, not sure whether to act upon the urge within her. "Can I make a strange request?"

"Of course."

"Do you mind if I touch him?" Although she did not understand it, Virginia had felt compelled to reach for Mikha'il since she'd first come into the room.

"That's fine. I'll introduce you and tell him you're here. I should've when you arrived anyway." While Virginia lifted herself from the wheelchair and approached the bed, Jasmine leaned over Mikha'il and stroked the side of his neck. She kissed the cheek she'd shaved earlier and brought her lips to his ear. "Hey, baby, it's just me. The U.S. secretary of state has come to say hello."

Virginia touched Mikha'il's forearm. Her body tingled with emotion. It was the same feeling she'd had when she'd struggled to cling to life. Confused by the overwhelming sensation, she jerked her hand back and looked into Mikha'il's face. Tears were rolling down his cheeks. "He's crying! But I thought . . ."

"I know. Dr. Ben says it's just an involuntary response—because his eyes are dry. I don't believe that, though. It only happens when I whisper in his ear."

TWENTY

TWELVE SAYERET COMMANDOS ENTERED the fifth floor of the building from the stairwells at either end. While the other members of their squad secured the entrance, elevators and fire escapes, the soldiers had deployed without resistance.

Moving as an army of clones in black, the commandos reached their preassigned positions in the hallway. In front of an apartment door, two members held a heavy iron battering ram. The team leader held his hand up high for all to see. His black-gloved fingers showed three, then two and then one, and his fist violently thrust forward.

The ram crashed through, and flash-bang explosives were tossed in, creating a brilliant burst of light and a deafening blast.

Hussein and Hasan shrieked and pressed their hands to their ears as the sting shook their heads. Terror replaced their initial shock when fearsome black-suited apparitions rushed through the smoke, thin, red laser lights criss-crossing the air. Beside the boys, their momentarily blinded mother scrambled on the floor for the boys' screeching baby sister, whom she had dropped in shock.

Fatima yelled as her boys were scooped up and thrust against the wall. Her vision returning, she tried to grab her daughter, but the weight of a heavy boot pushed her onto the floor. She yelled out, kicking in desperation as her hands were ripped away, bound together behind her back and tethered to her feet.

While the intruders ransacked the room, Fatima watched helplessly as her baby, lying unattended on the floor, screamed and kicked into the air, and her wailing boys clutched at each other where they stood, pressed against the wall by two commandos only a few feet away.

Pink blossomed in the sky as the ocean released the morning sun from its grip. Leaning on the rail of the two-hundred-and-fifty-foot recovery ship *Neptune Endeavor*, Captain Andy Thomas squinted momentarily but otherwise paid no attention to the radiating presence.

Routinely, Captain Thomas welcomed the break of dawn. For the past twenty years, the oceans had been his home. Whether plowing unimpeded through the doldrums of a flat calm or riding the crests of a raging storm, he preferred the liberty of an unrestricted sea to the confinement of land, and regardless of conditions, he greeted most mornings with the same free-spirited enthusiasm. But this morning was different.

He watched his crew lay bloated and burned bodies in black bags, zipper them shut and then place them next to the others—the many others—in neat rows along the ship's deck. These bodies were the ones newly collected from the still waters. Those casualties removed from the fishing and commercial vessels, first to arrive on scene, had already been bagged, catalogued and stored in refrigeration holds below deck.

Soon after the first crash, a soothing sky had settled over the north Atlantic. The winds had ceased to less than a puff, and the waves became eerily still. The weather had remained calm with the arrival of the recovery ship thirty hours later and was not expected to change for two more days.

From the bridge, a junior officer joined the captain, watching the crew working below. They knew the days ahead would be long, with double shifts and sleepless nights.

After a minute, the young officer broke the silence. "It's weird, isn't it, sir?"

"What's weird?"

"It's like something calmed the waters precisely when we needed to recover the bodies," he said, an odd optimism in his voice.

"What do you mean—*something?*"

The officer hesitated a second before he mumbled tentatively, "Some of the men are praying to God to keep it calm until our work is done."

"God, or the weather forecasters," Thomas said grimly. His voice took on a bitter tinge. "Son, right now I don't know how anyone can even say there's a God. In fact, I doubt there is. So many of those bags are filled with children. What God would allow that?"

The officer did not answer. An awkwardness between the two men grew until a screeching roar shattered it.

The officer looked up.

Captain Thomas's eyes remained fixed on the rows of bags below. He abruptly turned and went back to the bridge, leaving his officer on the balcony watching the sky above.

Jetting by, a pair of F/A-18 Super Hornets tipped their wings in respect of the bodies that lay below.

The officer tracked the fighters across the ocean and then looked to where they had come from. Ten miles away, the approaching ships of the Truman Carrier Group were silhouetted by the new sun.

At the sound of a knock, David Caplan looked up from the photos on his desk. With a quick nod to the seat across from him, he gestured for Mort Milner to sit down. For most of the morning, Milner's interrogators had been with the doctor who had treated Abdul-Qadir. Only hours after Fatima caved to the bombardment of their questions was the doctor arrested trying to enter Gaza.

As soon as the Sayeret commando raid failed to apprehend Abdul-Qadir, security forces along every checkpoint were tripled.

The elderly doctor was an easy arrest in the tightened security web, even in the middle of the night.

"He's confirmed the girl's story." Milner sat down. "Abdul-Qadir had been there for the past three weeks. He says he was taken against his will and that Abdul-Qadir was in bad shape, a gunshot wound to the stomach." He leaned forward in the chair. "But get this. The doctor was grabbed shortly after Rubenstein's attack in the Old City."

David brushed his eyebrow with his forefinger, processing what he'd just heard. "Abdul-Qadir was hit there?"

Milner nodded. "It checks out. We've got Tariq Nur al-Din on security video carrying a bloodied Abdul-Qadir out the Zion Gate."

"So he was among the crowd watching the speeches."

"Sure as I'm sitting here."

"Jacob would've been happy to know he shot Abdul-Qadir," David said wryly. "What did the doctor say about his condition?"

"Weak, lost a lot of blood, and infection set in after he removed the bullet. At first, the doctor didn't think Abdul-Qadir would survive, but the infection subsided, and by the time he saw him last, he was stabilizing."

"He didn't look so good in the video."

"He still has an abscess pressing against his spleen. The doctor said the infection could easily return, so I'm surprised they didn't take him with them."

"Abdul-Qadir is too proud to be seen needing a doctor," David said assuredly.

"Proud as he is, we almost got the cockroach. We missed him by only a couple of hours, and with security forces on high alert, we'll turn his rock over in no time."

"No, Mort, he's taunting us."

"How do you mean?" asked Milner, confused.

"I've been thinking about the picture in the video. Abdul-Qadir is too smart for that to be an oversight. It was intentional. He wanted us to know he was there. I guarantee your cockroach is long gone."

"If he knew we were coming, he would have at least warned the girl."

David shook his head. "She's Shia, right?"

"Yes . . ."

"It fits. Abdul-Qadir despises the Shia, so he used her. This has only furthered his cause. The story that will spread is that twenty heavily armed commandos stormed in on a young Muslim mother caring for her two little boys and baby daughter. How's the woman, anyway?"

"She's a lot tougher than the doctor—that's for sure." Milner shifted in his seat. "We questioned her for close to ten hours straight. Eventually, the threat of losing her children loosened her tongue. She seems to hold a lot of resentment toward Abdul-Qadir and any armed resistance, but she loathes us more. We've had her husband in custody for almost a year."

"Poor woman," said David. "Damned on both sides."

"Her husband has a kid brother living with her. He allowed Nur al-Din in with Abdul-Qadir."

"The woman didn't object?"

"She and her children were away, visiting family. We're confident that she knew nothing about the circumstances of Abdul-Qadir's shooting, and wasn't happy with the situation."

"Anything more on the brother-in-law?"

"Not much beyond his driver's license." Milner handed a photocopy to David. "IBA identified him as the one who delivered the video. He's only seventeen. Other tenants in the apartment building heard him boasting he was recruited by Abdul-Qadir and to the cause of jihad."

David briefly inspected the license and gave it back. Ramzi looked like any young Palestinian teenager. "Any idea where he is now?"

"No. She doesn't think even he knew where he was going."

"What should we do with this doctor then?"

"Arrest him and toss away the key." Milner raised his voice. "If he's innocent, why would he be running for Gaza?"

David nodded. "And the girl?"

"Her, too. She may not have liked it, but she did cooperate with them."

David didn't reply. He lifted the photos on his desk before him—the twin boys, mouths open in frantic screams; the tiny rundown apartment; the young mother curled up on the floor with her hands tied to her feet; a single commando looking down at the baby on the floor. "No, Mort. Abdul-Qadir used her, just as he's used us."

David tossed the photos back onto his desktop. "*He* pushed her to the ground, not us. Give her back her children. Let her go free."

TWENTY-ONE

IN THE WEEKS THAT FOLLOWED, the constant media bombardment of real and imagined terrorist threats intensified public anger and anguish. The West was outraged at the audacity of Abdul-Qadir's warning—and the fact that no trace of him had been seen or heard since.

Two weeks to the day after the airline attacks, the American carrier group prepared to depart from the waters of the crash sites. It was ordered to continue on to its initial Mediterranean destination at dawn the next day.

At 4:25 p.m., eight hours after the *USS Harry Truman* received new orders, United Airways Flight 84 departed Newark. Ninety minutes later, Air Canada 084 rose from a runway in Toronto. The planes shared not only the same flight number but, on this night, their doom. In nearly parallel routes, both flew over the Atlantic and were to land within two hours of each other the next day at Ben Gurion Airport in Israel.

The United plane fell first. The FAA immediately grounded all flights. The Air Canada Boeing 767 turned toward Newfoundland, a return to safety. It was not to be.

Just as happened in the Second World War, despite German U-boats' targeting allied ships, transatlantic travel could not be stopped. Flights resumed after a week, and in a seemingly unpreventable chain of events, five more planes were targeted over the next four months.

An El Al flight bound for Israel from Miami was lost with all souls. After a short reprise, an Emirates Boeing 777 from Dubai did not reach its American destination, and soon, routes between Europe and America were no longer immune. Flights to London and from Paris and Istanbul were downed, as the jihadists targeted passengers connecting to and from the Middle East.

Along with the U.S. carrier group, a flotilla of recovery ships waited in the Atlantic for more carnage to drop from the skies. International police and security forces worked twenty-four/seven in a futile attempt to determine how explosives were getting aboard.

Deep-water cameras and wreckage recovery indicated each plane had suffered an intense mid-air explosion at the intersection of the wings and fuselage, and, falling separately, the parts had come to rest at varying distances on the ocean's bottom.

The theory held unanimously was that a massive explosion in the fuel reservoir was caused by a smaller explosion in the cabin above. Although many hypotheses were offered, no evidence of the method of ignition could be found.

Israel's El Al was the first to implement major changes. Other airlines quickly followed. The midsections over the wings were restricted from passenger seating and access, and heavy doors around the bulkheads were locked, essentially separating the entire midsection of the plane as it left the gate. Armed commandos flew on every plane, and cameras were installed throughout, transmitting live images to land-based security centers.

Airfares almost tripled due to soaring insurance rates, the investment in onboard changes and reduced passenger capacity. Local news networks were quick to report a further negative— that cameras were also installed in all onboard restrooms. Already frustrated by the increased thoroughness of body and carry-on searches, the public sneered at the undignified loss of privacy.

Although intelligence agencies and defense forces from many countries had been united in searching for Abdul-Qadir and known jihadi operatives, their efforts met with little success.

Yazid Abdul-Qadir had fulfilled his oath of terror and inflamed a Holy War against his declared enemy.

Media reports of an embittered Islam multiplied exponentially, and accordingly, all of Islam was blamed for the terror in the skies, sparking more outcries and transforming anguish into hatred. To the people of the West, the threat came not just from an extremist terrorist cell but from the entire Muslim world.

A dark storm of panic swept over Europe and North America, stifling any confidence in the West's ability to defend itself and avert an impending economic disaster. Oil prices soared and financial markets plunged, with billions of dollars lost in real value affecting even the average household. For the first time, a generation went to bed fearing that the very fabric of the society they had woven was tearing and might, in fact, rip completely apart by morning.

The alliance Israel had enjoyed with many nations suddenly became tense. For many, the sacrifice of life, liberty, safety and happiness was becoming a cost too great to bear.

TWENTY-TWO

MIKHA'IL LOOKED AROUND from the mountain he found himself on. He was not afraid. He was beginning to sense a purpose to his visions, though he did not yet know what it was.

The mountain was not as jagged or as high as those of the world's greatest ranges, but the beauty of the view stole his breath. Most of the slope and lands surrounding it were devoid of large trees, but an occasional bush bowed to the wind, and cottony clouds floated through the sky, their shadows passing over the golden-hued terrain.

A large body of water narrowed into a river at the mountain's base, and Mikha'il could see a humble town resting on the other side. Rudimentary stone walls enclosed low and uneven buildings. No roads seemed to lead in—there were no smokestacks, antennas or water towers associated with modern civilization.

Making his way down the slope, he paused at a clearing to inspect a modest campsite. A blanket, some animal skins and hide pouches surrounded a fire pit. Seeing no evidence of anyone nearby, he continued toward two large boulders, four times his height.

Bracing himself along the second rock, he stopped, startled.

An old man, no more than ten feet away, sat staring out over the land below.

Mikha'il said softly, "Excuse me. Hello."

Slowly, the man turned his head, showing no surprise at Mikha'il's arrival. He gave a slow, crooked smile before returning to his view.

Mikha'il drew nearer. "Do you mind if I sit for a while?"

The crouched figure tapped the end of his walking staff, which had been lying upon his crossed legs, against the ledge at his side. "This spot is free, young man. Come, rest yourself. Would you like some water?"

Mikha'il took the hide bag. The feel of water in his mouth was wondrous. It had been so long since he remembered swallowing.

"Slow down. You're no camel. You'll cramp yourself." The old man pulled the animal skin from Mikha'il's hands with surprising strength. "Besides, that has to last me for, well, I don't know for how long."

"I'm sorry. It's just been some time since I've been able to drink like that." Mikha'il panted from the refreshing sensation. "What is this place?"

"It is the land promised to my people by our Lord," the old man proudly claimed.

"By your Lord? Who is your Lord?" Mikha'il asked, trying to determine where he was and with whom he was speaking.

"My Lord is the one Lord, the only God." The elderly man turned. Despite his clouded eyes, he seemed to see everything. His face was weathered, and deep lines gave evidence of a long and hard life. Yet his words, raspy and spaced as they were, emerged noble and strong. He raised his staff and passed it over the valley. "The Lord made all of the beauty you see.

"He is the God that created earth and heaven. He created man and woman, and blessed them, and gave them the dominion over all. This, truly, is the one God, the God of Adam, Noah and my people's father, Abraham. This and more I have scribed in the Torah, the sacred word for my people."

Mikha'il smiled, in awe of the ancient man beside him. "You're Moses, the leader of the Jews."

"I am Moses, the Hebrew. And you, young man, what is your name?"

"Mikha'il," he replied meekly.

"Welcome, Mikha'il." Strands of long white hair and beard jostling in the breeze, Moses turned to Mikha'il.

"Thank you." Mikha'il hesitated. "I don't really know how I got here, though. Where are we?"

"We sit on the Mount of Nebo, and what you see before us is the land of milk and honey. It is the homeland of Abraham, the father of our religion. He was the first to recognize the one true Lord. As a newborn, Abraham was abandoned and left to die. The Lord sent an angel to provide for the infant. When the child grew, he pledged his life, and those after him, to the grace of God."

"The baby Abraham—was he left in a cave?" asked Mikha'il.

"Yes, in a dark and damp place. But, in the presence of the angel, milk flowed from his finger and he fed himself."

So that's what I saw. "What happened to Abraham after that?"

"He became a shepherd and lived a righteous life. Although his wife was barren, the Lord blessed him with a son, Isaac. But the Lord called upon Abraham to demonstrate his faith by sacrificing his only child. Abraham took Isaac to an altar atop Mount Moriah, which is where the sky meets the land, there." Moses pointed his staff toward a cloud touching the horizon. "That place is sacred. It is where God made Adam."

"But Abraham didn't sacrifice Isaac, did he?"

"No. The angel appeared and stopped Abraham. The Lord is merciful, and witnessing Abraham's intent was enough."

"And then the Lord tested Abraham in the same way again?" Mikha'il pressed, remembering the second time the angel had stopped Abraham.

"No, just that once," replied Moses, looking at him curiously.

"Abraham didn't attempt to sacrifice another?"

"No, only Isaac, his son," Moses answered quickly.

Mikha'il was perplexed at the lack of explanation for the second vision he'd had but fell quiet as the old prophet shared more about his people.

Moses told of the plight of the Jews: how, facing drought and famine, the descendants of Abraham, the Israelites, had fled their homeland westward into Egypt. At first they were welcomed as equals, but the Jewish faith in the Lord conflicted with the beliefs of the pharaohs, who deemed themselves incarnates of the gods.

He recounted soberly how the Hebrews were soon regarded as lesser, and their faith in only one God as meek. They were enslaved and oppressed. Still, the light of the Lord shone over them. Through many generations under tyrannical rulers, the Israelites were fruitful, and their numbers multiplied. And, after five hundred years, the might of the pharaoh collided with the power of the Hebrew God.

Moses asked the pharaoh to release the Hebrews from slavery. The pharaoh resisted, and the wrath of God was brought down upon his people. The Lord sent plagues of terror upon the awaiting Egyptians, but the pharaoh refused to free the Hebrews.

And then one night, the angel of the Lord came to kill the firstborn son of every family. The Israelites were warned and ordered, in the darkness of a new moon, to place the blood of a lamb on their doors so death would pass over. By morning, every Egyptian family had lost their firstborn son, including the pharaoh. Overwhelmed by grief and despair, the pharaoh gave the Israelites the freedom they had sought.

During their exodus from Egypt, the Lord gave to Moses a list of commandments. Among them was absolute loyalty to the one and true God, forbidding the worship of any other. As reward for their loyalty, the Lord promised them the land pledged to their forefather, Abraham.

But the naïve Israelites, celebrating their new freedom, defied the covenant they had made. Some made worship upon a cow forged in gold and were punished with death. Many who remained then revolted against Moses and his God. So enraged was the Lord that he banished them to forty years in the Sinai Desert before they could enter their promised land.

As the sun neared the earth in front of them, Moses continued, "That river is the Jordan, and hiding behind the walls of that city are the evil ways of Jericho. Our forty-year sentence has ended, and we will relieve the treachery that exists there. The city and the lands beyond are those promised to my people."

While Moses was concluding his story, a man, shadowed in the brilliance of the setting sun, approached, climbing up the steep grade of the hilltop, and Moses stopped talking.

Mikha'il used his hand to shade his eyes from the glare and, squinting, saw the tall man leaning forward as he negotiated the rough ground.

The man wore a long robe of white, tied at his waist, and a small rounded white skullcap on his head. His beard, also white, was neatly trimmed to the sides of his face, unlike the long unkempt beard of Moses.

As the man drew closer, Mikha'il thought he recognized him. *Could it be?* He watched a few seconds more. *Yes, yes, it is!*

Mikha'il smiled broadly and quickly left Moses to assist the man struggling up the incline. As they neared each other, Mikha'il yelled out, "Hello, Grandfather. It's me. Just wait—I'll be there in a second."

The two men embraced joyously. With his arms around his grandson's shoulders, Mikha'il's grandfather pulled his head back and grinned. "I'm glad to find you well. I have been so worried for you."

"Oh, it is so good to see you." Mikha'il pulled his grandfather to him in a second embrace. "Come, I want you to meet somebody."

His grandfather glanced toward the figure above them. "I know who he is."

Mikha'il looked at his grandfather questioningly.

"I was told you would be here."

TWENTY-THREE

CLOSING THE COMPUTER ON HER LAP and placing it on the table, Jasmine rose from her chair at Mikha'il's side. She had become so familiar with his pale complexion, dry lips and stringy hair that his appearance no longer alarmed her. She ran her fingertips along the top of his forearm and over his hand. The muscles in his arms and throughout his body had softened noticeably; even the skin on his fingers was loose and wrinkled.

Jasmine walked to the window.

In the courtyard below, large barricades topped with barbed wire surrounded the perimeter of the Hadassah. Two tanks sat with cannons pointed outward, and soldiers stood guard behind machine guns mounted on camouflage-painted combat vehicles. This type of scene had become common throughout Israel in response to the terrorist risk over the past months.

Overhead, black clouds merged in the sky, which was fast darkening into night. Lightning momentarily gave brightness to the canopy, but with the crack of thunder, it immediately turned black again.

Droplets beaded down the window in front of her.

Jasmine focused on the tiny rivers meandering along the glass, steady streams of tears, tracking down the reflection of her face. Sliding a finger down the pane, Jasmine remembered the afternoon she'd first met Mikha'il, how she'd quickly felt the kindness in his warm words and the joy of life in his laughter, already wanting him to kiss her. And that midnight in a gentle rain, when he did.

Kiss me again, Mikha'il. Make me alive once more. I'm here, waiting. So come back to me and just kiss me again.

It was under the shade of a tree, only a few miles past the tanks below, that they'd fallen in love. But as quickly as their relationship had come, so suddenly had it changed.

Jasmine knew this rain would not bring the same happiness. Her life's joy had come, and it had gone. Now, she was truly alone.

Soon, Dr. Ben would enter the room, and she suspected she knew what he wanted to discuss with her. She would have to make the decision she had, until now, tried to ignore.

Mikha'il and his grandfather reached the small plateau where Moses was waiting. Mikha'il introduced the two men, who shook hands in greeting.

"It is good to meet the source of seed in this fine man." Glancing at Mikha'il, Moses raised himself slightly, arching his old back and shoulders.

Mikha'il's grandfather, his joints, too, showing their age, awkwardly sat down.

Before Mikha'il could join them, Moses said, "Can you retrieve my blanket? It's not far up the mountain. You may have passed my campsite when you came down."

"Yes, of course. I know where it is."

"Thank you. I did not expect to be here this long, and the coolness is sapping the strength from my bones." The two old men watched him depart around the boulder, and Moses said, "Your grandson is an astute student. He listens well."

"It's good to see him have such interest in faith and religion."

"He hasn't always?" pondered Moses.

"No. His grandmother and I were of different religions, and we were each determined to have Mikha'il's father embrace our individual beliefs. Ultimately, our son rejected both, and eventually us, too."

"And where is your son now?"

131

"In defiance, he left us to fight a faraway war. He never returned. He was killed there."

"It is said that, 'In peace, sons bury fathers. In war . . . fathers, their sons.' Although war is a necessary evil, I am most sorry for you," said Moses, adding softly, "There is no loss greater than that of our children. But we cannot keep them protected in our nests forever."

"No, I understand that," said Mikha'il's grandfather, trying to hide his anguish. "At least in that land where he died, he left a son."

"And Mikha'il's mother?"

"She died when he was seven. That's when his grandmother and I brought him to live with us. Mindful of the mistakes we made raising his father, we decided to leave our religions out of Mikha'il's upbringing. We celebrated local holidays, but beyond his grandmother occasionally bringing him to her church, we never discussed our beliefs with him and did our best to separate him from all religion and worship."

"And still, he is full of faith," Moses said, nodding. "I can feel it embedded deep in his soul."

"He's always been full of a natural goodness and, as an adult, a believer in the high morals and true virtues in all mankind. I don't think he could ever tell a lie in malice or watch a living soul suffer."

"A good way to live," reassured Moses.

Both men sat in silence, taking in the panoramic view before them. Mikha'il's grandfather chose the opportunity to pursue his purpose. Turning to Moses, he asked, "And you, then?"

Moses hesitated. "I am sorry. I do not understand your question."

"Do you believe in the goodness in all mankind?"

"Yes, of course I do."

"*All* mankind?"

Not sure of how to answer, Moses again paused.

"It's getting cold up here," said Mikha'il, interrupting them. He gently wrapped the blanket around Moses's shoulders. "There, that should bring some warmth to your bones."

"Thank you." Moses reached up and pulled the blanket tighter.

Mikha'il sat beside his grandfather, who renewed his questioning of Moses. "Do you believe in the goodness in all mankind?"

Moses turned to meet his eye.

"You are God's chosen people, right?" Mikha'il's grandfather pressed.

"Yes, all the Hebrew are."

"And by *chosen*, you believe you are chosen over other people?"

"Presumably so," conceded Moses.

"And your God is a just God?"

"He is."

"And in his justness, he is fair?"

"Yes," Moses answered confidently.

"If he is fair, why would he choose you over others? Where is the justice in that?"

Moses's response was prompt. "As Abraham, the father of our religion, first did, we continue our covenant with God. As such, we obey all that the Lord has spoken."

"And for that he has promised to you the land before us?"

"Yes. It is the homeland of Abraham, the root to the branches of our tribes."

"Your families have been gone from this land for almost five hundred years. What of the people who live here now and call it their home? If your God is a fair God, where is the fairness in stealing it from them?"

The calm began to leave Moses. "The people who call these lands their home are evil in their ways. They worship many gods and foreign idols. They live in corruption and follow an immoral path."

"How can you say that? Are they not of the same creation as you? Did your God not create all man as equals?"

"Yes, but these people have come to live in wickedness and treachery." Moses straightened his back, his words growing stronger.

"What? Each and every one of them, the old and the sick, their innocent children? How can they all be living in treachery?" asked bin al-Rashid, slowly shaking his head in disagreement but still maintaining a tone of respect. "And what gives you the authority to judge them?"

The swift response came from an alert and strong mind. "It is the punishment of the Lord for their blunder."

"All right, let's make the mental leap that they all live in sin, and by *all*, we mean every single one of them. Your people have heard the Lord, right?"

"Yes, he delivered rules for us to obey, and we made a covenant of commandments with him."

"And very soon afterward, your people sinned and broke that covenant," Mikha'il's grandfather continued, unrelenting. "They chose a foreign God and idol to worship. A golden cow, I believe."

"For that we were judged, and those thousands who committed the sin were blotted out with death."

"And, still, only a short while later, all the remaining Israelites rose up in revolt against your leadership and once again defied the power of your God."

"Again, we were punished. We were banished to a life of exile in the desert," Moses countered, confident in his words and resolve. "Now our time in the harsh Sinai has ended, and we have come to claim the land promised to us."

"You see, with all due respect, that's just what I don't understand. The people of these lands have not yet had the same opportunity to hear the message from God and won't for another two thousand years. Yet when they unknowingly sin, they lose their homeland. You kill them all. Is that fair? Is that just?"

"Grandfather, please," said Mikha'il anxiously, reaching for his arm. "Perhaps this is not the time and place."

"That's just it, Mikha'il. This is the time, and this is the place!" Ignoring the grasp of his grandson, he kept his eyes fixed on Moses, waiting for a reply. When none came, he persisted. "Your people have escaped from the tyranny and oppression of Egypt, only to become the tyrannical oppressor of the people of these lands. The oppressed now become the oppressor."

"How dare you!" Moses shouted, raising his staff and slamming it against a rock, as if calling for its transformation.

"How dare I? How dare you! You will destroy this city of Jericho. You will massacre all of its people, the old and the young, the poor and the sick, the women and the children. The flock of Abraham's grandson, the legitimate eldest, whose rightful inheritance was stolen from him, will be among those you attack next. The violence you breed will not stop for four hundred years. The slaughter and bloodshed will continue. You will impale their leaders and behead their kings until all the land promised to you belongs to you. Your David will have defeated their Goliath. You will crown your kings and build a great temple to celebrate victory.

"But with your crimes against humanity, your kingdom and mighty temple, too, will fall. You will not heed the pleas of your own prophets. People of a distant land will conquer you. You will pray for a Messiah to again deliver you from oppression, but in grave error, you will see him crucified. And this will bring to the land a new religion—one that most of the known world will come to accept."

"Where do you come from, that you pretend to be so wise? Have the people of the valley below sent you?" Moses's words were quieter but seemed more fierce.

"Before I answer, tell me—when does the cycle of oppression end?"

"I will not answer any more of your questions. This is trickery. You come from the evil of the valley below," Moses scoffed.

"I do come from the lands below." Mikha'il's grandfather paused and looked over the land and then back to Moses. "But I, too, am a descendant of Abraham, our forefather."

Dr. Ben opened the door and stepped inside. "Excuse me, Jasmine. Is this a good time?" he delicately asked.

She wanted to scream out, *No! This is not a good time.* Yet she knew no time would be good. She walked to Mikha'il and held his hand in hers, touching it to her cheek.

135

Dr. Ben followed and, moving the guest chair at the foot of the bed closer to her, sat down.

"I know why you're here," Jasmine said bluntly.

Dr. Ben nodded.

"It's not fair. He looks so alive, like he's just sleeping. I keep praying he'll wake up. He must wake up . . . But, he won't, will he?"

"No, Jasmine, he won't."

"You know that for sure, don't you?" She felt hot blood sear her heart and the limbs it passed through. Her palms grew wet and sticky as she tried not to cry.

Dr. Ben's voice was slow and atonal. "We have done so many tests. All of them, doubled and tripled, far more than we would ever do for another patient. The people of Israel are beholden to him and his great courage. Just know, we are willing to give him the very best care through all of his remaining years, and to you, as well. We will always do all we can for you. You know this is so. Prime Minister Kessel has pledged it to you and repeated it to me."

"Yes, I am grateful, and I know Mikha'il would be, too." Jasmine slowly nodded.

"I have tried to choose my words very carefully with you as I have not wanted to upset you. But in doing this, perhaps I have given you false hope. I am sorry for that." Dr. Ben pulled his chair closer. "Mikha'il has virtually no functional activity. Medically, his conscious brain is nonexistent." He drew a quick breath. "He is, in fact, brain-dead, and that won't ever change."

"You're here to say we should let him go, aren't you?"

"It's the humane action and perhaps the best way for you to move on."

Barely able to breathe, she spoke hurriedly. "I don't want to move on. I want to stay right here, with him."

"Would he want that? Or would he want you to pursue a fulfilling life?"

"I don't know. I don't know," Jasmine sobbed. She could no longer control her tears.

"What if it were the other way around and you were lying there? What would you tell him, sitting here at your side, day in and day out?"

Her heart did not want to accept that Mikha'il had slipped from her, but she could no longer deny he wasn't coming back. "Can you give me a few more days with him? Maybe this Friday. It will be five months since that terrible day."

There was nothing the doctor could do or say that would ease her grief. A full minute passed before he continued. "We'll need to have his grandfather sign some papers."

"He's gone." Jasmine wiped the tears from her reddened face with both hands. "I'm sorry. I thought you knew. He had a stroke and died last week." She looked up at Dr. Ben with a watery smile. "At least Mikha'il was saved that loss."

"So there's only you?"

She nodded. "Do you mind leaving us alone for a bit?"

"Of course not." He left his chair, stopping at the door to look back toward them.

Sensing him still in the room, Jasmine called for one last request. "Dr. Ben."

"Yes."

"I don't want the press, or even the prime minister, to know until after Mikha'il is gone, and I'm sure Mikha'il wouldn't either. He wouldn't want all the fuss."

"I understand . . . only those needing to know will be told."

Moses scowled at the abrupt disrespect from Mikha'il's grandfather and berated him. "You are not of Abraham, for you are not an Israelite. You come from none of our tribes. For if you did, you would not dare talk to me in this way."

Mikha'il's grandfather held back his emotion. "I am not an Israelite. But just like my people, I am a descendant of the son of Abraham—but not Isaac, rather the other son of Abraham."

Moses hesitated and then responded, the force taken from his voice. "Ishmael?"

Mikha'il's grandfather did not react. In the silence, Mikha'il spoke up, questioning Moses. "You said Abraham had only one son."

His grandfather ignored Mikha'il and spoke once more to Moses. "You cannot deny it. You yourself wrote it in the Torah."

Moses turned slowly to Mikha'il. "Ishmael was the son of Abraham and his servant. The boy and his mother were banished when he was thirteen, after the birth of Isaac."

Mikha'il's grandfather then spoke the words Moses himself had scribed in the Book of Genesis. "The Lord said to Abraham, 'Also of the son of the servant will I make a nation, because he is thy seed.' "

"Yes, but—"

"But you didn't think the seed of Abraham and Ishmael lived in the lands your people aim to conquer and are those they will kill?"

"No, this cannot be." Moses shook his head in disbelief.

Mikha'il's grandfather continued, his tone respectful, "Ishmael and his mother were exiled and almost died in the desert. But the Lord sent the angel Gabriel to protect them and ensure their survival. Abraham knew that they had survived and occasionally visited them. He kept this quiet as he chose not to offend his wife.

"Together with Ishmael, his son, they rebuilt a shrine to worship their God. That shrine became the Kaaba, the most sacred site to the descendants of Ishmael, and near it, the Lord called upon Abraham to again demonstrate his loyalty by sacrificing Ishmael, as he was to do with Isaac."

"But he didn't kill him, did he?" Mikha'il asked, remembering what he had seen. "The angel stopped Abraham, just as it had done before."

"You're right, Mikha'il. The angel intervened and held back Abraham's blade."

Mikha'il nodded. "Abraham's obedience was again evident to the Lord because he was also willing to sacrifice his first son, Ishmael, Isaac's brother."

"So you see, Moses. The people your Hebrew take the land from, and make an enemy of, are, in fact, your brethren."

"It matters not—our destiny is written!" Moses replied coldly. He looked away from them and stared into the orange sky, the sun's rays weakening over the land.

Mikha'il stood and reached for his grandfather. "Let's go. This is of no use. He's right. Even I know it is written. Let's leave this place."

"No, Mikha'il, I will stay and address these concerns with my brother."

"For how long?" asked Mikha'il, clearly worried for his grandfather.

"Until we debate no more. Until he takes my hand and walks this land with me, each with our children safely at our sides."

"Grandfather," Mikha'il said sadly, "that may be a long time."

"Then so be it."

TWENTY-FOUR

JASMINE RETURNED TO THE SOLACE of the window. The thunderstorm had blown westward. The soldiers still stood guard, ignoring any change in the weather. Their M-16 rifles pointed out from drenched ponchos, and under the artificial brightness of heavy floodlights, large halos glowed in the misty air over them and their instruments of destruction.

She surveyed the scene below, aware of the irony of a force dedicated to the annihilation of life protecting a place built for the preservation of it. *Perhaps it is better for Mikha'il not to see this.*

Despite her desire to block out the ills of the world while cocooned with Mikha'il, she could not avoid the news that filled her laptop every day.

She watched as despair spawned loathing in the lands that God created. As in the time of Moses, greed tore nations apart, and the open wound poured red.

In retaliation against all Muslims for the terrorist attacks in the sky, mosques and Islamic community centers were bombed. And in turn, Muslims attacked not just planes but synagogues and churches, restaurants, shopping malls and office buildings. The conflict spread like a brushfire, darting wildly and burning everywhere: London, Paris, Madrid, Rome, New York, Chicago, Washington. Mourning and worry had turned to revenge, rage and death. None were immune to its effect.

Jasmine was angered by the media, which relentlessly reported every attack over and over, serving only to instigate more fear and conflict. Deteriorating economic conditions were blamed on the unrest, and the media predicted further strife and turmoil.

In Israel, conditions were much worse. Not a day went by without Jerusalem being rocked by explosions. Jasmine often heard the thunderous attacks followed soon after by the wailing of ambulances approaching the hospital. She knew of rockets from Gaza raining down over southern towns and of the Islamic Insurgency swelling in nearby Syria, threatening all around them. She'd heard of dreadful terrorist actions, people burned alive and beheadings.

Throughout the Hadassah, medical staff talked, without remorse, of retaliation.

Apache helicopters hunted suspected terrorists, and martial law was implemented over every Palestinian in East Jerusalem and the West Bank. Israeli defense forces patrolled the streets flexing muscle with tanks, armored attack vehicles and troop transporters—the young soldiers storming suspected safe houses, killing or arresting their occupiers.

So many had suffered. Every family mourned the death or injury of a close member. Despite public appearances and pleas from leaders on all sides, nothing could prevent the deadly onslaught of the Third Intifada.

"The nights are colder than I remember." Sitting with his legs crossed on one blanket and with a second pulled over his shoulders, Yazid Abdul-Qadir warmed his hands over the tiny fire.

Nur al-Din dropped another log onto the flames. "Are you sure you're all right here?"

"I've spent many a cold night in the desert," Yazid said, pulling his hands back from the fire. He grinned at Nur al-Din. "Besides, in my heart is a warrior half my age, so perhaps it is you who should show concern."

Nur al-Din returned the smile and nodded in whimsical agreement. "I'll get you a tea. It'll help you sleep."

"Thank you, but my sleep's fine," snapped Abdul-Qadir, any jesting gone.

"I'll get it anyway." Nur al-Din returned to the tent behind them.

Abdul-Qadir became transfixed by the flames. *Sleep . . . If only I could sleep. The bullet may be gone, but the sickness and spirit that came with it remain. The poison of one tortures my body and the memory of the other haunts my soul.* He let his eyes close, trying to free his thoughts.

On his lids, he felt the heat of the crackling fire calling back his attentive stare. He opened his eyes, the memory of being shot impossible to avoid—falling to the hard ground of the plaza, the pain piercing his side. As his blood pooled on the Old City square, he remembered the second intrusion, one that he could not explain.

The force penetrated deeply into his soul. It was as if an energy protected his wounded body. The force had persisted as Nur al-Din carried him through the streets of Jerusalem. That spirit, whatever it was, had held death at bay until the doctor took over.

Just as the poison from the wound did not leave him, nor did the memory of the spirit. Both now pained him, and his bitterness toward the spirit that had abandoned his soul just as quickly as it had entered it only grew.

Abdul-Qadir's thoughts were interrupted as a cup intersected his sightline and Nur al-Din's voice broke the trance.

"Here, this will warm you."

"Thank you, Tariq," Abdul-Qadir said softly. With both hands, he brought the cup to his lips. He downed the tea, and his face flared with life. "We will not have to stay much past the winter. The West shall soon fall to the will of Allah. The infidels do not have the strength in their faith to resist."

"We have had great success thanks to your guidance. Even here, they look at you with great respect. You have inspired our people."

"It is not I that they follow but the will of Allah." Abdul-Qadir's back straightened, and energy filled his voice. "All of Islam has risen in unity to strike at the evil and treachery of the infidel. The insurgency here is modest compared to what we have unleashed.

Around the world, Muslim brothers have taken up arms to fight the tyranny of the Western oppressors. Their corrupt cities cry out in pain as their wealth turns to dust before them.

"In the weakness of their greed and vanity, they will fall to their knees to save the material possessions they have embedded into their lives. They will retreat from their protection of the Jew and the oppression of our people. Israel will crumble without them, and our lands and culture will be returned to us. The will of Allah shall be done."

"And the people of Palestine will rejoice," Nur al-Din added. "We will have our nation."

"I want to demonstrate to Palestine the true strength in their faith and the might of Allah over the infidel God," continued Abdul-Qadir boldly. "In this, all of Islam will find encouragement to march unrelenting into victory."

"What do you have planned next?" asked Nur al-Din, poking at the fire with a thick stick.

"We will attack their soul in Jerusalem—the soul of Christianity."

Nur al-Din removed the stick. "The tomb of the Christ?"

"Yes, the Church of the Holy Sepulchre. Where the body of their beloved Jesus was entombed and supposedly rose from the dead." Abdul-Qadir yanked the stick from Nur al-Din's hand and thrust it into the embers. "In his sacrifice, one Palestinian will be immortalized among Islam and find eternal reward in paradise."

"It will be an honor for that freedom fighter to serve both Allah and his people."

"I'm pleased you agree . . . because I have chosen Ramzi for this."

"Ramzi! Isn't there another you can choose?"

"No, it has already been arranged. He leaves tomorrow. He will fly to Paris and, from there, to Israel."

"I've told you before, he's too young. He shouldn't even be here!" Nur al-Din raised his voice in anger.

"You were young once, and still you fought in defiance for your cause."

"I was twenty when I killed my first Jew. He's only seventeen. Let him mature into the cause and role he aspires to. Right now he wants only to please you."

"It is not me he wishes to please." Abdul-Qadir spoke calmly. "He is ready to serve Allah."

"For a mere boy, he has already served enough," argued Nur al-Din adamantly. "He defied his brother's wife and opened their home to you when you were near death. He has greatly contributed to saving your life, and for that, you take away his? I should never have taken you there."

"It was the will of Allah, just as this is," Abdul-Qadir responded, smiling and nodding, his thin brows raised and eyes sparkling. "Ramzi's youth will serve our cause well."

"Yazid, you pledge too many around you to serve Allah, and again you have planned around me." Nur al-Din withdrew the stick from the fire. Frustrated and suddenly disgusted by his leader and mentor, he threw it into the desert night and started to get up.

Abdul-Qadir grabbed Nur al-Din's arm and tugged him back down. Then he spoke softly yet firmly. "I also send him to protect and prepare you."

"Protect and prepare me? For what?"

"Your concern for him weakens you. His family is too close to you. And in this, you, too, will sacrifice, for there may come a time when the will of Allah calls upon you to lead your people as I have. You must be hardened for that time."

"You are too clever with your words, dangling this in front of me. Sometimes your will is stronger than that of Allah," sneered Nur al-Din. "You have much strength and many years ahead of you yet."

Abdul-Qadir did not respond, allowing his protégé's anger to ease. Nur al-Din waited for a moment longer and then tried to leave but again felt the vicious claw trap his arm.

Abdul-Qadir glared fiercely up at Nur al-Din. "You, too, grace me with your compliments. We both know my health is not readily returning, so it is you who puts cleverness in your words. But Ramzi goes. I have decided. Now collect the men for midnight prayer."

TWENTY-FIVE

HIS GAZE MOVING SIDE TO SIDE and up along the columned walls in awe, Mikha'il strolled through a magnificent court. The open plaza was at least three football fields wide and equally long. The stone walls, both far to his left and directly to his right, soared upward fifty feet at least.

Atop the walls, guards wearing bronze helmets and chest plates, with crimson capes attached to their backs, held out ten-foot spears in straightened right arms. The sun broke over the roof, and the scent of dew still drifting in the air led Mikha'il to guess it was early morning.

In the plaza, scores of tables held an array of clay pitchers and cups, tin plates and ceramic bowls, but all were left unattended. Tethered goats and sheep, and crates holding poultry, had also been deserted. Mikha'il looked around, trying to make sense of the scene. By the look of the overturned chairs and abandoned stools, the plaza had been vacated in a hurry. In the center of the plaza and directly in front of him, a massive temple towered behind a walled perimeter. Unmanned turrets stood at each of the corners and in the middle of two longer sides.

Mikha'il approached and paused in front of double golden doors. He knocked loudly and stepped back, looking up. A tapestry hung from the temple's sculpted roof. The rich red and purple of the heavy fabric complemented the blue sky. When no reply came, he continued along the portico, following an echo of voices and cheers.

The plaza opened onto a second esplanade, and diagonal to him, a large group of people gathered in the opening of what appeared to be a garrison. Curious, Mikha'il hastened his pace and soon drew close to the swarming mob. Some were crying, but most were yelling and jeering at whatever spectacle was holding their attention. More Roman legionnaires stood shoulder to shoulder, lining the wall overhead, with spears pointed toward the crowd.

Upon reaching the entrance, Mikha'il pushed his way through, stopping once he could finally see the focus of the horde.

Limping slowly, a lone man was prodded along by a dozen legionnaires to an open gate at the opposite end. Some of them jabbed at his back and sides with the blunt ends of their spears. Others clubbed at his bruised and bloodied body. Two muscular soldiers snapped whips into his open wounds.

The man dropped to his knees.

A centurion kicked him until he fell to his face.

The crowd cheered.

The slender man struggled to his feet. He did not cry out in pain. He did not speak.

The bridge of his nose gaped wide, exposing the white of the bone, and blood had dried around his nostrils and upper lip. Underneath his crimson-soaked and shredded tunic, the skin on his arms and legs was ripped. Blood flowed freely from the frayed flesh.

Again the whip snapped.

Again he made no noise beyond the slow, deep breaths of exhaustion. The punishments continued, the crowd yelling for more.

The man's eyes were half shut with pain, but they did not close. He looked up to the sky momentarily and continued, hobbling toward the open gate.

Please leave him alone. Mikha'il wanted to come to the man's aid, but when he stepped forward and shouted at one of the centurions, the soldier was oblivious to his presence, and Mikha'il realized he was only an observer. Nobody was aware of his existence.

The beaten man was perhaps thirty, though his age was difficult to determine. His beard and shoulder-length hair were knotted with sweat and matted with a mix of dirt and drying blood.

His hair! Suddenly, Mikha'il noticed a ring of thorns piercing the skin of the man's forehead. Mikha'il had no doubt what he was witnessing.

Jasmine stood with her back pressed tight to the closed door. It was not that she didn't want anybody to enter the room. Rather, she did not want to be there. She watched in a strange haze, as if her mind tried to protect itself from the unbearable scene before her.

Dr. Ben, a second doctor and two nurses moved quietly at the bedside, speaking in whispers. They removed the tubes that had nourished Mikha'il and disconnected all the wires, except those attached to the heart monitor.

The sterile smell of disinfectant, which Jasmine had ceased to notice during the months she'd spent here, returned to her nostrils. The room appeared so much smaller as the walls, floor and ceiling closed in. Her protective numbness had vanished. She felt her mouth go dry and a deep nausea fill her stomach. Although she'd been dreading this day for five months and had had a week to prepare, she was not ready. She never would be. This was not how a couple should be wrenched apart. She could not watch him go this way, with a simple flip of a switch.

No! She wanted to scream out or open the door and flee into the loving arms of her mother.

Jasmine's parents were waiting outside. They'd flown in two days before to support their daughter. Although her parents were proud of her devotion, she could tell they were relieved by her decision and hopeful that soon she could carry on with regular life.

Jasmine controlled her urge. She just had to get through these next minutes. Fists clenched and teeth gritted, she watched and waited.

———————

Jesus did not falter, despite the pain so evident in his face. Determined, even in the midst of such brutal torture, he limped onward.

Mikha'il, the soldiers and the crowd followed.

The gate opened into the middle of a narrow street, where more had gathered to witness the spectacle. Soldiers pushed the restless horde back, opening a pathway.

As Jesus reached the center of the street, two legionnaires placed a broad wooden cross over one of his sloping shoulders and wrapped his arm around it. The sheer weight of the heavy pine forced Jesus's knees to buckle, and he started to fall.

He braced himself, placing his free hand onto the ground and, for a moment, his body shuddered, battling against gravity. He drew a deep breath, pulled his head back and, with heroic effort, straightened to bear the full burden.

The crowd cheered.

He stumbled past them, down the cobblestone path, following the commanding centurion on a dark stallion and the higher-ranking tribune on a pure white mare. Blood spatters and puddles were left in his wake. The soldiers continued to prod him with spears and clubs. The mob marched behind, through the pools of Jesus's blood, tracking it into the porous stones of the street.

Mikha'il's stomach lurched in disgust.

A few voices cried out in concern and shame, pleading with the soldiers to stop. Of this minority, some buried their eyes in their sleeves, not wanting to witness the inhumane treatment of their Messiah. One woman broke through the cordon and ran to Jesus with a cup in her hand, but the soldiers gave her a shove and she fell back.

Jesus turned his head to her. His eyes rolled and he dropped. Under the heat of the morning sun and the weight of the cross, he lay still.

The mob hushed while the two officers on horseback turned and steered their horses back. "His sentence is crucifixion," the tribune yelled to the centurion at his side. "By law, he has to be kept alive until then!"

The people cheered.

"Get someone to help him," bellowed the centurion to the soldiers. The black horse under him reared. "And keep that crowd back!"

"You!" the legionnaire shouted, grabbing at a burly man standing next to Mikha'il. "You'll help him carry it."

The small woman who'd tried to assist Jesus before slipped through a crack in the wall of the legionnaires' shields. She darted to Jesus, and this time, the guards stood back as she knelt to wipe his face and pour water between his parched lips.

"That's enough," said one of the soldiers, yanking her out of the way so the large man could help Jesus up with the cross.

They stood, adjusting the balance of their shared burden, and their eyes locked. There was no sound until their reverie was broken by the snapping of whips across their backs.

The two men carried the cross through the outer gates and headed for a nearby hill. The spectators trailed along, the sounds of grief-stricken women, shrieking and sobbing, rising unbridled from their midst.

Mikha'il noticed one woman in particular, who seemed to attract respect from those around her. Dressed in black, she was held up by young men at each side, and the people stepped back to ease the trio's progress through the crowd.

At the base of the rugged hill, Jesus paused. His companion took the full weight of the cross to allow him to turn and face the people. The soldiers and crowd fell silent as Jesus held the attention of every eye.

Through swollen eyes, Jesus panned the crowd for the women grieving for him. He drew strength and cried out, "Daughters of Jerusalem, don't weep for me but for yourselves and for your children."

In the obstetrics wing of the Hadassah, a nurse held the hand of a young mother-to-be. "Okay, deep breaths. You're doing fine. Just relax."

"Oh, God, help me!" the woman cried, her hair drenched with sweat, and panic filling her face.

"You're very close," the older nurse reassured her.

"How much longer? I can't bear this."

"Not long, dear. Don't worry. You're doing great. Stay calm."

The mother-to-be grimaced and grunted with the pain of the next contraction. Her teeth ground together, and her face turned a raspberry red.

Atop the hill, two soldiers held up the sagging form of Jesus while others ripped the blood-soaked tunic from his body, leaving only a loincloth around his middle. They placed him on his back along the cross, which they'd laid flat on the rocky terrain, and stretched his arms across the wide center beam. They held his unresisting hands down and hammered a spike into each. With every swing, blood sprayed from his open palms but Jesus did not cry out. After hammering his blackened feet to a block on the cross, the soldiers began to lift.

"Wait," barked the commanding tribune from his white horse, and the soldiers let go. The cross dropped, wrenching Jesus's body as it thudded to the ground. The tribune threw a small wooden placard at the centurion. "Have them put this above his head."

After they nailed the plaque to the top of the cross, the centurion nodded in satisfaction. "There, raise him!"

Four soldiers pulled at ropes tied to the sides of the cross while another two guided the base to a hole in the rock. They let go and the cross fell into place.

With the jolt, Jesus's body collapsed, his raw abraded knees buckled and both shoulders dislocated.

A wail rose from his followers as they watched the cruelty inflicted upon their teacher and read the words above his head: *Jesus of Nazareth, King of the Jews.*

He had been placed between two criminals, also sentenced to execution.

The crucifixion was complete—only death had yet to come.

Waiting, some from the city shook their heads in mockery and shouted abuses up at Jesus. "You can destroy the temple and rebuild it again in three days, can you? Then, if you are the son of God, save yourself."

Several officials, gowned in elaborate garments and headpieces of black, gold and purple, made their way through the crowd. One stopped at the foot of the cross and to those walking behind proclaimed, "He saved others, but he can't save himself."

The group of priests and teachers of religious law scoffed at Jesus.

The high priest waved to quiet his entourage. He glanced up to Jesus and commanded, "Come down from that cross, and we will believe you truly are the Messiah. Prove this."

Even after such physical abuse, Jesus was conscious and comprehending. He looked up to the sky and rallied his strength. Blood misted from his mouth as he spoke. "Father, forgive them, for they know not what they do."

The priests, annoyed by Jesus's relentless defiance, shrugged and left the hilltop.

One of the criminals was awed by the courage and empathy exhibited by the man beside him. Awaiting the onset of death, the criminal pleaded, "Jesus, remember me when you come into your kingdom."

With all of his might, Jesus struggled to pull his body up. He sucked air through his broken teeth and swollen gums. "I assure you. Today you will be with me in paradise."

Jasmine watched Dr. Ben and the others hover around Mikha'il, their activities complete.

Dr. Ben turned to her. "Jasmine, it's time."

She did not speak. She could not. Yet somehow, her feet took small steps forward and carried her back to the bedside. This was the first time Jasmine had seen Mikha'il so natural-looking since that awful day. He didn't have the tubes and wires attached to his body anymore—other than the trach tube attached to his throat and the wires from the heart monitor neatly tucked under the sheets.

His chest rose and fell in a simple rhythm, and his face was perfectly shaven. She had shaved it one last time earlier that morning. He looked peaceful, as if only sleeping. Perhaps he was dreaming of her. Or, possibly, of all the good in the world, wherever it was.

After the departure of the Jewish leaders and priests, three women approached the base of the cross. One, red-haired and frail, and the second, noticeably older, led the third, the woman in black Mikha'il had noticed before.

This woman stood frozen in shock, her face pale. She touched Jesus's feet and fell to her knees. Her companions tried to help her up, but she refused their aid. Trembling, she held her hands to her face and wept uncontrollably.

Mikha'il watched her lower her hands to her lips and, with tears streaming down her face, stare into Jesus's unfocusing eyes. Although she only whispered, Mikha'il heard the tender appeal. "Jesus, why?"

Hearing her words, his eyes flickered, and he fought to open them wider. As a man, Jesus, the son, looked upon his mother for the last time.

In the delivery room, the expectant mother dug her nails into the sheets. This was her first child, and although she'd taken all the prenatal classes, she didn't truly know what to expect. Her husband brushed away the beads of sweat from her forehead.

"Count with me. One, two, three and push!" The gray-haired nurse held her hand. The tone of the nurse's voice had turned strong and firm. "Breathe one, two, three and push again!"

The doctor raised his eyes. "We're almost there. Keep her pushing. Don't let her give up."

———————

"My God, my God, why have you forsaken me?" Jesus cried out, raising his head to the sky above.

The soldiers below were oblivious. Mikha'il watched them, playing dice and arguing over their wagers, who owed whom and who was winning or losing. Behind them, a man soaked a sponge and placed it at the end of a long branch. He lifted it up to Jesus.

In his transient state, Mikha'il did not know how much time had passed since he'd first seen Jesus in the temple courtyard, but at that instant, the sky over the rocky hilltop changed violently. The brightness of the sun fell behind heavy black clouds, and an eerie stillness blanketed the land.

Fighting to hold his head up once more, Jesus shouted out, "Father, it is finished. I entrust my spirit into your hands."

A twisted line of lightning cracked the sky, followed immediately by an explosion of thunder. An eastern wind tore through the curtain hanging from the Jewish Temple and howled over the hilltop, swirling clouds of sand through the dark sky. The land trembled in torment, and boulders split apart.

The tribune was thrown from his horse and, landing on the ground, joined the legionnaires, centurion and bystanders, hugging the earth in fear for their lives. A single soldier stood and fought against the wrath of nature. He leaned into the gale and thrust a spear deep into the side of Jesus.

As the soldier withdrew it, no reaction came from Jesus's body, only clear liquid and blood rushing from a gaping wound.

Mary alone ignored the forces of nature, as if immune to them. Her face twisted in torment and, silent cries clogging her throat, she fixed her gaze on her dead son.

Mikha'il's stomach was tight with nausea, and a pasty dryness filled his mouth. Like so many of Jesus's followers, he could not prevent his tears from falling. He understood what he had just witnessed and considered the magnitude of its consequences on all of mankind.

Behind Mikha'il, an intense light split the darkness. He turned and shielded his eyes so he could peer into the blinding glare.

There did not seem to be anything there, only the glowing brightness.

No one else noticed the light. They were still distracted by the storm. But then Mikha'il realized that another might be witness to the strange light. As he watched her, Mary gazed toward him.

Her face tightened in disgust, and her anguish turned to fury. She got to her feet and approached, her determined stare never leaving Mikha'il.

Can she see me?

The brilliant illumination behind Mikha'il strengthened in intensity until, from it, a hand landed on his shoulder. Mikha'il did not have time to react, not even to turn his head. He was pulled backward.

In an instant, both the light and the scene before him were gone.

TWENTY-SIX

"LOOK, HE'S CRYING. He knows!" Watching the tears roll from Mikha'il's closed eyes to the pillow, Jasmine called out in one last desperate plea.

Dr. Ben winced in discomfort. He squeezed her hand but didn't look to her. "No, Jasmine, he doesn't know. What we are doing is what should be."

He'd prepared her for what was next to come. They would disconnect the ventilator tube from the fitting in his trachea. Jasmine herself had chosen this over having the artificial breathing machine simply turned off. She wanted Mikha'il to die as naturally as possible.

With the tubing removed, his lungs would exhale—an involuntary response as the air exited his chest cavity. But he would not inhale. And without oxygen, his heart would slow. The monitor would indicate a descending rate until it stopped beating. This would take only two minutes. Dr. Ben had warned her that they would be long minutes, but there would be no pain. Mikha'il could no longer feel pain.

Waiting for Jasmine to stop him if she truly wanted to, Dr. Ben hesitated. When no indication came, he subtly tilted his left wrist and glanced at his watch. Then he nodded to the doctor across the bed. "Go ahead."

With one last hard push, the young mother uttered a high-pitched scream, and her baby was born. The doctor cut the cord, and the exhausted new mother finally relaxed.

The doctor delicately rubbed the body of the infant, but no cry came. Quickly, he gestured to the nurse at his side, and she immediately pushed the red button on the wall. It lit up and flashed on and off while an alarm wailed at the nursing station down the hall.

The panicked mother lifted her head and called out. "What's happening?"

"It'll be all right. It'll be all right!" Her husband tried to reassure her, but fright, too, revealed itself on his face.

The nurses and doctor shoved a narrow tube into the baby's mouth to suck fluids from its lungs. Another doctor and nurse darted into the room with more equipment. Together, they desperately tried to induce breathing, a heart rate or any reaction from the newborn.

Across from Jasmine and Dr. Ben, the assisting doctor unscrewed the fitting on the pipe attached to Mikha'il's throat and removed the transparent tubing. A nurse turned off the ventilating machine, and then both stepped back and lowered their heads.

Mikha'il exhaled. In a natural reaction, his body jerked slightly, and the white line on the heart monitor jumped irregularly.

But Mikha'il's body stilled. The peaks of the graph narrowed and slowed.

Jasmine prayed for the soul of her beloved. With her eyes closed tightly, she listened to the heart monitor gradually lag and then stall. Then she heard a loud beep, followed by a second stronger one. Her eyes opened wide.

Mikha'il took a breath. His chest rose, fell and rose again.

Dr. Ben and his staff watched in disbelief.

Jasmine was speechless, unable to force a single word out. She was mesmerized as Mikha'il sucked in air through the plastic pipe in his throat. He shuddered, and his throat moved.

He swallowed. He actually swallowed! I just saw him swallow. Before her thoughts could turn into a rejoicing shout, Mikha'il's body spasmed and the heart monitor screeched.

In the delivery room, the neonatal and obstetrics teams ceased working on the lifeless baby. The doctor glanced up at the clock and whispered to his nurse, "Time of birth and death: 3:00."

The elderly nurse came to the side of the young mother. "I am so sorry, dear." Her tone was delicate. "We did everything we could."

"Oh God, no, no, please, no!" she cried out. She reached for the wrist of the nurse beside her. "Please, let me hold my baby, at least for a little while."

The nurse passed the baby to its mother. The distraught woman pulled the tiny, motionless body to her chest.

The instant the baby was held near the heartbeat of its mother, it kicked and then arched its back, and stretched out its arms before sucking in a small breath.

Life had entered the baby.

Dr. Ben pushed past Jasmine and held Mikha'il's thrashing body down. He felt Mikha'il's heart beating rapidly. Hurriedly, the rest of the team strapped a blood pressure band to his arm.

Typically, a racing heart rate was countered with a tranquilizing sedative. But this wasn't an ordinary situation. Dr. Ben didn't want to risk arrest, but considering the force with which Mikha'il's heart was pounding, he couldn't delay. Over the sounds of the alarms, he shouted to his team, "Prepare to sedate on my mark!"

Holding for the order, a nurse readied the needle and handed it to the other doctor. "Okay, Ben, I'm ready."

"Wait, wait!" He hesitated as he felt Mikha'il's heart rate slow. "I think he's stabilizing on his own."

They listened as the alarms stopped and the spikes on the heart monitor leveled out. Dr. Ben stepped back to Jasmine's side. Mikha'il's blood pressure returned to normal, and his body relaxed. He breathed on his own.

"What happened?" asked Jasmine, emotionally drained and exhilarated all at once.

Not knowing exactly how to answer, Dr. Ben, bewildered and fatigued, could think of only one thing. "He didn't want to go."

"He's not going to die?" she asked, a hint of excitement in her voice.

"Not today."

TWENTY-SEVEN

THREE DAYS LATER, through the early morning hours, Mikha'il's body remained motionless. After seeing her parents to their hotel, Jasmine had returned just past midnight to kiss his cheek and then retire to her suite.

Other than a brief nursing check, Mikha'il had been left alone when, from the corner of his room, a shimmering glow spun in circles.

With it, Mikha'il's spirit swirled.

Suddenly, the light burst into brilliance.

Mikha'il shielded his eyes and, remembering the stories from Moses and his grandfather, spoke out. "I know who you are."

For a moment, no reply came. But, then, the transcending brightness answered, its words slow and firm. "I am Gabriel, servant of the Lord. I stand at the left hand of his throne and come here to do his work."

"Please, can you show yourself?" Mikha'il timidly asked. "I can't see. It's too bright."

The emanating light dimmed, just enough that Mikha'il could openly look into its source.

Mikha'il saw, seated in Jasmine's chair—now at the end of his bed—the tall white figure that he'd first seen in the damp cave.

Even with lowered intensity, the glowing light radiated throughout the room. The holy figure sat perfectly straight, hands gathered around a white flower resting in its lap. Its expressionless face atop a slender neck was framed in long, flowing white hair.

Mikha'il calmly addressed him. "You allowed the starving baby to feed itself from its finger. That baby was Abraham, and in his older years, you stopped him from sacrificing his two sons. First you saved Isaac, and then you saved Ishmael."

"It is not relevant if it was I or one such as I. Just as it is not relevant who was saved first," said Gabriel softly. "What is relevant is that it all was. And it is I who am here with you now."

"Okay. Then why are you here? What's been happening to me? Is Jasmine all right? Where's my grandfather?" Mikha'il asked in rapid progression. "And why did you pull me back from the crucifixion of Jesus? I know it was you that did."

The angel answered only the last question. "I was sent for you. To pull you back to this place. In that very moment, all of your strength was needed here."

"So, do I have my strength back, here, now?"

"Only somewhat—I am here now so that you may come with me, to witness and to learn, as I help a mother grieve."

With the mention of a grieving mother, Mikha'il's concern turned to the new life that had come so close to being lost. "I didn't think the mother lost her baby. I thought the child took a breath and lived."

Gabriel leaned forward. "You are aware of them, the young mother and her newborn?"

"Yes. I felt them just after you pulled me from the hill where Jesus died. The baby was declared dead. The doctors couldn't stimulate life, but—"

"Stop there," interrupted Gabriel as he raised his hand. "You felt them?"

"I did. I sensed the struggle in the soul of the stillborn and the fear in its mother as she watched. Then, with the touch of the mother, I felt the baby's spirit surge."

"Touched by the mother?" Gabriel asked inquisitively.

The light of day had not yet come.

The Hadassah halls were quiet while Dr. Ben walked along the hallway to Mikha'il's room, reading the recent reports. He had taken the weekend off and returned early Monday morning, curious whether the inexplicable recovery of his patient had continued. While Jasmine's mood had been transformed from somber to jubilant, he remained concerned that any new hope may be short-lived. Mikha'il's breathing was improved, but neurological tests showed no change.

Although he could see that his patient's door was closed, just as it should be that early in the morning, he noticed an unusually bright light seeping under it. The light was far more intense than what should normally come from the room.

Dr. Ben quickened his pace.

"Yes, the mother. Are they all right, she and her baby?" Mikha'il was now more worried for their well-being than about learning what was happening to himself.

"Yes, they are," answered Gabriel with a slight smile and caring eyes.

"Why are you here then?"

"As I told you, to take you to a grieving mother."

"But you just said . . ." Mikha'il was baffled.

Standing at the door, Dr. Ben glanced down at his shoes. They were illuminated by the shimmering light. He turned the handle. It was locked. *The door can be locked only from inside. Would Jasmine have arrived this early? What's that light?*

Still trying to turn the door handle, he knocked three times. And got no reply.

Before Gabriel could explain, they were interrupted by a knocking on the door.

The pounding continued. Mikha'il's wide-open green eyes remained fixed on those of the angel until the white light from within Gabriel burst forth in all its brilliance.

The angel spoke gently, his words clear. "The mother I was referring to is not the mother of the newborn. She is another. Come, follow."

The sudden flare of light caused Dr. Ben to jump back. He rummaged through his coat pocket and removed a small ring jammed with keys. He selected one and unlocked the door.

As he opened it, his eyes were stabbed with another burst of light that extinguished in a split second, leaving the room in complete darkness.

He blinked rapidly until his eyes could adjust and then flicked the light switch on and searched the room. Everything was as it should be. He checked all the vital signs on the monitors and reviewed the charts. Noticing the last nursing round had been only twenty minutes earlier, he was pleased everything was as he'd hoped.

For a moment, Dr. Ben wondered about the strange phenomenon he had just experienced but shrugged it off as his eyes playing tricks on him. He watched the tranquil breathing of his patient. *If you continue to breathe on your own, we'll remove that fitting from your throat in a few days.*

As he turned, Dr. Ben noticed Jasmine's chair had been moved to face the foot of the bed, and a single white flower sat on the seat cushion. It was the first time the chair had been moved since he had brought it in for Jasmine five months before. *She must have moved it to make room for her parents.*

Dr. Ben pushed the chair back beside Mikha'il and picked up the fresh flower. He turned off the light and left the hospital room, dark and still.

Mikha'il and Gabriel walked along the broad hallway of an ancient church and through a series of high marble archways. A deep aroma of spice filled Mikha'il's nostrils and lungs. Burning incense had permeated the porous stone walls through the centuries before.

"What is this place?" asked Mikha'il, looking up and around him.

"One of the first churches of Christ ever constructed. It was built on the very location I pulled you from," answered Gabriel, his luminosity greatly dimmed since their arrival in the church.

"Where Jesus was crucified?"

"Yes."

"I know it now," Mikha'il said, putting his hand on the cold stone. "It's the Church of the Holy Sepulchre. It still stands in the Old City, only a ten-minute walk from the plaza." He looked around. "It's beautiful."

"It is full of much beauty," agreed Gabriel. As the two followed the hallway, the white angel continued, "In the time of Jesus, this site was just outside the walls of Jerusalem. Many decades after his death, the city was expanded, and eventually, the Roman Emperor Constantine, deeming the idol worship of paganism improper and blasphemous, declared the religion of Christ the true religion of the Empire. In celebration of Jesus and the sacrifice he had made here, the emperor had this church built."

The pair strolled under the final arch, which opened to a magnificent rotunda with high stained-glass windows encased in dark stone frames. Faded mosaics adorned the cold floor.

Mikha'il and Gabriel passed a security guard. Dressed in a gray uniform with white shirt and black tie, the guard stood against the wall, quietly laughing into a small phone.

"He has a cell phone." Mikha'il whispered to Gabriel. "We're in my time!"

"Yes, it is present day, just at sunrise," said Gabriel calmly.

"What's the date?" Mikha'il demanded, dropping the whisper.

"You are right, no need to whisper."

"How long have I been in a coma?" He persisted, grabbing at the holy angel's sleeve.

"Spring and summer have passed. It is now your autumn," said Gabriel, looking down at the hand clutching his sleeve. He then raised his other arm and pointed. "But this is of no importance to you now. Look there."

Mikha'il let go of Gabriel's sleeve and, with his gaze, followed the outstretched hand of his heavenly guide. In the center of the rotunda, a small, dark, gothic-style chapel rested under the high, domed ceiling.

"This is where Jesus rose in spirit. His tomb is inside that chapel," explained Gabriel. "And that is why I brought you here. See how she grieves."

In front of a darkened pine bench facing the chapel, a woman garbed in black knelt in prayer.

Mikha'il looked closely. "I know her," he exclaimed.

Gabriel nodded.

"It's Mary," Mikha'il said, falling back into a whisper.

"It is."

Mikha'il was filled with a rush of emotion at the memory of her at the crucifixion, her grief, her anger and the way she had stared him down just before he was snatched away. "But how can she be here now? Has she followed me to present day? You know, she saw me when no one else could."

"She can't hear or see you, Mikha'il, not now, not then."

"So why is she here?"

"It is for me she has come," answered Gabriel. "It was me she saw and recognized in the light when I pulled you away. Hers is a determined spirit. A part of her has chased after me to, as you say, your time."

"She wants you?"

"She is angry and seeks to confront me. She was permitted to follow me to you so that you could learn from our meeting in this holy place. I knew she would be here."

"At her son's side."

"Yes, her spirit prays for her son here, at the location of his death and resurrection. And with the grace of his sacrifice, she also prays for them."

"Them?"

"Good morning, Dr. Levine. You're in early." The head duty nurse greeted the doctor with a smile as he approached her nursing station.

"I know. Couldn't sleep much." Dr. Ben held out the flower. "This was in Mikha'il's room. Can you have one of your nurses place it in some water and put it back?"

"How nice—a lily." From below the sink, she removed a small vase and, filling it with water, asked, "Where was it?"

"It was just lying on Jasmine's chair," said Dr. Ben while reaching for the coffee carafe.

The nurse placed the flower in the vase and paused. "Are you sure? I was just in there with one of my nurses doing rounds. I didn't see it."

Dr. Ben lowered the steaming cup from his lips. "You probably missed it. The chair was moved to the foot of the bed."

She looked up, a puzzled expression on her face. "It wasn't thirty minutes ago. I actually sat in the chair, watching Mikha'il while the night nurse checked on him. The chair was where it always is. Other than you, no one has been down that hall since our rounds."

"Someone must have been. That chair was definitely out of place. And, just as strange, the door to his room was locked, and the lights were acting up. They were on and flickering when I got there but shut off when I opened the door."

"We certainly didn't leave the lights on. And the door wasn't locked," she insisted.

"Yes, it was. I had to use my master key to get in."

"And no one was inside?"

"Just Mikha'il. As I said, strange."

"Dr. Levine, you know the door only locks from the inside. Maybe it was just jammed."

He looked at the expression on her face and realized how foolish he must sound. With a chuckle, he gave in, putting the episode down to his lack of sleep and the early hour. "I guess you're right."

He picked up the stack of files waiting on the counter for him and started to shuffle through them.

"And you mentioned something wrong with the lights? Maybe I should call maintenance."

"No, never mind. I'm sure everything's fine. What time will Jasmine be by today?"

"She knows you're back to work, but she won't be in until later this afternoon. She's taking her parents to the airport first. It's nice to see her so happy," said the nurse with a smile. "How fortunate Mikha'il made this recovery right when Jasmine's mother and father were visiting. And spontaneously, all on his own. Makes you wonder what difference we nurses and doctors really make."

"Well, I wouldn't go looking for a new career just yet. I don't think we'll be out of a job anytime soon."

"I'm not too sure about that, if what's been happening around here keeps up."

"Really? What's that?" asked Dr. Ben, looking up.

"We haven't had a death in almost three days."

"That's not terribly odd. After all, our job is to prevent death." Dr. Ben continued his perusal of the file folders.

"Not just on the intensive care floor, but the whole hospital."

He put the folders down. "You mean no one has died in the entire Hadassah since Friday?"

"Not since Friday afternoon. A cardiac arrest was the last. A woman died down in the ER at 2:45. A little while after that, a baby was declared stillborn over in OB but then breathed on its own."

Dr. Ben was stunned. "I haven't heard anything about this!"

"Well, you've been off all weekend."

"What time did the stillborn come to life?"

"Three o'clock, on the dot."

Dr. Ben stood in silent bewilderment at the coincidence, remembering how he'd readied himself to call the time of Mikha'il's death.

To his new student, Gabriel explained, "She prays for those in the hour of their death, here and now, in this holy city. In her anguish and loss, she holds on to those souls near this place. And in doing so, Mary has held back all death in Jerusalem since she followed me to you almost three days ago. Her healing energy first restored life to the stillborn infant you sensed. It was with her prayers that air rushed into its tiny lungs.

"Like the baby, all the souls dying in Jerusalem, from those too young to those aged beyond their years, in the hour of their death—they unknowingly hail to the grace of Mary, the blessed mother of God. She feels their prayers and, in resistance to the horrid loss of her own son, has defied death."

"How long will she stay?"

"That depends on whether she will heed me. She knows her actions will bring me to her. She beckons me to come and persuade her to stop, to allow those souls to pass as nature wills."

"And if she leaves, all those people . . . they'll die?"

"Some will. Or perhaps they will be spared for a time, maybe a day or a month or for many years to come. Death is natural and does not always follow order. Its grasp can be of destiny or purely random."

"And the newborn?"

"The baby, I know, will be fine."

"And . . . me?" Mikha'il asked hesitantly, thinking of Jasmine.

"You were saved when I pulled you back from the crucifixion. Mary followed immediately after. The stillborn was the first that she saved," explained Gabriel. "There is one greater watching you."

"Vishnu?" asked Mikha'il.

"In a way, yes." The angel's light flared, causing Mary to turn to the brilliance. "She sees me. I must go to her. Come with me and hear my words."

TWENTY-EIGHT

MIKHA'IL WATCHED AS the mother of Jesus rose from prayer and wiped the tears from her face. She straightened her small body and readied herself to meet the angel of the Lord. Under the thickness of her full hair, still dark with youth, though speckled with gray, Mary's somber face tightened in pain.

Instead of graciously accepting the arrival of the angel as she had upon their first and only meeting, she angrily snapped at him, "You have deceived me."

> The Bible, Luke 1:27–33, 38 Gabriel appeared to Mary and said, "Greetings, favored woman! The Lord is with you!" Confused and disturbed, Mary tried to think what the angel could mean. "Don't be frightened, Mary," Gabriel told her, "for God has decided to bless you! You will become pregnant and have a son, and you are to name him Jesus. He will be very great and be called the Son of the Most High. And the Lord God will give him the throne of his ancestor David. And he will reign over Israel forever, his Kingdom will never end." . . . Mary responded, "I am the Lord's servant, and I am willing to accept whatever he wants."

"Please, my child," Gabriel said as he reached for her, holding out both hands.

"I am not your child," she scorned, stepping back. "You have taken the life of my child in brutal torture. Where were you then? Where was your Lord that he could not save the life of his beloved son?"

"We suffered with your son and grieve with you your loss."

"No, you only came afterward. I saw you there," she accused.

"The Lord cried out and all of his force in nature did so with him. You must have seen and heard his torment. The sky shuddered, the wind wailed, and the earth roared."

"It does not matter," Mary argued. "You have broken your pledge. 'The Lord is with me,' you said. 'Don't be frightened, for God has blessed me,' you said. How could you—" she shook her head in disgust "—one of such supposed goodness, allow this evil to take place?"

"Near the evil, goodness prevails," Gabriel said gently. "Through the Lord, we brought his life to you so that your son would grow to shine a new light in this world. As the servant to the Lord, you accepted his will upon any course."

"I am not the young girl I was then." Mary boldly stared into the eyes of the divine figure. "It is not natural for a mother to outlive her child. A mother does not just give life. She nurtures it. He is my son and my son alone. No father would allow his son to suffer like that."

Gabriel paused, gathering his words. "The purpose of your son was foretold. He was born to give great testimony."

"Not in his death, not like that!" Mary struggled to retain her composure, her voice cracking. "I watched and could do nothing! I could hardly recognize the broken body of my own son. It was only in his eyes that I could see him. Oh my poor Jesus."

"You know he could have prevented his own death. But he did not. Jesus accepted his destiny and welcomed his fate."

"You told me that he would be given the throne of Israel. Instead he was crucified like a criminal."

"No man's destiny is completely preordained, nor was his. Each determines the direction of his life based on what exists in his heart. Jesus's heart was filled with love like no other before him—for in it was the seed of the Lord. On the day of Jesus's sacrifice, you say you could recognize your son only through the love in his eyes?"

Mary nodded slowly.

"Could you also recognize his love through his words and the grace of his actions?"

"He was so strong and yet so gentle," she answered quietly, her lower lip and chin quivering.

Without emotion, Gabriel continued, "Not just in death, but in all his time. This was the beauty of his life. Jesus delivered a message of peace at a time of great need. He stood by the suffering, spoke of the meek inheriting the earth. He called out to peacemakers, that they are the children of God.

"He fed the hungry, healed the sick and chased away evil from those possessed by it. The lame walked, and the blind saw. The blemished became whole. He preached that forgiveness would overcome vengeance and peace would rule over war. He encouraged all to do good upon their fellow man, not just those who could better their station. You see, love is the life force of the human soul.

"He delivered a message to all of mankind, and all of mankind will hear it. They will rejoice and celebrate in his name because you, holy mother, are correct. He did not sit on the throne of Israel. He was not the Messiah, rather something far greater. Your son was not just your son, but the son of all and the savior to all of humanity. And in time, the known world will praise Jesus, for his spirit has arisen and lives. The followers of his teachings will become the believers in the Holy Spirit, your son, Jesus, the Christ."

Without rest from anguish and prayer, and overwhelmed by Gabriel's words, Mary sat down on the bench behind her. The angel stood patiently by the exhausted mother's side, waiting for her suffering to ease. After a moment, he reached for Mary's hand, and this time she did not refuse it.

"Why did his death have to be so violent," she asked quietly, "and why on the cross, like a traitor to his people?"

"The cross came to symbolize the sacrifice he made and the freedom in salvation of his followers. And with it, the new covenant of Jesus spread throughout the world. Eventually, the pagan ways of idol worship in Rome ended. The way of Jesus, the Christ, emerged throughout the Empire and the known world as the preeminent religion of faith."

Mary's eyes had not left the face of the angel as, sitting at his side, she listened to his words. When Gabriel finished, she did not respond right away, and as she looked to the chapel, tears again fell from her eyes. Her chin once more quivered as, finally, she spoke with some gratitude and respect for the divine servant of the Lord. "I hear your words. I understand the purpose of Jesus's life and in it, the value of his death. But you have to understand that he was my son. I miss him too much and think his sacrifice was unfair, at least to me. Perhaps someday I will see it as just, but not now."

Gabriel sighed. He knew that, in time, the mother would appreciate the sacrifice of her son. For now, the angelic servant was content that, with the understanding of her son's purpose, perhaps he had brought her some comfort to ease her grief.

Gabriel let go of Mary's hand, and she lowered herself to the damp stone floor of the rotunda to kneel once more in prayer.

The morning sun shone in a perfect sky. At the security checkpoint of the Dung Gate, an armed Israeli officer studied the passport of the student standing in front of him, while another rummaged through his knapsack. At three other conveyer belts, guards did the same with the many people who'd reached the checkpoint after waiting close to an hour.

Security had been enhanced at all seven gates leading into the Old City since the beginning of the violence that now plagued it. Several dozen Israeli soldiers, most less than twenty years old, with M-16s in hand, stood alongside the security team and monitored the line.

"Remove your glasses and both earphones," ordered the officer. "You're studying in France, are you?"

"That's correct; at the Paris Sorbonne University," Ramzi answered with just a hint of a French accent, while removing the other earphone and leaving them both to hang over his shoulder. He slid his glasses up to rest on his forehead. Even these actions had been planned to give Ramzi the appearance of a common, carefree student.

The officer glanced up and, as expected, said forcefully, "No. Completely remove your glasses and earphones."

Ramzi had left the Iraqi desert a week earlier and had been rigidly trained for his martyrdom by loyal operatives in a Paris safe house. He was questioned and drilled until he had perfected each answer and every detail of the mission awaiting him. To alter his appearance, his thick hair had been cropped close to his head and his stringy beard shaved off. Wire-rimmed glasses were added to reinforce an intellectual image.

In seven days, Ramzi had been turned into a shrouded killing machine.

Waiting for the security officer to finish, Ramzi's stomach turned in a tightening twist of knots. Since he'd inserted the two condoms of liquid nitroglycerin into his rectal cavity two hours earlier, the nervous ache in his stomach had intensified. Concentrating on the heavenly paradise that awaited him, Ramzi tried not to think of the pain.

"Where are you from originally?" the officer asked.

"Haifa." Ramzi swallowed, keeping a straight face.

He'd been instructed to arrive at the Old City just before 8:00. The operatives knew security would be the busiest at that time, with the rush of both Jews and Muslims heading to their holy sites for morning prayer.

"How long will you be in the Old City?"

"Just a few hours."

"Purpose?"

"Sightseeing and some shots of the Dome of the Rock." Ramzi smiled, taking a breath and glancing toward another officer inspecting the video camera from his backpack.

Watching for any reaction, the questioning officer studied Ramzi's face.

He shrugged and smiled again.

"Go ahead, but stay away from the Western Wall." The officer waved to the next person in line.

Ramzi casually walked through the metal detector and body scanner, replaced his glasses on the bridge of his nose and collected his belongings. Sauntering into Jerusalem's Old City, he put his earphones in and turned the iPod on.

Reaching the famed mosque, he removed his video camera and passed the next thirty minutes filming the hallowed ground.

After believing he'd diverted any possible suspicion, he exited the Temple Mount grounds and continued west along a narrow laneway. This tiny street would lead him to the front steps of his target, the Church of the Holy Sepulchre.

Unknown to Ramzi, this was the exact route another had followed. Two thousand years earlier, Jesus, suffering the pain from his torture, carried the cross along the same cobblestones to his final sacrifice.

Ramzi tried to fight the burning pain that rippled through his body. The throb of anxiety was intense and pulsed with his every breath. Trying to force away the nauseating feeling of dread, he concentrated on his reason for being there. In his mind, he repeated the teachings of Abdul-Qadir and his continued quotations from the Qur'an. "Slay them where you find them. Fight in the cause of Allah against those who fight against you. Drive them out from where they have driven you out."

Ramzi had reveled in the quest of his sacrifice and martyrdom. He was honored to offer his own life in the name of Allah and Allah's messenger, Muhammad.

Walking briskly along the narrow corridor, he thought of his family, his coming memorial and his eventual destination. *My brother and nephews will forever be proud of what I do for them and our people today. Oh, what pleasures await me in paradise.*

Gabriel knelt in prayer beside the mother of Jesus.

Confident in the knowledge that she could not see him, Mikha'il joined them. He had never really prayed before—at least not like this—kneeling in a church. He thought of Jasmine and his grandfather, and those souls touched by Mary, asking that their suffering be eased. He prayed to Jesus, respectful of his sacrifice.

Their heads bowed in silence, the three faced the tiny chapel in the center of the church's main rotunda. Around them, a dozen tourists and devout followers had entered the vestibule. They walked quietly around the chapel and the sacred foyer.

The small chapel had once been open to the public. But with the recent instability and violence, the chapel's heavy iron door had been closed and was guarded by two armed security officers.

Mary raised her head and said to the angel beside her, "I would like to enter and be nearer to where my son was laid."

Understanding her desire, Gabriel nodded, but before her departure, he graciously asked, "And what of those souls awaiting death so near this place?"

"They are free to follow their natural course."

"Thank you, my child. Go in peace. I shall remain here for a moment and continue to pray, not just for your son but for you, hallowed mother, and for those souls you have just released."

Ramzi walked up the steps and into the ancient church. He marveled that after so many centuries, he alone would bring the walls of the Church of the Holy Sepulchre tumbling down. Entering the first vestibule, he saw from the corner of his eye a small door, almost concealed in a nearby alcove. The floor plan of the church had been drilled into his memory. This was the rest room he knew would be there. Quickly, unnoticed, he scurried for the door and entered.

"After Jesus's death, they soon forgot his words," said Gabriel under his breath, still kneeling, head bowed.

Mary had been gone only a few minutes, and the angel and Mikha'il remained, praying together in front of the chapel.

Gabriel stood, motioned to his student and said, "Please, sit with me."

175

With Mikha'il next to him, the angel began, "Sadly, some in the Christian religion succumbed to the imperfections of man. In the triumph of their new way and religion, they became self-righteous, like those before and after, believing theirs to be the only ordained religion and true path to the Lord. They condemned other practices of faith, decreeing them blasphemous.

"The new church overlooked the roots of its religion, the teachings and meaning of Jesus's words. As the followers of Jesus came to believe in Christ and his resurrection, his self-sacrifice overshadowed his teachings. Selfishly, some concentrated worship on their own redemption and salvation in the afterlife.

"In time, the Christians were oppressed by their own church. The church held a monopoly on forgiveness and implied the way to salvation was through them alone. Their leaders made the people God-fearing rather than God-loving. Instead of living freely and understanding the mercy of Jesus and his father, believers dreaded the church's judgment. Those resisting the church were labeled heretics. Some were banished, others tortured and still many more killed.

"For over a thousand years, the scriptures of the Bible were not even provided in a language the vast majority could read and comprehend for themselves."

While Mikha'il listened, disturbed, to every word, Gabriel detailed the oppression and loss of innocent life that came with Christianity, including the deadly Crusades and Inquisitions.

Twenty yards behind them, on the other side of a series of thick stone walls, Ramzi sat in the privacy of the isolated rest room. A single toilet and tiny sink were crowded into the closet-like space. After carefully removing the latex condoms containing the deadly liquid, he broke off the ends of his earphones and peeled back the white plastic covering on each end, exposing the thin copper wire. Holding one condom, he untied the knot—a small string looped through, making it possible to loosen—with precision and cautiously placed the ends of the wires inside.

Just as he had practiced countless times until his technique was perfect, he retied the condom into a tight knot. He then taped the two bulging condoms together. To the battery he'd already taken from his video camera he taped the end of one of the wires hanging from the condom.

Taking care not to touch the other loose wire to the battery, Ramzi placed the bomb into his knapsack. In the smaller front section, he placed the battery. He closed the zipper as much as he could, leaving the connecting wire exposed and running through the small opening and then put the knapsack on the floor. Ramzi rubbed the bristled hair on his head, remembering not so long ago when it was long and flowing freely.

Although he'd been ordered to work quickly, he hesitated. His heart raced and blood pounded into every muscle of his body. Looking down at the knapsack between his feet, he recalled Abdul-Qadir's directions and the orders from the operatives in Paris. He'd been repeatedly told any delay would increase the risk of being caught and left in never-ending disgrace.

What he didn't know was that the true reason for urging haste was to eliminate the possibility that the jihadist might lose his resolve.

With a sudden lurch in his stomach, Ramzi leaped up and then knelt to vomit violently. With his head bowed over the bowl, he spit and threw up again.

Trying to regain his composure, he got to his feet and paced the tiny, tomblike room. He stopped at the rust-stained mirror and stared into his flushed, sweaty face. This was not how he'd expected it to be. Gone were his feelings of excitement and glory. *I'm going to be dead in five minutes. I don't want to die. I should run. But what of my family? I will have dishonored them. What have I done?*

In a state of shock, Ramzi realized he had come too far to have any options and, painfully, accepted his destiny. He picked up his backpack and left the sanctity of the rest room. *Allah, please let there be a paradise.*

"Finally, in your time, and almost two thousand years after the sacrifice of Jesus," Gabriel continued, "the Christian church has redeemed itself, seeking to right these wrongs and asking for forgiveness.

"But still, some followers prefer the trappings of worship and holiday celebrations to the meaning of Jesus's teachings. Even more sadly, many in the church continue to position theirs as the only true way to the Lord. They do not attempt to understand other religions and instead, in their ignorance, condemn others as wrong, making enemies of them. These enemies, in turn, counter with hatred."

"*Hate* is a vicious word," said Mikha'il coldly.

"Yes, it is, and, in its evil, terror and death are unleashed."

Mikha'il thought of the words Gabriel had spoken to Mary. "This isn't how you talked before."

"As I told you, Mikha'il, we came here to help a mother grieve, not add to her suffering. Through time she will know, and in this, she will pray for all those who sin."

"When does this sin of hatred end?"

Gabriel didn't have time to answer the question.

Twenty-five feet away, standing near a group of tourists, Ramzi placed his knapsack on the cold stone floor at his feet. He undid the zipper and pulled the loose wire from the back compartment. Holding the wire, he reached into the front pocket and touched the free end of the battery.

TWENTY-NINE

DR. BEN STOOD OVER MIKHA'IL. Everything in the hospital room was as it had been when he'd left it almost six hours earlier, apart from two exceptions: the white lily now stood in a vase on the bedside table, and the morning sunshine replaced the dark stillness of night.

Studying the information and readings on the monitors above Mikha'il's bed, Dr. Ben noticed a third exception. Mikha'il's vital signs had been somewhat erratic, though not drastic enough to set off alarms. The data indicated that his heart rate had increased to as high as 120, with a corresponding rise in blood pressure and accelerated breathing. All had peaked only fifteen minutes earlier, but had since returned to normal. Regardless of the changing vital signs, Dr. Ben remained pleased with his patient's condition.

However, his delight in Mikha'il's recovery was mixed as he struggled with the coincidence in the timing of it as well as the simultaneous unusual lack of deaths.

Dr. Ben had checked that morning with other hospitals in Jerusalem and the city coroner's office. He'd also made phone calls to colleagues in Tel Aviv and Haifa, asking them to do the same in their cities. He'd found that the incidence of death throughout Israel was as usual, but no deaths had occurred *anywhere* in Jerusalem since before 3:00 Friday.

He knew that in the Jerusalem area, which had a population of just under one million, it was only a matter of time before the media picked up on the anomaly. Rumblings could already be heard among the hospital staff; soon reporters would be rushing to the Hadassah to verify the rumors.

Dr. Ben felt a growing uncertainty overpowering his professional skepticism. He stared at his peacefully resting patient. *Are you somehow involved? This thwarting of death? It's not natural.*

His only response was the serene sound of breathing. For another moment, Dr. Ben stared, mesmerized, at Mikha'il. His concentration was broken by a voice calling urgently through the open door behind him.

"Dr. Levine, you have to come quick! There's been another explosion."

"God, will this never end? Where?" he asked the nurse.

"In the Old City, about fifteen minutes ago. It's the old Christian church!"

"How bad?"

"Several dead and casualties on the way, many critical."

He nodded and glanced down. *No, it couldn't have been you. Death, after all, is inevitable.*

"Ramzi did it!" yelled the courier as he entered the large tent and waved the newspaper.

Abdul-Qadir plucked it from his hand and, showing off the front page, proudly added, "See, I told you all he would do this."

Four bodies could be seen covered in blood-soaked white sheets. Emergency personnel were bent over several other victims, and police and armed soldiers stood among the carnage and debris. In the background, jagged holes gaped where ancient stained-glass windows had been.

Although charred and chipped, the stone walls and columned archways of the church remained intact, as did the small chapel. Inset into the top of the page was a photo of Ramzi. It was a school picture taken two years before. His hair was long and his face sported a broad smile.

"Fourteen wounded and six dead, including Ramzi. He was so young . . ." said Nur al-Din solemnly, lowering the paper to the table. "And it's as I said. He didn't have enough nitro to cause much damage in such an open space. It may have worked on the planes, but no way would it work there."

"I know." Abdul-Qadir grinned. "You can't really think I didn't know that, can you?"

"What? You argued with me over and over, not even caring that the Israelis might figure out how we're getting the nitro past security," stormed Nur al-Din, not caring to temper his fury. "What's worse, you convinced Ramzi he would bring down the Church of the Resurrection and that he would be remembered for an eternity by all of Islam for his martyrdom."

"He needed to believe that, and you needed to know he did," Abdul-Qadir replied insensitively. "It wasn't bringing down the church that's critical to our cause. It's the message we are sending by attacking this place."

"He was just a boy. You show no respect for those who serve you!" In his outrage, Nur al-Din jumped up from the table, sending his chair crashing to the ground, and stalked off.

"Don't you walk away from me! Come back here and sit down."

Nur al-Din ignored the order and, passing the courier and two other men watching the confrontation warily, continued through the tent's opening.

"Tariq, I demand it!" Abdul-Qadir shouted. "Get back here now!"

Nur al-Din stopped. He was treading on dangerous ground, he knew. Reluctantly, he returned to the tent. He picked the chair up and sat down.

Abdul-Qadir motioned to the others to leave. When the two were alone, he spoke in deliberate tones to his second-in-command. "I have told you before not to question my reasoning. We are like the wolf. We gain our strength as a pack. And as a pack, we hunt and attack our prey as one. You see, my trusted friend, as in the wilderness, if a lone wolf ever strays, that wolf immediately becomes a threat. As such, the pack will relentlessly hunt that stray. Then, together as one, the pack will rip the flesh from the stray's body until no resemblance or memory remains, only a bloodied clump of fur and bone. Do you understand?"

"Yes," said Nur al-Din respectfully.

"Good, so let's not do this again. Besides, the measure of one's worthiness is in his intent. Ramzi is still a hero of our people. He celebrates his victorious death in paradise with the praise of Allah."

"And what of his family?"

"You mean his brother's embarrassment, that Shia woman?"

"The Jews will never let him out of prison now. And they'll likely keep her locked up, too. There will be nobody to care for their children."

"She is Shia. Her children are better off without her." Abdul-Qadir returned to the newspaper with a self-satisfied smirk. "Look at what we have done. We continue to show the West our might and resilience."

Nur al-Din sat quietly. Then, attempting another approach, he countered, "About the Shia, I don't know that we should alienate them."

"How do you mean?"

"Perhaps we should reconsider our separation from them," said Nur al-Din, more energy in his tone. "Allying with the Shia may strengthen our bite. Reports are that Iran may be preparing nuclear weapons after all."

"I've read that, too." Abdul-Qadir laughed and peered over the newspaper. "The West will never allow the Iranians to have the bomb. If Iran gets close, the Americans will strike, and our cause will only be made stronger."

"So, Mort, what am I looking at?" asked David Caplan, holding a photograph taken in the Shin Bet forensics lab.

"They're minuscule pieces of latex from the ringed end of a condom. They were found at the scene around the assailant's body—or I should say, mixed with the pieces of him."

"So the kid had a condom in his backpack."

"Not exactly in his backpack. If the condom was in its package, packaging fragments would have been found. But they weren't. Nor were there any other pieces of latex. Only these bits from the ringed end."

"So where's the rest?" asked Caplan, giving Milner his full attention.

"The only explanation is that the rest of the condom completely melted away, leaving not even a microscopic trace. From the lack of residue and debris, we know the explosion was caused by a concentrated amount of high-intensity liquid nitroglycerin."

"You think the nitro was in the condom?"

"That's right—likely stuffed into his rectum. It's the only way he could have gotten through security. None of our scanning equipment would pick it up. It would only read as bodily fluids. We've also determined that earphone wires and a video camera battery were used to detonate it."

Caplan rubbed an open hand across his face. He rose from his desk and looked out the window briefly. "So that's how they've been getting explosives on the planes." He leaned back on the windowsill. "Yes, it makes sense. And now Abdul-Qadir is showing off. He didn't care that we'd figure out what they were doing. In fact, he wanted us to. He's bragging about how he carried out the airline bombings, and now that we've prevented them, he wants us to know that even our toughest security screens can't stop him."

"Perhaps you give him too much credit. We haven't heard from him in five months. He could have died from the bullet wound."

"No, he's alive," insisted Caplan. "Did you find out anything from the kid's brother?"

"We pulled him from his jail cell yesterday and have been questioning him all night. We're confident that he didn't know anything."

"Okay, send him back then."

"Should we bring the woman in again for questioning?"

"No," Caplan said. "She's no friend of Abdul-Qadir's. Besides, we've already put her through enough."

THIRTY

THE AMERICAN PRESIDENT'S OFFICE was just that, an office—a place of work. Documents, some as hefty as five hundred pages, sat piled on top of the desk, coffee table and various shelves and cabinets throughout the impressive room.

Never removing or loosening his tie, the president spent as many as sixteen hours a day reviewing the documents around him. Although the tall stacks of bound paper seemed disorganized, he knew exactly where to find what he needed.

With the upheaval in the world, his days had been longer, and although his mind was still sharp, his body was beginning to show the effects of the unrelenting stress and lost sleep. His red hair had whitened around his temples, and the lines on his face had become much more pronounced. He'd also dropped a few pounds from his tall, lean frame, which showed in the bagginess of his clothes. Regardless, his resolve was unaffected. President Robinson carried on with ever-increasing determination and purpose.

He sat on one end of a sofa, reading over a report and awaiting the arrival of his CIA director.

After a faint knock, the door across from him opened, and his secretary leaned her head in. "Mr. President, Ms. Adams and Mr. Whelan are here to see you."

He had not been expecting them but, without looking up, he answered, "Send them in. And when Vasquez gets here, let him in, too."

"Good morning, Virginia. Hey, Matt." President Robinson placed the papers on the table. "What's up?"

"Sir, there have been two major bombings. The Blue Mosque in Istanbul and the mosque at Saladin's Citadel in Cairo," reported the secretary of state, approaching the center of the office.

The president scowled as he sank down onto the sofa. Such reports had become a daily occurrence.

"CNN's reporting," added Matt Whelan. "Want me to turn it on?"

"Don't bother. I've seen enough shootings and bombings," Robinson said flatly and gestured to the sofa across from him.

The chief of staff began, "They were hit ten minutes ago, thirty seconds apart—mostly cosmetic damage to the façades and surroundings. Only a dozen or so injuries."

"Who's responsible this time?"

"Probably Christian radicals retaliating against the church bombing in Jerusalem," Virginia answered readily.

President Robinson shook his head and said solemnly, "So, in the words of Moses himself, an eye for an eye."

"Or in this case, two eyes for one," Whelan remarked.

"With two eyes poked at the exact same time, but a thousand miles apart, I'd say these attacks were well coordinated."

"Yes, sir, and bolder in their targets," Virginia continued. "These mosques are two of the most famous in the world. Their people will be outraged."

"Just as Christians the world over were four days ago. It seems the pope's plea didn't do much good."

"No, sir."

"Virginia, we have to get Israel's prime minister and the P.A. leader talking again. That's where this all started, and that's where its end has to begin."

"I've convinced Prime Minister Kessel that they need to meet again," Virginia began quietly, "but Abu-Hakim still refuses. He usually abhors acts of terror, but he's outraged that his people are suffering. He holds Kessel personally responsible for Israel's aggressive stance and the recent deaths of so many innocent Palestinians. Abu-Hakim is concerned that, unless Israel relaxes its grip, meeting with any of the country's officials will only damage his reputation."

After a brief pause, President Robinson straightened. "Maybe the pope can help after all. Matt, you're still working out the details of the papal visit to Washington next year, right?"

"Our staff has it tentatively planned for mid-March, just before Easter, but they haven't confirmed a date yet."

"Let's get it moved up as early in the year as possible and invite Kessel and Abu-Hakim. An informal setting may help to start a new year in the right direction. Matt, get the date set with the Vatican first, and then, Virginia, you can invite the other two. We don't want it to seem contrived. It's a long shot that they'll both come, but it's worth a try."

Before either could reply, the door opened.

Behind the technicians, Dr. Ben and Jasmine observed the video screens filled with digital images taken from various angles. It was unusual for visitors to join doctors during MRI procedures, but Jasmine had come to be a fixture in the Hadassah, and to Dr. Ben, Mikha'il was no ordinary patient.

Inside the scanning cylinder, an electromagnetic field surrounded Mikha'il's still form. To protect his brain from the bullet fragments still lodged in his frontal lobe, Mikha'il's head was firmly secured by a heavy plastic brace.

Jasmine had seen so many scans of his brain that she knew what to look for. Dormant brain cells appeared yellow, while blue cells indicated involuntary function such as breathing. As brain activation was heightened with more complex function, colors would change to orange and then to red.

To incite brain cell activity, gentle pulses of electricity were aimed randomly along Mikha'il's skin while hot and cold air was intermittently blown over the soles of his feet, and different sounds played on speakers near his ears.

With her hands to her lips, Jasmine watched the monitors with hopeful anxiety.

"Mr. President, it's Iran," said Vasquez, as he entered. "Analysis of this week's satellite footage indicates that the construction of Iran's nuclear facility has progressed, and our covert recon confirms it." He opened his attaché case and removed a DVD container, placing it on the coffee table. "We have video of twelve trucks towing covered trailers into the facility. We're confident they're all carrying medium-range missiles for nuclear warhead armament."

"Confident?" asked President Robinson. "I need to know for sure."

"Yes, sir. That's why our ops-team leader risked detection. At a narrow curve in the road, he jumped into the back of the last trailer as it slowed. The photos he took are indisputable." He tapped the disk container on the table.

"How long before these missiles are armed?"

"Could be as soon as ten days. We believe the facility is nuclear-ready, but not launch capable."

"So, once armed, they'll be moved?" the president asked.

Vasquez nodded. "And taken underground to unknown locations, making an attack against them difficult. Sanctions and Mossad actions haven't worked. Neither has diplomacy. Iran can't be trusted. The facility should be the prime target now, taking it and the missiles out together."

"So we have a ten-day window to strike?"

"Less if we want to avoid a nuclear explosion in the facility. The first missile could be nuclear-ready sooner," Vasquez said with authority.

"And if they aren't knocked out?"

"They'll be in range of Israel. And if they're used against Israel, Kessel will have to counter, perhaps in a nuclear exchange. War would break out, and with the added support of Iran to the Arab cause, Israel, after giving one hell of a fight, would likely lose. Even if Israel doesn't counter, the country will sustain grave, perhaps permanent, damage from the nuclear blasts, and the Arabs would take full advantage. Either way, Israel loses."

"Virginia?" The president turned to the secretary of state.

"I agree," she said. "If there is war and the Muslims are united—Sunnis and Shia together—Israel, left on its own, will lose. The entire land, including the portion Israel holds, would revert to the Palestinians, forcing all Jews to flee. Iran could emerge as the hero in the eyes of the Sunni majority, which could pave the way toward the spread of theocratic influence. With the recent insurgencies, the whole region could turn to Sharia law. Imagine what would happen if control of all the Middle East oil fields fell to newly volatile nations. But if we—"

The president cut her short. "But if we, the United States and our Western allies, rush to save Israel by entering the conflict, the leadership of Russia, bent on returning their country to the glory days of the Soviet Union, will surely do the same on the side of the Arabs and Iran, soon after which, the Chinese, with their thirst for oil, will follow Russia, its once communist cousin." Robinson paused, swallowed and, shaking his head, continued, "Doomsayers will have their Armageddon of Revelation."

The four sat quietly, weighing their dilemma.

Virginia broke the silence. "Mr. President, I still need to point out that, with the bombings of these mosques, an attack on Iran will seriously damage our role as mediator for peace."

"I realize that, Virginia, but I'm concerned that the fruit is ripe for the Iranians now. In an attack on Israel, Iran will have support from all of Islam."

"Well, we need to do something," implored Vasquez, "and soon."

Generally, a functional brain MRI lasted twenty minutes, but Dr. Ben had now allowed more than double that time to pass. He knew Jasmine refused to relinquish hope, and he had some curiosity of his own to appease. The colors in the images of Mikha'il's brain scans were predominantly yellow, with a few tiny black spots representing the bullet fragments. Occasionally, various yellow areas were speckled with blue.

Jasmine finally spoke. "I think there's more blue than before. That means there is more brain activity now, right?"

"Yes, because of his breathing. But there's no other evidence of increased activity or cognitive function. Beyond the fact he no longer needs life support, Mikha'il's condition remains unchanged."

"So, that's it. The only improvement is his breathing?"

Dr. Ben debated whether to tell her of Mikha'il's irregular heart rate and blood pressure changes, but as these had occurred only once, and briefly, he believed them to be anomalies. "We have done many tests over the past week, and they all indicate the same thing. I'm sorry, Jasmine. I understand you had your hopes up." He hesitated momentarily. "Although this is very difficult for you, is it all right if we stop the procedure now?"

Jasmine didn't answer.

"It's been a long week, and it's Friday evening," he pressed delicately. "We have to let the technicians go home."

She finally nodded, clearly upset.

Dr. Ben signaled to the technicians to shut off the stimuli inside the cylinder, but before the technicians could respond, flashes of orange suddenly appeared on the video screens above.

The stunned technicians pointed at the monitors indicating Mikha'il's heart rate and blood pressure were also increasing. Dr. Ben leaned forward, hardly believing what he was seeing as the orange flashes sparked to red.

"We're agreed, then, that our first priority is to maintain neutrality so as not to jeopardize the effectiveness of our role in any peace talks," said President Robinson. "But through unofficial channels, I'll inform Prime Minister Kessel of the imminent threat to Israel. I'm confident that he'll act accordingly."

"It's our only option," agreed Virginia.

"This conversation did not take place. Any action the Israelis undertake has nothing to do with us. I'll make that clear to Kessel."

"Of course, Mr. President," all three answered simultaneously.

"Good. Now, Matt, see what you can do about moving the pope's visit up sooner and let Virginia know as soon as it's set so she can invite Kessel and Abu-Hakim."

THIRTY-ONE

FAR AWAY FROM THE HOSPITAL, Mikha'il felt the burn of the hot sand under his bare feet and the scorch of the sun's rays on his face and arms. Around him, dunes mixed with uneven formations of rock. Both rose from the heat of the dry earth and shot toward the clear blue sky. He walked along the dusty path until he heard the call of his name bouncing off the walls of stone around him.

"Mikha'il, Mikha'il, Mikha'il," the voice repeated, softening as it echoed from an unknown direction. He looked around, scanning the high, rocky slopes for the source.

"Here," the voice echoed again, growing fainter each time.

Finally, Mikha'il caught sight of a single figure, standing on a ledge two-thirds of the way up the rocks to his left. He shaded his eyes to better see.

The white figure waved at him.

His curiosity piqued, Mikha'il increased his pace. After only a dozen steps, a burst of light flashed in his eyes.

When he was able to regain his focus, the sand below his feet had been replaced with shale, and he, too, stood high on the ledge.

"Welcome," said Gabriel serenely. "You are well?"

"As well as can be expected," Mikha'il answered. The memory of the explosion came back to him in a rush. "Why didn't you stop the bombing?" he asked angrily. "It happened right in front of us. You could've done something."

"I see only what I am shown and do only what I am asked. Preventing the bombing was not my purpose and not the will of the one I serve."

"It should've been his will! Innocent people died there."

"The innocent die every day. But this is not the time for you to question it."

"If this isn't, then when is?"

The angel raised a placating hand. "Slow down. Control your alarm. Again, you get ahead of yourself."

"Sure, right," Mikha'il said, irritated. He looked about him. "So where are we now?"

"We're in the Arabian Desert, not far from Mecca."

"And what are we doing here?" Some respect returned to Mikha'il's tone.

"We are not in your time," replied Gabriel without expression. "Jesus was not the last messenger of the Lord. Another followed, six centuries later. It is his time we are in, and it is he who now awaits us."

Beyond the shadow of a modest opening, the rock broadened to create a tidy space about twelve feet deep. At the end of the cave, a lone man sat in the darkness, his back to the opening.

"Salaam. Welcome, friend," said the stranger without turning.

"Salaam," Mikha'il answered, bending to accommodate the low ceiling.

"Gabriel told me of you, and I have been expecting your visit. I am Muhammad."

"The prophet of Islam?" asked Mikha'il curiously.

"Yes," he answered. "Please sit with me, Mikha'il, as meek as my lodging may be."

Mikha'il found a small rug at the back of the cave. Only a dormant fire pit separated him from the sacred man.

"Our teacher has told me much about you," said Muhammad, nodding to Gabriel, still standing just inside the opening of the cave. "Apparently you and I have similar backgrounds."

"How so?" Mikha'il asked, unable to make out Muhammad's features, his head wrapped in a desert scarf and his face hidden in the silhouette created by the light from the cave's entrance.

"Like you, my father died before I was born. I was with my mother for only a short time before she, too, died. I loved her very much, but I have only a few memories of her. Again, like you, after she died, my grandparents raised me, but they soon passed, and it was my uncle who raised me to manhood."

"You're right. Your upbringing was much like mine, though I don't have an uncle, and my grandfather is still alive." Mikha'il remembered the strange arrival of his grandfather during his encounter with Moses. "At least, I think he's still alive."

"I'll leave you now," interrupted Gabriel. "You two have much to discuss."

Neither objected as the shining figure ducked under the overhang and departed.

"He can be both intimidating and gentle at the same time," murmured Muhammad.

"Yes, he can," Mikha'il agreed, feeling at ease with the warmth of the man before him.

"You get accustomed to it, but his stubbornness . . ." Muhammad laughed with a shrug. The prophet's tone became more reverent as he continued, serious now. "It was here, in this lonely cave, that Gabriel first came to me. At first, I thought I was having some kind of strange dream, but I was soon convinced otherwise. Gabriel has come to me now for twenty-two years. He has delivered to me the words of the Lord, and I have in turn taken them, word for word, to my people."

Qur'an, Al-Najm, 53:4–10 The Qur'an is nothing less than a revelation that is sent to him (Muhammad). It is taught to him by the angel Gabriel with mighty powers and great strength, who stood on the highest horizon and then approached, coming down until he was two bow lengths away or even closer, and revealed to God's messenger (Muhammad) what he revealed.

Mikha'il listened as Muhammad told of life for the Arab people at the time of Gabriel's arrival in the cave.

Muhammad explained that, after the discovery of riches in the Far East, the Mediterranean populace required safe passage of goods through the harsh deserts of Arab lands. The nomadic Bedouins acquired wealth and power as their mighty caravans established the spice road, bridging the East and West.

Unfortunately, the economic gain was not accompanied by the establishment of government or religious law. Without restraint, corruption became infectious, spreading through every Arab community until, finally, all social order collapsed. Deadly feuds erupted between warring tribes. The rich and strong oppressed the poor and weak. There was no sanctity of marriage. Men could take as many wives as they wanted, with no financial responsibility whatsoever. Regarded as property, women were exploited and their children suffered in poverty. Unclaimed orphans roamed aimlessly and resorted to begging in the streets for survival. Crime, murder, rape, infanticide, gambling, drunkenness and debauchery ran rampant, engulfing Arabian society, as the strong craved greater decadence and were free to acquire it as they wished.

The people were pagans, believing in desert genies, and their focus was on attaining riches. The religious laws and moral orders of Judaism and Christianity had not found their way into Arab society.

Mecca, the economic heart of the Arab world, had grown from an oasis where an ancient shrine had been established thousands of years before. Most accepted that the shrine—the Kaaba—had been reconstructed by Abraham, to worship his single God, but it had long since become a haven to the many idols representing the deities of the pre-Muslim world.

"To bring hope, salvation and peace to my people," Muhammad continued, "Gabriel brought to them, through me, the way of Allah. And Allah is God and God is Allah, for he is the one God, the only God, the God of Abraham."

After listening attentively, Mikha'il quietly said, "You believe in the same God the Jews and Christians do?"

"Yes, Mikha'il, the very same. Muslims believe in God and all the prophets of the Holy Book, the Jewish Torah and Scripture, and the Gospel of Jesus. We accept Ishmael, Isaac, Moses, Jesus and all of the messengers of the Lord. However, we do not make any distinction between these prophets. They are all equal in the eyes of the Lord."

Qur'an, Al-Imran, 3:84 We (Muslims) believe in God and in what has been sent down to us and to Abraham, Ishmael, Isaac, Jacob and the Tribes (The twelve tribes of the Israelites). We believe in what has been given to Moses, Jesus and the prophets from their Lord. We do not make a distinction between any of these prophets.

"Jesus is not seen any differently from the prophets before him?" Mikha'il asked.

"Special among all the others, yes, he is," Muhammad replied, "for Jesus was made of the Lord. Our teacher, Gabriel, told Jesus's mother that, although no man had ever touched her, of her would be born a pure son. Her son would become not just the Messiah to the people of Israel but a blessing to all of mankind."

Qur'an, Al-Imran, 3:42; 3:45–49; Maryam, 19:19–21 Gabriel said, "Mary, God has chosen you above and made you pure: He has truly chosen you above all women." . . . The angel said, "Mary, God gives you news of a Word from Him, whose name will be the Messiah, Jesus, son of Mary, who will be held in honor in this world and the next, who will be one of those brought near to God. He will speak to people in his infancy and in his adulthood." . . . She said, "My Lord, how can I have a son when no man has touched me?" The angel said, "This is how God creates what He will: when He has ordained something, He only says Be and it is. He will teach him (Jesus) the Scripture and wisdom, the Torah and the Gospel. He will send him as a messenger to the Children of Israel."; (At the birth of Jesus) The angel said, "I am but a servant from your Lord come to announce to you the gift of a pure son. This is what your Lord said; . . . We shall make him a sign to all people, a blessing from us."

His eyes never leaving the distinguished man seated across from him, Mikha'il was astonished by what he heard. "Then, like the Christians, Muslims believe in the Holy Spirit of Jesus Christ?"

"You are both Muslim and Christian, are you not, Mikha'il?"

"Yes, from my father's side, and I suppose some other religions from my mother's. But I remember very little of my mother's beliefs, and although my grandfather is Muslim and my grandmother Christian, they didn't share their views with me. Growing up, I developed a belief on my own, of one God. Not a specific God, but still, a God of mercy and goodness."

"Muhammad nodded in approval. "Jesus was not exactly the Holy Spirit as Christians believe him to be, for Jesus was not one with the Father, our Lord. It is true that Jesus's birth was miraculously brought about by the Lord. But the followers of Christ preach that Jesus, the Son, the Holy Spirit, and God, the Father, are but one. However, this cannot be, for our God is not only a specific God, he is the only God. Even Jesus knew this to be true."

Mikha'il remembered hearing Jesus's dying words from the cross. *My God, my God, why have you forsaken me?*

Unaware of Mikha'il's thoughts, Muhammad carried on, "Indeed, our Lord favored Jesus, for he delivered a new light, a path of peace and goodwill for all of mankind to follow. Regardless of how God raised Jesus up to him, the Lord pledged to Jesus that his work on earth would be rewarded, for those living in the light and following the path he laid before them would also find eternity with the Lord, while those who did not would be punished."

Qur'an, Al-Imran, 3:55–57 God said, "Jesus, I will take you back and raise you up to Me: I will purify you of the disbelievers. To the Day of Resurrection, I will make those who follow you superior to those who disbelieved. Then all will return to me and I will judge regarding your differences. I will make the disbelievers suffer severely in this world and the next; no one will help them."

"So it's not the way Jesus dies that matters; it's an acceptance of his teachings?"

"That's right. Although Jesus will eventually return to restore the world, my purpose is to unite people in his teachings, not divide them."

Qur'an, Al-Shura, 42:13–14 (Gabriel said,) "We have revealed to you (Muhammad) that which enjoins Abraham, Moses and Jesus. Uphold the faith and do not divide into factions within it."

"But like those of Jesus's time," Muhammad continued, "my people would not readily listen to this message. Although my wife and my cousin accepted the word, after almost ten years, only less than a hundred followers believed.

"And yet, with the threat of our moral change, the powerful in Mecca ostracized us. Our assets were confiscated, and we could not trade for goods. We became impoverished, hungry and sickly. My uncle and wife died under these conditions. For a time, I gave up hope, but one night when I was praying at the Kaaba for guidance, Gabriel came to me, and on a winged horse, we journeyed into the stars.

"We landed in Jerusalem, on the rock where God made man, the location at which the Israelites built the temple to house the ark holding the covenant of the Commandments given to Moses and the place Jesus was sent to death. From this hallowed ground, we ascended into heaven.

"In one night, I met with Abraham, Moses, Jesus and, ultimately, with the Lord. With their guidance, I became undaunted and committed to the destiny before me. I returned to deliver to my people the way of Allah, the one Lord, the only God.

"Eventually, the Meccan leadership let my followers go. We fled to the village of Yathrib, a ten-day ride north of Mecca, where we were unbound to practice our faith and the moral code God meant for us all.

"That there is no distinction between sex, race or class and piety and compassion for our fellow man are the keys to a fulfilled life. We pursue thought and learning. We promote justice, equality and peace, for all to be free to stand up for the oppressed. We care for our weak, the poor, the sickly, the orphaned child, and with mercy and compassion, we give them strength."

At these words, Mikha'il interrupted bluntly, "But what of Muslim women? You restrict them, keeping them segregated and completely hidden under their clothing."

"No, Mikha'il," Muhammad answered. "On the contrary. As I told you, before our new religion existed, our women were treated without regard—a practice I always considered unjust. Before moving to Yathrib, I loved only one woman, my dear wife. She was at least my equal, if not more, for I met her when I was in the employ of the successful caravan business she owned. Although she was fifteen years older than I, I cherished her and the children that we had together. My heart sank many leagues under the sand when she died. It was the lowest point of my days."

Mikha'il watched Muhammad as the great man lowered his head, as if to hide his emotion.

Muhammad took two deep breaths and continued, "Accordingly, with Islam, women are not inferior; rather they are cherished. After leaving Mecca, we gave them rights and protected them by sanctifying marriage. By the laws of Islam, men cannot have sexual relations with a woman unless they are married. Further, a Muslim man is limited to only four wives, and every woman must agree to the marriage, for women are not the property of men but independent, free thinkers."

"If men and women are equal, why can a Muslim man have four wives?" Mikha'il respectfully asked.

"We live in a desert where the lives of many men are taken by nature's ferocity, if not by battle, so our women outnumber our men. Before Islam, a man could take as many women as he pleased, but now, he must marry and be financially responsible to both his wife and their children."

"Do you not want all of your women covered head to toe, even completely hiding their faces?"

"In Islam, we adore our women, placing them atop pedestals, not hiding them and stuffing them under a rock," said Muhammad oddly, seemingly puzzled by Mikha'il's perseverance. "It only is my wives who cover their faces under a curtain or veil to protect their sanctity. Other Muslim women, much like the women of the Jews and Christians, need only wear garments to wrap the sensual parts of their bodies and hair, that which are alluring to men. Before Islam, many Arab women had to prostitute themselves for survival, allowing men to pilfer their virtue. But you ask much about our women. May I continue?"

"Yes, of course," Mikha'il said, embarrassed.

"Only two years after we had established our community in Yathrib, our new religion had spread through the Bedouin tribes and villages of the Arab peninsula. This angered the powerful of Mecca. Although we never wanted to overthrow them, only to bring social reform to those who welcomed it, they feared we would destroy their lifestyle. And so my Arab brothers attacked us, vowing to kill every Muslim or convert them back to pagan ways.

"We had to take up arms against them. Again, as happened with Jesus, it was my own people who persecuted us, but unlike Jesus, we fought back. Over the next eight years, we met our Arab kin in battle."

Qur'an, Al-Baqarah, 2:191–193 Fight in the cause of Allah against those who fight against you, but transgress not. Surely Allah loves not the transgressors. Once they start the fighting, kill them wherever you meet them, and drive them out from where they have driven you out.

Qur'an, Al-Anfal, 8:39 Fight the pagan idol worshippers until there is no more persecution, and all worship is devoted to God alone.

"It was your own people you defended yourself against and not the Jews and Christians?" asked Mikha'il.

"Yes, our Arab brothers of Mecca and those allying with them. They pursued and attacked us. We had no choice but to defend ourselves. Otherwise, our new religion would have been destroyed."

"A Holy War then?"

"How can a war be holy?" Muhammad tilted his head. "Isn't that a contradiction?"

"You fought for your religion."

"We fought for our survival."

"But what of jihad with the infidel?"

"I'm not sure what you refer to. *Jihad* means struggle. The only struggle for a Muslim is the personal struggle to strive in a life of peaceful submission and to surrender continually to God and his way. And the *infidel,* well, that is either one who doesn't believe in any God or is an idol worshiper of many false gods."

"The Christians and Jews are not the infidels then?"

"No, Mikha'il," Muhammad said, shaking his head in slight frustration. "How can they be infidels? As I said, they believe in the same God as ours, the God of Abraham. As such, some allied with us, eventually taking up arms by our side to fight against the armies of Mecca and our Arab brothers. I regret not yet uniting all believers in the God of Abraham, for this is my ultimate goal.

"But my efforts to bring the word of the one and only God to my people have been rewarded, for my brothers of Mecca have now, finally, accepted Islam. Their armies laid down their weapons and surrendered to the will of Allah. Twenty-two years after Gabriel started to deliver the word of God to me, my people are united in the practice of it."

Mikha'il sat silently, for what he was hearing differed much from his impression of Islam and what he had thought Muslims believed in. He wished his grandfather had shared more with him when he was younger.

Muhammad allowed him the time to absorb his teachings. When no further questions came, Muhammad gently said, "I tire you, my friend. Night will soon come, and it will grow cold. Let me give you a moment of rest while I get some kindling to start us a fire. We can talk more after I return."

THIRTY-TWO

THREE F-15 STRIKE EAGLE ATTACK JETS flew in tight formation, eleven miles above the Shia nation of Iran, and rapidly approached its controversial nuclear facility.

"Maestro, this is Tenor One," said Lieutenant Commander Joshua Ephraim into the built-in microphone of his visored helmet.

"Go ahead, Tenor One."

"Opera House is good for go. We're approaching stage," the squadron leader reported to his command control in Israel.

"Roger that, Tenor One. You have a full house and are good to go, repeat, good to go," was squawked back in Joshua's ear.

"Copy that, Maestro." The seasoned pilot immediately followed up with the two strikers flying on either side of him. "Tenors Two and Three, triggers to hot. Good for go on my mark."

The three copilots armed their weapons.

"Mark, set to go, and ready and, three, two, one, release."

Jasmine had spent the weekend next to Mikha'il, anxiously watching the monitors over his head, waiting for another change. But none came.

Still, she was pleased with his appearance. After a nurse had removed the few stitches from Mikha'il's neck, Jasmine had tenderly shaved the stubble, pausing occasionally to kiss his soft cheek. For the first time since the day of the Old City attack, he looked as she remembered him. Although he'd lost considerable weight and his complexion had grayed around his cracked lips, there were no bandages or tubes attached to him. The half-inch scar in the center of his neck was pink, but like hers, the scarring on the side of his face had mostly healed.

Jasmine rose from her chair and lifted his right hand. She held it between both her hands and squeezed it tightly.

Instantly, the graph line on Mikha'il's heart monitor jumped, and the machine beeped louder. The blood pressure and breathing monitors flashed.

Oh my God, he can feel my touch!

With one hand still holding his, she pushed the red alarm button on the wall.

Mikha'il's body jerked.

He was alone in the cave. It was pitch-black, though he could see some stars beyond the rocky entrance. Muhammad had not returned, and Mikha'il was uncertain how much time had passed since he'd left. A few hours, a day, a month, perhaps years. All seemed possible.

The dormant fire pit burst into flame, startling Mikha'il.

"Did you learn well from the messenger of Islam?" Gabriel materialized across the fire where Muhammad had been. "I did not wish to alarm you with the fire, but it had gotten cold in here with no one to care for it since his departure."

"Yes, he's taught me very much," Mikha'il answered, not surprised by Gabriel's abrupt appearance. "But where is he? Where did he go?"

"He has died," Gabriel said with no sadness or regret. "He fulfilled all that he could. Muhammad was of the line of Ishmael, firstborn son of Abraham."

"Yes, even Moses wrote of it!" exclaimed Mikha'il. "The Lord said he would bring a great nation to the son of Abraham and his servant. That nation is Islam."

"Correct."

"The Jews and Muslims are brothers!"

"And those of the Christ, too. Although there were prophets before Muhammad, he was the summation of their words and the last messenger of God, the same God as the Jewish and Christian God."

"But why such a vast difference in the divinity of Jesus, one that now separates so many?"

"A difference, yes, but perhaps one should consider the difference moot."

"Moot! How can that difference not be important?" Mikha'il demanded.

"Does it really matter whether Jesus was made and sent by God, or was God himself?" argued Gabriel. "Either way, to humanity, the message remains the same."

Mikha'il said nothing and stared at the angel. Mikha'il considered the devastation and atrocities that had befallen humanity over the centuries since Muhammad. He considered, too, that with true irony, these acts directly defied the purity of both Jesus's and Muhammad's messages, all in a struggle of superiority over what was, in effect, an irrelevant and unanswerable difference. He pushed the angel further. "But Muhammad's ultimate goal was to establish one religion under the one God of Abraham. In this, he failed. Why would the Lord not have let him succeed in uniting his new religion with the existing ones of Christianity and Judaism?"

"Muhammad did as he was required. His people accepted his word as the word of God. But most Christians and Jews did not. Perhaps the people of the Arab nation would not have accepted so freely if the others had."

"Why wouldn't they all accept it?"

"It seems it was not the time."

"Again you answer 'not the time'?" Mikha'il's frustration grew. "Then, when is the time?"

"In due time, and time comes due."

"And when you don't want to answer questions, you give me riddles," said Mikha'il, shaking his head. "It's sad that it wasn't in

Muhammad's time, as he suffered so much in his cause, as have so many since."

"It's possible more would have suffered. It was Muhammad's people who, in that time, needed to be brought to the way of God. After twenty-two years, he succeeded in delivering God's word to them through the establishment of Islam and the words of the Qur'an."

"All the words of the Qur'an, are they not from you?" asked Mikha'il. "They are, in fact, your words, aren't they?"

"They are from the one who sent me, the Lord your God. I do not possess free will, and I serve him in perfect obedience," Gabriel answered humbly. "For him, I came to Muhammad, and through Muhammad, the messenger to his people, those words flowed. By memorization and reiteration, the words spread amongst his peoples and were soon written, becoming the Qur'an, the sacred Muslim scripture, which has remained unchanged since."

"Muhammad told me that he almost gave up hope, but you took him to Jerusalem to meet Jesus and those prophets who came before him."

"This is so, and no more than seventy years after we rode together to Jerusalem, the religion of Islam had spread beyond the Arab lands and into all that is south of the great sea, into the broad expanse to the east and to all of the Holy Lands."

"The Muslims entered the gates of Jerusalem and, to celebrate Muhammad's journey to the temple ruins, built a spectacular golden domed mosque on the rock of life."

"The Dome of the Rock," Mikha'il added.

"But thirst for power had already gripped the Muslim leadership and divided them in bloody battle. After the unexpected death of Muhammad, there was no clear successor. Some believed the next should be related by blood to Muhammad. They proposed that Ali, Muhammad's cousin and companion since boyhood, be made caliph. Ali was the second in accepting Islam and was married to Muhammad's daughter.

"However, the majority felt that lineage was not relevant and selected another as caliph. But twenty-four years after the death of Muhammad, it was agreed that Ali, then aged, would become caliph. In the rapidly expanding empire, Ali moved his administration to Iraq. But he was soon murdered, and the caliphate forever fell out of Muhammad's line.

"This division in the Muslim nation remains to this day, Mikha'il. The small minority that believes the caliphate should have carried the bloodline of Muhammad, as intended by God, are known as Shia and still live in Iraq and adjacent Iran today."

"While the remainder are Sunni," said Mikha'il.

"You see, even in the successful completion of Muhammad's mission, believers fracture the purity of his religion," said Gabriel calmly.

Then the angel looked Mikha'il in the eyes. "Muhammad's mission has come to an end, but your purpose has just begun."

"My purpose? For what?"

"I have shown you the way of the Lord and, through his messengers, have delivered to you his word. Do not blend these truths with the festivals, holidays and cultures that followed—like your questions about Muslim women hiding their faces. Such customs emerged after. The way of Muhammad was for Muslim women to cover only those body parts that are alluring to men. Veiling themselves fully, including their faces, came with the influence of tradition.

"Tradition and ritual matter not to me nor to the Lord. These, with their differences and rivalries, are of the minds of men and that which separates those minds. Listen to me carefully. There is no separation in the path of the Lord. He is not the exclusive property of one religion but is the source of all life and human knowledge. Remember that above all."

"But what am I supposed to do? Why me?"

"Your heart is full of goodness, and your soul, pure. Many different religions lie within your background, and yet you have not been tainted or influenced unduly by them. Your faith has not been distorted. In you, all can rejoice. Kindness, wisdom and resistance to that which you see as wrong all live in you. You are a representation of free will. Without concern or hesitation, you were willing to give your life for the lives of others. You have shown pure sacrifice. Now you tell me: if not you, then who?"

Mikha'il, looking into the fire, kept his gaze from the divine angel. He said slowly, "I don't feel like I'm worthy, and I definitely haven't sacrificed like those before me."

"Perhaps you have yet to sacrifice what, in your own heart, will be enough. But only one claiming unworthiness can truly be worthy. In time, you will see. Now my time with you is complete."

"Complete?" Mikha'il looked to his mentor. "You're finished with me?"

"Yes."

"But . . . I'm not ready," Mikha'il said, panic welling up inside him. "What am I to do now? How will I know? I need more guidance. Will there be others after you?"

"There may be; there may not. It is not my place to say." Gabriel reached across the flames. The heat did not singe his sleeves.

Mikha'il placed his hand in his.

Gabriel gripped tightly. "May peace be upon you, one with God."

"He squeezed my hand! He just squeezed my hand!" shrieked Jasmine.

"Are you sure?"

"Yes, yes, of course I'm sure!" Jasmine practically shouted, holding Mikha'il's right hand between both of hers.

The nurse clearly didn't believe her, but then Mikha'il coughed faintly and tried to lift his head. He was able to raise it only an inch or so from the pillow before it fell back.

"You see, you see. I told you!"

They watched, stunned, as his eyelids fluttered open before quickly closing. Then he coughed a second time, and his dry lips parted in what seemed to be an attempt at speech.

Jasmine cried out, "He's trying to talk."

"Yes, yes, I can see!" The nurse grabbed at the phone on the wall.

Jasmine clutched his hand and lowered her lips to his ear. "I'm here, Mikha'il. I am right here with you. Please don't leave me. Stay right here. Oh, God, please don't go."

Dr. Ben ran through the corridors of the Hadassah, all thoughts of protocol gone from his head the minute he'd read the news on his pager. *Mikha'il conscious. Come quick.*

When he reached the open doorway, he halted in astonishment at the sight before him. It defied his faith in science and medical training. And yet, Dr. Ben could not deny what he was seeing— what he'd been taught was impossible.

Mikha'il was awake.

III

CITY OF
BROTHERLY LOVE

All wars are civil wars, because all men are brothers.

François Fénelon
Catholic theologian and writer
Paris, France, AD 1693

THIRTY-THREE

READING IN THE MUTED LIGHT from the single lamp at his side, Mikha'il sat in silence on the living room sofa of his grandfather's townhouse. Resting in his lap was an open Qur'an, which he focused on without regard for time. He couldn't sleep and had returned to the many reference texts surrounding him.

In the center of the coffee table were two Bibles. One, Jasmine had purchased for him in Jerusalem, and the other had been his grandmother's, which he'd found in the drawer of the desk when he'd returned to New York. Piled on the floor next to the table were dozens of other books. The subject matter ranged from ancient Hindu writings to the histories of Judaism, Christianity and Islam, from biographies of Jesus Christ and Muhammad to contemporary scholars' interpretations of religion in the modern world. Jutting from the tops of the closed pages were scores of small, torn pieces of paper.

Jasmine gripped the railing to guide herself down the dimly lit staircase. She entered the living room and stopped to watch Mikha'il. She wondered if he'd acknowledge her presence but knew he would not. After he turned another page, she walked to the end of the sofa and stood by him.

Mikha'il did not raise his head.

Finally, she lowered herself to the sofa.

He lifted his eyes from the Qur'an and she cuddled closer. "I woke up and you weren't there."

Mikha'il did not speak. He just gazed into her eyes and smiled.

Three months had passed since, to the amazement of the Hadassah medical staff and the media of the world, Mikha'il had awakened.

At the time, Dr. Ben explained that Mikha'il's injuries were extensive and that he would likely never live a normal life. But as had been proven, Mikha'il was no ordinary patient. A prognosis of only minimal motor function became a projection of near complete recovery within two years, which then went to eight months and then three.

Other than the occasional headache, only one handicap remained permanent. The bullet fragments lodged in his frontal lobe were impossible to remove. As a result, Mikha'il could only utter muddled sounds. He was mute.

Realizing early on that his speech was not likely to return, Mikha'il and Jasmine learned sign language. Both were quick studies, eager to find a way to communicate with each other.

Mikha'il's degree of determination was evident in all his therapy, his perseverance unprecedented at the Hadassah. A typical patient would be exhausted after four hours of physical therapy per day. However, Mikha'il would return for a second session after his cognitive skills retraining. Throughout the therapy, Dr. Ben kept close watch over his special patient. The two men formed a strong bond, each respecting the work ethic of the other.

In the early weeks, public response to the news of Mikha'il's recovery was overwhelming. People sent flowers and gifts, and some held prayer vigils outside the walls of the Hadassah. Virginia Adams and Aaron Kessel both telephoned Jasmine and sent personally written notes to Mikha'il.

When Jasmine told Mikha'il of his grandfather's death, she'd been stunned by his lack of surprise. It was as if he had already known.

Once Mikha'il no longer needed to spend the majority of his waking hours in rehab, he focused his attention on the study of religion. His interest rapidly grew into a fascination nearing obsession. After his morning therapy, he would read for most of the day and, often, late into the night.

While confused by the change in Mikha'il and a little jealous of the hours he dedicated to his therapy and newfound passion, Jasmine encouraged his study, tracking down obscure titles he wanted whenever she made trips into Jerusalem.

Despite the requests from Jasmine's employers, Mikha'il avoided all media. The most exposure he would agree to was to stand quietly at Jasmine's side while she fielded questions. Confident in front of a camera, Jasmine was articulate and engaging, and she quickly became the focus of the media during the early weeks of Mikha'il's recovery.

The media soon turned their attention back to the deteriorating state of the world. Mikha'il tried to ignore those reports, still believing bad news only bred more bad news, but couldn't avoid hearing of the shootings, bombings and violence. After the bombing of Iran's nuclear facility, Iran blamed not just Israel but all of the West for attacks on the Islamic people.

Any hope of peace seemed distant, and Mikha'il chose not to raise the topic with Jasmine—even though they were both well aware of the ignited crisis. With instability in the Middle East raging, oil prices continued their meteoric rise, thwarting any improvements in stock markets and further jeopardizing world economies by adding to the hardship of all.

While the intifada erupted into global Holy War and Yazid Abdul-Qadir's threat hung over the world, Mikha'il's physical and mental state rapidly improved. Once he'd completed three months of therapy, he and Jasmine headed home to London for the December holidays.

After only ten days in England, Mikha'il insisted on returning to New York City. Jasmine was reluctant to extend their stay in the U.S. for too long. She'd planned to return to work full time and hoped she and Mikha'il would resume a regular life together. Mikha'il seemed changed to Jasmine, and she'd thought that the familiarity of their London surroundings would help return him to his normal self.

He sighed and moved his hands and fingers, creating words. "Sorry. I couldn't sleep again. I didn't wake you, did I?"

"No, I just don't like it when you're not beside me," she said quietly, moving even closer and sliding both arms around his waist. "Can I get you a glass of milk or something to help you sleep?"

"Thanks. Milk would be great," he signed and kissed her cheek.

When she returned from the kitchen, she hovered for a moment. "Would you like me to stay down here with you for a while?"

"No, you go back to bed. I promise I'll be up soon."

Jasmine could not fall back to sleep. Instead, she lay in bed worrying. They were far from the care of Dr. Ben and the Hadassah staff. Although still ecstatic with his remarkable improvement, she was concerned that he'd hurried through his rehabilitation. Mikha'il's peculiar behavior and reclusive manner were becoming more marked. He did not sleep much, suffered from headaches and seemed distracted most of the time.

Not knowing many people in the United States, Jasmine felt isolated and quite alone. She wondered who she could turn to for help.

Downstairs, Mikha'il forgot about his promise to Jasmine.

Everything he read in the Bible and the Qur'an confirmed what he'd been told in his visions. He was surprised at the similarity in their scriptures and message of goodwill. The basic foundation of Islam was, in fact, identical to those of its predecessors, Judaism and Christianity. The Qur'an was indeed a continuation of God's revelations to the Hebrews and Christians, only this time to the people of Islam.

Just as explained to him by Muhammad, the only significant difference Mikha'il found was in the divinity of Jesus. Although the Qur'an described the virgin birth of Jesus to Mary, as made by the Lord, it did not suppose Jesus and the Lord to be one and the same. Yet the intent, the message and the description of all the prophets were virtually the same.

Every night, Mikha'il hoped for another vision. But the dreams did not return, and sleep came only with difficulty.

He stretched across the sofa, attempting to ease his mind, but he couldn't rest. They couldn't have been just dreams. *What about those dying in the Old City? I felt them. I can't deny that. What about the visions? If they were real, why haven't they returned? What am I to do? I can't even speak.*

THIRTY-FOUR

VIRGINIA ADAMS WORKED at the large desk in her office, preparing for a meeting at the United Nations the next week. There, officials would confirm the details for the upcoming summit meetings with the Israeli prime minister and the P.A. leader.

Matt Whelan had been successful in moving the papal visit to the second week of January, and Virginia had convinced both Prime Minister Kessel and Umar Abu-Hakim to attend. However, before any official announcement was made, the media aired rumors of the meeting at the White House.

The Muslim nation immediately accused the P.A. leader of being weak for bowing to the wishes of the West and claimed he wasn't worthy of representing the Palestinian people. Abu-Hakim denied agreeing to meet in Washington, claiming that if Israel and the U.S. wished to meet with him, they needed to come to him. The Muslim nation shouted victory in his defiance.

Virginia sprung into action. She graciously ceded to Abu-Hakim's demand, offering to meet with him wherever he wished.

After he chose Muslim lands near the disputed Israeli-occupied West Bank, Virginia pleaded with Kessel to join, and ultimately, a meeting with all three parties was arranged to take place in Amman, Jordan, with a follow-up meeting scheduled in Sharm el-Sheikh in Egypt's Sinai Peninsula. The summit dates were set for mid-February and mid-March. Virginia had accomplished a difficult task—the peace meetings would happen, and Abu-Hakim had remained strong in the eyes of the Palestinian people.

At her desk, Virginia was reviewing the agenda for the first summit meeting, only five weeks away, when the door to her office opened.

"Sorry to disturb you, ma'am. Jasmine Desai is on the phone for you. She's wondering if you're free to talk."

"It's all right. Put her right through," Virginia said without hesitation and picked up her phone when it rang. After exchanging pleasantries, she asked how Mikha'il was doing.

"He's well, but they don't think his speech will ever return."

"Yes, I heard that. I'm sorry," Virginia said. "Is there anything I can do for you while you are in the U.S.?"

"I'm not sure," said Jasmine hesitantly.

"Is everything all right?"

"Not really. I'm afraid it's Mikha'il," she replied, strength returning to her voice. "He's acting strangely, and I don't know where to turn."

"Have you talked to Dr. Levine?"

"No, Mikha'il claims he's fine and doesn't want to go back to the Hadassah. We were planning to return to London, but now he wants to stay in New York a while. He seems fine. Only he's . . ."

"What is it?"

"He's just not himself. He's preoccupied, odd. Obsessive. You must be wondering why I would be calling you," Jasmine rushed on, "but I was remembering our conversation back at the Hadassah, how close I felt to you. And frankly, I need to talk to someone I can trust, who isn't involved with Mikha'il personally. I wouldn't want him to think I was talking with his doctor or our friends behind his back. I don't really know anyone else here and—"

Hearing the distress in her voice, Virginia quickly cut in. "Jasmine, I'll be in New York next Thursday and Friday for meetings at the UN. Perhaps we can get together for a talk."

"That would be so nice," Jasmine said, her relief evident. "I'd like that."

Seeing her assistant open the door again, Virginia asked Jasmine to hold.

"Sorry to disturb you again, Madam Secretary. Mr. Whelan is on the other line."

"Do you know what he wants?"

"No, ma'am, but when I mentioned you were on the phone with Ms. Desai, he insisted that I interrupt you."

After asking Jasmine to wait a minute or two, Virginia switched lines. "Hey, Matt."

"Hello, Virginia. Are you speaking with Mikha'il bin al-Rashid's girlfriend right now?"

"Yes, why?"

"Huh. That's sure odd," said the White House chief of staff. "We received a call from the Vatican half an hour ago. The pope has requested that bin al-Rashid be present at the White House for his visit this weekend."

"The pope wants Mikha'il there?" Virginia asked, not bothering to hide her surprise. "Does the president know?"

"I've just passed it by him. He suggested we invite Mikha'il and his girlfriend to the dinner Saturday night."

"I can't see that being a problem. I'll ask her."

THIRTY-FIVE

GUESTS—MOSTLY CABINET MEMBERS, senior senators, prominent congressional representatives, and their spouses, as well as a few local clergymen—waited patiently in line to be introduced to the pope, who was seated on a heavy gold-leaf chair between the cardinal of the Washington archdiocese and the president.

Jasmine and Mikha'il were next and stepped to the waiting pontiff. Like those before her, Jasmine bowed and held her hand to him. "Hello, Your Holiness. I'm Jasmine Desai and this is—"

Before she could finish, the fragile pope gripped her hand tighter for support and unsteadily braced himself to rise from his chair. Once standing, he let her hand go and turned to Mikha'il.

Only eighteen inches apart, they locked eyes.

The cardinal, President Robinson and guests standing nearby watched the peculiar encounter in astonishment. No one could remember a pope rising to greet anyone like this.

Following the lengthy stare, the pope took Mikha'il's hand in his and, raising it to his lips, softly kissed the back of it. Still holding it firmly, he spoke quietly. "May peace be with you, Mikha'il."

Mikha'il helped the pope ease back into his chair and, gradually, the crowd's murmuring subsided.

Mikha'il and Jasmine sat with three senators, a congressman and their wives, while at the pope's table, Virginia was seated between the president and Matt Whelan.

As President Robinson engaged in conversation with the pope, Whelan excused himself and walked to the podium. The friendly chatter ebbed when the White House chief of staff began speaking.

After formally welcoming the pope and cardinal, and introducing a few VIPs, Whelan called for grace. "At this time, I would like to ask our honored Most Holy Father to lead us in prayer before dinner begins."

Across the room, a young steward carried a microphone to the pope. When she reached him, the pope turned toward President Robinson and spoke into his ear.

The president nodded and stood. "Our beloved pope has requested that Mikha'il bin al-Rashid, who heroically thwarted the attacks in Jerusalem last April and who is among us here tonight, say grace instead. Mikha'il, do you mind?"

Everyone turned to look at Mikha'il, but he didn't hesitate. He pushed his chair back and stood up, waiting for the aide to bring him the microphone.

Mikha'il glanced down at Jasmine, who responded by standing beside him and taking the mic. "Thank you, it will be an honor, Mr. President. However, I hope you don't mind if I interpret for Mikha'il."

Not waiting for approval, Mikha'il began to move his hands and fingers as if completely prepared for the duty before him. He paused only briefly to allow Jasmine to catch up. As she spoke, the nervousness left her voice and turned to proud confidence.

"Dear Lord, Allah, God of Abraham, and Holy Father of Jesus, please provide our leaders with guidance in our time of great need. Inspire them in the way you have taught through your messengers before them, for it is not our faith that separates us; rather, it is in our intellectual criticism that we segregate ourselves.

"Some say, love those close to you and detest those you battle against. But I say, love your enemies together with all of man, for where is the reward in loving only those who are like ourselves. Let us endeavor to celebrate the similarities that unite us and not hunt for, and brood upon, those that divide us."

President Robinson was the first to break the short silence that followed. He stood and began to applaud loudly. All those in the dining room did the same, while the president and cardinal bent to assist the pope to his feet as he, too, clapped for Mikha'il.

After they returned to their seats, Virginia leaned over and whispered to the president, "It's too bad that Kessel and Abu-Hakim didn't hear that."

"Yes, it is. They both could certainly learn from him," said the president, and both returned to the various discussions around the table. But despite the friendly conversation with the pope and others, President Robinson did not stop thinking of Mikha'il and his words of grace.

While dessert was being brought in, the pope was engaged in conversation with the cardinal and the first lady, and President Robinson turned back to his secretary of state. "Virginia, maybe there's a way they can."

"Who can what, sir?"

"Kessel and Abu-Hakim, together with Mikha'il," he answered. "Is there any chance that Mikha'il could be included in the peace summit, at least for the first meeting in Amman? I'm sure whatever words he shared would help."

"I suppose we could have him invited by the United Nations."

"Good idea. But do a thorough check on him first. We don't need any embarrassments at this point."

THIRTY-SIX

"HERE'S EVERYTHING YOU ASKED FOR, Madam Secretary. The Pentagon documents and files from both the British and Indian embassies just arrived," Virginia's assistant said as she placed a stack of folders on her large desk.

"Thank you. And hold my calls unless it's urgent."

The executive aide left and Virginia wasted no time in opening the folders. She examined the immigration, employment and financial records of both Mikha'il and Jasmine. Through internationally tracked passport usage, she checked the countries in which they'd traveled and worked.

She skimmed through the numerous news photographs Mikha'il had taken, most published more than three years before in acclaimed newsmagazine articles—no recent photographs had achieved significant recognition. Delving further into their private lives, she examined the family and education records of their pasts. There was a report on Jasmine's upbringing in Delhi, India, and her successful career with the BBC, another detailing Mikha'il's destitute childhood in Vietnam, the death of his mother and his immigration to the United States.

All seemed in order. She checked the military service record of Mikha'il's father, who, from media reports, she knew had died in Vietnam before Mikha'il was born. The records indicated that Corporal Salem bin al-Rashid was an army medic on a Huey medevac helicopter and had served two tours in Vietnam with distinguished service.

He'd been killed while aiding four downed airmen. The rescue helicopter couldn't land at their crash site due to enemy gunfire. Bin al-Rashid had jumped from the open door while the craft hovered over the site to tend to the injured airmen. Two hours later, after the site had been cleared and the rescue helicopter returned, the wounded airmen and bin al-Rashid had been found killed by the Viet Cong.

For his heroism, Mikha'il's father had been nominated for a posthumous congressional medal of honor, although it seemed to have been denied for unspecified reasons. Virginia looked to the photocopy on the next page—his military death certificate. His religion, circled in red, was listed as Muslim and his date of death, April 4, 1970.

Virginia felt a sudden chill.

Jonathon. Is that possible?

Jasmine and Mikha'il stood in line at the Dulles Airport, waiting to board their flight back to New York City. Jasmine was reading a magazine, and Mikha'il was leisurely glancing around the busy terminal.

Some people stood in conversation while others worked on laptops or relaxed with mp3 earphones in.

One person was distinctly removed from the others.

The young man, who looked to be in his mid-twenties, sat in a wheelchair beside a departure bench two gates away.

The man didn't notice Mikha'il, but the strong sense of compassion Mikha'il always felt for those challenged by disadvantages compelled him to keep watching. Although admiring the strength and courage they must have, he always thought it not right that some had to live with such difficulties and felt the randomness of those affected unfair. He wondered how God, or any god, could allow it and shook his head in disapproval. *Why do some have to live like this?*

The man in the wheelchair reached for the water bottle at his side but knocked it to the floor, where it rolled across the aisle. He pushed the toggle at his left side, but one wheel jammed into the leg of the bench beside him. He moved the control both forward and back but was unsuccessful in getting the wheel loose.

And now you let him struggle. It's not fair. Why can't you just allow him to get up?

The man tried the toggle three more times and finally gave up. He looked around the busy airport, but no one else seemed to have noticed his predicament.

Just as Mikha'il was about to walk from the line to go to his aid, the man raised his head and quickly scanned the scene around him, as if looking for someone.

Does he hear what I'm thinking? Mikha'il waited a moment.

But when the man looked in his direction, his gaze moved right by.

It's not me, but he feels something. Mikha'il wanted to go over and pick up the bottle. Instead, he stood still, watching, wondering what would happen next.

The disconcerted man looked at his feet, then his hands and then back around him.

Is he going to try on his own? Not taking his eyes from the man, Mikha'il frowned in concentration and prayer. *Let him get up. Please, let him walk.*

The man continued his search through the terminal, more anxiously now and with a baffled look on his face.

Come on. Get up and walk. Don't be afraid.

The man seemed to think for a moment before he pushed the breaks to lock the wheels, placed his feet on the floor and folded up the wheelchair's footrests. He sat back and, once more, glanced around the crowded terminal.

The man was clearly agitated. Mikha'il concentrated hard. *That's right, you can do it. Get up and walk.*

With his feet firmly planted on the ground, the man held both armrests and pushed down. Slowly, he rose from the chair. After steadying himself for a second or two, he took two steps to the bench, bent down and reached for the water bottle. Unbalanced, he wobbled a little, but after retrieving the bottle, he straightened.

With his prize in his hand, he walked back to his wheelchair and stood next to it in astonishment. No one paid any attention to him. He was just a man holding a bottle of water.

Then a young woman ran toward him, leaving behind the steaming cup of coffee she'd just paid for.

Mikha'il watched her hysterical joy. The terminal was far too noisy to make out what she was shouting, but somehow he could feel the words. *You're walking! Oh my God, you're actually walking!*

People nearby watched with curiosity as the woman embraced the absolutely mystified man. Mikha'il couldn't believe what he saw—or his apparent role in it.

Not noticing the couple two gates away, Jasmine put the magazine in her bag and tenderly punched Mikha'il in the arm. "Come on, you, we're boarding."

Blankly, Mikha'il headed for the gate, wondering how long the stranger had been in a wheelchair.

Mikha'il closed his eyes. *Thank you.*

Virginia unlocked a drawer in the high credenza that stood along the wall in her office and removed a folder, brown with age. Yellowed tape covered the label, which read *Captain Jonathon James Adams.*

After her election to the Senate, she'd obtained the file of her husband's exemplary military record. Although she had not opened the folder in several years, the nearness of it comforted her, strengthening her sense of duty and patriotism.

She quickly flipped through the pages until she found what she was looking for. *April 4, 1970. Killed in action with his crew and army medic, Corporal Salem bin al-Rashid.*

Virginia felt her legs buckle. It had been Mikha'il's father who'd sacrificed his life trying to save her husband. The coincidence was overwhelming. She thought about the sensation she'd had when touching Mikha'il at the Hadassah and the memory of some force keeping her alive in the aftermath of the nightmarish events in the Old City.

There was somebody Virginia needed to talk to.

It was 5:00 a.m. in Washington when Virginia's encrypted satellite phone rang. Awake in anticipation of the call, she picked up quickly. "Virginia Adams."

"Madam Secretary? It's Dr. Levine."

"Yes. Good morning, Doctor."

"You wanted to talk."

"I'm inquiring about Mikha'il bin al-Rashid." She described the highlights from the papal dinner and the plans for Mikha'il's inclusion in the upcoming summit.

After she finished, Dr. Ben responded, "I'm glad Jasmine and Mikha'il are well. But may I ask, what does this have to do with me?"

"It's a delicate matter, but I'll be frank. Do you see any reason that we may not want to invite Mikha'il? Or something in his behavior that would complicate his involvement?"

"Other than his loss of speech and the odd headache, Mikha'il's fine. It's common knowledge, though, that the speed of his recovery was nothing short of miraculous."

"Yes, of course. But . . . is there anything else?" Virginia probed further. "Let's say, anything peculiar, off the record."

For a long moment, Dr. Ben said nothing, which made Virginia think there was something, something he wouldn't say. "I know you must be concerned about patient confidentiality, but you can see that, under the circumstances, we need to be sure that Mikha'il represents no risk to the summit or to himself." She stopped, selecting her words carefully. "Jasmine has expressed some . . . concern about his recent behavior."

"I know Jasmine well," Dr. Ben said slowly, and Virginia sensed him still stalling.

"Yes, I suppose you would," Virginia continued, trying to coax him along. "She tells me that she often finds Mikha'il distant and removed from everyday life, like he's not really there."

Dr. Ben hesitated, but then responded with assuredness. "I would say that could be expected given all that he's been through—especially when coupled with his loss of speech. I'm sure whatever it is, it will soon pass."

"There's nothing else?"

"No," he said confidently. "But if you're worried about him, I have some vacation time. I could join you in Jordan, just to make sure."

"Oh, Dr. Levine. That would be ideal."

THIRTY-SEVEN

AT THE UNITED NATIONS COMPLEX, Mikha'il stood in the lounge outside the secretary general's private greeting room. He looked out through the ceiling-to-floor window at the array of skyscrapers of Manhattan.

He felt a soft tap on his shoulder and turned to find a young woman smiling up at him, her big eyes sparkling under dark eyebrows.

"Hello, Mikha'il. My name is Aisha. I'll be interpreting for you. Madam Secretary is ready. Can you follow me?"

Mikha'il smiled in return. "Of course," he signed.

When Aisha and Mikha'il entered the simple meeting room, Virginia rose from the modern leather sofa to greet them. "Hello, Mikha'il. It's good to see you again. Thank you for coming."

"It's nice to see you as well," Mikha'il signed, with quick interpretation from Aisha.

After shaking hands, Virginia gestured toward Aisha. "So I see Aisha has already introduced herself. I asked her to attend. She's a UN interpreter from Cairo and is fluent in Arabic, English and Hebrew, both spoken and signed. I hope you don't mind that she joins us."

Mikha'il nodded politely toward Aisha, who returned the gesture.

After briefly chatting about the papal dinner, Virginia did not waste time. "I wanted to meet with you today to talk about the role we're hoping you will accept at the upcoming peace summit in Jordan. As an envoy for the UN, you'd have full access to all meetings. It's imperative that these meetings next month and the month after be successful. If nothing else, your presence in Amman should ease both sides, making for a more relaxed and, therefore, progressive atmosphere. This is the first time since you stopped the attack in Jerusalem that Prime Minister Kessel and Umar Abu-Hakim will be together. You saved many lives last April, and quite possibly theirs, too."

Virginia gazed at Mikha'il.

Holding the stare, Mikha'il tilted his head in curiosity.

Before any real awkwardness set in, she brought herself back to the purpose of the meeting. "Jasmine mentioned that you don't like to watch the news anymore. I respect that, but I brought along some footage I think you should see. Just to give you some background as you decide—to show you what the world has come to since the derailment of the peace initiatives. Do you mind?"

He shook his head.

Aisha started the player. The video recording of Abdul-Qadir came up first. While Mikha'il watched, Virginia explained, "The jihadists' leader, Abdul-Qadir, made this from an East Jerusalem apartment eight months ago. No intelligence agency has heard from him since. But you'll find this interesting.

"Israeli agents discovered he was in the Old City the day of the attack. Abdul-Qadir was shot by Rubenstein before you took him over the balcony. He was taken to this apartment, where his wounds were treated by a local doctor. It seems he survived."

Mikha'il sat motionless, not giving away any sign of the shock that rippled through his body. *It was him! He was the thirteenth.*

While he watched more of the footage, Virginia periodically added commentary, but Mikha'il rarely looked at her, instead remaining fixed on the monitor.

His eyes widened when reporting from the Church of the Holy Sepulchre bombing appeared. Behind several emergency workers and covered bodies, he saw the charred remains of the wooden bench he and Gabriel had been sitting on.

After the seven-minute video ended, Virginia reviewed with Mikha'il the details for the upcoming peace meetings and the role he might play. She answered his questions and explained that if he accepted the invitation, Aisha would accompany him to ensure he could communicate freely and that Dr. Levine had volunteered to attend.

Mikha'il found it odd that Dr. Ben was invited, but he didn't question it.

"I don't want you to decide now," Virginia concluded. "You've already done so much. Take a few days to consider it. You should discuss it with Jasmine, as she is, of course, welcome as well."

Although his mind was already made up, Mikha'il decided to comply with her request and signed, "Thank you, Madam Secretary."

As he started to get up, Virginia stopped him. "Before you leave, there's something I'd like to share with you." She opened her briefcase, removed an envelope and passed it to him. "Inside is a photocopy from my husband's service file. I'd like you to open it."

While he read the contents, Virginia waited for his reaction.

Oddly, Mikha'il's face revealed no emotion. Choosing his words gracefully, he answered, "They both fought for the freedom of others."

The weather was unusually warm for mid-January, and Mikha'il chose to enjoy the forty-minute walk back to the Upper West Side rather than jump into the nearest taxi. Reveling in the sunshine, he strolled across United Nations Plaza and, on reaching Fifth Avenue, joined the throngs along the busy sidewalk.

Noon was fast approaching, and many were already on lunch break, eager to appreciate the weather. Just after passing

Rockefeller Center, Mikha'il stopped at a crosswalk beside St. Patrick's Cathedral. The historic church stood out in regal contrast to the towering buildings, modern stores and expensive restaurants.

While standing at the red light, he leaned his head back to take in the full view of the cathedral's two soaring spires. As the light turned green, he noticed that the tall church doors were open.

Not in any hurry, Mikha'il decided to go in and found that the 12:00 mass was about to begin. He headed down the center aisle and entered an empty pew, halfway down.

Mikha'il hadn't been here since his grandmother's funeral twenty-four years before. In his youth, she had occasionally brought him with her to Sunday mass. But as he got older, he thought it odd that she never explained anything of the service. All she'd tell him, time and time again, was that her older brother had been named for St. Patrick, he'd died when she was a young girl, and that was the reason she'd given Mikha'il his middle name when he first arrived in the U.S. So at each service he attended, Mikha'il Patrick just sat patiently, his mind wandering as he waited for the long hour to pass.

Although as a young boy he hadn't appreciated the splendor of the church the way he did now, Mikha'il felt certain that the interior hadn't changed much in thirty years.

While he took in his surroundings, an old man walked carefully down the aisle and stopped near Mikha'il. Seeing that he held a white cane, Mikha'il stood and guided the blind man to the pew. After expressing gratitude, the man removed his overcoat and wool scarf, set the cane to his side and knelt down in prayer next to where Mikha'il sat.

As the mass proceeded, Mikha'il noticed that the sequence of the service, much like the appearance of the beautiful cathedral, had not changed much. There was, however, one difference. Just before the mass ended, Mikha'il watched all those in attendance amiably shake hands with those around them.

Reaching out for Mikha'il, the blind man said, "Peace be with you."

Unable to give his reply, Mikha'il took the old man's bony hand in one of his and placed the other on the man's right shoulder in a subtle embrace. Mikha'il could not speak and the man could not see.

After leaving St. Patrick's, Mikha'il continued along the hectic streets before entering Central Park. The park was particularly busy for a Friday afternoon in January. The benches were full of those reading books or eating their lunches, the pathways crowded and the playgrounds buzzing with activity.

Mikha'il stopped to take in the pleasure of the children playing happily in the balmy weather. In front of him, a group of a dozen or so laughed and ran after one another, dodging puddles and mud as they engaged in a friendly game of tag.

But as Mikha'il watched, it became clear that the game was not as innocent as it first appeared. One child—a girl—was ostracized by the others.

In her white coat with matching hat and mittens, she was easy to spot, and it seemed that she was always "it." The others would approach, laugh, jeer and poke at her, forcing her to chase them.

Finally, two kids ran toward Mikha'il with her in pursuit, and he was able to see what made her so different from the others.

One side of her small, sweet face was stained dark purple. Starting at her forehead, the port-wine birthmark ran around her left eye, across her cheek and halfway down her neck.

Mikha'il grimaced with sadness and empathy for her. *No one should be branded like that, having to endure taunts, so marked from others, especially at such a young age. She's much too pure.*

Still, the little girl laughed along with the other children, not seeming to mind the ridicule, as if she were totally accepting of it. But her laughter came to an abrupt halt when a boy, much larger than she was, shoved her to the ground. She landed face-first in a puddle. Struggling, the little girl finally managed to get out of the dirty brown water and stood covered in mud. But she didn't cry; she'd clearly been pushed often before.

Only this time was very different.

The boy stood in utter shock and then called out excitedly to his friends. As they came closer, pointing to her face and talking animatedly, she heard their words in disbelief and desperately wiped at her cheek, clearing the mud from her face.

Her transformation was undeniable. The terrible birthmark was gone.

At first, the children stood bewildered; then with the innocent acceptance of youth, they giddily jostled around her and, holding her by the arms, ran with her back to school.

THIRTY-EIGHT

"IT'S HIM!" Abdul-Qadir threw the newspaper to the table. "It's him. I know it is! Where's Nur al-Din?"

A young jihadi soldier answered timidly, "He's outside with the men."

"Don't just stand there. Go get him. Now!"

The revelation still pounding through his body, Abdul-Qadir looked down upon the open newspaper on the table. He stared at the caption under the small black-and-white photograph. *Mikha'il bin al-Rashid to attend Amman Peace Summit as UN Special Envoy.*

Abdul-Qadir's scowl turned into a wince of pain, and he doubled over. With one hand clutched at his side, he slammed the other onto the photograph.

Jasmine passed Mikha'il the magazine article she was reading. "Here's another one. Your attendance is fast becoming public knowledge."

Mikha'il glanced through the article and signed, "I told Virginia that I don't want to deal with the press. She suggested you handle all the necessary media relations. She thought you did a great job while I was in the hospital."

"I can do that. It will give me a reason to be there with you. But this time, I won't do it for free," Jasmine said, giving him a devious smile.

234

Mikha'il raised his eyebrows.

"That's right. I'll need some sort of payment," she stated flatly, her face turning playfully stern before a softness broke over her expression, and she nestled close to him. After kissing his lips, she said, "But I'm sure we can negotiate something."

Mikha'il grinned. He removed the books from his lap and placed them beside those already stacked on the bedside table next to him. He shut off the light and turned to Jasmine.

In the three weeks following his meeting with Virginia, Mikha'il continued his research with new purpose. He concentrated on the Holy Land, the conflict between Israel and Palestine and, more specifically, Muslims and the West.

He took part in a series of meetings in Washington and at the UN, some of which included the secretary of state, and these helped him quickly become familiar with all of the issues.

At night, Jasmine and Mikha'il never separated. On visits to D.C., she traveled with him, enjoying their hotel stays and quiet dinners together. Regular sleep returned to Mikha'il, and Jasmine relished being able to once again cuddle up alongside his warm body.

For both, not only had a bond of friendship and passion returned, but, perhaps more than before, Jasmine admired the ease with which Mikha'il carried himself. A genuine optimism came over her, and Jasmine felt sure that after the summit, their life would return to normal and they would stay together.

For his part, Mikha'il could not stop thinking about the recent incidents with the disabled man and the disfigured young girl. Although he tried to brush them off as coincidence, Mikha'il could not deny what had happened. He searched his mind, hoping to find meaning in the visions he'd had—visions he could no longer pretend were just flights of imagination. There was too much truth in them.

"You'll be assigned to Mikha'il, code name Shepherd," David Caplan said, briefing Special Agent Deborah Barak, sitting across his desk. "Although he's insistent that he not have a security detail, Ms. Adams is demanding it."

"You want us covert?"

"Completely hidden unless necessary. Your detail will be minimal—yourself, a U.S. Secret Service agent and two Jordanians. Mikha'il will be staying with the delegation at the Le Royal Hotel, and the meetings will be in the palace of the King's Court. Any breach will likely come during travel between each. Since Mikha'il's refused dignitary status, he'll use the shuttle buses. Any problem, you call me immediately."

"Tariq, look at this!" shrieked Abdul-Qadir, pointing to the newspaper as if frightened by it.

"It's the photographer who stopped the attack in Jerusalem," replied Nur al-Din while skimming the article.

"It's because of him. I know it now. I can feel the venom."

"Venom?" Nur al-Din asked, confused.

"He's the snake. It was his bite that left this poison inside me. I know it. I could feel him after I was shot. Then he was gone, leaving a poison to rot inside me. This bin al-Rashid, he is a great threat to our purpose. He must be stopped."

"Yazid, you're a smart man—in fact, the smartest I know—but what you're saying is not logical," Nur al-Din said calmly, worried more than ever for the well-being of his mentor. "You haven't been sleeping well. Perhaps you're just a little overtired. I can have some medication brought for you."

"Nonsense! Don't demean me with your concern. I'm as strong as ever," the jihadi master shouted violently. "And don't tell me what's logical and what isn't. Hear me! He poisons me, just as he will poison us all. He'll soon be delivered to us. It is the will of Allah that brings him close to me."

"Think of what you're saying, Yazid. This can't be real."

"This is real, and Mikha'il bin al-Rashid needs to be dead."

"You want him killed?"

"Yes, at the peace summit." His master was adamant. "And I want to be there to make sure it happens."

Defiantly shaking his head, Nur al-Din openly argued, "It's too dangerous for us in Amman, particularly with all the security for the summit."

"I don't care. Organize the men. We leave for Amman."

"But, Yazid—"

"Don't contradict me. Don't you dare." The anxiety and panic had disappeared from Abdul-Qadir's tone. His unrelenting resolve had returned. "Or I'll have the pieces of your remains scattered through the empty desert."

THIRTY-NINE

THE SUMMIT MEETING began in early morning. Three long, narrow tables of equal length formed a giant triangle under a spectacular chandelier in the grand assembly room of the palace.

Seven people sat along each of the three tables, with Aaron Kessel and the Israeli representatives at one and Abu-Hakim and his Palestinian delegation at another. The United Nations mediators sat at the third, with Virginia Adams seated in the center and Mikha'il next to her.

Each delegation was supported by numerous staff members seated in rows behind them and along the perimeter of the large room. From the balcony galleries overhead, invited guests and correspondents observed the meeting.

Mikha'il concentrated on the proceedings, listening to everyone. As the first day progressed to its end, he was both surprised by and concerned with the lack of cooperation and progress. For hours, each side had postured and debated with the other, their bouts of aggressive rhetoric remaining unchecked by the UN mediators for several minutes. At times, the squabbling arguments heated to a boil, each side blaming the other for the current state of the world. In this meeting for peace, they struck just as fiercely with words as their people had with hatred and violence in the weeks and months before.

A ray of hope shone on the second day. Virginia had a podium placed at the point between the Israelis and the Palestinians—only one member was to speak at a time. The plan, though agreed upon, unfortunately, didn't succeed, as negotiations quickly bogged down in trivial details.

Virginia attempted to arbitrate, stressing the importance of a positive outcome, unfortunately to little avail. Just before the day's meeting drew to an end, Mikha'il passed her a note: *Can I share a few words?*

Ten minutes later, before adjourning the meeting, Virginia called upon him.

Carrying a single book, Mikha'il approached the podium, and Aisha followed closely behind. He set the book down and twisted the microphone to point toward Aisha, now standing at his side.

In tandem, they began.

Mikha'il moved his hands with refined fluidity and Aisha interpreted his signs with soft confidence. "Thank you, Madam Secretary, and I thank each of you for including me here at such an important and historic gathering. Before I begin, I ask your forgiveness if what I say does not follow proper protocol or is in any way offensive—but peace cannot be built upon a foundation of discord.

"I remind you that you are today's leaders, standing at the crossroads of our yesterdays, and it is the tomorrow of the Holy Land that you decide this week here, in Amman, named *Philadelphia* in biblical times, ironically meaning "city of brotherly love." Ironic because you are mastered by self-serving agendas—your words are proof. There is no brotherhood here.

"You have taken the battlefields not only to your streets but from there to this assembly, which as you know, is meant to be a summit of peace. Here, one should find shame, but not surprise, that the instruments of war have outpaced the instruments of peace. The taunting in our words remains as it has for centuries, but our rocks have been replaced with bombs, our swords with missiles, and our valiant with the innocent.

"In our haste to feed self-centered interests, we find conflict the easier choice. I remind you, though, the prize often lies in the difficult choice and the most valuable reward in the most challenging path.

"You debate over the smaller issues facing your peoples and ignore the larger, saying that they are too great to resolve at this time. But why not first tackle the most difficult issue? Then, in shared celebration of its resolution, the other issues' answers may readily follow. You see, in talks of peace, cooperation is more important than the details of negotiation."

Mikha'il hesitated as every person in the grand room watched him. He knew that his next statement would stir those seated before him, and he boldly continued. "The Old City of Jerusalem. Does it not belong to all?"

Gasps and whispers filled the room and balcony overhead.

"Is it not the place that the Lord made Adam, where the angel stopped Abraham from sacrificing Isaac, where David built his city, where Solomon raised a temple to house the Ark and Commandments, where Jesus was crucified and resurrected as Christ, and where Gabriel brought Muhammad on his night journey and ascension into heaven? It is surely the hallowed ground of our Lord's house, God's highest mountain. As such, it does not belong to any, but to all."

As the commotion grew more distinctly obvious from the Israeli side of the room, Mikha'il looked directly at Prime Minister Kessel and addressed the Israeli delegation.

"And in modern times, this tiny piece of land was at last to belong to all of man. The 1947 United Nations vote that the Jewish citizens of Palestine prayed would pass—delivering to them the independent country they so yearned for—proposed that Jerusalem be made a free and independent state, open to all people. You eagerly accepted the plan for not only the Old City but all of Jerusalem, as it had not been under Jewish influence for over eighteen hundred years. You lived in fear when the Arab League rejected the vote and war broke out between your peoples. In Israel's ultimate victory, all of Jerusalem was reclaimed for Israel. But still you live in fear."

The Palestinians applauded.

Mikha'il turned to face them. "Remember, for your Jewish brethren, their temple was as sacred as your Kaaba is to you. In an establishment of a new, independent Old City, they should be free to return to the site of its mount and not be forced to pray only huddled along the ruins of its last remaining foundation wall. Perhaps someday you will allow the Hebrew to build a new temple on its original mount, and the majestic grace of its presence can stand together with the two great mosques already there. In this new time, you may even find it in your hearts to give up your beloved Dome of the Rock for your brethren to rebuild their temple on its true site.

"I refer to the Hebrew as your brethren, for you should not deny that you are of the seed of Ishmael, brother to Isaac. Your Allah is not distinct from the Hebrew God. You are all of the same God, the Lord of Abraham, father to both Ishmael and Isaac. The Qur'an is a continuation of the Torah, Jewish scripture and Holy Bible. You should not only accept this but also preach the bond that unites you, rather than seek and dwell upon that which separates you. Muhammad is, after all, the Lord's messenger, who followed the Hebrew and Christian prophets before him."

Mikha'il turned and faced all those before him. "In your pride and stubbornness, how long can you resist these prophets and messengers? Is this not the time for you to accept their words? The answer may lie among your peoples, but the responsibility for it is with you, their leaders. It will be with your energy and conviction that you can once again shine a brightness over Jerusalem, and in the halo of its glow, truly light the entire world.

"Let the goodness shown to all humanity be your true victory, and the Lord, the real judge of your actions. I beg of you—strive as brothers, together, and heal the land that you love. Jerusalem is meant to be the City of Peace."

Mikha'il stopped, and while he reached for the book from the podium, a hushed moment followed, only to be broken by the loud mumbling of excited voices as the delegates turned, talking with those beside them.

Virginia watched Mikha'il unassumingly leave the podium. He walked behind the Israeli delegation, looking at no one, and when he reached Aaron Kessel, Mikha'il placed the book in front of him.

In the close quarters of the alleys beyond the palace grounds, a middle-aged man loitered around a cluster of small shops. Surrounding their cramped open entrances were mounds of colorful spices, photocopied DVD covers, various leather goods, ceramics and rugs.

It was into the crammed carpet shop that he occasionally glanced. In between stacks of rugs, piled on the narrow, dusty floor or rolled into columns around the shop walls, the lean man periodically met the eyes of one of the two men working inside. He waited for the nod that would indicate that the summit's motorcade was departing and, with it, the security forces that guarded the dignitaries.

FORTY

JASMINE HURRIED FORWARD when Mikha'il and Aisha arrived at the bottom of the stairway outside the assembly room where she and Dr. Ben had been waiting for them.

"I'm so proud of you." She beamed, sliding her hands under Mikha'il's arms and squeezing him tightly. "You were amazing."

He pulled back and signed, "Let's just hope they listen."

Waiting for the motorcade to leave before the shuttle buses could arrive, they wandered through the palace corridors, admiring the floor mosaics and elaborate artwork adorning the halls.

With Dr. Ben and Aisha a few steps behind, Mikha'il signed to Jasmine, "Did the media leave you alone up there?"

"Yes, nobody's been too difficult."

"Maybe they've finally grown tired of our story."

"They'll probably ask me what you gave the prime minister."

"Let him tell them."

"Will you tell me?"

"My grandmother's Bible."

Atop a ten-storey building across the boulevard, the lone militant, holding a carpet under one arm, exited the rooftop doorway.

In the shadow of a large sign overhead, he cut the ties binding the carpet and unrolled it. Inside was a long-barrelled rifle. The assassin slung it over his shoulder and climbed the sign's ladder. Stepping off the rung, he crawled to a hidden ledge directly under the base of the rusted frame. On his belly, he looked through the high-powered lens of his weapon and panned those exiting the palace gate below.

From his high perch, the killer watched the meeting's attendees fill the various shuttles. One by one, the buses left the driveway, heading for their respective hotels. And he lay silently waiting for his prey.

Only steps ahead of Aisha and Dr. Ben, Mikha'il and Jasmine walked through the open gates toward the last empty shuttle.

A single gunshot cracked through the dry air.

Mikha'il felt the impact as the bullet went through his body, his shoulder crashing into the wall behind him.

Frozen in shock, Jasmine heard screams from the streets and laneway as she stared uncomprehendingly at Mikha'il, who lay motionless at her feet.

"Shot fired, Shepherd down, Shepherd down," Deborah Barak yelled into her cuff microphone. She and a Secret Service agent sprang from the dark sedan parked halfway down the driveway. Behind them, two other men rushed from a similar vehicle, and the four ran, sidearms drawn, toward Mikha'il.

Clearly stunned, Mikha'il moaned and looked up to Jasmine. He caught his breath, blinked a few times and attempted to get up.

Forcing him back down, Dr. Ben said, "Just wait, Mikha'il. Not so fast."

Anxiously, he searched Mikha'il's body for a bullet wound but found none. Nor was there any sign of blood. He tore at Mikha'il's suit jacket and shirt. Bullet holes in the front and back of both garments provided ample evidence of a bullet's entry and exit.

"Is he all right?" Jasmine gasped. "Was he hit?"

"He's okay! I—I don't think he's been shot. I can't find a wound."

Dr. Ben removed his own overcoat and placed it over Mikha'il's shoulders. He hoped Jasmine had not noticed the bullet holes, or worse, anyone else. "Quickly, quickly," he shouted, "Let's get him out of here."

Aisha picked up their belongings, while Dr. Ben and Jasmine guided Mikha'il toward the waiting shuttle.

"I'm all right. I just fell, that's all," explained Mikha'il with awkward hand gestures as he shrugged off their assistance.

"Hold up. He's okay!" Deborah Barak slowed, watching to confirm her observation. "He wasn't hit. He must have just tripped."

Officers and soldiers had rushed to the scene, and the four agents mingled with them long enough to ensure that Mikha'il was safely on the shuttle bus before racing back to their vehicles.

Mikha'il didn't know how to explain the incident to Jasmine, nor did he want to. As the shuttle drove them to their hotel, Mikha'il refused to engage in discussion, and Dr. Ben, too, sat silently watching out the window.

Jasmine and Aisha calmed each other in low voices as Mikha'il sat in deep concentration. He'd almost convinced himself that he'd only fallen until he shifted in his seat, and Dr. Ben's coat, still draped over his shoulders, slipped slightly to reveal the bullet holes in his clothes. He remembered the intense sting in his chest.

Mikha'il pulled his shoulders inward, casually tucked his shirt in and closed his suit jacket.

After Mikha'il and Jasmine reached their hotel room, Mikha'il went straight into the bathroom and prepared a shower. The hot water felt good. Remembering Dr. Ben's silence on the bus, he wondered if the doctor, too, had noticed the bullet holes.

The phone rang, and Jasmine knocked on the bathroom door. "It's the police. They want to ask you some questions."

Mikha'il wrapped himself in a robe, rolled his shirt and jacket into a bundle and stuffed them into a plastic bag before leaving the bathroom.

Jasmine talked with the officer and interpreted Mikha'il's answers. The conversation was cut short by a call from Virginia on Jasmine's cell phone. Mikha'il repeated the same thing—he had only fallen and was quite fine.

After the two phone calls, Mikha'il brushed the incident off and, wanting to avoid any further conversation about it, suggested that Aisha and Dr. Ben join them for an early dinner.

"You have failed me, Tariq," growled Abdul-Qadir as he sat on the side of a cot in the dingy cellar.

"I don't understand." Nur al-Din paced the basement's dirt floor. "He used a hollow-point bullet and saw bin al-Rashid take a direct hit. I don't know how he's not dead."

"This assassin, you're sure he can be trusted?" Abdul-Qadir coughed and twisted in pain.

"The man is one of our best and very loyal to the cause. There's no reason that he would lie."

Abdul-Qadir rubbed at his stringy gray beard. His swirling thoughts mixed with the piercing ache in his belly and colored his words while he grew excited and adamant. "Perhaps our shooter was successful." He paused, deep in thought. "I should have considered this before. Of course! Of course that must be it. It's the only answer."

Nur al-Din stopped pacing and waited in front of the sickly man, clearly expecting him to continue. When he did not, Nur al-Din asked, "What? *What's* the answer?"

"He can't be killed," Abdul-Qadir replied calmly, certain. "This Mikha'il bin al-Rashid, or whatever he is, cannot be killed, at least not like any man before him."

"Yazid, that doesn't make sense. He's a man just like any other."

"Don't tell me what makes sense and what doesn't! His venom doesn't poison your body as it does mine. I know what I say is true!"

"It's not this man who poisons you, Yazid, but the abscess and infection from the gunshot. Your condition has deteriorated with the trek across the desert. I'm telling you we should send for a doctor."

"I don't want a doctor. I want bin al-Rashid to answer for this." Abdul-Qadir yelled, gasping for breath. He cleared his throat and spit on the ground. As he did, the wheezing turned to an uncontrollable cough and his frail body heaved with the effort.

"Let me get you some water."

"No, get me bin al-Rashid!" Abdul-Qadir held up his hand, waiting for the coughing to subside. When it did, he continued, "If he can't be killed, I want him. Bring him here before they put an impregnable ring of security around him."

"But you're risking everything."

"Do not fail me, Tariq, or it will be *I* who next fails *you*. If it has to be the last thing that I do, I surely will."

After a short dinner—at which everyone thought about the attempt on Mikha'il's life but spoke only of the peace summit—Dr. Ben and Aisha walked Jasmine and Mikha'il back to their room. As soon as the door closed behind them, Jasmine turned to him. "Why do you insist on telling everybody you're all right? I don't understand. What's going on with you?"

"I told you, I'm fine."

"But you were shot. I saw it."

"No, I only tripped."

"You didn't trip! Your body flew back into the wall." The anger in her tone was fueled by fear and worry. "Mikha'il, please be honest with me. What's happening?"

"It's okay, babe." He walked to her and tenderly put his arms around her.

She pushed him away. "I saw holes in your clothes. Dr. Ben saw them, too. That's why he threw his coat over you—to hide them. I know it. He acted so strange at dinner. I could tell. He just kept staring at you and not saying much."

"I must have snagged myself on the wall when I fell. That's all."

"No, it's like somehow the bullet went straight through you. Give me your jacket!" she challenged, tears of frustration streaking down her face.

Mikha'il did not respond. It troubled him to see Jasmine so upset, knowing he was the cause of it. *Oh, baby, please don't cry. I wish I could tell you what's going on, but how would you believe me? I'm not even sure I do.*

She persisted. "Do I need to get your clothes myself?"

"You can, but what will it prove? What you're saying isn't possible."

"That's just like you, always so logical." She wiped at her tears.

Again, Mikha'il tried to comfort her. "Let's go for a walk."

"No. You go."

"I don't want to leave you like this. Come on." Mikha'il smiled cheerfully.

"No, I want to be alone," she snapped in defiance. "Go. I'll be all right."

FORTY-ONE

MIKHA'IL WALKED DOWN THE AVENUE and into the Amman night. He paid little attention to the small shops and rundown storefronts he strolled past. Instead, his thoughts focused on Jasmine. He was ashamed of his dishonesty with her. Even though he knew she wouldn't find his clothes—he'd buried them in a trash can by the ice machine in the hallway while she was freshening up for dinner—he decided that he would tell her the truth when he returned.

Hands in his pockets, he contemplated just how he'd explain all that had happened to him and considered the many ways she might respond to the coming conversation.

Suddenly, his concentration was broken by a loud knocking on the window he was passing. Mikha'il glimpsed the shadow of a figure inside the small storefront. Most of the signage was in Chinese, and oddly, no Arabic was visible, but a small neon light dangled in the window and flashed red in English: *The Red Tearoom. Open.*

Once more, the figure inside knocked at the window.

An old Asian man, out of place in the Arab country, merrily waved at Mikha'il and pointed to the door of his shop.

Mikha'il walked back three paces, opened the door and stepped inside.

The sound of chimes welcomed him, and the thinly bearded storekeeper sauntered over to greet Mikha'il. "Just the man I've been waiting for. Come in for some hot tea and a wee game of Wei-Chi."

"Excuse me?" Mikha'il said, shaking his head in confusion. "Tea and a game of what?"

"I, too, have always found that to sound so funny together—" the old man giggled "—and it's even more amusing when you say it."

When I say it . . .? His confusion transformed into excitement. *I'm speaking out loud!* "You heard me, didn't you?"

"Of course I did. I may be old, but I'm not deaf." The little man looked up to Mikha'il and grinned. "Come in! Come in before the wind snuffs out my candles."

Passing under the door chimes, Mikha'il followed the man into the cluttered room. Several lamps hung low over their heads, and Mikha'il ducked his way through them. Their dim glow was augmented by lighted candles, which shed enough light to reflect off several colorful ceramic pots and create shadows that danced around the crimson walls.

Picking up two steaming cups, the storekeeper passed one to Mikha'il. "Here, I've just finished making you one."

The cup warmed his hands, but Mikha'il didn't raise it to his lips. Instead, he watched the frail Chinese man gulp from his.

Beyond his broad forehead, he had a ponytail that fell like silk over his slanted shoulders. His face was disfigured, not to the point of being grotesque, but giving him an odd look. His eyes were unevenly close together, and a thin crooked nose separated his twisted cheeks.

Nevertheless, the old man seemed at ease, radiating calm and friendliness. His eyes twinkled under wiry brows, and his smile seemed permanently fixed on his face, making it difficult to resist his charm.

The Chinese man drained his tea before Mikha'il had touched his and, waddling to the corner of the room, gently announced, "Come. The game awaits us."

"But who are you?" Mikha'il asked politely.

The storekeeper nodded at the acknowledgment of his oversight. He paused but did not turn around, offering, "I am he that many refer to as such that I say."

"Pardon me?" Mikha'il asked, more confused. "You're who?"

"You know, Confucius says this; Confucius says that," said the old man, walking away, making fun of himself, bobbing his head back and forth. "Oh, well, it is not a bad mark to leave."

"You're saying you're Confucius?"

"Correct, but why so puzzled?" Confucius stopped and turned. "Have you not met others before me?"

"Yes, but only in a coma. This isn't even a dream."

"Dream it is not. I am here just as you." Confucius winked. "Besides, how else can you explain that you are able to speak?"

Hiding in the shadows, just down the street from the tiny shop, Nur al-Din waited with three militant operatives.

Another rounded the building's edge. "He entered a shop halfway up. The security team is parked a few doors away. Two cars, four agents."

"All right, you keep watch from here. We'll wait in the alleyway behind for your signal that he's left. If he's in there for long, we'll switch up every ten minutes."

In the corner of the tearoom, Mikha'il sat on three cushions with his legs crossed, in front of a block oak table that rested on ornately carved knobby legs, while Confucius sat across from him on several gold-colored pillows. Most of the tabletop was etched with vertical and horizontal straight lines, and each man had a hollowed wooden bowl filled with small stones in front of him.

"The conflict in man parallels that of a simple game," said Confucius, playing with his skinny beard. "Before I explain the rules, what do you see before you?"

"A game board, much like a chess board, but with more squares." Mikha'il began counting. "Eighteen squares by, I guess, eighteen, since the board seems even on all sides."

"Yes, a total of 324 squares," the Chinese master enthusiastically confirmed. "The area we do battle over."

It did not take long for Confucius to explain the rules. "And as my able opponent, what is your objective?" he inquired.

"To take your stones and control more area than you, thereby winning."

"Correct! My objective is to overcome you, just as it is yours to overcome me. Really quite simple. Let's begin."

When Mikha'il began placing his stones on the board, Confucius quickly reprimanded him. "You aren't doing that with the force of a confident warrior. When you put the stone down, you snap it in your fingertips and slap the board with determination in the face of your opponent."

Mikha'il chuckled and snapped his next stone with delight. "There, how was that?"

"Much better. Now, what difference do you notice between your side and my side?"

Mikha'il took a moment to scan the setup before them. "They look the same. I'm not sure what you mean by a difference. I don't see any."

"We sit on opposing sides of the board, and our stones—do you see anything different about them?"

"I suppose the colors. Yours are white and mine black."

"Precisely. They define each of us. Opponents engaged in conflict. It matters not the color of each, only that we are different." Confucius placed a stone on the board. "Conflict in man begins with differentiation. The most defining criterion has been, and still is, the religion of man. With it, we segregate ourselves, poised for opposition and conflict."

"Our faith separates us."

"No, no, no." The ancient Chinese teacher slapped his own knees and asked with some disgust, "Have you not learned anything from those before me?"

Mikha'il didn't answer and sat back, refraining from placing a stone on the board.

The wise philosopher calmed himself and began speaking with gentle conviction. "Faith does not divide us; it bonds us. Faith is inside all man. It is innate, placed in us for purpose. With faith, man stands out from all other living things and, through his advancement, is poised to ensure goodness and to protect the earth. In his quest for knowledge, he understands more of himself, his relationship with others and that with nature. We evolve.

"All men are bound by the force that created them. With the essence placed inside of each, we understand the difference between right and wrong, good and evil. This is not taught. It is embedded in our existence. We strive for goodness and seek the ultimate reward for our deeds. This is common among all people. This is the faith of man."

"By faith, you mean our soul, placed in us by God, our Creator?" Mikha'il asked astutely.

"From the will inside you—you will call it what you will." The Chinese master laughed, pleased by the play he made on his own words. He leaned forward and raised his stringy eyebrows. "Still, one cannot reject the notion that man and the world around him have progressed through the ages. The history of the planet, its relationship with the universe and the development of nature's species are scientific facts, proven through the knowledge of man. They are man's reality.

"However, if only the science of evolution explained man's progress, one would find a hierarchy in nature consistent from the simplest of organisms to the complexity of man. Although this hierarchy progresses throughout all of nature, it does not extend to man. The consistent linear progression of species stops just before man, and then leaps bounds to man. Man is far more advanced than even those species closest to him. We cannot deny the existence of man's vast superiority over all others. This defies the logic in pure evolution. The reason must lie inside, with the faith of man."

"The typical debate between science and divinity," Mikha'il added.

"Not exactly," Confucius countered, waving a spindly finger. "Evolution and faith are not opposite sides of an argument. Rather, they coexist. Both show the wonder of creation—one is the natural code of developing progress, the other the distinguishing spirit of purpose in man. Just as you cannot defy evolution, you cannot deny faith. They exist together."

"What about those who argue absolutely against faith?"

"Even those few who outwardly reject faith often embrace it during the time of their greatest need. Whether it is at the death of the mother that bore them or in the instant threat to their safety, they may stir the faith that rests deep within."

Jasmine's anger had receded, only to be replaced with worry.

She'd called Dr. Ben, and he spent much time soothing her concern, insisting he saw no bullet holes and that she was probably mistaken about the clothes, even though she couldn't find them.

Although he suggested joining her to wait for Mikha'il's return, she declined his offer. But after two hours, her concern persisted, and she called Virginia.

"Don't worry, Jasmine. Reports are that he just fell. That's all it can be."

"I suppose you're right, but I don't like the thought of him out there alone."

"He'll be okay."

"How can you be sure?"

Virginia hesitated. "We have agents trailing him. I know he refused a security detail, but we had an undercover team assigned to him anyway. They'll be watching him right now."

"Were they at the palace gates this afternoon?"

"Yes. I'm sorry to interfere in your privacy this way."

"That's all right. I'm glad," Jasmine said with relief.

Caught up in their discussion, Mikha'il ignored the tea, now grown cold, that he'd set on the floor beside him. Enthusiastically, he said, "So regardless of how it's identified, whether it is faith, an essence or a soul, it is embedded in all man."

"That is correct." Confucius nodded, clearly pleased with his student's progress. "But religion—well, now, that's quite different. Religion is artificial. It is made by man and comes with the imperfections of man. Religion is an interpretation of man's faith and founded in a quest for answers.

"Faith is universal, so the questions incited by it are identical. But in the answers provided by religion, differences emerge. While all religions explain when and how the world and man were created, provide examples of good prevailing over evil and promise that goodwill is ultimately rewarded and evil punished, these explanations differ by religion. Man is united in the questions inspired by faith, but in the answers provided by religion, man is divided.

"For each people, religion is authenticated with history and scripture and maintained with law and celebration. The stories and legends of strong leaders influenced those who followed. The old taught the young, until the young became the old and passed what they'd learned to their own young. Through generations in each land, distinct religions grew into differentiating scriptures, traditions and cultures. Even in my land, some follow my teachings as religion, separating ours from others."

Mikha'il sat deep in thought as Confucius continued. "And the land currently dividing you from me consists of the squares of this game board." The master waved his hand over the table. "As opponents, we battle for control of it."

"I'm sorry," Mikha'il said. "I guess it's my turn. I lost track."

"That is of no matter." Confucius drew Mikha'il's attention back into his teachings. "As nations meet in conflict, their peoples become enemies. They each seek victory. Their faith is the same, but their religions differ.

"The leaders of nations unite their peoples through their religion. It is entrenched into their culture and existence. All peoples believe they fight on the side of good and on behalf of the only true religion, understanding little of their opponent's motivation. This is an advantage for leaders. Each side is encouraged to fight for its faith and preserve its religion from the threat of the other."

"If they all believe they fight on the side of right, how can the loser explain defeat?" Mikha'il interrupted.

As if expecting the question, Confucius didn't hesitate. "For the generals on the battlefield, both victory and defeat can be easily explained through religion. Victory is the reward for fighting on the side of good, and defeat is the punishment for some previous wrong. When their own wrong is righted, with, of course, the guidance of those governing, their people can return to fight with confidence, with reassurance.

"Conflict ebbs and flows. There are points in time when balance shifts—one becomes stronger, the other weaker. Like this game, man battles over borders. Whoever controls the land has the power. From the land comes resources useful for food, shelter, energy and security. It is not for religion that man fights. No, it is for land and power. Religion is just the simplest, and most motivating, differentiation on the field of battle. Like the colors of our stones, it does not matter which of us is black or white, only that we are not the same."

Mikha'il remembered his previous lessons. He thought of all that troubled the world, the centuries of warring nations.

Confucius didn't allow his student much time for recollection. "And now I must encourage your departure."

"Excuse me? You want me to leave, just like that?" Mikha'il asked, feeling suddenly rejected.

"This game, I sense, will not be completed, but with you, fortunately, I have finished." The comforting smile vanished from Confucius's face, and his tone turned abrupt. "I have said what is to be said, and your blanket grows impatient."

"My blanket?"

"You see the gentleman standing by the window? This is the fourth time he has peeked inside since you have been here. He is an agent from your surveillance team. Go ahead . . . See for yourself."

Mikha'il navigated a short path to the window. He saw the man walking toward two cars. "I didn't know I was being tracked."

Confucius joined him at the window, in time to see a second man leaving his car and joining the first. Watching, Confucius said to Mikha'il, "But you don't need a blanket if the cold can't hurt you."

"What do you mean?" asked Mikha'il, turning toward his teacher.

"Take the alley behind the store. There is a back door you can go out. They won't follow you there."

"Now?"

"Yes, now!"

"Thank you, I guess. I have enjoyed our—"

Before Mikha'il could finish, Confucius shooed him to the back of the shop. "Take with you one last thought. Even with this talk of conflict, inside the faith of all man is the hope for peace. I suggest you make haste."

The Jordanian agent didn't look into the window this time. Instead, he and his partner nonchalantly entered the shop. The chimes rang and the storekeeper glanced up.

From behind the counter of the jammed tobacco shop, the middle-aged Arab clerk politely asked, "Can I help you?"

"Where's the American?" demanded the first agent, looking for some sign of Mikha'il.

"There is no American here."

"Shepherd gone. Shepherd gone," the second agent blurted into his sleeve as both agents pulled out their sidearms.

"Where did he go? I saw him through the window only a minute ago. He was playing some game in the corner with an old Asian man," the first agent barked at the man behind the counter as he glanced around the musty shop. He saw his partner searching near cracked tobacco cabinets and dusty displays of pipes and Arabic hookahs. In the corner of the shop, two stools sat beside a flimsy table with black and white dominos scattered on top.

"Honestly. I've been alone in here for more than two hours. It has been a quiet night," the frightened shopkeeper responded.

"I thought you said this place was a tearoom," the second Jordanian agent said.

Confused, his dumbfounded partner looked out the window to confirm he was in the same store.

"Tearoom?" the clerk replied. "I've owned this tobacco shop for sixteen years, and there isn't a tearoom anywhere around here."

Deborah Barak and the American agent burst through the door.

"He's not here!" the second Jordanian agent reported.

"Where'd he go?" Deborah asked urgently.

From near the window, the first agent nervously answered, "I don't know. He just disappeared, like he wasn't here, but I know what I saw."

"Right." Deborah ignored him and asked the second, "Have you checked for another exit?"

"There's no back door, and the store's clear. The only way in or out is the door you just came through."

FORTY-TWO

MIKHA'IL IGNORED THE SMELL of rot and decay filling the alleyway. He had no idea how much time had passed while he was in the tearoom, but it was dark, and he knew Jasmine would be worried. Not far ahead, he could see an opening between the buildings; he turned toward it.

As he took a step over a pile of garbage, he caught a movement in the shadows. In the split second that it took to register in his mind, a form leaped forward and brought him to the ground.

A knee rammed into the base of his neck and his face was shoved into the loose gravel. He felt a wrenching in his shoulders as his arms were pulled behind him. His captor, breathing loudly with exertion, knotted a rope around his wrists.

A hand grabbed at his hair and violently yanked him backward, and Mikha'il caught a glimpse of another pair of hands as a small sack was dropped over his head.

Mikha'il choked and gagged as it was tied tightly around the back of his neck.

He inhaled. The rancid air from the alley was masked by the dirt embedded in the burlap of the sack. From the sounds of other voices nearby, he guessed there were at least four, perhaps five, men. Too many.

"You lost him?"

"Yes, Commander," Deborah Barak replied meekly into her telephone.

"I've just finished talking with the prime minister, and I assured him that you had Mikha'il safely protected. And now you tell me this."

"I'm sorry, sir. It doesn't make sense. We had him, and then he just—"

"He just what? Disappeared?"

"That's right, sir."

David Caplan snorted in frustration. "Listen, Deborah, it seems that somebody wants him dead. We just got word from the Jordanians. They found a sniper rifle on the rooftop across from the palace gates. They haven't apprehended anyone yet, but it appears Mikha'il was the target. The single bullet shot from the weapon was found lodged in the wall directly behind where he fell. Apparently, Mikha'il tripped right before the shooter fired, and that's how he was missed. It was pure luck."

"Yes, sir, a lucky escape. Don't worry, sir. Mikha'il is on foot, so he couldn't have gotten far. We'll find him."

"Well, make it quick!"

With his hands still bound and the sack over his head, Mikha'il was marched into the basement of a crumbling warehouse. A metal door leading to a dark storeroom was opened. Two men pushed him inside and slammed the heavy door shut.

A local operative, left to watch over Abdul-Qadir, promptly strode from the opposite end of the cracked-cement hallway to meet Nur al-Din and the others.

"Go back to Yazid," Nur al-Din ordered. "Tell him we have his prisoner."

Shaking his head, the middle-aged Jordanian did not answer.

"What is it?" Nur al-Din frowned in frustration.

"He's gone." Reaching Nur al-Din, the man whispered, not wanting to alert the others.

"Gone where?"

"He's dead, Tariq. Just now, when you arrived."

Nur al-Din grasped him by the shoulder and pulled him aside. "You're sure?"

"Yes. Come."

Nur al-Din turned to the men and gruffly ordered, "Wait here until I return."

As they walked swiftly down the hall, the operative frantically explained, "He started calling out, talking crazy and choking. I thought he'd awoken from a nightmare and was bringing him some water. He sat up in the bed, eyes bulging. Then he cried out, 'Allah, have mercy on my soul!' and just dropped dead. I didn't want to touch him, even to close his eyes."

Aaron Kessel leaned back into the tall chair in the sitting room of his hotel suite. He closed the Bible and set it, along with the handwritten note from Mikha'il he'd found inside, onto the table beside him. He closed his eyes and considered the verses that Mikha'il had written from. He could still visualize Mikha'il's lean form at the podium, fingers signing elegantly, and the sound of the voice of the interpreter beside him.

Kessel's mind wandered. Having just learned of the shooting attempt on Mikha'il's life, he worried about the safety of this strange messenger.

"Excuse me, Mr. Prime Minister," his executive assistant said, entering the room. "It's about Mikha'il bin al-Rashid."

"What about him?" Kessel leaned forward.

"He's all over the news."

"That was quick. The assassination attempt?"

"Not just that, sir," his assistant replied with hesitation. "There's more, so much more. You really need to see for yourself."

Nur al-Din looked down at the face of the jihadi master—sunken eyes wide and mouth half-open. He waited to feel something. Nothing came: no emotion, no sense of loss. *Perhaps at one time*, he thought, *but not now.*

He returned to the hall where his men waited, guarding the prisoner's door as instructed. Speaking in tones of respect and sorrow, he announced the death of their leader while maintaining a posture of purpose and command.

Without waiting for a response from the shocked men—two dropping to the cold floor to pray—Nur al-Din gestured to the door.

One of the men fumbled with the lock, and Nur al-Din entered.

Mikha'il saw a glimmer of brightness through the burlap sack as the rusted hinges on the door frame squeaked open.

He heard people entering, one dragging what he thought might be a chair. Moments later, someone helped him stand and untied his hands before removing the sack from his head.

Mikha'il took a full breath of air and blinked as his eyes adjusted to the light.

"I am Tariq Nur al-Din. I hear you can't speak," said Nur al-Din, throwing a pencil and pad of paper on the chair opposite him while two other men left the room and closed the door.

Mikha'il lifted the pencil and pad and sat down on the wooden chair.

For a few seconds, each man sized up the other.

Nur al-Din wondered why Abdul-Qadir had wanted this man so badly and what he would do with him now.

Mikha'il wrote on the pad, tore off the top sheet and handed it to his jailer.

There is no God but Allah, and Muhammad is his messenger.

Nur al-Din scoffed. "I know you have a Muslim name, but you're not one with us. You don't share our faith or our cause."

Again, Mikha'il wrote and held up the pad. *He's dead, isn't he?*

"Who's dead? Muhammad?" asked Nur al-Din, forcing a chuckle. Although outwardly showing amusement, Nur al-Din didn't understand how this man could know about Abdul-Qadir or his death. The room was soundproof. There was no way bin al-Rashid could have heard.

No—Yazid Abdul-Qadir is dead.

"Why do you say that?"

Mikha'il wrote. *I felt him die.*

"When?"

When we arrived here.

"That's not possible!"

He cried to Allah for mercy on his soul.

"How could you know?"

Mikha'il busily pushed the pencil along the pad.

"Never mind. This is nonsense," Nur al-Din said icily, standing to leave. "You can sit alone in the darkness! I'll return when you have found your senses."

Mikha'il wrote briskly. He gestured urgently for Nur al-Din to wait, but Nur al-Din dismissed him with a brusque wave and left the room, closing the door and leaving Mikha'il in darkness.

In the absence of light, Mikha'il scribbled away. *I saved him when he was shot. I kept him alive. I felt him struggle for his life while you carried him out the gates, just as I did when we entered this place. Hatred and mistrust devoured his faith. The fear created by his own demons caused him to misinterpret my presence, and as I neared him, he resisted.*

A few steps away, Nur al-Din stopped and put his hand to his head. While one of the guards locked the door, the new jihadi leader remained, absorbed in the quiet words that sounded in his mind.

"Tariq, are you all right?" asked one of his men.

Ignoring him, he turned around and calmly said, "Unlock the door."

Grabbing a second chair, Nur al-Din reentered the room, turned on the light and closed the door behind him. "You say you tried to save him?" he asked softly. "That you felt him when I carried him from the Old City."

Mikha'il nodded in surprise. He scribbled once more. *You know what I'm writing?*

Before Mikha'il raised the pad, Nur al-Din answered, "Yes, I know what you're writing."

Mikha'il left the pencil aside. *You can hear my words?*

"Yes. I don't know how . . . The mystery makes me curious. But unlike my master, I don't fear you."

The two men conversed through the late hours of night. At times, they agreed, and at other times, they did not. Nur al-Din complained of the oppression against the Palestinian people and detailed all the injustices heaped on them. Unrelenting, he justified the actions of their jihad and those fighting for freedom. Both men referred to verses from the Qur'an, and impressing each other with their knowledge, they debated over the meanings.

Mikha'il looked on the man who would now lead Islamic jihad. *Just as your mentor misinterpreted my presence, he has misinterpreted the message in your Qur'an and twisted the words of Muhammad. Worse, he hid behind them. For your cause, your jihadists terrorize the innocent and slaughter the young, the women and those unable to defend themselves. In doing so, they act against all of humankind. This jihad is not the way of your prophet.*

Qur'an, Al-Ma'idah, 5:32 If one kills the innocent, it shall be as if he has killed all of mankind. If one has saved them, it will be as if he saved all of mankind.

Nur al-Din adamantly defended his cause. "Even the Israelis made Menachem Begin their adored prime minister. And he was by any definition, a freedom-fighting terrorist who ordered the bombing of the King David Hotel in the forties, killing a hundred innocent people. And what of the Palestinian people? Is it not Muslims who are the oppressed now? Should I not fight for them the same way?"

I sense that you are one who believes in what is right and stands against that which is wrong.

He swiftly responded, "And my people are wronged."

I am mindful that your people feel great misery because of the injustices laid upon them. However, you satisfy your thirst for their freedom by drinking your wine from a cup of hatred, and in spilling it worthlessly, only hated can you become.

"Hated? I don't think so!" Nur al-Din laughed boldly. "When we are successful, my people will declare us great heroes."

Will they?

"Yes, most definitely."

Or is it because of you that their oppression worsens? Have you had success in your approach so far?

"We will have victory," Nur al-Din said with determination.

And if you are successful in your way, then what?

"Our people will have freedom."

And those you have terrorized? Those who, in defeat, have not given freely—will they not strike back at you? The terrorized will become the terrorist. As you become them, they will become you. The cycle of violence will only continue.

Nur al-Din shook his head and rose from his chair. "It will be of no matter. The land will belong to us."

Ah, yes, the land. This is not a Holy War. It is a struggle for the control of land. Mikha'il looked up to him. *It is not religion that divides you. It is the land. It is only in losing it that you have declared your enemy.*

Nur al-Din walked behind his prisoner. "They have been our enemy before."

Mikha'il did not turn. *Only for a couple of years, before the establishment of a Muslim nation, when a tribe allied with the Meccans battling Muhammad. For those few Jews, it was about land, not religion.*

"And the early Israelites stole the land from our ancestors," Nur al-Din exclaimed, coming back around to face Mikha'il. "That you can't argue!"

Three thousand years ago, only to lose it afterward. Your people weren't Muslims for another sixteen hundred years. You didn't become enemy with the Jews until 1948, when they took Palestine from you.

"So, you agree they have taken the land from us," Nur al-Din said victoriously, clapping his hands.

It does not all legally belong to them.

Nur al-Din returned to the chair across from Mikha'il and, leaning forward, asked, "Then what do you suggest we do? How do we fight fairly against a foe when we have nowhere near the forces that Israel and its Western allies have? Where is the fairness in that?"

Like the great prophet of your people, you should resist with honor. Through diplomacy and understanding, you will gain the support of the world for your plight. What you are doing now is only forcing the world against you. Not against your cause, but your path.

The tall Palestinian sat back in his chair. "You can follow the path you believe in. I'll follow the one I know. I will not give up until we have justice."

All Arabs are called by names with meaning. Does your name not mean "the star and light of faith"?

"Yes, it does. You know your Arabic well. And your name, bin al-Rashid; it translates to 'the selected one, the knower and undeniable teacher.' So what?"

Mikha'il was unmoved. *Your people have been devoid of a great leader for too long. There is no star in the sky to follow. But you represent the Muslim nation through your actions. Be responsible, be honorable. Be—*

A loud knock sounded, and Nur al-Din stood to answer the door.

The guard whispered in excitement, "Tariq, this man is all over the news."

"Do they know he's missing?"

"No, I don't think so."

"Then what is it?"

"Something isn't right. As soon as he arrives here, Yazid dies. The men are concerned. You really need to see."

Closing the heavy door behind him, Nur al-Din joined his men, huddling over the screen of a cell phone. Several minutes later, all eyes were on him.

Their new leader wasted no time. "We return to Iraq immediately. Release this man. He means nothing to us. Take him near to where we found him and let him be."

"What about Abdul-Qadir?"

"It's already too dangerous for us. Leave his body here . . . and get a camera."

FORTY-THREE

TIRED AND WITHOUT SLEEP, Mikha'il strolled through the quiet streets of dawn's peaceful stillness, thinking of the day and night before—his transformation from student to teacher. Passing along the lane where he thought the tearoom had been, he looked for the storefront but couldn't locate it. The morning sun rose above the horizon, and Mikha'il approached the base of the hill where, halfway up, the hotel stood over the city.

He walked up the gentle incline toward the entrance, eyeing the crowd of press scrums and camera crews, which had dramatically multiplied since he'd left. At least a dozen trucks and scores of reporters waited in front of the hotel entrance.

He wondered what had happened during his absence.

The instant Mikha'il was recognized, the media swarmed around him, thrusting cameras and microphones into his face. He stopped, confused by the frenzy of questions, unable to comprehend, let alone voice a response.

Rushing into action, Deborah Barak, the other agents of her security detail and several uniformed police officers forced their way through the crowd. Reaching Mikha'il, they formed a protective ring around him.

Deborah held up her credentials, shouting above the noise, "Mikha'il, I'm Special Agent Deborah Barak with the Israeli prime minister's security force. Are you all right?"

He nodded twice.

"Good. Then let's get you safely up to your room."

Nur al-Din stood by the body of Abdul-Qadir one last time. Some memory of the respect he'd once had for his mentor returned as he readied for the role he'd accepted. Nur al-Din considered the strange conversation with the man his leader had grown so paranoid about. Although Nur al-Din accepted there was some truth in Mikha'il's words, he remained determined to fight for his people.

"Excuse me, Tariq," one of his men interrupted respectfully.

"Is your camera set?" Nur al-Din did not turn.

"Yes, whenever you are ready."

Waiting with Dr. Ben and Aisha, who had both joined her late in the night to soothe her worry, Jasmine heard the door unlock and leaped from her perch at the end of the bed. When Mikha'il walked into the room, she ran to him and threw her arms around him.

They stood that way for a long moment until Jasmine lifted her head from his shoulder and met his eyes. "Where have you been, leaving me alone like that?" she asked, softening her voice to take the reproach from it.

Even after the long night, Nur al-Din's men noticed the force evident in their new leader. Contrasting his strength with that of his ailing predecessor, they shared relief in his ascension. When the camera began recording, Nur al-Din needed only one take, and the jihadi warriors watched the performance with admiration and instant loyalty.

"I am Tariq Nur al-Din, the star and the light of faith. Our Yazid Abdul-Qadir has left us for the reward that Allah has bestowed upon him in paradise. We remain to fight for the cause of our people.

"But hear me now. This is not a Holy War. It is a battle for the equal rights of man. We fight against injustice and oppression. We fight for the freedom of our people and the liberation of our land. For this, we declare war on Israel and its allies.

"No more will we rain terror on the innocent of our enemy, but we will fight, hard and endlessly, until the oppression of our people ends. We do not fight for today but for tomorrow, for the opportunity for our youth and the generations to follow.

"To our people, I plead that you do not strike out against the weak and innocent, or from the timid and easy shadows of violent hatred. But, instead, join as brothers and sisters, Sunni with Shia, to fight freely and fiercely against only those soldiers assigned to fight against us. And, to our foe, I pledge to you a bloody struggle that will last until you heed the right of freedom for all people, not just your own. I am Tariq Nur al-Din, and I am the star and the light of faith."

The senior member operating the camera turned it off and asked, "What should we do with the recording?"

Not hesitating, Nur al-Din replied, "Leave the camera with Abdul-Qadir's body. Three hours after we've left, have the Jordanian police tipped off. They'll make sure the video gets to both the Americans and Al Jazeera. I don't care who gets it first."

Mikha'il shrugged and signed, "Sorry, I went for a walk and got lost."

Jasmine didn't say anything. For a long moment, she just stared at him. From behind her, Dr. Ben and Aisha did the same.

Sensing the awkwardness, Mikha'il signed again, "What's with all the media? They were all over me. I was only gone one night."

A troubled look replaced the anger in Jasmine's face. "Mikha'il, the media didn't know you were missing. That's not why they're here."

Mikha'il raised his eyebrows in question until, finally, Aisha broke the uncomfortable silence. "They're reporting again."

Jasmine sat on the end of the bed, where she'd been watching the television most of the night, and said, "Turn it up, so we can all hear."

"Minutes ago, Mikha'il bin al-Rashid walked up this sidewalk alone and was immediately escorted into his hotel by local police and special security forces. It is not known where he's been—only that he was gone most of the night.

"We've been investigating the story of bin al-Rashid since he was appointed as a United Nations envoy to attend the peace summit between Israel and the Palestinian delegation, which started here two days ago.

"After delivering what witnesses are calling a game-changing speech in the final hour yesterday, our cameras recorded this assassination attempt on Mikha'il's life at the gates of the Jordanian palace.

"As you hear the gunshot, you can clearly see bin al-Rashid being hit. He's thrown backward into the wall by the impact and then slumps to the ground. In the moments after, those tending to him placed an overcoat around him and helped him to a shuttle bus, which was driven here, to this hotel. When we inquired into his condition, we were told by officials that he'd tripped with the sound of the gunshot. The evidence seems to suggest otherwise."

Jasmine's eyes went back and forth from the television to Mikha'il. She waited for him to show any reaction, but none appeared. He only watched, stone-faced, the story unfolding before him.

"I'm sure many of you remember that Mikha'il bin al-Rashid was the hero who almost sacrificed his own life in stopping the attack of the Israeli security officer on the Old City of Jerusalem last April. Miraculously, the only person killed that day was the terrorist, but bin al-Rashid was left clinically brain-dead. Beyond the news of his mysterious recovery four months ago, what we are about to report is the story we've been investigating over the past few weeks.

"Many of the victims seriously wounded during the attacks in the Old City claimed to have sensed an unidentifiable but peaceful force enter them after they were shot. All described a similar feeling, and all insist this 'spirit' helped them cling to life, saving them from sure death.

"We've learned that five months later, at exactly 3:00 on a Friday afternoon, with absolutely no hope of recovery, bin al-Rashid was secretly disconnected from life support. Rather than peacefully passing away as expected, he lived.

"What few know, however, is that, in fact, there was not a single death in Jerusalem for three days—not until the church holding the tomb of Jesus Christ was attacked.

"Exactly one week later, and on the same day Israel's air force bombed a nuclear facility in Iran, Mikha'il amazed the medical world when he defied science and awoke. Not only did he awaken, but other than losing the ability to speak, he almost immediately made a complete recovery."

Mikha'il stood frozen, watching attentively as the investigative feature continued. Eventually, he looked at Jasmine, a sense of relief flooding through him. He had not known how to explain to her all that had been happening to him, or how she would react. The need for deception was over.

He crossed the room to sit beside Jasmine on the end of the bed, and after tenderly rubbing her back, as if to say that all would be okay, he reached for her hand.

Together, they watched the remainder of the news report.

The investigative story followed Mikha'il to Washington and back to New York. It covered the White House dinner, where the pope stunned those watching by rising from his seat to greet Mikha'il and kiss his hand, and later relinquishing the duty of saying grace to him.

A young man and his wife, an old man, and a couple with their eight-year-old daughter were all interviewed. Each explained the remarkable miracles that had happened to them recently. A paraplegic man, unable to walk since a car accident twelve years before, got up and walked while waiting for a flight at Dulles Airport. An elderly man, blinded by disease in childhood, saw for the first time in sixty years at Manhattan's St. Patrick's Cathedral. An eight-year-old girl's disfiguring birthmark suddenly vanished while playing in Central Park.

The reporter then tied Mikha'il to each wondrous event.

Security camera footage from a departure lounge at Dulles Airport showed the man walk from his wheelchair while another camera, two gates away, recorded Mikha'il watching from a line boarding a flight to New York.

News articles reported Mikha'il's meeting at the United Nations the following Friday, and Security records indicated he left the building at 11:45 a.m. Only a ten-minute walk away, the noon mass at St. Patrick's Cathedral started. The elderly man claimed his sight was restored just as the service ended. The first thing the once-blind man saw was a stranger leave from the pew he'd been in. The man identified Mikha'il from photographs shown to him as this stranger.

It was twenty minutes after the mass had ended, a short walk away in Central Park, that the port-wine stain on the schoolgirl's face disappeared, as if it had never been there. Even though Mikha'il was not seen in the park, the location was shown as roughly halfway between the church and his grandfather's townhouse.

"Although these miraculous stories were reported to local press, they were not linked together until this investigation." The footage of the assassination attempt on Mikha'il at the palace gates was repeated, and the reporter concluded his commentary. "Regardless of whether or not you believe in God, or which religion you belong to, you have to admit, Mikha'il bin al-Rashid seems to be one extraordinary man."

The three waited in anticipation for Mikha'il's reaction.

When he showed none, Jasmine urged, "Can you at least tell us what you think?"

Although Mikha'il couldn't deny the truth, he wasn't ready to explain what had happened to him—at least not to Aisha and

Dr. Ben. He slowly motioned his hands in a few signs and then rested them in his lap.

Aisha waited for more, and when none came, overwhelmed with emotion, she lowered her shoulders, bowed her head in prayer and whispered to herself, "Praise be to Allah."

Hearing her, Dr. Ben spoke for the first time since Mikha'il had entered the room. He asked, curiosity evident in his voice, "What did he say, Jasmine?"

Not moving her gaze from Mikha'il's face, she answered, "He didn't know the blind man regained his sight."

FORTY-FOUR

ONLY TWO HOURS LATER, Aisha and Mikha'il were ushered through the hotel lobby doors by Agent Barak and a reinforced security team. Aisha was caught off-guard by the shoving and bumping of reporters and cameramen, but this time, Mikha'il paid no mind to the throng as they were rushed into a black SUV surrounded by armed soldiers.

"Good morning, you two." Waiting inside, Virginia Adams cheerfully smiled.

Returning the smile, Mikha'il nodded, and Aisha replied, "Good morning, Madam Secretary."

"I'm glad you're well, Mikha'il." As the motorcade proceeded with lights flashing, Virginia added, "We've confirmed that there was an attempt on your life yesterday, and we aren't going to take any chances. You'll be riding with me."

Virginia, too, had watched the news reports, and now she took a fleeting moment to look casually at the man seated so normally beside her. *You saved me? Can all this be true?*

She didn't betray her thoughts, though, as she firmly pressed on. "There have been some changes for today's proceedings. Prime Minister Kessel has requested that the balance of the meeting be limited only to those officials at the table. There will be no support staff, press or observers, and the palace will be closed to everyone else. Aisha, you'll squeeze into our table to interpret for Mikha'il."

"Yes, ma'am."

"Mikha'il, in light of everything that's been reported, we hoped you'd give a statement and take questions at a press conference later today."

Mikha'il signed and Aisha interpreted, "I'd rather not. They'll only twist anything I have to say."

"I see." Aware of Mikha'il's mistrust of the media, she'd been prepared for him to say no. "Well, then, perhaps Jasmine and Dr. Levine could answer the questions I'm sure the press are eager to ask."

Remembering the pact that Jasmine had insisted upon with Aisha and Dr. Ben earlier that morning, Mikha'il accepted.

"Good. We'll set it up in the hotel for this afternoon. It'll keep the media away from our meeting. You seem to be the bigger story anyway."

When Mikha'il entered the assembly room and took his seat, a hush fell over those officials already present.

Soon after, Prime Minister Kessel entered and joined the Israeli delegation. From his seat in the center of their table, he wasted little time in addressing the room. "Thank you for accepting the changes to today's meeting. What I want to discuss with you needed to be within the confidentiality of this small gathering. May I continue?"

With acceptance from all sides, he approached the podium carrying the Bible Mikha'il had given him.

Knowing all in the room would be aware of the assassination attempt, as well as the media reports through the night, he made no mention of them. Instead, he held up the Bible. "After Mikha'il spoke to us yesterday, he gave me this Bible, with a note inside. In it, he had written from three verses: two from the Hebrew scriptures of the Old Testament and one from the New. What he underlined is short and to the point, so it won't take long for me to read."

Jasmine stayed seated on the bed, only periodically asking a question or rising to pace the hotel room. All that she and Dr. Ben could agree upon was holding to the promise of denial they'd made with Aisha and Mikha'il before they left earlier that morning.

Dr. Ben, for his part, had come to Amman to address a curiosity but now had no answers for the questions asked of him or, for that matter, the questions pressing on his own mind.

He considered the many prophets in his own religion. He hadn't given much thought to the Hebrew messengers since he'd studied scripture as a youth—it had bored him.

Although neither he nor Jasmine had accepted Mikha'il's apparent transformation as simply as Aisha had, he was surprised at how comfortable Jasmine was with it. *Perhaps a reaction of shock.* He'd seen shock before, but not caused by something so unexplained.

Prime Minister Kessel took the note from the Bible and unfolded the pages. "The first is from the Book of Ezekiel." He wasn't sure if he would have read these or recommended what he was about to if he hadn't seen the news reports the night before. Either way, he was compelled by his own faith to proceed. Israel's prime minister looked up to ensure he had the attention of the entire room. "Thus says the Lord, God, 'I placed Jerusalem at the center of all nations, but she has rebelled against my regulations and has been more unjust than her surrounding nations.'

"And the second, from the prophet Isaiah." He lifted his eyes momentarily and returned them to the note. " 'In days to come, the mountain of the Lord's house shall be established as the highest of all mountains and shall be raised above the hills. All nations will stream to it. For out of Jerusalem shall go forth instruction and the word of the Lord to all of the world. The people shall hear and beat their swords into plowshares and their spears into pruning hooks.' "

Kessel flipped to the next page. "And finally, from Revelation, the last book of the Christian Bible. 'I saw the Holy City, the New Jerusalem coming down out of heaven to rest on this mountaintop. And I heard the voice, look, I am making all things new.' "

He folded the note, placed it in his jacket pocket and set the Bible on the podium. Hearing the murmurs coming from those in front of him and expecting certain resistance from his fellow Israelis, he continued, "So I say to you, the leaders of our Holy Land, there may be some merit in Mikha'il's suggestion. Regardless of what has been reported about Mikha'il—but rather because of what is right for all—perhaps it's time to deliver to the world a New Jerusalem. A Jerusalem that is not just the center of Israel's future, but the world's. As the highest mountain, it will draw all nations to it. Jerusalem can be the city of peace, of shalom, and of salaam.

"Accordingly, I would like us to devote the remainder of our day to this possibility—here, now and in the privacy of this gathering of like-minded, faithful and caring people."

The press conference at the Le Royal Hotel was, as expected, jammed with cameras, microphones and reporters. Summit officials did all they could to maintain control. From behind a curtain, and with prepared statements in hand, Dr. Ben and Jasmine approached a draped table and sat on either side of a moderator.

Dr. Ben went first and addressed the issue of the supposed lack of death in Israel as purely random. He also confirmed that Mikha'il's recovery, although uncommon, was easily explained by science and totally accepted by the medical community. After outlining Mikha'il's injuries, Dr. Ben reminded the audience that the human brain was a vastly complicated organ, capable of much and yet still little understood. He cited several examples of similar recoveries and detailed the reasons for his patient's inability to speak. He pointed out that Mikha'il's recovery was not complete, which was why he was in Amman. As directed, he took a few questions and gave brief answers.

When Jasmine stood, camera flashes lit the room.

At ease, she waited for them to subside. Unlike Dr. Ben, after referring to the prepared statement given to her by Virginia's staff, she folded it, placed it on the table and spoke with graceful sincerity, holding back any apprehension. She thanked the press for their obvious concern but assured them that Mikha'il was just a man, as any other, and insisted that any reported events, as marvelous as they seemed, were only coincidences. She patiently and comfortably answered all the questions fired at her.

Smiling with humility, she agreed that Mikha'il was a special individual, filled with selfless goodwill, and she wished more people were blessed with his noble virtues. She shared hope for a successful summit meeting and an end to the troubles affecting so many. She accepted the compliment, on behalf of Mikha'il, to any reference of divine association, but chuckling, she denied any possibility of it.

Exhausted at day's end, Mikha'il returned to his hotel room to find Jasmine, who'd only just arrived from the press conference. The couple hadn't had much time alone that morning when, in the awkward quiet, both chose not to discuss what they were thinking. Beyond Jasmine's insistence on a pledge of silence, they did not talk about the investigative report.

Mikha'il hesitated in the doorway. His head ached, and he didn't know how Jasmine was going to react now that they were alone again. He wished he was sure what the future held for them.

He was relieved to see Jasmine's smile. She rushed to him and gave him a long hug, as if nothing had changed.

He could see she was drained, though. She couldn't hold her smile, and lines of fatigue showed around her eyes.

After a gentle kiss, Mikha'il signed, "I heard you were a star this afternoon."

"All they wanted to talk about was you."

"Virginia told me that her staff thought you were a natural."

Jasmine shrugged off the compliment. "Babe, I don't care about today, or last night. I'm just so tired. Can we stay in and order room service?"

Delighted with her suggestion, Mikha'il grinned. "Whatever you'd like."

He had planned to tell her about his visions and the amazing incidents that had been reported. He wanted her insight, her understanding. However, as the evening progressed, he sensed she'd rather delay any discussion and instead enjoy a night together as a normal couple.

"Have you seen the Nur al-Din video?" Robinson asked.

"Yes, sir." Virginia Adams held the secure satellite phone to her ear. "Prime Minister Kessel and I watched it at the hotel after today's meeting. It sure makes for a lot happening here these past two days."

"Definitely. Vasquez has confirmed with the Jordanians that the body they found is Abdul-Qadir's. The Nur al-Din recording was leaked to Al Jazeera television before it was forwarded to the CIA for authentication."

"That doesn't surprise me," she commented. "The Jordanians are sympathetic to the plight of the Palestinians, particularly since they're supporting over a million of their refugees."

"What does Kessel make of all this?"

"Shin Bet believes Abdul-Qadir's presence indicates he was likely responsible for the attempt on Mikha'il's life. However, other than causing disruption, his motive is unclear."

"And what about Nur al-Din?"

"In some ways, the Israelis are relieved, and in others, quite concerned. They believe he'll make good his elimination of terrorist attacks on the innocent. He is less fanatical and irrational than Abdul-Qadir but just as committed and defiant. Apparently, he's regarded as an honorable man by his people, which worries the Israelis. They're not only concerned that he'll encourage more attacks on military forces but that, under his leadership, Islamic support for their cause may strengthen, bringing Sunni and Shia together. He might even ally with Iran, which Abdul-Qadir would never have considered."

"That wouldn't be good. Vasquez has intel that indicates the Iranians have moved their nuclear development underground but are having difficulty determining where."

"Let's hope we make progress here before the Iranians get too involved," said Virginia optimistically.

"Agreed. How'd the meeting go today?"

"Surprisingly, Kessel didn't discount Mikha'il's suggestion. In fact, he praised it. After Abu-Hakim and his Palestinian delegation got over their shock, and the other Israelis got over their knee-jerk resistance, things moved forward. Each side has much to deal with before the next summit, particularly Kessel, who'll need more support from his government. Making the Old City of Jerusalem an independent state, much like Vatican City, will be the focus of the second meeting next month."

"And Mikha'il? Will he be included?"

"I hope so. He's very much a part of this now."

"And all this talk of miracles?"

"I've gotten to know Mikha'il quite well and can confirm that he's very righteous. But to suggest he's divine?" Virginia paused, considering the impossibility of what she'd been thinking. "Well, that's another thing altogether."

Jasmine realized Mikha'il had fallen asleep. She was grateful to have him with her when he'd so nearly been taken away. Regardless of why or how he'd recovered from his injuries and the assassination attempt, Jasmine cared only that he was there.

She ran her fingertips along his chest and then softly pushed her palm in slow circles until she felt the beating of his heart fall into rhythm with hers.

Wondering if their lives had forever changed and praying that they wouldn't be parted, she rested her head just under his chin and joined him in sleep.

FORTY-FIVE

AFTER THE AMMAN MEETING, international media bounced from the story about Mikha'il to news of Yazid Abdul-Qadir's death to Nur al-Din's video. Very little time was devoted to the summit meeting, particularly since the major developments considering the future of the Old City were being kept strictly confidential.

In the thirteen days that followed Nur al-Din's video declaration, terrorist attacks around the world halted, and a general sense of relief started to take hold. Hope of an end to the intifada evolved into a true possibility of peace when no further word came from him.

But grand appearances weren't necessary. Muslim communities began to back Nur al-Din's leadership, and the jihadists acted through the vast network of covert cells and new supporters. The hiatus from violence, in effect, was only short-lived.

Bombings against both Israel and the West quickly accelerated. Attacks were escalating not only at checkpoints and military bases in Israel and occupied Palestine but also on Western forces established in the Middle East and southeastern Europe.

The world was shocked by the audacity of the strikes on peacekeeping soldiers abroad. Army barracks and troop transport vehicles in Saudi Arabia and Jordan, a sentry post at the French Embassy in Turkey and two jet-fuel tanks at the U.S. air base in Bulgaria were targeted and bombed. Although only nine civilians were lost in the mounting assaults, over two hundred peacekeeping soldiers were seriously wounded or killed.

Shia had joined Sunni. The Islamic Insurgency in Iraq and Syria gained in strength and turned outward, threatening all. And all eyes were on Iran, waiting for their next move.

Nur al-Din's led intifada had fast become greater than that of his predecessor's.

With the rapid increase in violence, Prime Minister Kessel received pressure from opposition parties to postpone the second meeting. The politician doggedly refused. In the four weeks following the first summit, he and his staff had made significant progress with both the United Nations officials and Abu-Hakim's P.A. delegation. Making the Old City an independent state had evolved from a proposal into a distinct likelihood.

Boundaries were easily defined for the less than one-half-square-mile city, completely enclosed by its ancient walls and seven narrow gates. Preliminary details for self-governance and elections, financial transfers and taxation, UN-supported policing and dual citizenships for its thirty thousand residents had been resolved. Still, the developments remained highly confidential.

After Amman, Jasmine and Mikha'il returned to New York only to find the press waiting outside the townhouse. Joining the media vigil were scores of people bringing sick and handicapped loved ones, believing in, and praying for, a miracle in the presence of Mikha'il.

The couple quickly realized a normal home life was temporarily impossible, so Virginia's staff arranged their secure travel to guarded accommodation in southern India, where Jasmine had vacationed as a young girl.

Expressing his feelings like never before, Mikha'il revealed to Jasmine insecurities carried since childhood, shared his innermost thoughts and vowed his devotion to her. She accepted all that she heard, and her love only grew stronger. He was the soul mate she'd wanted him to be.

In the privacy of their beachside bungalow, Mikha'il explained as best he could the strange occurrences that had happened to him since he'd fallen off the balcony of the Yeshiva School. He told Jasmine that he didn't have control of the happenings, nor did he know when to expect them. But he did believe they were real and couldn't understand why nothing had happened since Amman. Mikha'il tried to concentrate on a specific subject and attempted to send his thoughts to Jasmine as he had to Tariq Nur al-Din, but regardless of how hard he tried, she didn't hear him.

With no more recent mysterious occurrences, Jasmine felt convinced that the purpose of Mikha'il's visions had been fulfilled by his address at the summit and Kessel's acceptance of his proposal for the Old City. Grateful that Mikha'il had finally opened up to her, she now hoped their life together would become normal. For the first time, she accepted that Mikha'il had truly committed to her. These were the only thoughts she wanted to hold on to.

In the Red Sea, two miles off the tip of the Sinai Peninsula, the Aircraft Carrier *USS Harry Truman* and two escort destroyers cruised at idle speed.

The ships were part of the carrier group, their six-month tour extended after being delayed in the mid-Atlantic, where they'd supported salvage and investigation crews working through the waters where the commercial jets had gone down.

With the latest attack on a U.S. army base in nearby Saudi Arabia, President Robinson, demonstrating a commitment of force, deployed the three ships into the Red Sea to provide aerial reconnaissance and defense for the summit meeting.

The atmosphere in Sharm el-Sheikh contrasted significantly with that at the conclusion of the first meetings in Amman. Tension and trepidation matched any expectations for a successful outcome. The vacation oasis in the Sinai Desert was transformed into a heavily fortified military zone. Egyptian and American forces lined major roadways and every intersection. Overhead, recon helicopters and pairs of fighter jets crisscrossed the cobalt-blue sky.

The meetings were moved from the Congress Center to the Four Seasons Resort, where summit participants and officials were staying, eliminating the need for ground travel. The gathering was limited to those who'd attended the last day of the meeting in Amman. Other guests and media were prohibited from the resort, although on the first day, access was granted to a BBC crew from London.

Given that so much was still being reported about Mikha'il—especially in light of his refusal to appear publicly, sparking rumors about the reasons for his attendance—Virginia hoped Jasmine could serve as an appropriate diversion.

Knowing what her coworkers wanted, and how to give it to them, Jasmine once again performed flawlessly. The interview was immediately aired on the BBC, and segments were shown on other networks around the world. Jasmine spoke of a normal life with Mikha'il, their family histories and the time they'd shared over the previous five years. She showed photographs and video of Mikha'il and their life together. She constantly stressed that her and Mikha'il's desire was a freedom for all peoples and a peaceful solution to the pestilence enveloping the world.

In conclusion, Jasmine criticized the media for reporting on so much violence and suffering, seeming to show only the bad in the world and, perhaps, adding to it by sensationalizing events. She challenged her colleagues to emulate the conscience of man and also present the good that existed.

Virginia's hunch had been more than accurate. While Mikha'il had ironically become the voice of hope, Jasmine had fast become the face of it. Unfortunately, Jasmine's success was not paralleled at the summit meeting.

Israeli concern over strengthening Muslim support for Nur al-Din marred the Old City discussions. Umar Abu-Hakim was accused of losing the endorsement of his people.

Sympathetic to the growing unease, while concerned about their own support faltering, Virginia and Kessel both had difficulty focusing on the purpose of the meeting. At times they, too, got caught up in the bickering.

"How can we consider such an offering when more than seven hundred million Muslims surrounding Israel don't want peace?" stressed a senior Israeli delegate.

In defense of his people, Abu-Hakim responded, "By far the vast majority of Muslims are law-abiding and peaceful people, living in accordance with the words of our Qur'an. Like you, we only seek a peaceful outcome."

"Okay, let's agree that ninety-nine percent are peaceful, as you say," rebutted the Israeli official. "That leaves one percent that aren't—seven million potential terrorists bent on our destruction."

Mikha'il, who'd only observed until then, stood up. He waited until he had the attention of all those in the room. He did not have to wait long.

As a moment of relative quiet began, Mikha'il gestured to Aisha for interpretation and then started signing to all. "Tell me, which of you is the dove, and which is the fox?"

The two men, vehemently opposing each other in argument seconds before, remained silent, not daring to reply.

Mikha'il opened his arms to everyone in the room before signing, "I invite any to answer, from either side. Which of you is the dove, and which is the fox?"

As he'd anticipated, no one spoke up. Each considered himself or herself as fighting on the side of right—and each was sure the other side was immoral and unjust. Not wanting to openly insult the other, all in the assembly chose the same response: to sit quietly.

When no reply came, Mikha'il responded, "Each is the same, as you are each the same. Both the dove and the fox are motivated, as all species are, by the natural instinct to provide for and protect their young and future generations.

"When you tear at the nest or the den, threatening the safety of those inside, will the dove and the fox not strike out? When one is provoked, is retaliation not inevitable? Is it not the desire of all man to provide a better existence for their children?"

Into the quiet, he continued, "When a man—no matter what man—is taught he's superior to another, is his fellow man not made lesser? When one is told to fear the lesser and at the same time shown how to hate him, will this hatred not fester into those generations that follow? The pain spares none, and all of mankind suffers.

"Are you the fox or the dove? It does not matter. You only believe the dove is pure and the fox not because of what you've been taught through stories and tradition."

After Mikha'il and Aisha sat down, Prime Minister Kessel recognized the opportunity. "You're implying that we're the same? Neither of us is right or wrong?"

"It would appear as such," Mikha'il responded. "Even here, you act the same."

"And this Nur al-Din?" asked Kessel. "Is he the same?"

Mikha'il signed, "He strikes as he believes best and with only that which he can."

"So what do you suggest?" the Israeli prime minister asked.

"Extend your olive branch."

Following Aisha's interpretation, the senior Israeli official forcefully questioned Mikha'il. "If we do, will we not appear as if we are giving in to terrorists?"

Kessel countered on Mikha'il's behalf. "Or simply making a peace offering to our enemy."

A few minutes later, during a brief hiatus in the meeting, the young prime minister succeeded in convincing his respected statesman to withdraw his challenge. Once the delegates returned, dialogue in the meeting room quickly focused on the independence of Jerusalem's Old City. The resistance eased, and eventually, the assembly reached agreement and began to consider how to announce news of the intended free state.

Evaluating each alternative raised, Prime Minister Kessel suggested a celebratory announcement in the plaza of the Old City itself. "We need to act immediately and end this conflict. Friday, three weeks from now, is exactly one year since that day in the Old City—the day when violence ignited this crisis. I recommend that on the anniversary of this dreadful event, we extinguish this inferno and officially announce the commencement of a new era of peace and goodwill."

In solidarity, everyone in the assembly stood to applaud.

When the second day's meeting ended, late in the evening, Aaron Kessel approached Virginia and Mikha'il. "I thought you'd like this back, Mikha'il. It seems to have served its purpose."

Smiling, Mikha'il nodded and took his grandmother's Bible.

Turning to Virginia, Kessel added, "Abu-Hakim and I have decided that we should hold a press conference tomorrow to publicize these developments and the official announcement in Jerusalem next month."

"I agree," she replied. "I'll make the arrangements."

Kessel looked to Mikha'il. "And I was hoping you and Jasmine would attend tomorrow."

Virginia interjected, "I have a better idea. Jasmine's already done a great job with the press here these past two days. Perhaps Mikha'il can publicly deliver a message of hope at the official announcement in the Old City next month. He was, after all, the hero there a year ago."

"You're right. That'd be far more appropriate," enthused Kessel. "Mikha'il, would you?"

Finding the encouragement in the faces of both Virginia and Aisha hard to resist, Mikha'il reluctantly signed, "I guess I could."

Virginia was quick to reply. "We don't have to make it official now. You can decide the week before."

Realizing his journey was ending and that he would soon share a regular life with Jasmine, Mikha'il expressed more optimism. "If I do give an address, and if it is truly to be a free city of peace, can we allow access to all peoples and not shroud it with a show of military might as we have here?"

Prime Minister Kessel answered with optimistic assuredness. "We'll do our best, Mikha'il. We'll do our very best."

IV

THE MESSAGE

So that the Messenger can bear witness for you,
And you can bear witness for others.

Muhammad
Qur'an
Al-Hajj, 22:78
Medina, Saudi Arabia, AD 630

FORTY-SIX

SITTING WITH DAVID CAPLAN in the informal parlor next to his office, Aaron Kessel waited for the arrival of his guests. By a large bay window, overlooking a perfect garden in which spring flowers bloomed in the midday sunshine, the two men discussed the prime minister's plans for Mikha'il that day.

"It's important that Mikha'il understand the struggles of the Jewish people, particularly during the past century, and that he recognize the magnitude of what we're about to offer."

"We've made the arrangements at the memorial."

"Good," replied the prime minister as a soft knock sounded on the door.

"That'll be them, sir."

Both men stood and approached the double doors.

"Good morning, Mikha'il, Jasmine," Kessel said cheerily, opening the doors. "I'd like you to meet Commander David Caplan, the director of the Shin Bet, responsible for all national security."

"We last met under very different circumstances, Ms. Desai," David said respectfully. "I'm glad all is so much better now."

"Thank you, Commander. Mikha'il and I are appreciative of everything your people have done for us."

It was the first time David had seen Mikha'il since he'd ordered him evacuated from the Temple Mount. David gripped his hand firmly. "It's an honor, Mikha'il."

Once the four were seated in the cluster of tub chairs by the window, Prime Minister Kessel said, "Thank you for putting this day aside for me. Is everything to your liking at the hotel?"

"Yes, very much so," replied Jasmine. "We didn't expect such a large suite, and the white roses are my favorite."

Proudly, Mikha'il signed, "We are, in a way, celebrating our anniversary. We first met during your reception for the press at the King David five years ago, when we were here covering your election."

After Jasmine interpreted Mikha'il's words, Kessel chuckled. "I remember that day, and with all the media coverage of you two, how could I not know that? Speaking of the media, Mikha'il, I'm glad you did, but I was surprised to see you make such a public appearance this morning."

The couple had arrived at the King David Hotel early to spend a few days celebrating their anniversary. An hour before leaving for the prime minister's office, they'd met with reporters at a breakfast press conference planned by summit organizers. It was the first time the press at large had been given the opportunity to direct questions to Mikha'il.

Standing rigidly at Jasmine's side, he'd awkwardly signed short answers that she interpreted on his behalf. Together, they announced that he would deliver a public address the coming Friday during the speeches in the Old City.

Mikha'il signed, "Virginia thought it would be good preparation for me."

"Very prudent of her. She'll be arriving tomorrow evening with most of the others. We've done our best to meet your request, Mikha'il. Other than the hotel, the city will be open to everyone. We're expecting more than double the fifty thousand who attended last year's meeting." Kessel turned to David and invited him to continue. "Commander."

David addressed Mikha'il and Jasmine with calm professionalism. "Starting tonight, after the last of the regular hotel guests have checked out, the hotel will be fortified with forces to protect the dignitaries arriving as early as tomorrow morning. Security forces in the city will be minor by comparison. Local police, undercover agents and a minimum of soldiers will line the streets. During the announcements this Friday, other than the command trailer, military forces will be held back and discreetly camouflaged. Our air force will be on high alert, but not visible. The only aircraft in the skies will be prescreened media helicopters, and we're expecting only two."

Pleased, Mikha'il signed, "I'm grateful for your efforts."

"It's obviously important to you, and you've steered us well these past two months," the prime minister said squarely. "But be assured that, although Muslim attacks have ceased in anticipation of this announcement, we still expect the usual protesters, and at the slightest indication of concern, Commander Caplan will release our defense forces without regard."

Mikha'il nodded in acceptance.

Kessel's tone lightened. "As for the speeches, other than the Temple Mount, which we'll keep clear for obvious reasons, loud speakers will be spread throughout the Old City, and video screens will provide written translations in Hebrew, Arabic and English. With the assistance of your interpreter, your words will be heard by everyone in attendance."

"Thank you, Mr. Prime Minister," Jasmine replied for Mikha'il, reaching for his hand. "I'm sure that will be fine."

"I'm confident, as well, Jasmine. This day will be monumental for so many, but especially for Jews around the world. It's important that you understand what exactly we're offering.

"I'm sure you know no people have endured as much as the Jewish people have. Still, through our perseverance, unity and conviction in our beliefs, we have survived. Not only have we survived, but we've made great contributions in every corner of the world, from the arts to the sciences, from invention to discovery.

But it's only been in the last decades that our ancestral lands have been returned to us, and with them, we have pledged never to be defenseless again. Now, after only a short time having them in our possession, we offer our beloved Old City to all."

Mikha'il began to move his hands.

Before Jasmine could start interpreting for him, Kessel gently raised one hand and interrupted them. "Please don't comment yet. I have asked Commander Caplan to accompany you to the memorial dedicated to those lives stolen in the Holocaust. If you don't mind, you'll be brought back here afterward. We can have an early dinner, and I'd be most interested in your comments then."

"Whatever you think is best," Jasmine interpreted for Mikha'il. "We've cleared the day for you."

"Thank you," said the Israeli prime minister, "and remember, while this evil can lurk in the distorted faith of one soul, its madness can overwhelm many."

Letting their guests view the exhibits in their own time and appreciate everything they represented, Deborah Barak and Commander Caplan followed Jasmine and Mikha'il through Jerusalem's Holocaust museum.

Although Mikha'il felt uncomfortable that the museum had been closed for their private viewing, he didn't dwell on his uneasiness. Instead, with Jasmine close at his side, he moved slowly and quietly along.

The needless loss of life sickened both of them.

Faded photographs showed people with cheerful faces, bright eyes and smiles, eking out a living just as any other would. The stories printed beside the black-and-white photos told of the everyday and the mundane—men and women working and living together, barbers, farmers, bankers, bricklayers and garment makers, parents and children, husbands and wives, brothers and sisters, family and friends, old and young alike.

There were displays of objects, remnants of unforgotten lives: shoes, many with laces still untied; eyeglasses, some cracked and others chipped; hairbrushes clinging onto a few last strands; unfinished knitting; little toy trucks and china dolls, never to be adored by tiny hands again; aged books with bookmarks unmoved.

More photos depicted those same people locked behind heavily guarded barbed wire fences. Their smiles were gone, their joy extinguished. Men, women and children starved and humiliated beyond recognition—dignity, rightfully belonging to all, stolen. Victims of the brutality of loathing and prejudice, unable to defend themselves, these people waited for their deaths as they smelled their loved ones burn.

Detailed lists gave accounts of those marched in and the naked bodies carried out, piled into heaping graves or incinerated into fine ash and gray smoke. An entire nation of people, nearly snuffed from existence.

Mikha'il and Jasmine carefully studied the displays and photographs. The enormity of this unimaginable tragedy hit the couple as crushing grief, chilling their bodies.

Mikha'il began to swing his head in different directions. A faint, yet bothersome, ringing had come to his ears, and as the noise grew, he looked around, trying to locate where it was coming from. Soon, the sound transformed itself into a crying, an eerie jumble of voices, sobbing and calling out for help. The plea grew louder and louder and came from every direction.

He gripped Jasmine's hand tighter and looked at her. But she just went on, silently reviewing the articles in the display. "How can you bear it?" he signed and pressed his hands tight over his ears.

"What? The photographs?" Jasmine said, immediately concerned for him.

He shook his head hard and signed, "No, no. The voices. The crying."

"I don't hear anything."

As she spoke, an intense shaking wracked his body. His face contorted in pain, and he clutched his forehead.

"What is it? Are you okay?" she cried out.

He fell to his knees and braced himself with his forearms. Jasmine desperately tried to hold him up. Struggling for control, Mikha'il sucked in deep breaths and fought to push away the image of the unbearable torture these people had suffered.

FORTY-SEVEN

COMMANDER CAPLAN AND ONE OF HIS AGENTS held Mikha'il up as they guided him from the memorial and onto a bench near the exit.

For long moments, Mikha'il attempted to regain his composure.

Leaning into him, Jasmine gently rubbed his back. "What happened? Do you feel better?"

He nodded and raised his face to the sky.

A gentle rain fell, and it felt good on his closed eyes.

"Well, I'm not taking any chances," declared Caplan. "We're taking him to the Hadassah. Agent Barak—"

Mikha'il shook his head in disapproval and signed, "I'm all right. I just needed some fresh air."

Caplan watched him closely. "Let's go back to the hotel then. Maybe we can have Dr. Levine meet us there."

Outside the King David, the media and public had already begun gathering. Security was minimal, as Mikha'il was not scheduled to return for hours, and the heavier forces wouldn't arrive until later in the evening. The few agents on the scene formed a protective cordon around the couple. Inside the human wall, Caplan firmly held Mikha'il's left arm and Jasmine his right while Agent Barak pressed from behind.

Progress through the crowd was slower than Caplan liked. Cameras and cell phones were shoved too close. David realized the potential for danger, and it worried him. He barked forward to his men, "Push them back harder. We need to get through quickly."

Seconds later, Deborah saw the unmistakable sheen of metal. She screamed out, "Gun!"

The loud snap of gunshot echoed as she and Caplan leaped to take Jasmine and Mikha'il to the ground.

For Mikha'il, now lying on the wet walkway, this was very different from the shooting at the Amman palace gates. Blood was quickly seeping into his clothing. He could feel its warmth against his skin, and yet there was no pain. He could see pools of crimson rapidly spreading around him and wondered about his condition until he heard the awful, unimaginable words.

"She's been hit!"

The crowd was screaming in panic, some trying to escape, others to see what happened. A pair of agents held a struggling man firmly in their grasp. Assured that they had the shooter, Agent Barak yelled to the crowd, "Back off, back off," while rising to her knees and cautiously turning Jasmine onto her back. She opened Jasmine's blazer and tore at the bloodied lower buttons on her blouse. Seeing the blood gushing from Jasmine's abdomen, Deborah tried to stanch it.

"Move! I'll take over! You get help," shouted Caplan, jumping off Mikha'il.

David ripped off his jacket and, making a ball of it, pushed it against Jasmine's wound. Within seconds, his hands were soaked.

At first, Mikha'il did not move. He could only stare at Jasmine's beautiful face as red rolled out of her mouth.

She seemed calm, almost serene, her eyes open and alert. Caplan spoke to her. "You'll be fine, Jasmine, just keep breathing for me. That's all you have to do. Help is on the way."

Every cell in Mikha'il's body was tight with fear. *No. No! This isn't right!* He slid beside her. *This can't be.*

As best she could, Jasmine smiled up at him. *I can hear you now, Mikha'il.*

Then let me help you, the way I helped those in the Old City!

I prayed we'd stay together. She gazed into his eyes intently.

Let me save you. You know I can.

No. This is the way.

No! It's not. Let me help you! Mikha'il concentrated, exerting his will.

You can't save me, Mikha'il. That's not how this must be. Jasmine somehow blocked his efforts, and he desperately tried to break through.

He held her rain-drenched head off the cold sidewalk. *You can't go, Jasmine. Please let me help you. I can't lose you!*

It's all right, my love. We must sacrifice. Stay strong. The color was rapidly leaching from her face. Her breathing was weak, but she managed one final smile. *It's so peaceful, Mikha'il. It's wonderful.*

No. No. No. Don't go. Please don't go. No! You can't go!

She closed her eyes. Her body did not twitch. It did not jerk. It simply lay still.

Mikha'il looked into the gloomy sky and screamed at the dark, turbulent clouds. The rain intensified and washed away the tears that rolled down his face.

He shook and sobbed like an infant, not daring to let go of the one woman he'd loved. At the steps of the King David, and in a hardening rain, Mikha'il kissed Jasmine's lips for the last time.

FORTY-EIGHT

HER HAIRBRUSH.

Mikha'il stared at Jasmine's hairbrush. He ran his fingers through the bristles, feeling the entangled strands of her hair, remembering a similar brush he'd seen in the museum.

He picked up her favorite perfume and gently sprayed it in the air. He shut his eyes and inhaled. Her scent filled his lungs. He sensed her presence and quickly opened his eyes.

He was alone.

In the mirror of the vanity, Mikha'il saw Jasmine's clothes hanging in the closet behind him. He turned and slid his hands through the hanging sleeves of a black silk dress before sinking to the floor beside her shoes, neatly lined up in pairs. He reached for one that he knew she liked best. He guided his fingers along the opening and placed his hand inside. Sitting on the cold ceramic floor, Mikha'il began to cry uncontrollably, as he had many times throughout the night.

"We're not leaving this time, Mikha'il." Dr. Ben called out from the other side of the door.

"We're staying until you let us in. Please, Mikha'il," begged Aisha.

Although each felt puzzled that he couldn't save her—if he truly was what they thought—they were more worried about their friend and, for hours, had been returning to his door, knocking and trying to talk to him. Regardless of who or what he had become, whether he was or was not, they knew he'd been through much more than any could bear, and they didn't want him to be alone.

Dr. Ben knocked again.

Wearily, Mikha'il opened the door.

The heavy clouds had blown through overnight, and the new day's brightness could not be blocked out by the translucent sheers covering the high windows. Croissants, fruit bowls and three glasses of orange juice sat untouched on the sideboard. Dr. Ben and Aisha spoke in subdued voices to Mikha'il, doing all they could to relieve his grief.

He sat in a chair across from them, his face expressionless.

Trying anything, Aisha broke the growing silence. "Ms. Adams has moved her flight up. She's been flying all night and will be here this afternoon."

Dr. Ben added, "I spoke with her just before she left Washington, and she agrees with me about the pain you experienced yesterday afternoon. That's not just another headache. We'd both feel much more comfortable if you were checked out at the Hadassah. What happened to you in the memorial was caused by something."

For the first time, Mikha'il showed emotion, signing abruptly with a shake of his head, "I've already said no! I am not going to any hospital."

Not needing an interpretation from Aisha, Dr. Ben said gently, "I don't think that's wise."

Mikha'il changed the subject. "Tell me about him."

"About who?" asked Dr. Ben, after Aisha told him what Mikha'il had signed.

Showing no fatigue, Mikha'il's eyes narrowed and focused on Dr. Ben. He firmly signed in reply.

"He wants to know about the man who shot her," Aisha said.

The doctor hesitated but then nodded. It had been all over the news. "His name is Emmanuel Judkowitz. He's known to police as a local vagrant. It seems he was acting alone. All that's being reported is that he's homeless and has drifted between prison and institutions all his life."

"Where is he now?" Mikha'il signed.

"He's being held by the Shin Bet."

"I want to see him—now."

Dr. Ben delayed answering, trying to assess Mikha'il's resolve. Seeing the determination, he said, "All right. I'll call Commander Caplan."

In the stark gray interrogation room, Mikha'il waited for Jasmine's murderer. He wanted to meet the man face to face, stare into his evil eyes and peer into his icy soul. Mikha'il required justice and redemption. The anger surging within him needed to be released.

Three agents escorted a handcuffed man wearing orange coveralls into the room. The agents did not speak. They seated the man directly across from his visitors at the small metal table and left the room.

The prisoner was not what Mikha'il expected.

Not much older than Mikha'il, he was tall but wiry and thin. His bony face, partly covered by frizzled graying locks and a shabby beard, was blank, and he paid no attention to Mikha'il. Instead, the man jerked his head from side to side, his gaze darting around the room.

You're Emmanuel Judkowitz? Mikha'il thought that this meek-looking man could not have committed such a heinous act. Perhaps the agents brought in the wrong prisoner.

The twitching man, not seeming to mind that his hands were cuffed, said cheerfully, "Yes, that's me, all right. Emmanuel Judkowitz, but my friends call me Manny. Yup, they call me Manny, or sometimes they call me Jude. Manny or Jude, Jude or Manny. That's what they call me."

Manny or Jude.

"Yup, you said it right," he answered, nodding with a friendly smile. "Manny or Jude, Jude or Manny."

Aisha looked at Mikha'il curiously.

"I won't need you," he quickly signed to her. "Would you mind waiting outside for me?"

She stayed seated for a second, confused, and then stood up. "Of course."

How about I call you Manny?

"That's me, Manny." The man fidgeted.

You can hear me then, Manny?

"Yes. Why? Can't you hear me?"

Yes, I can hear you. Mikha'il did not flinch. *So tell me, why did you do this terrible thing?*

"Do what? What did I do now?" Clearly agitated, Manny twisted in his seat.

You killed her. Mikha'il was careful to refrain from showing any emotion or inflection.

"Who? Killed who?" Manny nervously rubbed his thumbs against the callused underside of his fingertips. Fear entered his face, and his eyes widened. "Who'd I kill now?"

The woman at the hotel. You killed her yesterday afternoon.

"Oh, you mean her," he said with relief. "It was the voices. The voices told me to do that."

Voices—whose voices?

"The voices in my head." He bounced his cuffed hands off his forehead three times.

Voices in your head, like my voice?

"No, I don't hear your voice in my head." Manny laughed giddily. "I hear your voice in my ears."

Mikha'il understood that this simple man could not distinguish between hearing words through his own ears or in his thoughts. *Then whose voices do you hear in your head?*

"I always hear voices in my head. Even now, I hear the voices."

What are they saying?

"Run, Manny, run!" he yelled out.

You say you always hear voices?

"Yup, they're always there. Except when I take the pills, but I don't like them pills." Manny's grin became a sour frown. "The voices stop when I'm forced to take them, but the pills make me feel so sad."

Sad?

"Yes, aren't you ever sad?" The prisoner peered into Mikha'il's face.

I'm sad now.

"I'm sorry that you're sad." Manny's frown deepened and his face cringed. "I don't like being sad."

Neither do I, Manny. Neither do I.

"What're they doing?" asked Morton Milner, after joining his commander, who watched through the one-way mirror and listened on the speaker.

"I don't know," replied Caplan quietly, not taking his eyes off the two men in the interrogation room.

"It's like he's answering questions, but Mikha'il isn't saying anything."

"Look at Judkowitz. I don't think he even realizes what he's saying. He's just hearing voices again."

"I guess you're right," agreed Milner. "It's the only logical answer."

"Anything from the gun?"

"Nothing. An old Colt, the serial number cleanly filed off, like it was never there. No prints—somehow, not even his." Milner hesitated. "He's sticking to the story?"

"Still says he found the gun in a trash can," David said, exasperated. "He insists voices told him it was there."

Mikha'il, too, observed Manny. Although sadness and guilt remained, Mikha'il's anger toward the prisoner had been replaced by empathy. He realized that Manny was too delusional to know either evil or hatred. Rather, Manny's true spirit was hidden behind a deforming mask that only distorted his understanding of faith.

Mikha'il reached across the table and cupped both of his hands over the worried man's trembling ones.

Within moments, Manny relaxed. "The voices. The voices are gone," he cried out.

Yes, Manny. And they won't come back. Mikha'il smiled placidly into the joyful man's face.

"But your sadness." He tensed. "It was me that did this terrible thing. I know it now. Oh God, no! Please no."

It's okay, Manny. All is well. I forgive you, and so will he.

FORTY-NINE

WITH AISHA INTERPRETING, Mikha'il spoke on the telephone with Jasmine's parents. Respecting Jasmine's Hindu beliefs, Mikha'il sadly agreed on the details of her funeral arrangements.

Jasmine's body would be flown to Delhi and cremated immediately. Mikha'il was to remain in Jerusalem for his speech, although he was unsure whether he still had the will to deliver any message. Afterward, Mikha'il would depart for India, as Jasmine's family had agreed to delay the funeral ceremony until his arrival.

For the Hindu, death was just another path. Jasmine's ashes would be returned to the source of life. With Mikha'il next to them, Jasmine's parents would scatter their daughter's ashes over the rippling waters of the Ganges River, where her soul would be freed—born again into a new and unknown life. A life that Mikha'il would not be a part of. And yet he felt comforted to think that her precious spirit would be rewarded in its next existence.

Still, without Jasmine, Mikha'il felt no purpose. Life for him was meaningless. When he walked, it seemed as if his feet didn't touch the ground, for Jasmine was his gravity, and with her gone, there was no reason to stay bound to the earth.

In his deeply saddened state, he shared only a few words with Virginia after she arrived. Condolences came in from everywhere, including the Vatican and President Robinson, but Mikha'il responded to none. He refused to have anyone around him, not even Dr. Ben or Aisha. He sought the isolation of his hotel room but didn't turn the television on, knowing what he'd see. He tried to eat, but had no appetite. Eventually darkness set in, and Mikha'il endured another sleepless night.

Once the thin light of dawn had crept into his room, Mikha'il left the insulating walls of the suite. Many of the dignitaries and event officials had arrived through the night, but at this early hour, the King David's halls and lobby were quiet.

Unnoticed by security and hotel staff, Mikha'il slipped into the hotel gardens. He felt the warmth of the sun on his face and drew in a heavy breath, his lungs sensing the fresh spring dew. But after spotting the bench under the broad canopy of the oldest tree on the property, his brief tranquility was shattered, replaced by the painful memory of laughing with Jasmine the day they'd met there.

Mikha'il walked to the bench and sat down. He closed his eyes, reliving every detail of the wonderful day his life had bonded with hers.

"Excuse me, this is my tree that you doze under." Mikha'il heard the firm voice resonate from very close by. "If it is under my tree you choose to lie, you cannot sleep. You must awaken."

Feeling a slight poke in his arm, Mikha'il struggled to open his eyes.

Next to him, a man draped in orange robes sat with his legs crossed. The man smiled. "Ah, it is good that you raise your eyelids to welcome the sunshine that surrounds you."

Mikha'il and his host sat next to the twisting trunk of a mighty tree, under its thick boughs. All about them, golden grasslands blew in a nimble breeze, and a stream, meandering alongside them, sparkled in the sun. The bench, the hotel and the city were gone.

"Who are you? Where are we now?" asked Mikha'il, with slight annoyance.

"I am the one my father called Siddhartha," the man replied. "I am the ninth incarnation of the Lord Vishnu, and in his embodiment,

I am the Hindu who became the Buddha. And you, you are the one sent to me for awakening."

"I suppose that maybe I am," said Mikha'il, tiredly readying for yet another lesson. "But what's the use?"

"You have come to this place deeply troubled. I sense much struggle and sadness within you."

Mikha'il bowed his head, but this time it was not in respect but, rather, as a way to gain control of his emotions. He slowly lifted his chin. "And this place? What is it?"

The Buddha opened his arms as wide as he could. "This is the center."

"Center of what?"

"It is the tree at the root of all life. In an effort to find the secret of fulfillment, I have found the truth here and achieved enlightenment. And what is it that brings you here, suffering as you do?"

Frustrated, Mikha'il did not respond. He coldly looked at the annoying man seated next to him.

The Buddha patiently returned his stare. At the top of his head, his black hair was tied tightly. He had a broad physique that displayed strength and confidence, and his clear bronze complexion, perfect looks and dark shining eyes radiated sincerity and purity.

"It matters not when you answer. Time is not relevant here," said the Buddha, slowly turning away from Mikha'il and resting the backs of his hands on the knees of his crossed legs. He tilted his head down and closed his eyes.

Mikha'il once again felt alone. As the discomfort of isolation intensified, his obstinacy yielded, and he said quietly, "You found truth here. Well, I've lost my only truth—what I loved most."

"Jasmine." The Buddha opened his eyes.

"She's all that matters. It's not right that she's been taken from me."

"Not right?"

"No, definitely not. I've come to realize that both life and the world we live in are unfair. I feel cheated. I've been chosen to deliver great purpose and given wonderful abilities—powers that I can't understand, let alone control. And still I couldn't save her."

"You could not save her, or she did not want you to?"

Ignoring the question, Mikha'il carried on. "I tried so hard to, but she died anyway. I accepted my destiny with an open mind, but now its cost is too high."

"In your loss, you seek answers, but unable to find them, you are tormented by frustration. Your mind is no longer open. You have closed it."

Mikha'il shook his head and shrugged. "I can't erase the guilt and anger I feel."

"Where does the guilt lie?" the Buddha asked.

"With myself, for exposing her to danger."

"And the anger?"

"With whoever laid this burden upon me." Mikha'il again shook his head, this time with vehemence. "It's not right. It's not fair."

"If there were sunshine every day, there would be no rain, and the earth would become dry." The Buddha paused. "May I tell you a tale of two farmers and two sons?"

Mikha'il didn't answer.

Regardless, the Buddha started. "Both farmers were bountiful. They each had a son whom they loved with all their hearts. Neither farmer loved his son any more than the other did.

"The first farmer did everything for his son, gave to him everything he could. Each year, the farmer cultivated all the lands and delivered the harvest himself. Every day, the farmer worked alone. The son was pampered, protected from the earth, from hardened windstorms of dust to the mud brought by torrential downpours. In the evenings, the son feasted upon glorious foods prepared for him. The son took the bounty that the land bore and never knew struggle, pain or hardship. All came easily to him.

"The second farmer shared responsibility for the lands with his son. The son learned how to seed and prepare the earth. He worked hard, over long hours. Together with his father, he struggled through the deep mud and battled fierce storms. In the evenings, the son soothed his aching back and wretched body by a warm fire. Then early each morning, the son rose with the father, and together, they returned to the land. At the end of each year, a wonderful meal of thanks was prepared.

"The first son never experienced joy or celebration. He was completely dependent upon the father and, as such, did not know pride or worthiness. The first son did not come to respect the glory in the land nor realize any of the virtues within himself.

"But the second son accepted the struggle required to garner the bounty of the land. He was soaked by the rains needed to nourish the soil and was moved by the winds necessary to change the seasons. He learned to relish the satisfaction of achievement and worked to improve both the land and himself.

"Without suffering, there cannot be joy. While the first son never experienced emotion, the second son was filled with it, the most splendid feelings being worth, happiness and, above all, love. Without knowing emotion, one cannot freely choose to give it up and truly realize so much more."

As the wise man spoke, Mikha'il's petulance was gradually replaced by humility, but his fury did not easily retreat. Apologetically, Mikha'il responded sadly to the parable, "I understand the moral of your story and appreciate its purpose, but I've sacrificed far too much."

Showing no sympathy, the Buddha said sternly, "Although it is the greatest sacrifice that is most noticed, it is not in the loss itself but, rather, one's willingness to detach from it, that adoration can be bequeathed."

"But my anger remains."

"A mere fable will not persuade your mind to surrender that anger. The struggle is your responsibility." The Buddha looked deep into Mikha'il's green eyes. "You must resolve it yourself. Even as you speak, you do so with *I*'s and *my*'s."

Mikha'il winced and shrugged helplessly.

"Close your eyes and hold your breath for as long as you can."

He followed the instruction.

"Good. Now try to remove the *I* from your thought. Do not think of the self. The self is limiting. Concentrate on the space that surrounds you. The space is limitless."

Mikha'il did so. But after a moment, he exhaled and opened his eyes.

The Buddha shook his head in disapproval. "No, do not open your eyes. Do not breathe."

"How can I not breathe?"

"Ignore the instinct of the body. Connect to the world around you with your mind. Come, once more."

Mikha'il tried again.

"Very good." The Buddha's voice had lightened, his words slowed. "Now, transport yourself deep into thought and leave the loneliness and sadness behind you. Wipe away not only your sorrow, your anger and your guilt, but all emotion. Release yourself from all that you are attached to. Have no desire and no loss. Escape the self. Let what you love most go, and experience only the emptiness that remains. You must accept the noble truth. Suffering ends when craving for your attachments does. Follow this path and alleviate your craving. In the absence of all, you will find the absolute center, the real origin of everything that exists. Not only feel it but grasp the natural energy that exists there, only in *Nirvana.*"

Mikha'il did not open his eyes. He did not move. His breathing had completely stopped.

The Buddha continued, "Here is true enlightenment, the energy and the life source of the universe. You have lived many, many lives, and now, in this one, are blessed with enlightenment. Embrace it. See the pureness in the center of its light. Be mindful of its reality and speak its truth."

Mikha'il strayed from all time and all thought. Time no longer mattered. It was as if but a minute passed and, in the same instant, the entire age of the earth. As the days turned to darkness, the light that followed led into night and again into dawn. The cycle was infinite.

"Mikha'il, Mikha'il, wake up."

When he heard the delicate feminine voice, Mikha'il's heart skipped a beat, but he did not flinch. He did not react. He was not sad. He did not feel emotion.

He slowly raised his eyelids and saw the garden of the King David Hotel. He had somehow left the bench and now sat with his back against the tree's broad trunk. The Buddha was gone. Aisha stood before him.

Mikha'il struggled to sign. "How long have I been here?"

"Most of the day," Aisha replied. "Security blocked off the garden so you wouldn't be disturbed. Ms. Adams told them to let you sleep."

Although well rested, Mikha'il's body was weak. It did not readily respond. Gently resting his head against the rough bark, he took in a full breath.

"Mikha'il, they're coming—so many are coming," Aisha said with excitement.

"Who's coming?"

Aisha didn't have time to respond.

Virginia did instead. "It's because of Jasmine—her death, only hours after you announced together that you'd address those attending in the Old City this Friday. It's all that's been playing over the news." Virginia swallowed, trying to hold back her tears. "People are coming from all parts of the world to show their respect for both her and you. Every hotel is booked solid, and the borders are flooded. Hundreds of thousands are expected. They still don't know how many. Flights from everywhere are sold out. Charters are being added by the hour."

Aisha reached out to touch Mikha'il gently on the shoulder, "They're all coming to Jerusalem, just to see you! It's like Jasmine's asked them here."

FIFTY

IT WAS JUST PAST NOON FRIDAY when the motorcade pulled out of the King David's circular driveway and entered the cordoned-off street. Although flashing red lights signaled the approach of the slow-moving convoy, no sirens wailed. A calm had blanketed the city.

Security forces barricaded the designated route into the Old City. Every third police officer held an automatic rifle, and all stood at attention, shoulder to shoulder, along the curbs of the one-mile route. Within a two-mile radius of the ancient walls, every street and even the smallest of laneways were completely blockaded and closed to all vehicles.

Packed onto those roads, sidewalks, parks and lawns, people waited patiently for the dignitaries' arrival into the Old City plaza and the commencement of speeches. But above all, they waited for Mikha'il.

More than seven hundred thousand had swelled into Jerusalem to witness Mikha'il's public address. From many nations and every religion, they'd come to the hallowed city.

"There aren't many protesters," Aisha said thoughtfully. "And even they seem quiet."

Seated across from her and Agent Barak, Dr. Ben watched Aisha peering out the tinted window, fascinated by those around them, but no one else spoke.

Wearing a business suit, Dr. Ben was dressed much like the other men traveling in the limos. In contrast, Mikha'il looked informal in black trousers, a casual white shirt, open at the collar, and leather sandals. Not even Virginia had dared an attempt to convince him to dress otherwise.

Only Deborah responded to Aisha's observation, and then just with a slight nod and absent murmur. The mood inside the pristine vehicle remained somber.

In the silence, Dr. Ben glanced through the window. He realized all that had happened was far greater than science, that something more lay in the faith of man, and Mikha'il was its servant.

He turned to him and said quietly, "All these people have come, not just to show homage to you and Jasmine, or to watch you speak, but for something far more important to them. They've come to touch the hand of divinity and hope that the hand touches them in return."

But Mikha'il didn't respond. He just kept staring straight ahead, as if looking through an infinite destination.

Mikha'il had journeyed far and well beyond his companions. With the wisdom and enlightenment he'd acquired, he sensed that his destiny was near.

In the more than forty hours since his awakening from the Nirvana, Mikha'il had paid little attention to what surrounded him. Occasionally, he felt a sharp pain over his left eye, where the bullet fragments remained, but he chased it away, along with any comments from those who'd seen him flinch.

He was no longer overcome with anguish as before but was, rather, devoid of all emotion. He'd gone past grief and sorrow. His transformation was absolute—he had chosen. He folded inside of himself, to a space where anger and disillusionment did not exist. He sensed no loss, no desire and no attachment. Retreating from life, he grew nearer to the secret of its center.

Along the north wall of the Old City, the motorcade made slow progress through the crowds. From the east, it entered the Lion's Gate, rolling over the charred and blackened stones where the first Sayeret assault vehicle had exploded exactly one year before.

Inside the Old City, the procession followed the Via Dolorosa and turned left onto the El Wad. Along the narrow street, the rooftops and upper windows of the buildings were jammed with quiet spectators watching the activities below.

Surrounded by escort vehicles with lights still flashing, four limousines came to a stop at the southern end of the route. In orchestrated unison, the doors were opened as eight news helicopters jockeyed for position overhead.

On the ground, armed officers guarded the perimeter around the vehicles, while agents dressed in black suits guided the dignitaries through a tunnel to the rear of a five-foot-high platform. In front of it, the packed crowds in the Old City plaza awaited their arrival.

The stage was bordered by two rows of police officers in honor guard uniforms, standing rigidly at attention and tightly in formation. Behind them, atop the broad platform, other summit and government officials sat waiting with the anxious crowd.

"So far, so good," said Morton Milner, watching the walls of video screens. Around him, agents sat at two long counters and directed surveillance cameras feeding the stacked columns of monitors above them.

Standing to Milner's left, David Caplan nodded. "Let's hope it stays that way."

Inside the command control trailer, just outside the Dung Gate, the two men glanced from one monitor to the next, listening to the radio checks as they came in.

Every few seconds, camouflaged sniper teams on the rooftops and hundreds of undercover agents mixing among the crowds reported in with one of more than a dozen designated radio operators.

In the two days before the event, as the numbers of people expected to attend reached exorbitant highs, plans were made for a vastly expanded though well-hidden security force. David Caplan devoted long hours to ensuring his people were completely prepared for any potential occurrence. At the same time, banks of speakers and large video screens were placed outside the Old City walls and through nearby streets, guaranteeing that all of those gathering would be able to see and hear the official presentations.

As the proceedings were about to commence, David observed the feeds from a variety of camera angles on selected screens. He watched Prime Minister Kessel approach the podium and quiet the cheering masses. David checked the large digital clock above the monitors. "Okay, everyone, this is it. All eyes and ears open."

With his arms outstretched, Prime Minister Kessel waved his hands and finally silenced the applauding crowd. He lowered his arms and leaned into the many microphones atop the podium. His voice echoed, not only throughout the Old City but across all of Jerusalem.

"It was exactly one year ago that we last came to the Old City of Jerusalem, a sacred ground celebrated by so many. Today, I am honored to be the first to announce to you that there is to be a new and independent Old City of Jerusalem. This tiny walled city will once again come to represent the center of faith, peace and goodwill for all of humanity . . ."

While Prime Minister Kessel continued his historic address, directly behind him, Umar Abu-Hakim and Virginia Adams listened attentively. But seated at Virginia's side, Mikha'il did not. Instead, he quietly rose from his chair and walked toward the rear of the stage.

Concerned but anxious not to draw attention, Virginia casually turned to ensure that he was all right. Confused by the sight of Mikha'il walking away from the stage and down the stairs at the rear of the platform, she shifted her eyes to Dr. Ben and Aisha, sitting behind Mikha'il's now empty chair.

Equally surprised by their companion's strange and unexpected withdrawal, they both shrugged and shook their heads.

Dr. Ben attempted to follow Mikha'il, but Agent Barak gently pushed him back into his seat before following her assigned subject.

"Mikha'il," Deborah called out, quickly catching up to him. "Is everything okay?"

He did not slow but turned slightly, nodding with a nonchalant smile.

"Where are you going?" she asked.

Mikha'il ignored her and continued to make his retreat from the stage.

Deborah chose not to disturb him again. She followed a few steps behind and spoke into her cuff mic, "Barak to Control. Shepherd's on the move."

Inside the darkened command trailer, a radio operator swiveled in her chair and blurted, "Shepherd has left the stage. Agent Barak with subject."

David scanned the wall of video screens until he found the appropriate monitors. Without moving his eyes, he held out his hand to the radio operator. "Give me your headpiece."

David fastened it to his ear. "Barak, Caplan here. What's your destination?"

"Unknown, sir. Shepherd didn't respond to my questioning."

"Stay with subject. We have you on visual and are tracking."

Paying no mind to Deborah's presence, Mikha'il strolled eastward. Only a brief walk from the Western Wall, Mikha'il climbed a wide stone staircase. Atop the stairway, he approached four security officers, who moved to stop him, but several steps behind Mikha'il, Deborah flashed her credentials, and they stood aside to let him pass.

Without missing a step, Mikha'il passed under a columned archway and entered the rear courtyard of the Temple Mount, which had been kept clear of all spectators to avoid any altercations given the site's significance to both Jews and Muslims. Mikha'il hesitated and slowly scanned the open courtyard to where a corner gate and garrison would have been, only a few hundred feet away.

Mikha'il vividly recalled the horrid scene he'd witnessed there—the Roman soldiers viciously beating Jesus and the scornful horde cheering them on.

He turned to his right and walked in that direction. With its majestic golden dome visible throughout Jerusalem, the famed Muslim mosque, the Dome of the Rock, sat directly in front of him. Mikha'il wandered around the turquoise mosaic walls of the octagonal-shaped building, the color matching the vibrancy of the blue sky above, until he reached the large front doors. There he stopped and raised his head.

From around the cracks in the ancient doors, a bright light began to shine, framing him in its brilliance.

Deborah froze in surprise and whispered into her cuff mic, "Barak here. Positioned outside the Dome of the Rock and observing a strange light coming from inside."

"Copy that and hold," she heard David reply.

Inside the command trailer, David and Milner had been watching the appropriate monitors, but they saw no such light.

David pointed and spoke to one of the video operators. "Rewind that screen there and play it back slowly. Let's see what we get."

Still not seeing anything, David responded, "Negative on any abnormality. The light must be a reflection from the sun. We aren't getting it on camera."

"Nothing? Are you certain?"

"Roger that."

The three continued to observe Mikha'il—David and Milner on the live video feed and Deborah from the side of the mosque. They watched as he moved to the front doors and placed his hand on the handle, but then he appeared to hesitate.

Mikha'il heard a loud snorting from close behind him. He released the handle and turned.

Standing there was the enormous bull with the familiar figure of Lord Shiva, the God of Destruction, sitting on its back. The animal snorted a second time, but there was no ferocity in its manner nor in its rider's.

Mikha'il approached the bull and raised the back of his right hand to its wet nostrils. The bull bowed down its heavy head. Its master followed with the same respectful motion, and Mikha'il tenderly rubbed the side of the bull's face.

It was there, in the front courtyard of the Temple Mount that Shiva had stormed after Mikha'il the year before. Now, the Hindu lord raised his head to Mikha'il, and their eyes locked. Shiva gestured to the doors of the grand mosque.

With quiet grace, Mikha'il walked away from the bull and rider. He returned to the mosque and, this time, opened the door. The brilliant light radiated forth once again. Mikha'il shielded his eyes with his hands and walked inside.

The door closed behind him.

"Shepherd's gone inside! Request orders."

"Copy that. We saw him."

"Did you see the light this time?" she asked.

"Negative." David ignored her line of thought. "Confirm his movements. Was Shepherd signaling to someone?"

"Uncertain. I saw nothing and no one. He lifted his hand and then waved it up and down in the air. Then he entered the mosque while shielding his face from the light—or whatever it was."

In the instant that Mikha'il had disappeared into the mosque, David, too, had seen him raise his hands, as if to protect his eyes. Baffled, he asked, "What do you make of it all?"

"Unknown, sir. Should I follow?"

"Hold for directive," David replied. He cupped the mouthpiece with his hand and turned to Milner. "Mort, we don't have cameras in there, do we?"

"No, Commander."

"Damn." Aware it was forbidden for a Jew to enter the Dome of the Rock and the repercussions of any violation, David hesitated and then ordered, "Deborah, do not go in. Repeat, do not enter."

"Copy that. Waiting outside," she calmly replied.

13:58:14. David watched the seconds dropping from the digital clock. *Kessel will finish soon. After speeches by Abu-Hakim and Adams, Mikha'il is scheduled to speak.* David tightened his jaw. *What's he doing in there?*

Mikha'il blinked a few times and attempted to get his bearings. The grandeur of the mosque's beauty took his breath away.

Heavy gray and white granite columns formed an octagon that mirrored the mosque's outer shape. The stone pillars supported an arched ceiling surrounding the open cupola of the great dome, where gold leaf and ornate red floral inscriptions combined in meticulous glory. Elaborate mosaics depicting colorful gardens adorned every wall.

As he took in the splendor, Mikha'il thought to himself that the vibrant tiled artwork seemed to symbolize the gardens of paradise.

In the center of the mosque, under the domed ceiling, was a large exposed rock. The rock was enclosed behind a finely carved, dark, wooden screen, only about waist high. Around the screen and under the dome was lush red carpeting, but that bordering the columned outer space was deep green.

Mikha'il considered approaching the dark screened wall and sand-colored rock, but after taking one step forward, the white light shone directly behind him, halting his advance.

The brightness receded, and a bold but gentle voice said, "Hello, Mikha'il."

Mikha'il pivoted. Recognizing the figure before him, he resisted the feeling of joy that threatened to erupt and calmly said, "Gabriel."

"You have done well. The end of your journey nears. You enter the site of Mount Moriah, the Foundation Stone upon which the Lord made Adam, where Abraham was to sacrifice Isaac, where the Covenant Ark holding the Commandments given to Moses was worshiped, where the Jewish temples were built and where Muhammad rose with me to the heavens of our prophets and to the Lord."

"Is this my destiny, to leave this place for heaven or paradise or whatever awaits?"

Gabriel replied somberly, "In many nations, over the course of generations, few are watched. When the path of humankind is twisted to the point of rupture, when a dark flood rushes to cover the earth, then, one is chosen to intersect with the ill fate of humanity in an attempt to straighten that which has been bent. In your time, you are the one chosen by divinity to endure this burden. This has been your destiny."

"Does it end here?"

"That is not for me to answer." Gabriel raised his hand and pointed behind Mikha'il. "She waits for you there. Go."

Near the Foundation Stone, a woman bowed with her forehead to the red floor. She faced away from Mikha'il, toward a worn wooden niche carved into the wall of the mosque's interior.

Instinctively, Mikha'il removed his sandals in respect for the hallowed ground. Barefoot, he slowly approached the praying woman.

When he reached her, she ended her prayer and lifted her head. She looked directly into Mikha'il's eyes. She did not nod. She did not smile. Yet the expression in her face was somehow affectionate, welcoming.

Mikha'il knew her. "You were in my vision, just after I fell from the balcony. You left me in the desert. You're the Bedouin woman!"

The old woman replied gracefully, her words gently echoing throughout the entire mosque. "I am that I am. I am the one who always is and always has been—the Creator, the Protector and the Destroyer. I am the Maker of eternal energy, the God of Abraham, Father to the Son, Mother to life. I am everywhere and I am nowhere, but I am One, all in the same."

A rush of conflicting emotion burst through Mikha'il. Nervousness and awe blended with a contented tranquility of enduring love and peacefulness.

The old woman continued, "And with you, Mikha'il Patrick bin al-Rashid, I am well pleased. You have shown great willingness and sacrifice for my cause."

Mikha'il could not reject the honesty within his heart. He swallowed tightly. "But I was angry over the loss of the one I love most. I didn't willingly give her up and held much resentment. In my scorn, I have shamed you."

"You are not without the spoils of emotion. You are made to love and to protect those whom you love. You cannot remain emotionless and achieve this. This is the necessity of sustained life, to cherish and to provide for those who are loved so that they may endure. As such, it is not in a single wave splashing through the tiny granules of sand that one is judged but, rather, in the depth and breadth of the expansive ocean." Her tone softened. "Come, my child, pray with me."

Mikha'il lowered himself to his knees and closed his eyes, and the two bowed together in prayer.

With no realization of time passing, Mikha'il heard the query deep in his soul: *For whom do you pray, my child?*

I pray to you, the Lord of all man.

And it is to you, Mikha'il, that I now pray, and for them, the sons and daughters of mankind, that they may hear you. I send hope to humanity. Go to them now. I will be near.

FIFTY-ONE

"SHEPHERD'S OUT!"

"We got him," David answered Deborah immediately.

She watched as Mikha'il moved from the doorway of the Dome of the Rock and into the open courtyard.

Barefoot, he wandered close by her but didn't look at her or acknowledge her presence. He also appeared unaware of the helicopter tracking directly above him.

The news helicopter hovered lower with Mikha'il's reappearance from the mosque. Of all the helicopters jockeying for position, it had been the only one to follow Mikha'il to the Temple Mount. Still close enough to film the speeches in the plaza, it had moved to just west of the mosque, its news crew waiting for Mikha'il's exit.

Deborah looked up.

The clamor from its buzzing blades seemed muted as a large bird, perched atop the beautiful mosque, spread its wings and rose from the crest of the golden dome. The bird ascended and circled over the mount.

For a moment, Deborah forgot about her assignment. She strained her eyes against the bright sunshine, trying to focus on the soaring bird.

"Barak, report any irregularity," sounded the voice in her ear, but it was from too great a distance to heed.

Watching his agent on the video monitor, standing motionless, and Mikha'il walking away from her, David raised his voice to a shout. "Barak, is everything all right? Report!"

"Ah, affirmative," she responded. "It's only a large bird, sir. An eagle, I think."

Perhaps more surprised than his agent at her strange observation, David paused for a long second, and in contrast to his previous transmission, his response was gentle. "Please repeat."

"Roger that, sir. There's an eagle flying overhead."

With the confirmation of the irregular sighting, David pushed away his memory of a similar sighting. "Stay close to Shepherd. It looks as though he's headed back to the stage. He's scheduled to deliver his speech in about five minutes. We'll continue to track your position from here."

Concerned that Mikha'il would not return before she finished, Virginia slowed her closing remarks. She could stall for only a minute or two more, as her address, like Kessel's and Abu-Hakim's, was translated and captioned across the gigantic screens for everyone to follow. She allowed the excited cheering of the far-reaching crowds to carry on until the sentences crawling across the teleprompter finally ended.

She drew a long breath and continued, "I know so many of you are waiting for Mikha'il bin al-Rashid. We truly have so much to thank him for . . ."

Virginia glanced over her left shoulder one last time. Relief filled her as she saw Mikha'il climbing the staircase.

He walked past Aisha, Dr. Ben and several officials, and then by the two leaders who'd spoken before Virginia. The crowd saw Mikha'il's entrance and began applauding.

As he neared, Virginia, still standing at the podium and clapping along with the multitude, nodded at him with a smile.

Mikha'il inclined his head in return. He did not delay nor greet Virginia. Instead, he walked directly past her and beyond the teleprompter, to stop a few feet in front of the podium.

His appearance contrasted with that of the others on the stage. His white shirt hung loosely, untucked from his dark trousers and buttoned neither around the neck nor at the cuffs. More peculiar, he wore nothing on his feet.

After a long minute of cheering, during which Mikha'il did not move or acknowledge the great masses of people gathered around him, the deafening ovation faded until there was a serene stillness over the Old City.

Even the police officers and security forces, with their weapons firmly held at their sides, and the isolated groups of protesters waited in silence.

Only the throbbing sounds of news helicopters could be heard.

Virginia, realizing any further introduction was senseless, walked back to her seat, and Aisha hurried to the podium.

Mikha'il scanned the peaceful crowd, from those standing far away to those nearer by, taking in the sight of them. They were all equal, just a single people. No difference. Except . . . Mikha'il's gaze stopped at a figure who stood out from the rest.

Standing by himself, in the center of those in the front row of the plaza and only inches from the lines of police officers that separated the stage from the crowd, was a young Hasidic boy.

Mikha'il advanced two steps, until his bare toes gripped the edge of the platform. He peered down into the face of the Hasidic boy. He remembered seeing the same boy in the plaza, the day before the attack. As then, in their moment of connection, Mikha'il recognized in the boy's face a resemblance to himself as a child.

The boy returned the look and waited.

Mikha'il was ready.

He lifted his right hand and began signing, moving his hand and fingers in scripted eloquence. "You join me here, at the crossroads of life and faith alike. In this holy, yet fickle city, that has both honored and condemned its prophets, you gather not to witness a victory for any nation or people, nor for a culture or for a single religion, but to rejoice upon the freedom of all man. We come together, on this glorious day, to mark an end, and to seed a new beginning. The time that has been foretold has arrived to cease the division. We are not many nations. We are one. And this land we stand upon is promised to all of us, to all of humanity."

Behind Mikha'il, all on the stage stood in applause, and the exhilarated crowds roared with jubilation. Mikha'il held up his left hand and stretched his fingers outward. Beyond that, he did not move. Understanding the universal gesture, the crowds quickly calmed, and there was silence.

He continued, with Aisha interpreting his every word. "In the generations since Adam, Moses, the Hindu who became the Buddha, Jesus the Jew who became the Christ, and Muhammad the Arab who became the messenger, we have observed much change.

"For too long, we were a divided people, born of a world where towering mountain ranges, and sprawling bodies of sand and sea, posed as natural barriers between our lands. Nations were forged and yet separated by beliefs, traditions and languages, dividing humankind. Now, in only a short span of time, we have developed technologies to cross with ease not only these geographic hurdles but every imaginable boundary. Communication and information gaps have been erased, and we are granted instant access to each other. We are separated only from the stars in the sky and by the many beliefs we worship under those stars."

The crowd watched and listened. Those close to Mikha'il in the plaza focused on him, standing on the stage so near to them, while the majority—crammed into the Old City and the surrounding streets of Jerusalem, through the gardens of Gethsemane and along the hillsides of Mount Scopus and the Mount of Olives—watched Mikha'il on the gigantic video screens. They listened to Aisha's translation on loudspeakers or followed the words of their respective languages crawling along the bottoms of the screens around them.

Soon, some of the spectators began to lower themselves to their knees.

Major news networks carried the event live with correspondents and cameras positioned throughout the Old City, on the streets or in the helicopters overhead.

And those scenes were transmitted around the world, to anyone with a television, computer or handheld device, in homes and workplaces, malls, restaurants and cafés.

"As a common nation under those stars, we are united in all that is seen and unseen, heard and unheard, felt and unfelt, for these are from our Creator.

"Humankind has been set far above, unified in so much more, to have been bestowed with faith, for it is faith that further bonds man. We all have it, whether we deny it or not. Deep within the spirit of each one of us is a conscience, a center that differentiates between right and wrong. Regardless of our differences, of whatever separates us, the distinctions between good and bad are known to us all. It is in the essence of our conscience that we are united. For, within it, we have faith that our actions will ultimately be judged and either rewarded or punished. It is not in the bindings of scripture and dogma that we act morally. It is in the divine gift of faith that we do.

"Faith is embedded within us, and from it, our instinct is to reach out and touch our Creator. At times, we ask for guidance or for support. We pray for our ill and for our fallen. We give thanks for our bounty and for our joy. We all do this, but where innate faith is the same in us all, our varying beliefs continue to separate us."

As Mikha'il continued, Aisha began to stumble, as did those working the closed-caption script. Mikha'il had altered his scripted speech and ultimately abandoned it.

Although confused, Aisha concentrated on Mikha'il's hand signs, diligently speaking his words into the microphones in front of her and mixing the three languages as she felt was appropriate. While she spoke, those keying the closed-captioning equipment hurried to type in the translations.

An increasing number of spectators, all through Jerusalem, were dropping to their knees and bowing in prayer. Some knelt with hands clasped, others leaned forward, touching their foreheads to the ground, and still others sat peacefully with crossed legs. They were no longer reading Mikha'il's words nor listening to Aisha.

Instead, they *felt* Mikha'il's words somewhere deep within themselves. Thousands at a time, they sank to the ground, closed their eyes and welcomed grace. Those feeling Mikha'il's presence were not limited to the spectators who'd come to witness the announcement.

Camera operators abandoned their equipment while reporters set down their microphones. On rooftops, sharpshooters put aside their rifles. Throughout the Old City and the surrounding streets, security officers and soldiers lowered weapons, and protesters, their signs.

Those still standing gazed about in concern and disbelief until they, too, dropped to the ground in acceptance of their blessing.

Aisha struggled on, even though most of the others on the stage knelt in prayer.

Mikha'il ignored the effect of his words and, like Aisha, continued in his duty. "But we cannot be divided in our Gods, for there is only one Creator. Our divisions come from different interpretations of creation and destiny. It has been through our prophets, sent to different communities at different times, that varying beliefs and cultures have emerged. We were once divided lands, unaware of the rest of the world, and we respectfully followed our individual messengers, each sent to a specific nation. Although these pathways became unique, they all originated from one light, with the same moral value and purpose of goodwill. But our world has changed.

"We are no longer physically divided, and in our new awareness and knowledge, the time has arrived to accept ourselves as one nation, and one people, for our paths have come full circle and meet at the same source of light. What you hear inside of you is that reality, which you know rests deep within your soul."

Aisha stopped, stunned to realize that Mikha'il was no longer moving his hands. Yet, she felt his words and continued to speak them into the microphones. She looked behind her.

All those on the stage, including Virginia and Dr. Ben, Kessel and Abu-Hakim, were on the floor in prayer. On the giant video screens, the now unmanned cameras continued to record the unreal scene of her standing behind Mikha'il.

Facing the plaza, he stood tall, unmoving, his arms open, fingers spread. The camera angles did not change, and the words that had crawled across the bottom of the screens were now gone. But Mikha'il's words were still heard and could not be ignored. Aisha felt every beautiful word through her entire body. She slowly sank to her knees.

Follow my hands, and I will reach for you. Feel my thoughts, and I will teach to you. Prepare the way, if not for yourselves, then for your sons and daughters and for their sons and daughters.

There is no god, but God.

The time has come that we recognize our union under one Creator. Still, it is a time to respect all of the prophets, their words and traditions, and all of the celebrations and choices of worship under the dominion of this one God, just as we do our varying languages. The messages of your prophets have been written in scripture and verse, depicted and painted in frescos and murals. Do not deny them. Embrace them, in their purpose and meaning. We may call out in a different way, but there is One who loves all the same.

For your God and your neighbor's God are the same. They are one.

In the Shin Bet command control trailer, the scene outside the trailer seemed even more unearthly when contrasted against the frenzied reaction of the agents crammed inside.

Radio operators frantically attempted to reach the agents and officers posted throughout the city, but with no success. Where possible, security camera angles were shifted to ascertain the status of those agents. In every case, the operators inside the trailer reported that the agents and officers were kneeling in prayer amid the worshiping crowd.

Deborah had been the last to report in. They replayed her recorded transmissions: "I don't understand it. I can hear his words. They're all through me. I can't explain the feeling, but I am not afraid. It's . . . it's wonderful . . ."

With Milner at his side, David looked from screen to screen, searching for any clue as to what they were witnessing.

He returned to the image of Deborah kneeling with bowed head just behind Prime Minister Kessel, who was doing the same. David spoke into his radio mouthpiece one more time. "Barak, report situation. Please report!"

As in his three previous attempts, no radio response came.

Milner pleaded with him, "We have to do something. We need to deploy military forces, quick."

"Not yet, Mort, not yet."

"Come on! That's the prime minister out there. We have to do something."

Another agent approached the men. "News helicopters are continuing to film. They seem unaffected and are reporting live to their networks. We're feeding their broadcasts through now."

While he focused on as many video monitors as he could, David's thoughts accelerated, scouring for answers and appropriate action. *What is this? What's happening here? Come on, think!* Just then, he saw a familiar face in the crowd on one of the screens. David pointed to the monitor. "There, right at the foot of the stage. Rewind that camera in slow-mo!"

The operator started backing up the footage, and David stopped him. "Right there, zoom in on that child, the one in the black hat, and freeze it."

"It's a Hasidic boy, sir," the operator said respectfully.

"Right. Now go live."

The boy knelt in the center of the first row in the plaza, among kneeling police officers. When the camera zoomed in further, the young boy looked straight up into the lens and smiled, as if knowing the camera, at least two hundred feet away, was focused directly on him.

It was definitely the same child he'd encountered in the Old City attack a year ago. David remembered thinking the child could have been his own twin, so similar were his features to those of his seven-year-old self. "It's you!" David whispered.

Milner was also watching the live video of the Hasidic boy. "Is that the same boy who witnessed Rubenstein's attack, the one we couldn't find afterward?"

"Yes," answered David quietly, eyes fixed on the screen. *Who are you? What are you doing here now?*

Morton Milner also watched the boy. "I think I might know him! He looks familiar."

"Let me guess—he reminds you of yourself, when you were a child."

"Yes, but how . . ."

Just then, the boy slipped backward into the crowd and disappeared. David grasped the shoulder of another video operator and demanded, "Focus that camera on the Yeshiva School."

"Got it, sir."

"Zoom in on the fourth-floor balcony, where last year's attack was launched. Hurry."

"What the hell is that?" Milner said, craning forward to get a better look. "It's an eagle. I think it's an eagle."

"Yes," confirmed David, expressing no surprise. "It is."

With unblinking eyes, the eagle scanned the crowd and then spread its mighty wings, but it did not take flight. Instead, the majestic bird resettled its wings, tucked in its feathers and remained perched on the balcony.

"What's it doing here?" Milner wondered aloud. "What the hell is going on?"

"I think you have that backward," David said. "You have command, Mort. But whatever you do, do not deploy any defensive forces unless you have a direct order from me alone or you see a blatant attack and I am completely unreachable. Otherwise, you stay on stand-down."

"Why? Where are you going?"

Calmly, David gestured to the video monitors in front of them both. "Out there."

FIFTY-TWO

DAVID STEPPED OUT OF THE TRAILER and walked down the steel staircase. Even though he had seen with his own eyes, and knew what to expect, the sight overwhelmed him. All was quiet. The gate into the Old City stood before him, and all around it, the masses of people, regardless of their age, color, dress or religion, prayed together in silence. Not one of them took notice, not even as much as a slight turn of the head or casual glance, of the lone man walking carefully among them.

Soon, David felt a warmth spread through him. His steps slowed as words gently filled him. He lowered his knees to the sidewalk, shut his eyes and dropped his head. With acceptance, he listened.

Our God watches over every one of us, with caring and abundant love. But still, our God looks upon a world, even now, plagued by suffering. Too many of our people starve in hunger, cry in poverty and ache in sickness. War and oppression continue to rob the innocent of their loved ones, of their homes and of their livelihoods but, worse, of their future and of their hope.

In such a world, we each have the ability to do such good, to work together, to bring relief to those who endure what they should not. God looks upon the weak with empathy and favor, and in our hearts, so should we all.

It is the moral duty, of those who are able, to protect those who are not.

It is our added duty, as a united humankind, to be guardians of this world, for our Creator has placed us far above all other creations.

So, stand in awe of the science and laws of nature. Consider the complexity of the human mind and the abilities bestowed upon man over all others. Although nature has been our primary guide through the ages, does not our core tell us that within nature there is a caring source? With the wonders of our planet and the cosmos above, how can there not be a Creator of nature?

Still, it is you, humankind, that reigns supreme over the balance of all other life and nature. Man has been created, graced with the essence of spirit and guided as part of a divine path. Man has evolved to both stand and think above all else, in order to safeguard all else. It is our purpose to respect and to protect our planet and all that exists on it.

The helicopters continued to fly above Mikha'il, the Old City and its surrounding streets. They provided the only sound filling the air, but those below took no notice. Mikha'il's words reached only those spectators in and around the Old City.

Just as those below were oblivious to the helicopters above, those onboard were completely confounded by what was occurring below. Nevertheless, they continued to film and attempt to explain the strange spectacle while their correspondents on the ground failed to answer any call. All those who weren't directly exposed to Mikha'il's words, those in the helicopters, those viewing on television sets or handhelds and those inside the Shin Bet trailer, could only watch and wonder, arriving at their own conclusions, miraculous or not.

In our lives, respect for God and nature are essential, but if we cannot first respect our fellow man, then respect for all else is inconsequential.

All men are created equal. We are not any one race from the other. We are the full and the starving, believers and nonbelievers.

We each sleep and dream like any other. Each day we breathe the air with every other. We arrived in the world the same, and in the end, we will leave the same. We are human beings, each made of thought, of joy and of suffering.

In discrimination and oppression, you, too, become discriminated against and, eventually, oppressed. Do not be full of hate, and do not seek revenge, for in these, only treachery is found. Do not look upon your fellow man as lesser, for he will look upon you with the same regard.

Do not judge, for with any judgment you make, you will be judged in return.

Truly feel your neighbor, as he may be you. Listen through her ear, see through his eye, walk in her step. Love your God with all of your heart, soul, mind and strength, and love your neighbor as yourself.

For among you, whoever is least, is greatest.

Be humble and seek humility.

In the Situation Room of the White House West Wing, President Robinson watched the news coverage with the members of his inner cabinet. All viewed it without comprehension, unsure of what was happening, or how it had come about, and curious as to what it would bring afterward.

In the corner of a tiny chapel in Vatican City, the Most Holy Father sought solitude. Kneeling upon a red-velvet padded pew, his hands tightly clenching a plain wooden cross attached to a loosely hanging rosary of beads, the pope prayed.

Also in isolation, but in a stark and dingy prison cell, a man in orange coveralls knelt beside his narrow bed. Manny Judkowitz gave thanks for the peace that he had found within himself and hoped that others might be blessed with the same.

Only a few miles from the Shin Bet detention center, the hundreds of thousands jammed in the center of Jerusalem continued to embrace every word they felt and embed the meaning into their own souls.

Let us all come together and accept this ancient ground, the very earth and rock sacred to so many. Let us praise it as our collective City of Peace.

The divisions of religion are not real. With your brothers and sisters, blaze a trail to tear down the dams that separate us. Allow our rivers to flow freely, for they spring from the same cloud in the sky, lead to the same ocean beyond and are of the same tear in every eye.

You all have the ability to do such good. Encourage each other to find the strength in fellowship and harmony, to live in peace. Faith breeds joy, and unity seeds freedom.

But not all of this is for you today; rather it's for your sons and daughters, for they are your innocence, the you of tomorrow, and they cry out to you today to consider their tomorrow. Think of them as you prepare to set your way. Think of a land where all the children of man can run free.

Let whoever is here, deliver to all who are not. Wherever you come from, to wherever they are, whether they are of your religion or not, whatever your color or theirs, whatever their status, rich or poor, go and awaken them.

Let your face shine, for your light has come and the glory of God has risen within you. Many will be drawn by the light and to the brightness of your dawn. To the people, spread these words of wisdom and let a new tree blossom. Do not deny its root, and it will not deny you. When you wake each day, the harmony of nature will ring through your ears.

Tell the people everywhere. Rejoice! Let them know what you know, what you have heard, what you feel. When the light goes dim, there will still be light that will shine upon you, and in the next day, that light will shine on all.

On that day, the children of God will sing together, chanting in harmony among the stars, with new meaning and brightness.
So from here, together, let us begin anew.

FIFTY-THREE

SLOWLY, MIKHA'IL LOWERED HIS ARMS to his side.

He opened his eyes and inhaled.

Those gathered around him felt their muscles ease, and they, too, took in deep breaths. Gradually, most opened their eyes, though some kept them closed in an attempt to hold on to the sensation within their bodies for as long as they could. None spoke, and none cheered.

Without looking to those behind him on the stage, Mikha'il lowered himself from the platform. The police officers below quietly shifted aside to make way for him. His bare feet touched the concrete tiles of the plaza, and still speechless, those nearby watched as he took a few steps forward.

Mikha'il did not acknowledge the people around him. He paused and scanned the crowds nearest him, looking for the Hasidic boy. After a few seconds, he realized he would not find him and slowly walked on.

It was not necessary for Mikha'il to weave or dodge through the crowd. People parted in respect and awe, allowing him a clear path. He headed south, straight through the center of the still hushed Old City plaza. As he walked, only one dared to touch him.

She delicately placed her fingertips on his bare foot as it neared the ground only inches from her.

Mikha'il stopped. He looked down at the young Muslim woman. A faded yellow hijab was wrapped loosely around her neck and head. The woman kept her eyes fixed on the ground, but the baby girl strapped to the woman's back with a dust-stained sling gazed into Mikha'il's face. Her twin brothers, not much older than five and squatting next to their mother, did the same.

Mikha'il touched the boys' heads and then that of their baby sister.

Their mother reached for Mikha'il's hand, and he did not pull it away.

Fatima touched her lips to the back of it.

Mikha'il continued through the crowd, sensing one among them. He altered direction and walked with purpose toward the man, not taking his eyes off him.

When he reached him, those in the vicinity moved back a few feet, but the man still knelt. He wore a hooded garment of tightly woven, light beige wool. His head, totally covered, remained bowed to the ground.

Mikha'il put both hands on the broad shoulders of the man, and slowly, the man rose to his feet before Mikha'il. He kept his head lowered.

Mikha'il hooked a finger under the man's chin and tipped his face upward, wanting to see into his eyes.

Tariq Nur al-Din didn't blink as he gazed into Mikha'il's face.

Mikha'il again reached for Nur al-Din's shoulders, drawing him into a tight embrace, which Tariq didn't resist. He lowered his head close to Mikha'il's, and their right cheeks touched.

Mikha'il closed his eyes in thought. *Your people need wisdom and leadership, not might and bravado.* He withdrew from the embrace and walked away, leaving Nur al-Din standing alone.

Mikha'il followed the path to the inner security checkpoint. The guards, like the others all around them, respectfully slid aside to give Mikha'il access. Not far away was the south exit, and the crowd parted to create a path all the way through the arched Dung Gate. Mikha'il carried on, as though he, too, knew where he was next headed—as though this was the path he was meant to follow.

After only a few steps, he paused and made a complete circle to look upon the people around him.

Those on the other side of the plaza and the greater majority who remained crammed in nearby streets and park lawns outside the Old City walls were unaware of Mikha'il's location. They could see only the quieted stage on the screens around them.

Some began to mill about, rising to their feet and stretching. They whispered among themselves about the wonder of what they had just experienced, comparing every detail. Most believed it was a private and miraculous encounter with Mikha'il, unique to themselves, and they were concerned that no one would believe them, but it didn't take long for them to discover that they had all shared the same experience.

Mikha'il felt the presence above him. Squinting, he glanced up to the sky. The golden eagle was circling over him. To Mikha'il, the sun behind the bird appeared brighter, and the sky bluer.

A faintness came over him, and he fought to focus on the soaring bird.

His eyes stung, and he felt an intense pain behind his scar. As had happened at the Holocaust Memorial, Mikha'il's legs gave out, and he fell to a single knee.

The people around him moved back, unsure what they were witnessing or what they could do to assist this special man.

Mikha'il bent forward. His lungs seized, and he struggled to breathe. He tried to push himself to his feet but couldn't.

Dr. Ben ran to Mikha'il. He'd been following from a respectful distance since Mikha'il had left the stage. Dr. Ben dropped to the ground beside him and cradled him in his arms. "It's all right, Mikha'il. We'll get you to the Hadassah."

"My head hurts," Mikha'il said in a raspy voice. "It really hurts."

Before Dr. Ben could process the fact that Mikha'il had actually spoken, he yelled out, "Someone call for help!"

Mikha'il's gaze was fixed on the sky above. Dr. Ben looked up to see an eagle pass in silhouette against the bright ball of sun.

"Have I offended any or left anything unturned?"

"No, Mikha'il," whispered Dr. Ben. "You have done well."

"Has the message been delivered?"

"Yes! Oh, yes, it has."

A smile came to Mikha'il's face. "I can hear her, Ben. I can hear Jasmine. She knew . . . She didn't want us to be apart. She knew. She's there, waiting for me. I miss her. I really miss her."

"I know you do, Mikha'il. Just hold on. Help is on the way."

"No, Ben, I don't want to leave her."

The eagle cried out.

Dr. Ben glanced up again to the large bird, circling low overhead.

"I can see Jasmine now," Mikha'il whispered. "She's in white . . . and holding hands with the Hasidic boy . . . They're standing close to us." He fought to get his failing words out. "She is so beautiful."

Fighting his emotions, Dr. Ben could say nothing.

"Jasmine is right," Mikha'il said without a struggle, his face growing pale and his voice softening. "I can see it now. It is so very wonderful."

Dr. Ben held Mikha'il tightly in his arms and watched as his eyes widened to behold the paradise that awaited him.

Dr. Ben reached down and carefully closed the glazed eyes. Then, as second nature, he looked at his watch: *3:00.*

A large man, with a hood over his head that shadowed his face, gently eased Dr. Ben backward so that he could reach for Mikha'il.

Dr. Ben didn't resist.

Without a word, the tall stranger picked up Mikha'il and carried him toward the Dung Gate. Once again, he carried a fallen comrade from the Old City of Jerusalem.

———

Seeing the man carrying Mikha'il, David and his guards hurried toward him.

When they reached him, the man raised his head to meet the eyes of the Shin Bet director. His back arching, Tariq held out Mikha'il to David. "May peace be upon him."

Staring into the eyes of his nation's sworn enemy, David considered his next move. He quickly gestured to the soldiers behind him to take Mikha'il's body.

Face to face, David and Nur al-Din continued to watch each other as the soldiers carried Mikha'il's body toward the open, waiting Dung Gate.

It was David who broke the silence. "Upon us all, let there be peace. Shalom."

Tariq Nur al-Din, realizing his fate might not be as dire as he'd expected, gratefully nodded to David and replied, "Salaam."

David said nothing further and watched Nur al-Din walk through the open path, until the large Palestinian blended with the crowd and disappeared into what was soon to become a new City of Peace.

V

A NEW CITY

The future glory of this Temple will be greater than its past glory,
says the Lord Almighty.
And in this place I will bring Peace.

Haggai
The Bible
Haggai 2:9
Jerusalem, 520 BC

FIFTY-FOUR

UNABLE TO SPEAK TO ANY, Mikha'il had spoken to all. He spoke without talking, and the people listened without hearing. The hundreds of thousands bearing witness to Mikha'il's message in Jerusalem that day, the three world leaders, the diplomats and officials, the old and the young alike, the privileged and the poor, all received Mikha'il's message.

In the days and months to come, they would recite those words to their families and neighbors, and to their communities and nations. Not only would they recall the meaning in Mikha'il's message, but they would repeat every sentence to the very word. Not a pause or syllable would differ.

Mikha'il's message would be written and rewritten, from lyrics sung in harmonic choirs, to sermons shouted from both street corner and pulpit. In its divine proclamation and in its pure truth, it would not be denied or forgotten.

In the irony of destiny and fate, the news media, avoided by Mikha'il late in life, would, in his death, spread his word to the far corners of the earth, pulling them to one center.

The world united, had found a common message.

Jasmine's parents did not scatter the ashes of their daughter into the flowing currents of the Ganges River. The essence of Jasmine's spirit would never be reborn as in Hindu tradition.

Instead, the morning following the announcement in the Old City and Mikha'il's death, her parents returned to Jerusalem, bringing Jasmine's ashes with them.

The yellow and blue ceramic urn sat next to the heavy pine coffin containing Mikha'il's body. For three days, their remains rested on a linen-draped table in the entrance hall of the Yeshiva School, where hundreds of thousands of people passed by to worship and pray, and to bestow adoration and respect upon the exalted couple.

On the third day, Jasmine's parents, joined by Prime Minister Kessel, P.A. leader Umar Abu-Hakim, Virginia Adams, Dr. Ben and Aisha, were left alone with the urn and the open casket. There, Jasmine's mother removed the top of the urn and carefully released Jasmine's ashes alongside Mikha'il. Into eternity, Jasmine and Mikha'il would lie together, their spirits forever entwined and their sacrifice forever celebrated.

In time, Mikha'il and Jasmine would be enshrined in a plain white marble mausoleum, built in the newly named center of the People's Square in the independent Old City of Jerusalem, where humankind would celebrate them and honor their message for generations to come.

Chiseled into the broad trim around the rooftop were twelve words—inscribed in the varied languages of the world—three words to each wall. It would not make a difference which direction a viewer started reading from; the meaning would be the same in any order.

Under One God
With Their Sacrifice
For All Humanity
There Came Peace

APPENDICES

Hinduism
Do naught unto others which would cause you pain
if done to you.
Mahabharata Veda, 5:1517

Judaism
Thou shall love thy neighbor as thyself.
The Torah, Leviticus 19:18

Christianity
Do to others what you would have them do to you.
The Bible, Matthew 7:12

Islam
No one of you is a believer until he desires for his brother
that which he desires for himself.
Fortieth Hadith of an-Nawawi 13

Confucianism
Do not unto others what you would not have them do unto you.
Confucius, Analects 15:23

Buddhism
Hurt not others in ways that you yourself would find hurtful.
Udana-Varga 5:18

WORLD RELIGION POPULATIONS

Christianity (53% Catholic)	2,200,000,000	31.4%
Islam/Muslim (90% Sunni and 10% Shia)	1,600,000,000	22.9%
Hinduism	1,000,000,000	14.3%
Buddhism (includes 100 million Japanese Shinto)	600,000,000	8.6%
Confucianism (Chinese Traditional)	400,000,000	5.7%
Judaism/Jewish	15,000,000	0.2%
Atheism	200,000,000	2.8%
Other	985,000,000	14.1%
TOTAL	**7,000,000,000**	**100.0%**

ISRAEL
1947 UNITED NATIONS
PROPOSAL

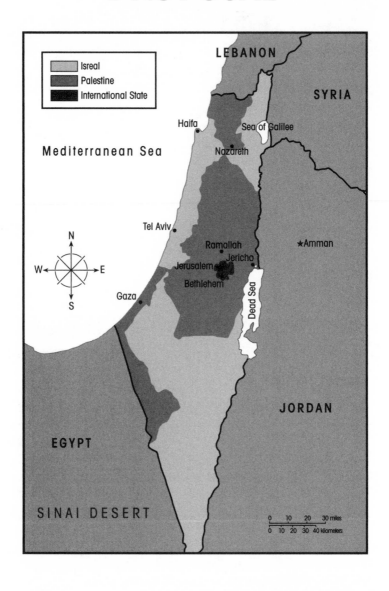

Isreal
Palestine
International State

LEBANON

SYRIA

Haifa

Sea of Galilee

Mediterranean Sea

Nazareth

N
W E
S

Tel Aviv

Ramallah
Jericho
Jerusalem
Bethlehem

★Amman

Gaza

Dead Sea

JORDAN

EGYPT

SINAI DESERT

0   10   20   30 miles
0 10 20 30 40 kilometers

ISRAEL
AFTER 1948 WAR OF
INDEPENDENCE

ISRAEL AFTER THE 1967 SIX-DAY WAR

ISRAEL
PRESENT DAY

Israeli Settlements

LEBANON

SYRIA

GOLAN HEIGHTS
Israeli occupied

Haifa

Sea of Galilee

Mediterranean Sea

Nazareth

WEST BANK
Israeli occupied

N

W E

S

Tel Aviv

Ramallah

★Amman

Jericho

Jerusalem

Bethlehem

GAZA STRIP
Palestinian controlled

Dead Sea

ISRAEL

EGYPT

JORDAN

SINAI DESERT

0   10   20   30 miles
0 10 20 30 40 kilometers

ABOUT THE AUTHOR, GREG MASSE

Greg Masse has dedicated many years of his life to learning about the world's religions. *And Then Came Peace*—a work of fiction—was conceived and written after Greg's intensive studies and thorough immersion in Middle Eastern cultures led him to conclude that, rather than being divisive, the world's religions in their purest, original forms actually have the power to unite mankind.

After an executive career in the marketing industry, Greg returned to college to study theology and comparative religion while, at the same time, starting a boutique advertising agency. Within ten years, the agency earned worldwide awards for outstanding creative, and in 2003, Greg sold it to focus on his personal interests: religion and creative writing.

A resident of Canada and Florida, Greg has been around the globe twice and explored the founding nations of the world's religions. In his most recent circumnavigation, he visited more than a dozen countries and got to know their peoples as he worked on this breakthrough novel. As a result, Greg is knowledgeable about the myriad of emotional, cultural, religious, historical, political and territorial issues complicating the ongoing crisis in the Middle East.

And Then Came Peace is the product of seven years of research and writing.